After She Left

AFTER SHE LEFT

RICHARD P. BRICKNER

A Donald Hutter Book

HENRY HOLT and COMPANY
New York

Published by Henry Holt and Company, Inc.,
115 West 18th Street, New York, New York 10011.

Published in Canada by Fitzhenry & Whiteside Limited,
195 Allstate Parkway, Markham, Ontario L3R 4T8.

Library of Congress Cataloging-in-Publication Data

Brickner, Richard P.
  After she left.

  "A Donald Hutter book."
  I. Title.
PS3552.R45A69   1988   813'.54   87-31090
ISBN 0-8050-0684-2

First Edition

Designer: A. Christopher Simon
Printed in the United States of America

10 9 8 7 6 5 4 3 2 1

ISBN 0-8050-0684-2

To Joy Harris and to Paul Zweig

Acknowledgment

I am profoundly grateful to Laura Jarblum-Margolis for her indispensable information, which she provided with so much generosity and patience.

Also to:

Don Hutter
Bob and Carole Zicklin
Richard M. Meyer
Ben Sonnenberg (*Grand Street*)
Sheila Lang
Carrie Smith

and many other crucial and cherished consultants

My deep appreciation to the John Simon Guggenheim Memorial Foundation for a Fellowship in Fiction, of invaluable help in the writing of this novel.

Contents

PART
ONE

PART
ONE

CHAPTER ONE

Amazingly Real

Emily's father took her to the theater almost every Saturday afternoon the year her sister left for college. By December, her life seemed permanent to her, as if she had gone to heaven and heaven were this winter. The snow, the slush, the sun, the marquees, the traffic, Columbus Circle, Times Square, all were high up and forever with her in heaven, in the penthouse of the skyscraper of the world, surrounded by sunny glass.

Emily did not understand why, feeling so excited and so grateful, she could not get rid of the stupid thought that bothered her each time she went into the theater. It had been in her life for nearly two years, since her fourteenth birthday, when, entering the orchestra at *Finian's Rainbow* with her father and sister, Emily had imagined she was stepping into a giant body, helping the audience to fill it with blood, and she had thought, "The theater is a body, the aisles are bloodstreams." The line had not left her alone from then on; it was as if she were being forced to say hello to someone she was trying to ignore, or to memorize a part she didn't want. If she ever managed to escape thinking the line, or if she were able to cut it off as she began to think it, then the line would shockingly interrupt her during the play, circling her brain like the moving electric sign on the *Times* tower: "The theater is a body, the aisles are bloodstreams."

She didn't tell her father. She didn't tell him any such thoughts, and she'd had quite a few. She wished she could say, "Daddy, I'm so weird sometimes," and hand over all her weirdness to him. She knew if she confided in him that way, he would only frown and say, "Don't worry about it. Behave." Like everything with him, his frown was quick. And his "Behave" was so automatic that it sounded like a calm warning not to do something she'd just finished doing. But even though he probably wouldn't pay much attention to what she confided, or to her wish to confide, she didn't dare begin to tell on herself.

If she wrote to Ellen, at Oberlin, "Sometimes I think about—while I'm—Is there anything wrong with me?," Ellen would write back, "Are you nuts?" meaning either that Ellen thought she actually was nuts or else that she was nuts to worry about anything so silly. Ellen had always thought Emily worried too much or got too excited about this or that. Ellen would complain, "What do you care? Nothing's that important. Do you know what your problem is? Everything means too much to you." Emily was famous in the family for having once screamed at Ellen, red in the face, "But I want it to mean too much to me, jerk!"

Coming home from school one day, Emily asked Jill Strauss if she ever thought things she would be embarrassed to tell anyone. "I don't mean about necking with Bobby Miller or something like that," Emily explained. "I mean things you think no one else is weird enough to think."

"Give an example."

"I can't think of any right now."

A week later, Jill told Emily that at the Yankee doubleheader with Bobby Miller, having guessed at the size of the crowd and the proportion of men to women, she had estimated to herself the total number of each item of clothing everyone in the Stadium had on, underwear included. "Not too idiotic. Is that what you meant?" Jill said.

"I guess." It was a good example, but not good enough for Emily to risk offering one of her own.

Jill said, "If you ever tell anyone, especially Bobby, I'll murder you."

"Why can't you tell him?"

"He wouldn't be the least bit interested. It sounds like the type of thing a moron would think."

"A moron wouldn't think it, though."

"No, Em. I guess not."

It made no sense to wonder if she would have been able to talk to her mother about her weird thoughts if her mother were here, since (she had decided), if her mother were not gone, the weird thoughts would have had no reason to occupy her time in the first place. They would have been bothering someone else instead. Emily did not think she appeared to be peculiar, but in her mind a hole had developed where peculiar thoughts collected. In retrospect it seemed to her that ever since her mother's departure she had felt privately strange. Her mother's dying while away had not made her any stranger. Even before her death, her mother had appeared to Emily as bleeding at the neck from bayonets or sharks, a mermaid bleeding; or as a bleeding moth fluttering toward her over the Pacific Ocean, but vanishing because the fluttering trip took so long, and because the trip was, after all, only a thought.

She remembered her mother's kiss on the back of her neck. Now her mother was the silvery photograph on the piano: short straight hair, somber small face, pearls.

Emily also thought she wasn't smart enough to be weird. Unless you were Andy Propper, and wrote poetry even when it wasn't assigned, how much good could it do you to think the theater was a body and the aisles were bloodstreams? Even Andy Profound might know better than to use such a pretentious line.

She didn't need a psychiatrist. She was popular enough to suit her; she didn't want to be too popular. Her eyes were hazel. She could have stood it if they were larger. Her mouth might be a little thin and wide, but her nose, complexion, and hair were an 'A' (the hair was long, fine and straight, pale brown or the darkest possible blonde, depending on the light and when she had washed it; Ellen's was wavier and darker), and her figure an 'A-minus' to 'B-plus,' on the slight side, but well proportioned. (Ellen had a bigger bust.) She did well in school. She'd played Emily Webb in *Our Town* last year and received an ovation on both nights (then swallowed her thoughts of being a real actress. She had time. No one would expect her to know what she wanted yet.) The vast majority of the world's people were poor; her family was "relatively" rich, as her father had once said, being careful in answering her question, "Are we rich?" (which she had asked him after Mrs. Shire, her social studies teacher, had said in class that to live on Park Avenue you had to be rich). Her father had then said, "And while we're on the subject, it's not nice to discuss money outside the home, so don't go around quoting me."

She had breakfast in the dining room every morning with her father, served by Margaret rain or shine, except for Margaret's day off, when Emily now made breakfast. Margaret said that without the Weils she would have no family that mattered to her.

Her father never lost his temper, at least not at home. He let her make necktie suggestions. He was only five feet eight and one hundred and forty-five pounds. He had dozens of suits. He was the best-dressed father she knew. Natty. He was prematurely bald, with a fringe. He had a delicate, straight nose, long eyebrows. Tortoiseshell eyeglasses. Her face was a miniature version of his, minus the specs and plus her beautiful hair. He said her hair was the most beautiful hair he had ever seen since he had given away most of his. He was so sweet, even though he didn't talk much. Had he been so untalkative when Mom was alive? At breakfast, he perused the newspaper. He usually came home for dinner, then went out again to play bridge. About once a week, people came after dinner to play bridge. Bunny the brainless bitch was invariably one of the players. (Did Daddy see just B. the b.b., or other women also?) At dinner, he always asked her about school. He always knew what courses she was taking, and when her tests were, and the names of her teachers. He almost never talked about his day at the office.

When Emily remembered Daddy appearing at Granny and Grand-pa's in the country, August 24, 1943, with the news that Mom had died, her heart felt as if it were being lowered into boiling water, and immediately she would get tears in her eyes, thinking how Daddy had restrained himself. It seemed even worse to her because he'd had to drive up on a weekday. She remembered his skin being white and shiny, like a raw potato. He never showed self-pity.

Usually they left together in the mornings. In the elevator or on the street, he brushed her cheek with his finger or kissed her quickly on the forehead, and said his "Behave." And then she was off to school and he was off downtown. Her father did not lecture her and he wasn't fat. He moved like a fly without a buzz. He was a conformist, she supposed, but if he was, he also happened to have a lot of guts.

After her father began taking her to the theater so miraculously often, after she started believing in her amazing good luck, she asked him one night at dinner (she had just suggested they go to *The Madwoman of Chaillot* the following Saturday afternoon and he had said that he would take care of it tomorrow, as if he were going to write her a simple note for school), "How come you like going to the theater so much, Daddy? I think you like it almost as much as I do." It was the kind of question she never asked him; a question that could land where she hadn't anticipated or he hadn't anticipated. And yet it seemed like such a basic question: Why, Daddy, do you like what you like?

Chewing (she had him figured at three chews per second), he looked at her, giving her no clue to his reaction. He swallowed his mouthful and said, "Why shouldn't I like it as much as you? I like going with you, cookie. Why do you like it so much?"

"I don't know if I can explain it." Heat filled her face. If she didn't have the right answer, he would stop taking her. "Everything's so sharp and colorful. Everything is beautiful no matter how sad."

"I couldn't have said it better. It makes life nicer, doesn't it?"

What she really meant, she thought, was that on the stage everything was so in focus that it was amazingly real. Then real life became amazingly real to her. Streets she knew very well became stage sets she had never seen before. Her eyes would take deep breaths. She couldn't say that to him. "You went with Mom? To plays?"

"Sure. Your mother and I went to almost everything over the course of a season."

"What was the first play you ever went to in your life?" (Hers had been *Life with Father*, interestingly, a year after her mother's departure.)

"That was *Peg o' My Heart*, with Laurette Taylor, with my parents. I was thirteen. I recall being captivated by her femininity." This was Daddy admitting that he had fallen head over heels in love with Laurette Taylor.

"What was the first play you went to with Mom?" Emily felt the risk spreading in her chest.

"Laurette Taylor was also in that. *In a Garden*, by Philip Barry. Nineteen twenty-five. The play was no great shakes. Nothing ever beat Laurette Taylor in *The Glass Menagerie*. I'm sorry Tennessee Williams didn't stop right there."

"I know, Daddy."

With the little condiment spoon, he tapped four helpings of horseradish onto his plate, and resumed eating his pot roast.

It was a joke of theirs. He hadn't allowed her to see *A Streetcar Named Desire*, which he had disliked because it was so "crude," and she had been too young to see *The Glass Menagerie*, which he would have allowed her to see if it were playing now. To think of asking him questions about him and Mom made her mind feel reckless. She didn't want to hurt him, she didn't want to remind him of the wrong thing. But one day there would be no one left to answer her questions. Ellen didn't seem to know more than she did. She didn't want to disturb Granny or Grandpa, either, and they hardly ever talked about Mom on their own. But you could tell from their faces that they talked about her silently. Emily was sure they were in permanent mourning. Sometimes she had more questions about her mother than she could keep in her head at once. "Daddy?"

"Yes, Cookie."

"What are you thinking about at the moment?"

"Nothing much. Why?"

"May je be excuzayed? I have a lot of work." She stood up in her gray skirt, short-sleeved teal sweater. "Thank you for getting the tickets tomorrow for *The Madwoman of Chaillot* for this coming Saturday matinee. I can't wait."

"Me too, darling. I want to thank you for reminding me."

She kissed his cheek on the way by, smelling lotion from his second shave of the day. At the dining-room door, she looped back to the swinging kitchen door and pushed it open. Margaret was eating her dinner. "Thank you, Margaret. You make the world's greatest pot roast. Superb." Emily nodded at her own words.

"I'm glad you enjoyed it, dear. No pie?"

"Ugh, I'm full. Thanks. See you in the morning."

"What a sweet young lady. Isn't she, Mr. Weil?"

"She's a perfect young lady," her father said.

Emily came away from every play or musical with fresh memories in need of relief, as if her new experience were a rash on her brain. In the days following the *Madwoman* matinee, given the most farfetched pretext, she would say to classmates with whom she could afford to be showoffy, "We are the friends of flowers," or, "At noon all men become Roderick." At home, entering kitchen, dining room or living room, or by herself in the hall on the way to her room, she would freeze in a grand, dotty, Martita Hunt-Madwoman pose and deliver one or the other of these lines, or moan the name of the Madwoman's long-gone and possibly imaginary lover, Adolphe Bertaut. Emily's father, as a rule, enjoyed her playful spells, or pretended to, or he ignored them. But this week she was dotty once too often for him, and he asked her to stop being so silly.

The trouble was that the play had irritated him. She, while conceding that the play was probably over-idealistic, thought the acting and the sets had been superb; they had made her believe the play. In the taxi after, he had said the play was dumb. Dumb! As far as she knew, he had never before disliked anything he'd seen with her. Emily said, "But the Madwoman wanted to make life better. You like that. Make life nicer."

"Cookie, it's too easy for her. All the businessmen in the play are stupid and greedy, all the bums are clever and good—the ragpicker or what is he, nosepicker."

Emily giggled.

"I'm afraid this one is just cheap."

She had thought cheap was for too much makeup. How would she be able to suggest another play? "Please forgive me, Daddy. I'll be more careful. I heard it was so good."

"That's all right. The playwright should have his royalties stopped, to see how little he really cares about money."

"Daddy, poor Giraudoux." Emily leaned her temple against the smooth, wintry-smelling shoulder of her father's navy-blue overcoat, then lifted her head and embraced his arm. The taxi ride had become fast and bumpy.

In the dark January afternoon, she was on her way to the evening she had been looking forward to sixty percent because it was excitingly comfortable to know it by heart beforehand (roast chicken, rice, and peas at home, then changing into her green velvet dress for Sue Freund's party, then going to Sue's, then the party) and forty percent because something different might happen. Tightening her entire face against the speed and the bumps, Emily found she was concentrating. She felt mature, as she always felt when she noticed she was concentrating; she could have been twenty-five instead of sixteen minus three months. Her father, she thought, seemed to care enough about disliking *Madwoman* to be right in his opinion of it. But he might subconsciously be upset because the play attacked people who reminded him of his materialistic clients. But if he was upset, he was also being somewhat funny. When he disliked something, but not too much, he was a different father from the father she knew most of the time. More boyish, but drier than boys. Andy Propper (Sue had invited him for tonight) was affected when he tried to be dry, and he did try. She loved her father for being funny when something irritated him. She gulped, because she was holding his arm and thinking of him.

She had happened to be standing near the foyer when Andy Propper arrived at Sue's, around eleven, not too pretentiously casual with his overcoat worn like a cape and his kelly-green muffler twirled around his neck and hanging about four feet down his front and back like an enormous ribbon he had awarded himself for being Andy. He wore a heathery crewneck sweater; all the other boys had on ties and jackets. But she didn't mind the sweater, actually. He said to her right away, "Let's talk," as if he had come to the party to see her. So while most of the others danced (thank God Andy didn't dance), they went and sat in the Freunds' breakfast nook with ginger ales. She hoped no one had noticed her going off with him, but she was also curious to find out what they would talk about. She liked hearing what came out of Andy's mouth. No one else she knew had a tenth of his nerve.

He more than lived up to expectations at Sue's. They had been in school together from kindergarten on, he was only a month older than she, and he said to her, sitting across the Freunds' breakfast table, "You are potentially the most interesting young woman I know."

A blush burst in her face. Her simultaneous, embarrassingly nervous laugh was the blush laughing. "Go ahead, Andy, I'll bite. What are my drawbacks?"

"No drawbacks. But it's because of what you could be that you're interesting."

"What could I be?" She didn't have time to predict what he would say.

"Unlimited, like me."

"Oh, well, that's too good to be true. How can you tell?"

"I can tell. You're scared to express yourself fully, your intensity."

"Oh for God's sake, Andy, isn't everyone? Except you? And how do you know I'd be interesting if I expressed myself fully? Maybe I'd be as dull as dishwater. And by the way, you didn't answer my question. How can you tell what I could be?"

"It's a hunch. It's a hunch based on the not-so-friendly way you're friendly to me. I don't think you dislike me. I think you're interested in me. But I think you fear me, true? When I recited Whitman in Mr. Duke's class, I noticed that you giggled. But you weren't really hostile. It was more because it moved you. True?"

"You were a bit overdramatic, don't you think?"

"Not at all. 'The armies of those I love engirth me, and I engirth them; they will not let me off till I go with them, respond to them, and discorrupt them, and charge them full with the charge of the Soul.' Not exactly a commercial jingle, you have to admit."

"I do admire you, you're right, but sometimes you embarrass me a little. You're so willing to be conspicuous, I worry someone is going to punch you. But I couldn't write poetry if I tried."

"I've been punched. The world is full of cretins. Another way I can tell about you is from your magnificent performance last year. Thornton Wilder is a third-rate playwright, but you made him look good. It was heartbreaking."

He had said the same thing to her at the time of the performances. Still, it was very sweet that he remembered. "I loved the part. It would

have been terrible if I couldn't have done it well." She didn't understand at all about third-rate playwright.

"You have talent, and you have courage."

He meant because the play had to remind her of her mother; but
actually, she had done the death part best, she thought. "Have you
seen *The Madwoman of Chaillot?*"

"Why would I see that crap?"

"You should. I saw it this afternoon. My father hated it. Sometimes
I feel when I go to a play that the sets and costumes would be delicious,
if they weren't sets and costumes, that is. Today would have been like
eating dawn or twilight. Some very delicate vanilla wafer. Sometimes
everything on stage is so bright and sharp it almost hurts. But today
it was pastel. And it still hurt." She laughed. "Anyway . . ."

"Eating dawn or twilight. Now you see what I mean by unlimited?"

"Are you going to use it, Andy?"

"It's brilliant. But it's yours. Use it."

While he was gazing at her, she wondered if she should give him
The theater is a body, the aisles are bloodstreams, and she remembered that
the line had left her alone today. Was she getting more mature in the
afternoons?

Andy said, "You fill my heart with joy."

"You do?" (She was sure she had said, "You do?" How could she
be such an idiot?) With the blood sliding from her cheeks, she watched
him rise and bend over the table and over her face. He kissed her
for about two seconds on the mouth, with his eyes squeezed shut. To
her relief, when he sat down again he did not say anything or hold
her hand. With her right pinky fingernail between her teeth, she
watched him smiling at her, his lips turned all the way in on themselves,
so that he looked sure that she would go far in this world because he
had kissed her. His face was so white. Chalky. Bony. His hair stood
straight up, like comic-book hair. His blue eyes were his only feature
girls were willing to rave about. His eyes belonged to someone more
easily liked than Andy was. She felt nothing from the kiss. She said,
"I'm going to go in, I think." He didn't know anything about her
future any more than she did.

"Suit yourself. What's in there?"

"I don't know, the party." But it was confusing, because he wasn't
really a phony, either. He noticed everything, remembered everything.

"We've never had a good talk."

"We just did, I thought. I'm certainly going to remember it."

"I may leave, go to another party. Some poets downtown. Care to join me?"

"I'd like to, Andy, but I can't leave. And I want to be home fairly soon. See you Monday. Thanks for the encouragement." No one disputed that he had the best brains in the class. "I'm flattered."

"I'm Andy."

She left him alone there.

When, later in the week, her father told her to stop being silly, she decided to make him treat her like an adult. She would present the subject after dinner. She didn't want him to be sitting. She did not think it would have crossed his mind that taking his daughter regularly to the theater could mean he was stimulating her interest in a theatrical career. He had quite a few well known actors and actresses for clients. He had once said to her, "Actors make such disgusting messes of their lives. They're sloppy people offstage." She stood behind him in his bedroom as he prepared to go out. "I think I'd like to try summer stock this summer, at the theater Jill's uncle owns. It's in New Hampshire."

"Who's Jill's uncle?"

"Maurice Boehm. He's a Broadway producer."

"What do you mean, 'Try summer stock'? You could try parachuting."

"I mean be an apprentice. Jill wants to go too. You do some of everything, and if you're lucky you get small parts."

"I understand that." He patted his pockets and left the bedroom. She followed his smart plaid suit, pale gray and blue and brown. In the foyer, he looked at her sideways, putting on his overcoat. A white handkerchief with three peaks stuck out of its breast pocket. "Want to be a leading lady?"

"I'd like to see if I'm meant to be an actress. I'm serious. Not a leading lady. I want the experience."

"You're much too good for it, Cookie."

" 'Life upon the wicked stage.' I'm not planning to be seduced or anything, Daddy. I want to see if I like it. It feels like the right time."

"I'd rather you went to Europe with some group."

The idea of going to Europe petrified her. Europe was on a different planet. "If you won't let me go to summer stock, I'd rather stay in the city and work. And sleep in Marlon Brando's dressing room. Europe is too far away from you."

"Let me talk to Boehm. I know who he is."

"It has to be soon. Lots of people want to go, Daddy."

"Well, not tonight. Behave." He patted her cheek.

She waited in their doorway while he waited for the elevator; he held his gray homburg. She looked him in the eye. "I want you to know this means an awful lot to me, Daddy."

He said nothing, watching her thoughtfully; but she knew he might not necessarily be thinking about her.

"Are you playing bridge tonight?"

"Yes."

"With Bunny?"

"I'm picking her up."

"Hope she's not too heavy. Yuck-yuck-yuck. Playing at the Wrights'?"

"Right."

She heard the elevator coming. "I love you, Daddy. Say hi to Bunny." The b.b.

At the instant she closed the door on her father, Emily thought of the toy stage her mother had given her, March 1941, an early present for her eighth birthday, before leaving for San Francisco on her way to Shanghai. (The perfect gift! A few years later, Emily began, more cynically, to understand the stage as the perfect gift in part because Mom might have been saying by it, "I'm going away. This is my replacement while I'm gone. While I'm gone, make things up, pretend.") When she thought of the toy stage, automatically she thought of what had happened on the radio. The stage had a working curtain of scarlet velvet, footlights, and little bulbs of different colors around the inside of the proscenium that turned on. Along with the stage came a carton containing batches of yarn the colors of her grandmother's marigolds in Newbury, cellophane and heavy paper of different colors, wire, clay, glue, paints and brushes, toy furniture. The first set Emily designed was of her own bedroom, where the stage lived on a bridge table. She played with the stage in the afternoons and on occasion all day for almost a year. She made up a play about an animal nurse in a jungle and a play about the Japanese army invading New York City and the Automat.

She was cutting paper one day for a set. She went to her bureau to turn on the little white radio. Out of the radio came applause. She returned to her chair in front of the stage-table. The applause didn't stop or even start to decline. She stood and bowed quickly, facing the radio, laughing at herself. She stayed standing, waiting for the applause to slow, to end, for the announcement of the performance or speech that had caused it. Then she got scared. Maybe God had been talking to the entire world, ending the war, the entire world was applauding. Emily yelled for Ellen, in the yell a throb of panic. Ellen rushed from her room saying, "What's wrong, for God's sake?" After Emily explained, Ellen moved the radio dial around and said, "It's static, idiot." She walked out.

Emily, when she got older, thought of the "applause" as electricity in disguise: something had been something else. The idea that the applause had actually been electricity sounding like applause seemed to her an excitement like spring fever, hidden somewhere in existence, a crucial mystery. She felt she could count on the mystery. What had happened to her once, even if it had happened almost eight years before, would happen to her again.

CHAPTER TWO

A Small Part

The summer at the Greenway Playhouse started off ideally. Emily was able to be envious of herself. She lived in a bright painting. The town of Greenway was filled with white houses and huge green trees. The playhouse, on a hill, was for Emily the castle of the town; the town's other buildings were the audience to the castle. When she looked at the theater in the morning as she approached it from her rooming house, one of its long sides visible through trees from Main Street, it could also seem to her an ocean liner that had docked overnight, or an enormous present, the trees through which she saw it like wrapping being torn away. She imagined it also as dangerous: if you touched its wooden hide, it would feel your touch and might kill you, but you wouldn't know unless you touched it.

During her first two weeks, Emily's assignment was to assist the stage manager, Carey, so she sat in on rehearsals of *Yes, Orson*, with a copy of the script, and watched the famous Freddy Krauss over and over, as if she were having a dream you could ask for anytime you wanted. She had seen Freddy Krauss in *Yes, Orson* on Broadway in the winter, and while the play was what people called "fluff"—and she agreed—Freddy's performance as the Hollywood composer deserved its great reviews, and she and her father were both glad they'd seen it. "Not everything has to be profound," her father said.

Freddy had a gloomy, wet voice and a European accent (he came from Vienna, she understood), in which he spoke beautiful English. She had never noticed such perfect consonants before, clear and delicate, his 't's and 'd's tapped with a tiny silver hammer. Freddy was

15

not so much fat as gradually paunchy everywhere, his belly a long slope, the skin from beneath his chin to his throat a miniature slope. His black hair, thick and straight in back, would get ruffled in front, cross-looking, as he got worked up during rehearsal.

Best of all about him was his clothes. He dressed as she imagined movie actors dressed, but Hollywood, as far as she was concerned, existed on a movie screen, while Freddy the Great lived before her eyes; he had burst through a movie screen. She wrote to her father that he might want to adopt Freddy's style. Freddy wore an avocado shirt with yellow slacks; a lemon-yellow shirt with sky-blue slacks; lavender shirt with pale gray slacks; prussian-blue shirt and dark gray slacks; scarlet shirt and jet-black slacks; white shirt and mauve slacks; chocolate shirt and beige slacks; shocking-pink shirt and cream slacks. He never ran out, it seemed.

The first thing she ever asked him was how he could travel with so many clothes. He told her (in exactly the same voice he used when he acted) that he owned only two shirts and two pairs of slacks and that he dyed them. When she said, amazed at her own nerve, "Sorry I asked" (and blushed), he said it was all right, everybody asked, leaving her sure that he was kidding and not completely sure if he was kidding. He changed his clothes between morning and afternoon rehearsals. What did he do, buy them in town? She went into Dapper Dan's, Greenway's fancy clothing store. They carried nothing like what Freddy wore.

For a week, after *Yes, Orson,* Emily drove around the countryside with Leo Rotunno, the prop man, in his jeep, finding the necessary furniture and accessories for the upcoming production of *Clutterbuck.* At night, she assisted him with the props for *Blithe Spirit,* the current presentation. *Moonlight* would follow *Clutterbuck,* and then a pre-Broadway tryout, *Mrs. Good Luck,* with Martha Rovere ("Miss Martha Rovere, star of stage, screen, and radio, but mostly radio," Dwight Hermann, one of the apprentices, described her, making Emily laugh hard and wish that Dwight weren't so fat; his breasts were bigger than hers).

Emily thought the other male apprentices were too silly or intense or conceited. She didn't attract their interest anyway. Maybe she was too young, or not free or friendly enough. She stuck with Jill a lot. She liked talking with Dwight. The only man at the Greenway who interested her was Carey, the stage manager. He intrigued her because he always said as little as possible but was never rude and could be funny, and because he gave the impression that he had carried a clipboard and a flashlight from infancy and gone through life without making an error. She wondered what he was really like, if he might be a homo, or maybe asexual and all work, as Jill thought. She awakened from a dream—she and Carey naked, backstage, on a couch in the wings—unclear if they'd gone all the way, crushed immediately by guilt. She knew him even less now; and she'd done something wrong to him through her dream, spoiled his reputation for being perfect, or cost him his job. Without him, she thought, the playhouse literally couldn't run. Everyone depended on blond, crewcut Carey in his spotless T-shirts and khakis. (He'd been in the army.)

Carey called the six female apprentices together one evening before a performance of *Clutterbuck* to tell them that *Mrs. Good Luck* had three bit parts for girls, and that the resident director, Shep Hamilton, needed to know if any of them would be available to audition. "Available," Maude Lofting said. The others laughed. "Extremely available," Maude said then. "Call my agent, pronto. Pronto Leibling, my agent." Only Jill hesitated. "I'm really more interested in the technical side." Emily gave Jill a lot of credit for being discreet, for not even bothering to say, "It would look like nepotism if I got a part." Then Giselle Pike, as if they were all at Girl Scout camp, said, "Oh, come on, Jill, be a sport, it'll be more fun." Carey said that Shep would hold auditions, with scripts, in a few days, and not to get too worked up, because they were talking about two or three lines apiece here, not Lady Macbeth.

In bed that night, in the rooming house, with Jill asleep in the other bed, Emily started taking bows of varying length, depth, and humility. For her two-line part (she assigned herself two lines instead of three to make her success even more earth-shattering), she was getting an ovation, the audience couldn't stop, her applause lasted three times, four times, five times as long as Martha Rovere's. Emily was called back by the audience after Martha Rovere had taken her solo bow. Martha Rovere threw a fit in the wings. "Get rid of that kid." But the production couldn't afford to get rid of Emily. Her debut in the tiny part was news around the world. *Mrs. Good Luck* became a smash on the summer circuit and the season's hit on Broadway, Emily repeating her two-line role for the Broadway run while finishing high school. She understudied the ingenue. She took over for the ingenue a few times. Emily Weil, no fluke. Astonishing maturity, individuality, versatility. Broadway waited for her to finish college. All the famous roles were lined up for her, a lifetime of star's costumes on an endless rack— Juliet, Blanche DuBois (Daddy would have to come), Amanda Wingfield, the Madwoman, Lady Macbeth, Nellie Forbush, Roxanne, Medea, Ophelia. She would play Lady Macbeth at twenty-three and Ophelia at seventy-three. Her career would never end. New parts would be written for her every year. She would always be bowing. If she didn't get one of the three bit parts, the rest of the summer would be a long disappointment, a waste of time. Maybe she would have to sleep with Carey to get a part. She imagined his chest, blond hair, her cheek on the blond hair on his chest. Her father and Bunny the b.b. would drive up to see her in the play. Critics would fly up, agents and producers, interrupting their vacations. Her mother would rise to her feet in the front row; a miraculous reunion would take place before the audience of tourists, critics, agents, producers. Her mother would start life again, overseeing Emily's career. Emily would never behave like a star, but a star's life would be granted her. Everything would be memorable, everything she saw, every room she entered. Every moment would be memorable. The dullest winter days. Every scene of her life would be a living painting of that scene.

Emily, Maude Lofting, Giselle Pike, Adrienne Tofanetti, and Polly Bull finally met with Shep Hamilton for the auditions (Jill now excusing herself on account of her superior charm and talent). Emily was asked to read the part of Dinah. Her first line, of two, after (*Door opens*) was, "Hi, are you Mrs. Parker?" Then Mrs. Parker (Shep was reading Martha Rovere's lines) said (*With dry exasperation*), "And which one are you, dear?" Emily's second line, the answer to Mrs. Parker's question, was, "I'm Dinah." Emily's ears predicted a polite, in-a-hurry giggle from the audience at this point, before the big laugh Martha Rovere would get on, "I'm sure Jim will call you if he ever gets home. Clear the threshold, Dinah, darling." (*Slams door*) The next day, Shep posted his decision. Giselle had the three-line part of Sandy. Emily and Polly would split the part of Dinah four performances each. Adrienne and Maude would split the part of Wendy four performances each. Very democratic, but understandable. Emily thought she wouldn't ask her father up to see the play.

As it turned out, she made a small success of Dinah. Without thinking about it, at the first run-through she gave her two lines (she called them her seven words) a bounce of obnoxious cheerfulness Shep and Martha Rovere both called perfect. When Polly took over for the last four performances, the effect was dull, and Emily was embarrassed for Polly by the audience's flat response. Polly got the quick giggle Emily had anticipated for herself; Emily had received warmer and longer laughter.

Martha Rovere autographed a program for her, "See you on the Great White Way! Love, Martha Rovere." Did "See you on the Great White Way!" mean that Martha Rovere would actually remember her if *Mrs. Good Luck* got to Broadway and call her up and say, "We must have you for Dinah, dear. Can't possibly do it without you"? Or did it mean, "Come visit me in the dressing room when you see the show on Broadway"? Or did it mean, "See you around," or even less? But the play was so stupid. It had taken two men to write *Mrs. Good Luck*, each with a tenth of a brain. And she didn't admire Martha Rovere that much, either. As an actress, competent, nothing special. In general, as a person, she was too willing to be silly in her idiot play. Just one of the girls, really. Martha Rovere and Bunny the b.b. would probably like each other. Emily decided that actors worked so hard on nothing just to be able to act that it was pathetic. But she couldn't be sure if she herself was simply ignorant about life or too smart to be in the theater. She did know that being too smart was no better than being ignorant if you couldn't tell which one you were yet.

Murderer's Row, the next play coming to the Greenway, was also not written by Shakespeare. It had gotten lukewarm reviews on Broadway last season, and run for a few months, starring Thom Blake, who was now touring summer theaters in it. Emily and her father had agreed they could manage to do without a mediocre play about a psychopathic teenage killer. ("It doesn't sound exactly edifying," her father put it.) Emily suspected that her father thought a profound play, like *Streetcar*, was not much better, simply because of its so-called crudeness. She didn't care if *Streetcar* was crude (and from reading it, she didn't agree with her father at all), but she didn't like being frightened for no worthwhile reason, even at the movies. And now, *Murderer's Row* was following her to summer stock. Help!

She would, however, be very interested to see Thom Blake. She had read interviews with him last winter about his ambitious, encouraging parents, his "moody good looks" (true, judging by the photographs), and whether he would ever be able to follow in his idol Marlon Brando's footsteps. Thom Blake was only three years older than she, and not long ago had probably been through exactly her fantasies. She was dying to ask him if he had dreamed of curtain calls and a career that never ended and if he thought of his life, being a star at nineteen, as memorable. And why did he have an *h* in his name?

But when she saw him, he seemed much farther away than nineteen, larger, taller than she'd expected. Also more handsome. Each of his eyes was big enough for two eyes, and they were unusually dark, either black or navy blue. They made her think of the petals of the pansies in Granny Luise's garden in Newbury. His very curly hair was also dark. He had the head of a large, beautiful baby. Full cheeks. Full lips of the kind Emily thought were called rosebud, more puffed in the middle, pursed (pucker up, Thommy) than wide. He looked like a prince, spoiled, yet considerate to the populace.

And all this was wasted on a sick part in a putrid play (even worse than she'd expected, but about average for the dismal summer so far). Emily was on the crew for *Murderer's Row,* and she passed Thom backstage all the time, as she ever so gracefully lugged flats or sofas with the other sweaty slaves, ready to look him in the face, ready to smile, rehearsing the look, rehearsing the smile, the "Hi." But either Thom would be preparing himself for an entrance (an actor getting ready to go on was a person whose whole body seemed to be holding its breath), or he would be on his way to his dressing room and talking with someone, or, once, talking with Elaine Salvage from the cast, with his hands just above her shoulders on the wall she leaned against, as if he were trapping her there; but Elaine Salvage was smiling, relaxed, in fact looked half-asleep. (Emily would never forget the scene.) Dwight Hermann said that Thom and Elaine were not an item. If anything was going on, Dwight said, it was between Thom and Erica Hammer, the mother in the play. Emily didn't believe the rumor. Erica Hammer had to be at least thirty-five. But if Dwight said nothing was going on between Thom and Elaine, Emily believed that.

On Wednesday night of *Murderer's Row,* Emily had finished with the first scene-shift and was starting up the spiral backstage stairs to the bathroom when Thom Blake, like a toppling mattress, swung around the bend of the stairs in sneakers and the New York Yankee uniform he wore when committing his murders, and carrying his cap and bat. She stepped sideways to let him pass, not breathing, and gulping as if she were swallowing a large hand. Smiling in his makeup, he rushed by her, then grabbed the railing and looked up at her. "Amy Weil, correct?"

"Amy? Sometimes people call me Emmy. It's Emily Weil." She thought of saying to him, Who are you?, but it would either be very funny or not at all funny, and she couldn't take the chance.

"Emily Weil. Can you meet me after the last act? I'd like to get acquainted. I've been observing you."

She shrugged. She felt sick in the chest, as if her heartbeats were tangling.

"See you right here," he said. He waved his cap and vanished.

She stood where he had passed. Why did he want to get acquainted with her in particular? Why had he been observing her? Maybe he had mixed her up with somebody. If he'd been observing her, why had he gotten her name partly wrong? How did he know her name at all? Who had told him? Maybe he and Martha Rovere knew each other, star to star, and Martha Rovere had phoned him to say that when he got to the Greenway in *Murderer's Row* he should keep an eye on Emily Weil, or Amy Weil, who had made a superb Dinah in *Mrs. Good Luck.* So now he had kept an eye on her and wanted to get her out to the pine grove in back and get acquainted, then strangle her, still in character from the play. Look at it this way: the worst that could happen would be murder. Murder was only murder, after all. She'd be dead. At least she'd be famous. Maybe they would sleep together in the grove, and after it was over she would immediately get her virginity back again, as if nothing had gone on. Maybe he'd forget he'd made the date and have to do something else. But if he meant it, where would they go? She didn't drink coffee. She was underage for drinking in a bar. Maybe they'd have strawberry sodas together, like George and Emily in *Our Town.* But would he be embarrassed to drink a soda?

After coming down from the bathroom, instead of going out front to watch Thom strangle Elaine Salvage, she went to find Jill. They sat on the door steps. Jill took a Chesterfield from the pack in her shirt pocket.

"May I have one?" Emily said.

"You don't smoke, remember?" Jill lighted up.

"I'll just hold it."

Jill shook her head and handed Emily a cigarette.

Emily simulated taking a drag, tapping ashes.

"It looks stupid," Jill said. "Don't get it wet."

"Here." Emily handed the cigarette back. "Uncontaminated." She could afford to be called stupid; in five seconds, Jill would be impressed with her. At the beginning of her announcement, her voice quavered. "Um, Thom Blake asked me to meet him after the play tonight. Don't you think that's strange?" Emily's lips wanted to smile, to admit embarrassment.

Jill didn't say anything.

"Don't you think it's strange?"

"What I'd like to know is why he doesn't think it's strange."

"He said he wants to get acquainted." Emily laughed. "He thought my name was Amy." She regretted instantly telling Jill he had called her by the wrong name.

"Did he say what he wants to get acquainted with?" Then Jill, in the fussy, nasal voice of their classmate Maxine Stone, said, "Emileeee." And together, Emily and Jill warned in Maxine's whine, "Don't do anything I wouldn't do. But if you do, name it after me-ee."

"Why did he single me out? Giselle has the bosoms. If I'm not home by one, call the police. Call Carey. I didn't even have a chance to say no, he asked me so fast. Do you think I should tell him no?"

"I guess. But I'm not your mother."

"Do you think I'd be foolish?"

Jill blew out smoke with a stiff sigh. The sound had become friendly to Emily. It meant irritation, but it also meant that Jill was involved, pondering. "I don't know. It's not foolish if he doesn't make a fool out of you."

"Wouldn't you be a little curious yourself?"

"Sure. But I'm suspicious. I'm not the no-business-like-show-business type. If you want, I can wait with you, and you can tell him you're too tired tonight but you could meet him for a hamburger tomorrow before the show."

"I know that's the right answer. But he'll forget about it, then. I really do want to talk to him. He'll have something else to do tomorrow."

"So suit yourself, then. Nothing'll happen. He's probably not a maniac."

"God, I think I've got stage fright, butterflies."

Jill squashed her cigarette in the parking-lot gravel. "If you throw up when he starts to kiss you, that'll solve your problems."

"I'll just make sure we go straight into Greenway for a soda, that's all."

"That's my pal. Live to the hilt."

CHAPTER THREE

A Big Part

So she wouldn't be standing and waiting for him like a prostitute, Emily walked around in the area between the dressing-room stairs and the stage door; whenever anyone passed her, she started looking for something on the floor, nibbling her nails. She had on the usual jeans and a short-sleeved plaid cotton shirt, socks, and low blue sneakers she liked. She carried a navy-blue sweater. Not a great outfit, and she'd been working all day, but she didn't smell, as far as she could tell, and anyway this date wasn't even a date, really.

Boyd Mullins came down. Erica Hammer. Wanda Philips and Matthew Chester and Alice Beringer. No Elaine Salvage. Hmmmm. Then Elaine Salvage came down with Vladimir Bilsky. Then Marianna Hugo. That made the whole cast, except for Thom Blake. He might have descended from his dressing-room window by rope. He might have come down the stairs disguised as another cast member. Was she now the sole person in the theater?

Then she thought he might be up there, waiting for her to look for him. She knocks. *Come in, Amy.* He's nude, standing with his thing sticking straight out at her like a sausage. She slams the door and flees. Then she thought she would find him sitting in front of his mirror, with his head hanging sideways and blood all over his neck. She comes close, to make sure he's dead. Then she runs, before she can be considered a suspect.

Then Thom appeared, strolling down the stairs, smiling gently at her, wearing quite short tan shorts, sandals, and a colorful sports shirt. His legs were tan and hairy. "Emily. Hi." He came straight at her, his gorgeous eyes and curls, his small, calm smile. He stuck out his hand. She took it quickly and weakly, uncertain if he was being too friendly or if she was being impolite.

"I don't have too much time," she said. "I have to paint sets tomorrow bright and early. The glamorous life." He didn't reply. The design on his shirt turned out to be red, green, orange, blue, and black bubbles of different sizes, so that the shirt looked like party napkins or a shower curtain. Don't judge a book by its cover. Why not? How could he dress like such a moron? "Do you mind if I ask you a question?" she said, taking the lead in moving toward the stage door.

"I can't wait to hear it."

"Well, I'm flattered you want to get acquainted with me, but I'm just an ordinary apprentice. Why me? Is that a fair question?"

"But you sound angry."

"I'm not angry. Why would I be angry? I'm"—she wanted to say "suspicious," Jill's word, but that would be getting things too much in the open, unnecessarily—"I don't know, I'm curious." She probably sounded as if she were flirting or fishing for compliments. But she had to have his answer, for her protection.

They were standing outside, on the landing of the stage-door steps, in the light from the bulb above the stage door. His face was just as handsome; his shirt refused to improve.

"Emily, I'm curious, too. You looked like a completely unphony, untheatrical girl, sweet and healthy."

"Doesn't sound that great."

"You look normal. I like to talk to people who aren't corrupted yet."

"Well, that may be me, true. But am I the only one in the world? Are we going into Greenway?" She felt that the stage-door landing was a miniature stage on which she was transparently struggling to make up lines.

"My limousine's this way. Where do you want to go?"

"We can try the diner for a soda, if that's okay."

"It's just what I would have suggested."

They walked over the gravel, toward a station wagon. His voice itself, she noticed—not just his words—was courteous. He seemed to keep it soft. Maybe he needed to save it. "What does normal mean, anyhow?" she asked him. "Do you like to talk to people who aren't corrupted yet because you aren't corrupted either, or because you are corrupted and need relief?"

"I'm very idealistic. There are people who would like to corrupt me."

He unlocked and opened her door. She got in. He shut her door. He went around and got in his side, shut his door, opened his window.

"May I ask another question?"

"You don't have to ask permission." He stuck the key in the ignition, but didn't turn it. He leaned against his door.

She couldn't ask him what he meant by people wanting to corrupt him, anyway. It would sound as if she didn't believe him, or it would sound too nosy. "Where did you get the shirt you're wearing?"

He looked at his chest. "How do you like it? I bought it last week in Ogunquit."

"I thought someone might have given it to you."

"Who? Someone you know?"

"Please forget it. It's not important."

He wasn't smiling. "Is it much too loud?"

"Please. I'm sorry. I don't know what's the matter with me." She wished he'd drive.

"I don't mind. I just want to know. I thought it was something a little different."

"It's just the design. It just doesn't seem like you."

"I have mostly plain clothes. I don't pay much attention."

At least people who didn't care much about clothes were supposed to be good, or not self-centered. By that criterion, she must be fairly bad. "I didn't even notice your clothes until tonight."

"Did you notice anything at all about me?"

She flushed. "What do you mean?"

"Were you aware of me even though you didn't notice my clothes?"

"Naturally. You're the lead." Now he would ask her how she liked the play. Yipes! "We'd probably better go, so the diner doesn't close."

"Your wish . . . is my command." He pulled his back away from the door and started the car, driving it across the gravel, up the stumpy hill; the car wobbled onto the road that would take them into town.

"Here's another question for you. Why do you spell Tom with a *Th?*"

"It's obviously a name you remember, right?"

"That's true."

"My agent thought it up, or someone. My folks, maybe." He seemed to drive with one finger. He looked at her frequently as they talked.

"I wonder why the *h* in Thomas isn't pronounced, anyway. Thom," she said, using the *h.*

"You've really got me there, Emily."

"Has anybody ever mispronounced your name that way?"

"Not that I recall." He laughed briefly. "So what else have you noticed about me, until this shirt?"

Did he expect her to tell him she thought he was unusually good-
looking? "Your performance, I guess. You're really good. Superb. The
play is so scary, I haven't seen it all the way through, but what I've
seen of you is excellent."

"Thank you very much."

She hadn't thought about his performance much, because she didn't
like to think about the play. She had some rudeness to make up for,
but she wasn't used to lying. She tried to figure out how dishonest
she was being. From what she had seen, he covered the stage all the
time, always dashing around. He had lots of different motions and
gestures, especially when he imitated different baseball players swinging, catching and sliding, at the same time doing a sports announcer's
voice. "In a way, your performance makes me think of a magician
who doesn't keep still and always talks."

"I haven't heard that. I appreciate that. The play is empty-headed,
though."

She didn't know what saved her. Instead of saying, "It sure is," she
said, "Do you think so?"

"Some of the critical fraternity thought so. Still, audiences like it,
and the movies bought it, so how empty-headed can it be? But it looks
like they don't want me for the movie, and I'm the whole play, so
something's empty-headed out there."

"God! Who would they want? Instead of you?" Suddenly she was
talking show biz. Why had he told her? Had it just happened? Had
he told everyone?

"It looks like Farley Granger. Picture Farley in a baseball uniform?
I don't get it. The movies don't want me for the part that I made
famous because I apparently am not famous enough."

She shook her head. "It seems so unfair."

"Nothing's unfair. It's just dumb. Empty-headed. It makes me want
to say fuck it and go to college or something. Pardon my language."

"It's okay." Her heart had jumped at "fuck it" as if the car had hit
a rock. Yet, she realized, he never raised his voice; no matter what
he said, his voice sounded calm.

"The producers don't know if they're coming or going. They don't
know if I'm right for this or right for that and they must have me for
this but first they have to sign Lunt and Fontanne, Katherine Cornell,
and Sarah Bernhardt, or they can't raise the money. I'm changing
agents next week. Let me tell you. People in this business don't know

what they're doing or they don't want you to know what they're doing. Two kinds. That's it."

"Then what will you do next?" She felt useless. She was frowning intensely, as if the problem were hers.

"That's what I'm saying. I don't know."

The softness of his voice made her feel worse for him and stupid for having asked the question. "I know. I meant it just seems so ridiculous." She realized that it might not be ridiculous; but it was awful anyway. Nineteen seemed even older at the moment.

"Once this big-deal stuff began, I didn't think my life was supposed to be over when the play stopped running. Maybe I have to keep doing this empty-headed play somewhere all my life."

"Your life isn't over. You just need to be patient. You'll get another part soon." How had he gotten the part? Maybe he'd have to play smaller parts. Or, if he studied, could he play Hamlet? He looked perfect for it.

"Let's drop the subject. Of course you're right. I'm supposed to be a find, for God's sake. Where's the diner?" They had reached Main Street.

"Down there."

"I can't tell you how I want this soda, Emily. My throat is begging for this soda."

She gulped. She thought of his throat again with blood on it. "Well, lucky you'll have it, then, I guess. There's a spot. No. There's a spot." A car was backing out of a parking slot facing the sidewalk in front of the diner. She thought of his throat as having a slash like a mouth in it, the blood coming slowly without stopping from the mouth, she having to put her mouth to the mouth and swallow the blood to prevent him from dying. She suddenly remembered her mother's bleeding mermaid neck. Her whole body squeezed for a moment, but nothing else happened. She wiped her mouth with her knuckles.

Thom took the parking space. She wondered if he would be recognized when they went in. She stepped out of the car into white light and the smell of hamburger grease. It seemed busy and noisy in front of the diner, but she didn't see or hear anything specific. She felt as if she had passed out into a different kind of consciousness, or that she was dead but alive on the other side of life, or arriving at the Academy Awards or something equally impossible.

Inside, Thom said to someone, "Do you have a booth in back?" and someone said, "Yes, Mr. Blake." Emily didn't look at anyone. She felt that she was being looked at. Her father had taken her to Sardi's three times. She had wondered there what it was like to be recognized and to pretend to ignore people looking at you. She imagined it now as other people's eyes hanging onto your skin and making you feel heavier. She sat down across from Thom Blake and his shirt. She thought of her father's exciting-smelling closet—cloth, leather, wood, sometimes camphor, and a slight perfumy sweetness. The smells weren't that strong, but they were strong in her head. To think of them gave her a little knock across the heart. Her father at the moment was either playing bridge or sleeping. Perchance with Brainless One? Ughh. "What do you like people to call you?" she asked.

"Thom, of course, What else? Mr. Blake? We haven't talked about you at all. Come on, what's your story, Emily?"

"I don't have that much of a story yet." Had Thom made a 'mess' of his life? Was Thom Blake an example of what her father meant?

"Where do you live? Who are your parents? And what are you doing up here?"

She thought of calling her father collect from a phone booth to tell him she was having a soda with Thom Blake and then they were going to rehearse a torrid scene from *Streetcar,* and at the same time she would find out if she was catching him and Brainless in the act. "The last one is probably the hardest. I live in New York with my father. My mother is dead. Your parents are both in the theater as I remember?"

"My father's a stage manager, correct. But my mother's just a plain ordinary English teacher out in Queens. How long has your mother been dead, Emily?"

"Years." It wasn't that long. "She's been dead since I was ten. Six years ago this month. Also, I have an older sister, traveling in France at the moment."

"How did she die?"

Emily shrugged. "It's a long story." She wouldn't mind telling him, but she wasn't used to telling it. She assumed most people in school knew. She didn't know that many people outside of school. And she'd only been to Camp Horrible for one summer.

"Is your father in the theater?"

"No! That's so funny. He's a stockbroker. He has some theater clients, though. And music clients. George Koenigsberg is a client of his."

"The pianist? Not bad!"

"And composer. The crush of my life." She wished she'd kept her mouth shut.

"Do you go to school?"

"I'll be a junior at Prentiss this fall."

"I'm sorry? Is that a boarding school?"

"No. It's just a private school in the city. You went to Performing Arts, right? I envy you."

"You want to be an actress, Emily? Way to go," he said, then, to the arriving waitress. "Emily?"

"Strawberry ice-cream soda, please."

"Something to eat for you?" he asked her.

"Maybe I'll have a hamburger," she said to the waitress. "Well done, please." Jill had taught her to order them well done; Jill's mother said it was safer. "No onions, please." Thom would think she'd ordered no onions to keep her breath fresh, but she usually didn't order them anyway.

Thom took over for himself. "I'll have a nice juicy cheeseburger, medium rare, grilled onions, a side of french fries. Thanks." He smiled at the waitress. "And a chocolate soda."

Emily said, "Excuse me, can you change mine to a cheeseburger, well done?"

"No onions," the waitress said, scribbling.

"No." Now that he had ordered onions, for her to order them would be even more conspicuous than it would have been ordering them in the first place.

"French fries?" the waitress asked.

"Okay, sure." The waitress left. "I have money with me," Emily said.

"I think I can cover this one."

"I'm sure everything's going to turn out fine for you, but I don't know if I'd be tough enough to be an actress, even though it's what I want to be." Tough enough partly meant tough enough to play junky parts.

"You need a tough hide."

"I'm sure some talent helps also. I just know I would hate to be sitting in an audience all my life. I'm very scared of not being able to use myself, that I'll end up being ordinary. I want what it's like watching a play, but not as a member of the audience. I want my life to be that way." She had never heard herself say anything that sounded so smart; at the same time, she wasn't sure it made sense, or if it sounded as if she wanted everything on a silver platter. "That doesn't make me an actress yet, but do you know what I mean?"

"You're a very intellectual person, Emily, not ordinary at all. I'm sure you'll make a fine actress."

"But I have no idea if I'd be talented enough anyway. I've done one play in school, and it was very successful, and I had a bit part here last week. It went very well, but it's not enough to tell anything. I love to act, but I'm worried that if I were an actress I might get lost in the part and not do what I'm supposed to. When I come out of a theater as a member of the audience, I don't ever want to let go of what I've seen." It was probably too weird to tell him. The sky sometimes, after a show on Broadway, would be orange-tinted, or rose, or violet, smoky, a silent storm of color looking like a big glowing body, visible and invisible, waiting to appear. "Coming out of the theater is like entering another play. Do you know what I mean? It seems to be another world, like a live stage set, but it's the actual world and I'm really there in it. I want everything to be that way all the time, so that I'm part of everything permanently, part of everything while I'm seeing everything, and something's always going to happen. I want it to be that way forever, with me there. If I could succeed in being an actress, then when I left the stage door my life would be the same as when I leave the theater with the audience, as if I'd been dipped in magic water or something. I don't mean everything's supposed to be the way I want it and great every second. I just want my life to be important. To me, I mean. And I always want to look forward to something." She meant forever. "I don't usually talk this way. I'm sorry."

"You have nothing to be sorry for. You're very intense, very ambitious. That's good! You'll achieve whatever you set your mind to."

"I'd like to know what being an actor is like for you. What does it do for you?" Then their orders were served. Emily was hungry, but it bothered her that the conversation would be interrupted. "How does it make you feel?"

"If I understand what you mean, sometimes it's the way you describe. Last winter on Broadway, I thought I was God Almighty coming out of the stage door, signing programs, people waiting for me."

"Did the world seem different?"

"It was different, people asking for my autograph."

He must mean girls. He just wasn't saying it. But what kinds of girls would go to a show like that? Girls with lousy taste. Girls older than she was. Women. Fans? He started to eat, crouching to bite into his cheeseburger. When his face lifted, he was chewing; ketchup appeared above the right side of his mouth. She started to indicate the ketchup by pointing to her own mouth, but then she thought she'd better forget it, after her comments about his shirt. She wanted to ask him if he'd dreamed of it. He took another bite of cheeseburger. She tried hers. She drew the pink sparkle of her soda into her throat. What did Thom think of her? Was she uncorrupted enough? Normal enough? Too normal? Had she sounded pseudo? Conceited? Too smart? Too spoiled? Was he thinking right now about finishing his food and getting the disappointing evening over with? She certainly hadn't expected to feel sorry for him; not sorry, but empathy for him. She liked it that he had told her about his problem. She liked the way he talked about himself. But he might not be too smart, either. He might be in trouble because he wasn't good enough. Also, he might be praising her too easily. He might be insincere because he was so handsome. He called her by her name all the time. Trying to remind himself not to call her Amy. She wasn't noticing his shirt as much, but she still couldn't ignore it. His head seemed to have gotten larger in the diner, to draw attention away from his shirt. What would happen if he kissed her in the car? Would she kiss his neck automatically, by mistake, trying to save his life?

"Was your mother an actress, Emily? Is it a sore subject?"

"Is it a sore subject?" She noticed he had wiped his mouth. She felt as if she were blanking during a test. "It's not a sore subject." She sounded exasperated to herself. "My mother was a social worker for the JRSA, which is a Jewish refugee organization. She went to Shanghai in 1941 to work with European refugees. She died there in 1943, in Shanghai." She heard the sound of her voice in her skull; she wasn't sure her words were leaving her.

Thom looked at her sorrowfully, and she could see him swallow even though he wasn't eating, so he must have heard her. "Was she killed?" he asked.

"She died of dysentery."

"That's terrible." He continued to stare with his mammoth eyes as if he were receiving the news through his eyes, and as if the news were about someone he knew. "Jesus. I've never heard of anything like that."

"Well, it's over, at least. It's a while now, as I said." She felt silly. It embarrassed her that he had stopped eating. She had thought she was understating it calmly, but it seemed as if she had made a big dramatic announcement, and as if she herself had died in 1943, not her mother.

"She's like a hero, a heroine. Do you know why she went there? Was she a spy? Do you know?"

"A spy?"

"I mean, she didn't have to go. She wasn't drafted, was she? Most people wouldn't do anything like that. Most mothers especially. It's amazing."

"My mother felt she had to do something. Her parents came to America before she was born, and all the relatives got over here from Hitler. She felt very strongly, obviously. That's the way she was. I'm sure she didn't expect to die." Emily wondered if she had a right to speak for her mother. "I'm sure she expected to come back, naturally. She was put in an internment camp by the Japanese. That's where she got sick."

"But doesn't it make you feel unusual to be the daughter of someone like that? It's like Eleanor Roosevelt being your mother."

"I didn't do anything unusual. My mother did." When Mrs. Roosevelt had come to speak at Prentiss, Emily had met her.

"I know. But you must wish she were around so you could enjoy being proud to be her daughter."

"I think about her." Emily had to shrug. Then she worried that she seemed phony-tough, flip. But the majority of the time these days her mother seemed like a boulder on her grandparents' sloping meadow in Newbury. Sometimes she missed her mother only because she worried that if she didn't think about her, her mother would know she wasn't thinking about her and her feelings would be hurt. "Someone did tell me once that my mother was Eleanor Roosevelt with a beautiful face." She couldn't help smiling.

"You should write a book about her."

"*I Remember Mama.*"

"She should be famous. I'm not kidding."

"She is sort of famous, among a certain group."

"What kind of certain group?"

"The people she worked with, in the JRSA, and the people she helped."

"Your father hasn't remarried?"

"No. But he has a friend, Bunny." Emily laughed. "Now that's a sore subject. Her real name is Berenice Kraft. My sister and I used to get on our knees and say, 'Dear God, please don't let our father marry Bunny the brainless bitch.' She's a real idiot."

Thom looked at her with a sad but amused expression. "Why is she an idiot?"

"She really means well, I suppose, but she tries so hard to be friendly to my sister and me and she doesn't even realize we can't stand her. And she writes these embarrassing poems all the time, thinking they're clever. 'Happy birthday, Emily Weil. I'd walk a mile for your smile. Here are four hankies to add to your pile.' "

"Okay, so . . . Your father must like something about her."

"She plays bridge well, for some reason. I guess they have a good time together. I'm glad he has companionship, obviously. I guess I sound really selfish, but she's not good enough for him, putting it mildly."

"She has a tough role to fill."

"True. If you met her, you'd know what I mean. I'm afraid I have to go pretty soon."

"Just let me finish my burger, and I'll get the check." He ate again.

"She's harmless, though. I'll have to try to be nicer. It's very immature."

Thom held up his hand as if to say, Now, don't be too hard on yourself.

She finished her soda. She tried to picture being nicer to Bunny and realized that if she were, then Bunny would infect her, try to take her over even more, want to go shopping with her, try to get her to confide in her. And then she would have to turn Bunny down all the time and feel even guiltier, so it wouldn't be worth it. She wished her father would find someone reserved, queenlike.

Thom said, his lips leaving his straw, "You're an intriguing person, Emily. I'd like to know more about you. Can we get together again tomorrow night?" He was smiling his small smile.

"I guess, sure. Since I've talked my head off, I don't think I have anything left for you to know, but I could probably ask you some professional questions."

"I don't have answers. Farley Granger has answers. Remember?"

"Stop. You really shouldn't talk like that. It's such a difficult profession. Things are going to get better again."

"Let's see a script, plus a producer, plus money raised, plus a cast, and a theater. But I appreciate your encouragement. I'll use it as good luck. I'm going to use you as a good-luck charm in my head."

"You don't need my encouragement. You won't." No doubt about it: what she definitely liked best was his voice. It was mysterious because it never got harsh or loud. It always stayed gentle. It made the parts of his personality she wasn't sure about less important. She had decided to think of him as his voice.

Ten minutes later, she was sitting alone, against a tree, on the lawn of her rooming house. Thom had driven away to the inn. She sat with her hands covering her face, trying to keep his kiss from escaping.

With each breath she felt a deep tingle, as if the kiss had fallen into her lungs. His voice had turned into his kiss. The softness of his lips was so strong she had felt as if it could have raised her into the air. He hadn't done anything with his tongue. Just his soft, plump, rosebud lips leaning against hers for five seconds, or ten seconds, with secret electricity in them. How could lips be so soft and so electric at the same time? Was it an actor's trick? She couldn't wait 'til tomorrow.

Between the day's set-painting and the evening's stage-crew work, she had gone home for a shower and to change. She wore her jeans and an emerald-green cotton blouse over which she had now pulled the honey-colored sweater Granny Luise had knitted for her. Thom came down the dressing-room stairs (not last tonight) wearing shorts like those of the night before, and a regular pale-blue short shirt. Maybe he dressed more sophisticatedly in the winter. He didn't seem to understand that it got chilly at night in New England, even in August. "Hi," she said. "Really excellent performance, what I could get to see of it." She really did appreciate his performance more. She might not exactly be objective, however.

Smiling, he bowed and kissed her hand. She blushed (as usual), as if they had not kissed much more significantly the night before. "What would you like to do?" he asked. "Drive around for a while? Or another soda."

"I'm not that thirsty. Drive around would be fine." It sounded risky in a safe way. "By the way, aren't you going to be chilly?"

"I'll borrow your sweater." In the parking lot, on the way to the car, he took her hand.

Instead of turning left on Main, toward the diner, he drove in the opposite direction, past her rooming house and through a leafy residential section, Greenway's oldest houses. They seemed to Emily like lace, the equivalent of lace. It had occurred to her that the main question she really had in mind, about whether he had dreamed of being an actor (not necessarily literally, but daydreamed, like her), was not a polite question to ask someone in his position right now, and the same would be true of similar questions. So her question instead would be why had he found her "intriguing"? Because of her mother? Or because of the way she had talked about what it was like leaving a theater? Was "intriguing" a polite way of saying "strange" or "arty"? Or did he just mean "different"? She had been different with him. She had talked more about herself at once than she ever had with any male of any age, and possibly with any person.

But then he said, "I thought about you a lot last night, Emily."

She refrained from saying, "Me, too," or "What about?" She said, "That's nice."

"About you, your mother, your family. What you told me about."

She didn't reply. She herself had gone to sleep thinking about the kiss and awakened thinking about the kiss, his perfect lips. She wished he were in her class at Prentiss, and her boyfriend, so she could show him off.

"It made me feel so badly."

"I'm sorry I told you, then."

"Do you mind if I ask some personal questions?"

"I guess not. It depends. What's personal?" She giggled, quietly but ridiculously.

"Just about your family."

"Go ahead. But could we stop? I can't talk seriously while we're driving. I can't explain it. Moving doesn't go with serious conversation. Do you know what I mean?"

"Wherever there's a good place to stop."

"We can stop right on the road here, I guess." They were out of Greenway now. "Or I know. Turn around and go back to where you turn to the inn. Go the other way instead and eventually we may end up down by Lake Lenore. I went swimming there once this summer, on my big day off. It's where a lot of the summer colony lives that's been coming to see you."

"We'll pay them back."

In about ten minutes, though she'd never given a driving direction in her life, he was turning off the motor and headlights within sight of the huge, moonless, secret-looking lake. They didn't belong there. On the other hand, just because they didn't belong there, and because they were parked in a sort of unsettled way, on a downward tilt, and also near bungalows, it seemed to Emily she couldn't get into any trouble that she couldn't stop.

She thought he would start talking, about her mother, but instead he surrounded her shoulders with his right arm and she slid straight to him. They were kissing again. She wanted the kiss to be an exact repetition of last night's. It was, except that she was noticing it, and this time her heart banged so hard she worried the banging might bump her head against his, and maybe it did, because his tongue had come through her lips.

She decided she had better keep her teeth together. If she let his tongue in further, he might be entitled to do whatever he wanted, or

something would happen to her brain and she would let him do anything. His tongue tried to pry her teeth apart. It climbed around on
her teeth. It vanished. He kept kissing her without using his tongue.
What felt very good now was his hand stroking the side of her neck.
Then he kissed her on the neck, where he had been stroking it, and
she shivered. With her wrist, she dried her lips of his wetness and
bent to kiss his neck lightly above the Adam's apple. His hands were
on her sweater, on her breasts; she jumped away. "I have to stop."

He curled sideways to face her, holding her hands. "We've stopped.
Take it easy. Are you a virgin, Emily?"

"Naturally. Aren't most girls my age you know virgins?"

"You're how old?"

"Sixteen."

"Sweet sixteen? A lot aren't. You'd be surprised. And you seem old
for your age."

"Thanks, but I'm very inexperienced. I hope you're not too surprised or disappointed. Luckily for you, you don't have to depend on
me."

"Do you want to stay that way until your wedding night?"

"I might. At least until I'm old enough to know I love someone and
I know him very well."

"And someone knows you very well?"

"That would be logical. Can we change the subject?" She laughed
it off.

He frowned heavily, as if he had a bad headache or as if he were
going to cry. His lips had tightened. He raised her hands. He lowered
her hands. He shook his head.

"What's wrong?" Was he going to tell her he loved her and had to
sleep with her?

He lowered his head. "Is your mother really dead?"

She was looking at his curls. The question sounded so familiar
because of the hundreds of times she had asked it to herself. But
the question belonged to her, not to him. And besides, she knew the
answer.

His head remained down. "Don't you think it's possible that your
parents weren't getting along and that your mother went away somewhere, but her going to Shanghai was a story your father cooked up
so he wouldn't be ashamed?" He lifted his face now, its anxious
expression still on it.

"My father wasn't ashamed of anything that I know. He was proud.
Do you really think I would lie?" She had used to upset herself with

the same kinds of thoughts Thom had just mentioned. She still didn't know how well her parents had gotten along, but she had always been able to remind herself of the cable and the death certificate. "There is a cable announcing her death. Also a death certificate. Okay?" She should never have told him in the first place. From now on she had to say to relative strangers, "I live with my parents and sister." There was something wrong about offering the real story.

"But Emily, don't you realize they could have been faked?"

"Why do you keep calling me Emily, damn it?" She tried yanking her hands away. He held them.

"You told me it was your name."

"That's why you don't have to keep saying it!" She turned her eyes to the lake—really romantic—unable to see what she remembered from her swimming visit, that the lake disappeared way down on the right, so that she had thought of the invisible part as an ocean. "Nothing was faked. The cable came from the Red Cross, from Switzerland."

"Maybe your mother was in love with a Swissman."

She looked at him. He had stopped frowning. His face was uglier than yesterday's shirt, even though nothing about it had changed. But it looked so stupid. She tried to ease her hands away; it was as if he had locked them. "And what about the death certificate?" she asked. She hated the sarcastic way she sounded, like someone in a fifth-grade argument.

"What about it? How do I know you're telling the truth?"

She felt as if blood were getting into her breathing. "I need to open my window. I feel funny."

"Go right ahead."

"I just want to breathe." He let go of her hands. She rolled her window all the way down and leaned her face out, resting her cheek on the edge of the door. He had moved over with her. She could feel his thigh against her backside. Either he was worried she would be sick or he was worried she would yell.

"After you get your breath, I just want you to tell me how I'm supposed to believe this story."

She breathed with her cheek on the door and her eyes closed for more than a minute, she guessed. She thought of her mother, in her white linen summer dress with the pale blue embroidery, appearing on the seat, slapping Thom and bawling him out so that he stuttered, and then apologized. When Emily brought her head in, her first instinct was to put it on his shoulder, to appeal to him. Instead, after rolling up her window, she sat back and waited, not looking at him.

"How does Shanghai get into it? From the movies?"

She sighed. Even though he was not touching her anywhere now, she stayed as close to the door as she could get. "Shanghai was a safe place for refugees to go. I think there were already a lot of Jewish people living there."

"And just how were the refugees supposed to get from Europe to Shanghai?"

"They went across Russia by train. That's what I've been told. Then they went to Shanghai. From Japan. They went to Japan, then to Shanghai."

"Is this the country of Shanghai?"

"What are you talking about? Shanghai is in China, in the country of China."

"Good. However, last night you said she was put in a camp by the Japs."

"She was. Shanghai was occupied by the Japanese. That's history."

"History. Anyway, your mother has two little daughters, a rich husband. What was so important to do over in Shanghai?"

"Not rich. Don't say that."

"Poor. A poor stockbroker."

Jill would tell her to stop answering the questions. But she wanted to answer them. To make him worse, to make him more of an ignorant idiot. To punish him. "As far as I know, she helped decide where the different kinds of refugees lived, how they could get kosher food, the orthodox ones, religious schooling, different problems like that. I think there were disputes between different kinds of refugees. I've never been questioned before in my life, you know. I'm telling you what I've been told. Anyone who's old enough to know anything about the war knows what I've told you. Do you believe there was a war?"

"I'll ignore that one. If you've never been questioned before, how can you know if people really believe your exotic history?"

"It's not the type of subject people are usually suspicious about."

"You wouldn't have any idea how suspicious they were if they didn't tell you, would you?"

She continued to refuse to look at him. She looked straight ahead. "Anyone who knew my mother said she was the greatest woman they ever met, particularly some of the people she helped who came over here after the war, who came to visit us. Maybe the problems sound minor to you, but obviously they weren't to the refugees. Their lives were completely changed, to put it mildly. How would you feel if you escaped from Hitler and ended up in China? My parents might not have gotten along so perfectly, either. I don't know if they did or not. My father's not the talkative type. He has enough to live with. There are questions I can't ask him. After she died, it didn't make that much difference how unhappily married they might have been or how happily. Sometimes I wish I knew more, I really do. But I know she went there because a lot of pressure was put on her by her organization. My mother was extremely highly regarded."

"Emily? Sorry. Do you even remember what you said last night? I'll save you the trouble. Last night you said she went because she felt very strongly. You didn't say anything about a lot of pressure being put on her for any reason."

"She wouldn't have gone if she didn't feel strongly, naturally. It's just not a contradiction." She couldn't tell him about Mom's earlier trip, to Havana. It would help explain things, but not to him. "Anyway, where do you think I'm making all this up from? I promise I'm really not that smart."

"Modesty becomes you. Partly from books, I suspect, partly from things you've heard, or someone else's story, who knows? I could tell you my father was Lou Gehrig and my mother was Tokyo Rose. The big tipoff is what you said last night. You said it yourself. You are scared of being ordinary. You've made up this stuff because it makes you someone with an exotic story. I kept thinking about the parts that don't make sense, and why it makes sense for you to lie. I thought I'd better find out the truth before I fell for you."

"Well, I'm glad you did." It was imperative that she didn't start crying in front of him. She felt the signs just as definitely as if she were getting a sore throat.

"I've given you every benefit of a doubt. I've tested every word you've said against my common sense. I've listened very carefully, and what comes into my ear is a fairy tale. Making things up is as easy for you as talking. I know other people like you, only not so daring, or not so crazy."

"Now that you know everything, could I please go home?"

"I'd still like you to tell me why this mother of yours was so extremely highly regarded?"

"There's no point telling you anything more." She turned her face toward her window.

"What choice do you have? I'm in complete control."

A bag of tears filled her head and broke. With her hands covering her face, she pressed against her window. Her own sobbing noises scared her. She was squealing away chunks of her throat. The car seemed to bump. It was moving. She thought she might be passing out. The car was backing up, then turning backwards. Into a side road. Was he stopping? Maybe he was going to drive them straight into the lake. They were driving on level road. After a short while, the car stopped. Emily sounded like a baby to herself, making squeaking sighs. She kept her hands over her face. She trembled, as if she were having chills. The trembling grew gentler, until it felt almost comfortable. "What are you doing?" she asked. Her voice wobbled. She rubbed the sleeve of her sweater across her eyes. Outside were road, trees, no houses. Dead green night.

"This is to prove to you that I plan to take you home when we're finished."

Anything she said might make her start crying again. She breathed carefully, until the breathing smoothed out. He hated her, for some reason. Or resented her. She shouldn't have gone along with his questioning. In some way, she had made a mistake, even though she was telling the truth. Telling the truth was almost irrelevant. In the process, she had also done something wrong to her mother, trying to explain how remarkable she had been, how selfless. It had made her less remarkable.

"Listen to me, Emily. I can believe your mother went away somewhere, that she left you and your father. She might be dead, too. She might have committed suicide. She might be in a mental institution. She might be married to someone else. I believe you're an unhappy person. You have something to cover up, and I was the victim. I picked the wrong person to get to know. But look at me." He put his hand under her chin and turned her head. "You picked the wrong person to tell your story to."

Could he be insane? No. She didn't do anything. She just watched him.

"Life is a big play for you, a big soap-opera tragedy, and you're your own star, playing the daughter of this noble exotic person. Not true?"

"Everything I told you is completely the truth." He was now holding her chin between his thumb and his index finger. She was ready to run if she had to. She could run back down to the lake. If he ran after her he might catch her, but if he did anything to her he would be ruined. His fingers slid off her chin. He rubbed the front of her neck slowly up and down with his knuckle. If he thought she was such a fraud, why was he doing this? She was sure she had locked her door when she had gotten into the car.

"I can't see you being an actress, I'm sorry to say. You think it's saying whatever you want when you feel like it, and making fools of people. If you're an actor, you have to work very hard, and you have to have respect for your audience."

"I know that." He was continuing to rub her neck with his knuckle, up and down, as if he were doing it because he could, because she hadn't stopped him. Her neck seemed to be numb.

"I don't think you do. Fibbing isn't acting. I don't think you're sixteen, either. You're too clever. I think you look young for your age."

She shrugged. "I was sixteen on April twenty-second."

"What's your mother's name?"

"Why?"

"Tell me."

"It was Janet."

"Janet. Now I have a surprise for you."

"What?"

"Guess."

"I have to go home, Thom."

"Just guess."

"The surprise is you believe me."

"Sorry."

"I give up."

"You can't guess?"

"I can't."

"Believe it or not, I'm your mother Janet in disguise, back from the dead." He gave a fake spooky laugh—"Meeuuahhahahaha"—the kind they used on the radio to pretend to scare you. "I've been watching over you, dear." His voice had switched to falsetto. "I've come to find out if you've been good. Your mother wants to find out if you've been a good girl."

His knuckle rested at the base of her neck. She turned to see whether her door was locked or not. His arm heavily covered her shoulders. He was pulling her toward him. She twisted her face away from him. The palm of his left hand pressed her breast. "Please stop it." She tried to push his hand off her. It stuck. She hadn't been able to imagine real danger.

"Before I return to the dead, I must inspect you, dear." His hands were on her belt buckle.

She jumped in her seat, pulling up the door lock, grabbing the door handle, springing the door open, swinging out her legs. He held her at the waist from behind, squeezing her.

"Get back in. I'm driving you home."

"Let go. I'll walk. I want to walk."

"Get back in."

"I can't."

"I won't let go until you get in. I don't want any trouble from you about tonight. I don't want to hear from Mr. Boehm or anyone that I tried to rape you."

"I don't want to get you into trouble. I want to go home. Let go. I'll scream."

"All I was doing was giving you a taste of your own medicine and trying to show you you can't treat people like suckers. If anyone says anything to me about tonight, you'll pay. If you don't pay up here, I'll get you back in New York. Then you won't have to make anything up. You'll have a real story to tell people."

"I told you I don't want to get you in any trouble. I'm not going to tell anyone anything."

"You still have to get back in. I don't want you walking alone late at night. It looks bad. Just get in. You don't have to worry. I'm finished with you. You're a cock-tease and a waste of time. All I'd have to do is tell people you asked for a drive and you were dying to be fucked but I learned you were jailbait."

She hadn't heard "jailbait" before, but she thought she understood. "Let go."

"Are you getting in?"

"I'd rather walk."

"Suit yourself. But I meant what I said. Any trouble you make for me I can make permanently for you. You'll get what you deserve."

"I'm not going to forget. I'm not going to say a word. You didn't do anything."

He rubbed her breasts as if he were drying her. She felt her cells freeze. Then he said, "This is your choice, to walk. I offered to drive you." His hands were off her, only air around her body.

She stepped out of the car. He was already at the steering wheel. She saw the lights go on. She shut the door. The car took off, in zooms. She waited until the taillights and noise disappeared before she started walking.

She walked without thinking about what had happened, because she was free to walk. The darkness seemed made of leaves, yet she walked straight through it, lightly. Her mother had hugged her and Ellen goodbye on her knees on the pale-green rug in the living room. Emily didn't remember what her mother had said to them. She thought she remembered that her mother's eyes were wet and red, but that she hadn't actually broken down in front of them. Emily wondered many times if her mother had been determined not to break down. Her mother had been wearing a navy-blue suit, white blouse, and small navy-blue hat. Emily could remember the smooth, hard finish of the suit, which must have been gabardine.

Walking in the dark, late at night, from an experience that could have killed her, Emily felt excited by strength. She belonged to life, even though life was so mysterious and dramatic, so important. It was as if, before her birth, or even before her conception, she had tried out for a big part and, amazingly, won it.

PART TWO

CHAPTER FOUR

A Sense of Asunder

Not far from her old childhood abode, Emily had found a studio apartment in a gigantic new white building that made her think of a prison; she expected to see guards with machine guns standing behind the turquoise plastic wall of the penthouse terrace. The building belonged in a modern nightmare. But from her own doorway, when she squinted over the room, the beiges, browns, lemon, rose, lavender and green of her furniture, drapes, rug, and prints allowed her to think of meadows decorated with miraculously subtle wildflowers.

"Cute, toots," Ellen said on a rushed visit. Ellen seemed to Emily brisk in general. Short, short-haired, buxom and brisk. She brought with her an old standing lamp Emily had asked for and as a gift a set of rather blah linen placemats and napkins. Emily didn't understand why her sister, being older and living as she did in a parkview apartment in the Majestic, with a priceless baby girl and a husband she inexplicably didn't find boring, needed to make comments like "Cute, toots."

Ellen deigned to stay long enough for a cup of tea, which she drank standing up. "When's the housewarming?" she asked.

Emily thought the question had a facetious undertone, but she answered straight. She was unable to do otherwise. "I don't know enough people to invite." And how she wished she were back in college, hanging around with her theater buddies and still involved with Timothy— in the middle of her time with him.

"You'll probably meet lots of exciting, intellectual people at work.

In a matter of weeks, your datebook's going to be crawling with Mr. Rights, Misters Right."

Crawling? "How I wish. How do you know? What do you think's going to happen to me? I mean it. When I was sixteen, I was almost positive I wanted to be an actress, a great actress. Then it turned out I didn't, or not enough, or I wasn't crazy enough, or something. And after that I didn't want to be anything. It really helped at college that I'd given up my grand ambition, because I had a wonderful time acting and I was pretty good. But in actuality I wasn't anything but an English major, and now I'm about to be a flunky in a publishing company. Is that really it for me?" Of course she might end up being the next F. Scott Fitzgerald's editor. But somehow she doubted it. "Seriously. How do you think I'll turn out? Where am I going to be in a year or two?" She didn't usually talk to Ellen about important personal things, so when she did, she always seemed to end up saying too much and sounding too self-centered. "Don't you ever wonder? About yourself, I mean?"

"Not much. Mostly I'm there already. In other ways, I know what I want and I'll have to wait and see."

"I'm nowhere."

"And proud of it, right?"

Was Ellen acting like a sister who didn't want to be asked unanswerable questions, like *How do you think I'll turn out?*, which one might normally ask a mother? Or was Ellen actually, as Emily sometimes suspected, on the cold side, pushed over to the cold side early in her life by Mom's departure? "Where are you off to?" Emily asked, gulping as she realized she was still trying to know her sister and that her sister might be permanently and confusingly not close.

"Meeting some political pals downtown for lunch."

Emily had once been asked along to one of these significant get-togethers. Egg salad sandwiches at Schrafft's. Ellen and a couple of fellow volunteers from New Yorkers for Stevenson from the 1952 campaign talking about how they prayed Adlai would run again in '56 and playing the game of what cabinet posts they'd be asked to fill if Adlai beat out Ike. "Have fun."

"When do you start your glamorous job?"

"Monday. Thanks for the lamp."

"Not to mention the placemats and napkins. They're from Stan and baby Jan as well, naturally."

"Tell them thanks. Send my love. When can I see my niece?"

"This weekend. Come Sunday afternoon. Call Sunday morning. We'll set it up."

"Does she need a sitter? What am I talking about? I'm too old to be a sitter."

"Toodle-oo. Listen to me. You're lucky to be starting out. Enjoy it. Maybe you'll hit the jackpot and meet a Stan of your own."

They hugged and kissed and Ellen left, Emily thinking then, maybe it wasn't so much that Ellen couldn't be close, but that Emily didn't have the power to make Ellen close to her. Or possibly not that she didn't have the power in herself, but that Ellen and she couldn't be close because they were daughters of the same mother, and Ellen didn't want a sister whose mother had gone away for good.

Her job covered the rent, with a little left over. Her father had put money in the bank for her, saying he would otherwise be paying for her graduate school anyway. She'd landed the job through college connections, the job being assistant to Wilma Cotton, the executive secretary to Duncan Sinclair, the publisher of Partridge House. If things worked out, Emily would substitute for Mrs. Cotton during her vacation. Emily loved watching Mr. Sinclair, because he had such a rich style. He was immense—too tall to be fat—and ebullient. All his features were thick, including his boyishly full head of wavy chestnut hair. Emily thought of him as British. He dressed in splendid double-breasted pinstripes and blazers, with which he wore intensely colorful striped or dotted ties, and always a silk pocket handkerchief, related to his tie in a surprising or offhanded way. He smoked cigars and pipes all day long; he smoked like the god of smoking. His lunches often lasted three hours and were, she had heard, like fancy dinners—not only preceded by drinks, but accompanied by wines and followed by cognac. For this hearty yet distant lord she typed and took phone calls; she sometimes sat in on and wrote up his meetings; and she rejected manuscripts sent to him (rather than to editors) by friends, friends' friends, and friends' relatives.

He had asked her to call him Dunc; she couldn't. Once she called him Duncan, as a compromise, and he told her, laughing, that only his mother called him Duncan. So while she thought of him as Dunc, she called him Mr. Sinclair. He was twenty years older than she, and in addition, his size, his clothes, his fancy life awed her. His friendliness did nothing to make her feel that he was friendly. He seemed to her like a wind that blew by her and above her.

Wilma Cotton, also imposing at first, became easier quickly. (Almost everyone and everything was imposing at first, important. Almost everyone Emily met soon after college impressed her as the mysterious original of someone she knew to exist but had not encountered until now.) Wilma appeared to be about sixty, with thin white hair, small, fine features. She was pretty, and delicate without being frail, just like the Florentine gold-and-emerald seahorse pin always attached to the lapel of her suit, always a fine dark suit.

Wilma's rank in life exceeded her professional rank. While she was undeniably a bit of a chatterbox, Emily liked hearing about the occasional opening nights she went to with Gifford, her lawyer husband, and the parties attended by people whose names everyone knew. (Emily saw Wilma as able to hold her own at such events. Emily thought it would be accurate to say that Wilma possessed ironic wit. Wilma called Dunc "a good sort who sometimes enjoys life beyond what is strictly necessary.") At the same time, Wilma treated Emily as almost her equal, probably bending over backwards not to treat her like a twenty-two-year-old novice. If that was the case, Emily didn't mind. Even when Wilma did call her "Emily, dear," it made Emily feel good. Wilma could do no wrong. Neither could Emily. In August, when Wilma went off to Blue Hill, Maine, with Gifford for three weeks, Emily was asked to "man the fort."

Since Dunc seemed to come in irregularly during August, Emily had some relaxed days, during which she could read for personal pleasure or chat with Daphne Rice, who had graduated from Pembroke the year before Emily had and worked in the publicity department, or with Bobbie Frost, the secretary in the contracts department. She had lunch or dinner sometimes with Bobbie. Bobbie was entertaining in a brazen way, but about as deep as a fingernail, interested in clothes and finding a husband. Emily would also have lunch occasionally with Daphne. She liked Bobbie better than she liked Daphne. Bobbie was sort of crude, but Daphne was too polite, ladylike, unctuous, a combination of goody-goody and slinky. Emily thought it best to stay friendly with her.

Then there was Robin Todd, a young editor who dropped in on Emily a fair amount, without ever staying long. He said very little; he wanted her to talk. He wanted to know what she read in her leisure time. (Right now, it was *Tender is the Night*, again.) Had she read *Pride and Prejudice*? (Of course.) *War and Peace*? (Yes.) *Anna Karenina*? (Emphatically yes.) *Portrait of the Artist*? (Yes.) *Dubliners*? (Most of.) *Ulysses*? (A little.) *Portrait of the Artist as a Young Dog*? (What?) *Middlemarch*?

(Loved it.) *Portrait of a Lady?* (Her favorite.) He recommended Proust, Gide, Kafka, Gertrude Stein, Djuna Barnes. He recommended novels she'd barely heard of, no less read. But he never lent her anything.

Robin was shy, to say the least, but he intrigued her. Considering his behavior, she found him surprisingly attractive—sparkling blond hair, slender. He had to be smart. He dressed somewhat oddly, in a normal seersucker or other summer suit or jacket, but always the same black knit tie (unless he used more than one black knit tie, which would have been odder). Anyway, his interest, if it could be called that, flattered her. It also kept her on edge. He didn't even ask her to have lunch.

The only man she had spent much time with since graduation was Byron Pecora, a fellow member of Sock and Buskin at college, and a definite homo. She went to the theater with him, standing room, or they went to the movies; Iris Gamble, also from Sock and Buskin, came with them sometimes. In August, Emily had dinner with Andy Propper. Disaster. Andy was starting medical school, of all things, preparing to be a psychiatrist. Andy had told her—his hand ever so tenderly on her shoulder—that they should get married. She had answered right away that she wasn't smart enough for him, while thinking: how could someone so ridiculously impulsive possibly be a psychiatrist? And so arrogant? He was the same old Andy, but his old attempts at maturity now seemed passé to her. He sounded irresponsible and yet having to be in control of everything. What did Andy know about marriage, for God's sake? Or anything else?

Thinking obsessively about the housewarming party she planned to give in October (having decided to take Ellen's unserious question seriously), Emily would imagine asking Robin, would imagine his being there, until she convinced herself he was too cautious to invite. On her list, from Partridge, were Wilma (with her husband, if he wanted to come); Daphne Rice; and just possibly Dunc, if she could get up the nerve. (There was a Mrs. Dunc—Emily had spoken with her twice on the phone—but Emily suspected that Mrs. Dunc would not exactly prize an invitation to her husband's secretary's assistant's one-room apartment.) The non-Partridge people were her father and Bunny the unwicked but no less brainless stepmother; Ellen (and baby Janet, if Ellen would bring her) and Stan, who smoked green cigars out of a mouth that Emily thought every time she saw him looked like a rectum; her grandparents ("grandparents" had always meant Mom's parents, Luise and Gus; Daddy's mother had died a long time ago and his father lived permanently in Miami, so, as it often occurred to Emily, the only parents, in effect, that her father had around were his dead wife's parents, leftover in-laws she knew he wasn't particularly close to, though she herself loved them a lot); Jill Strauss, "do-gooding," as Jill called it, at social work grad school and the Morningside Settlement House; and Byron Pecora and Iris Gamble, from college. She didn't have the nerve to call Timothy.

Emily couldn't conceive of those guests who didn't know each other talking to each other. Her father would be bored stiff. Bunny would read a poem (how could you prevent it?). Stan would stink up the place with his cigar. Her theater friends would make fools of themselves by being arty. Jill would disapprove of them. Wilma would be chirpy and tactful. Yet Emily wanted badly to give the party, gather her small collection of friends, relatives, and friendlies, her attachments, even if they didn't belong together, under the low ceiling of her dinky, viewless apartment.

Everyone accepted; she couldn't believe it. Dunc himself would "try to stop by." Jill was bringing Steve Farkas, a guy in the toy business she had met when he donated toys to the settlement house. They were going to see *The Diary of Anne Frank* and would be up right after. Emily wondered then if she should invite Andy Propper for herself, even though she couldn't stand him anymore.

She had decided on an after-dinner rather than a cocktail party, as being easier to prepare for after work and also because it would be longer, warmer. Cheeses, pâté, fruit, pastries, scotch, sherry, chianti, club soda, Cokes, ginger ale. During the week, on her way home, she stopped by her father's to fetch extra plates, cups and saucers, glasses, napkins, the big coffee maker. On D-Day, Friday the twenty-first, she bought the food itself, and the mums, zinnias, asters. The coat rack was delivered. She vacuumed, laid everything out, took a shower, dressed in her new floor-length plum velveteen skirt and cream-colored satin blouse.

At eight, seated on her tweedy oatmeal convertible sofa with a glass of Noilly Prat on the rocks, she waited, looking over the food and flowers, thinking of a paneled living room, paintings, canapés on silver trays, the many guests all talking, she the hostess with a name tag of reputation, the world-famous editor. In the real world, she had done a tremendous amount of planning, worrying, and carrying, given months of thought to a measly, probably awkward party that would be all over by one at the latest. Only Byron and Iris would stay, and she'd want them to go. Cracker crumbs, cheese rinds, glasses containing fractions of liquid and drowned butts. Dregs. At twenty-two, she felt as sad as fifty. When the party was over, her life would be exactly the same. Now that she was out in the world, things had stopped happening to her.

It was possible that the purpose of her life had already ended the year before graduation, with Timothy. She had a past, all right, but where was her future? And what would she be in it? She annoyed Ellen when she worried about her life this way. As a rule, though, she thought of herself as much more determined than pessimistic. She thought, as a matter of fact, that she still took life much more seriously than Ellen did. For Ellen, having a rectum husband and a baby named after their mother and working for Adlai (that's what you called him when you got to be a volunteer) meant you were automatically serious.

Timothy had called Adlai Stevenson "Sweet Adelaide." Timothy could never leave a name, word, or phrase unchanged. The first time she'd really met him was after the fall tryouts her junior year for *Ah, Wilderness.* (He was a junior, too, but a transfer student, so she'd never even seen him before the tryouts.) They had auditioned for the leads and received minor roles.

The cast sat in the Faunce House theater while Mr. Gillette sat on the edge of the stage telling them what he wanted to see them doing in the play, talking something about "a sense of wonder, a childlike sense of wonder," in the embarrassing shiny-eyed way Gillette had of saying things, as if he had just thought them up. Emily noticed that Timothy, sitting next to her in the second row, was taking rapid notes on his copy of the script. Then he tilted what he had written toward her. "Do I have a sense of wundah!" she made out. "I own a race horse named Sense o' Wundah. In storms I have a sense of thunder. When I make a mistake, I have a sense of blunder. When I steal, I have a sense of plunder. When I visit Australia I have a sense of down under. When I'm torn, I have a sense of asunder."

Since she couldn't laugh out loud, she blushed. She remembered her heart feeling as if it were sinking too fast into a featherbed, a feeling of alarming delight. Then, after a few seconds' panic that she wouldn't be able to play his game, she took his script and his pencil and wrote beneath his series, "When I went to Alaska last summer, I had a sense of tundra." He wrote, "Your reply gives me a sense of rejoinda." She answered, "Isn't this getting redunda?" and he, "Yes, and besides, I have to read *Daniel Deronda.*"

After the cast meeting, they went to the Blue Room to have the first of their hundreds of cups of coffee. He told her he was at work on a very long musical comedy called *Kiss Me, Nathan Detroit,* containing characters, stars, plots, and songs from some of the great shows of recent years. Among the numbers were, "Everything's Up to Nate in Detroit"; "Shall We Dance, Or Would You Rather be Doin' What Comes Naturally?"; "I've Got the Horse Right Here, So You'll Never Walk Alone"; and "Bea Lillie, Ha'i, May I Call You, Any Night, Any Day?"

She understood from the beginning that he tried too hard. He understood it, too. He would interrupt himself in the middle of some Gilbert and Sullivan song (he knew them all as if he had been born singing them—that is, he knew the words one hundred percent and the tunes approximately), and cry out, "Stop me, Oh, prithee, stop me! I beg you, I command you, stop me! Cut out mine tongue, cut out mine pastrami, cut out mine corned beef!" So it went. But the important thing was that she had never met anyone like him and was certain she never would. She could manage his being such a maniac because he was one of a kind. The way he behaved made her want him to be quiet, so she could find out what he was really like. Of course once he had quieted was when the real trouble began. Once she had gotten him under control, things had gotten out of control.

You could also say the trouble had started immediately, as soon as they took up with each other, because they liked each other so much and were barely ever apart when their schedules permitted. It comforted her that despite his being silly and even tiresome sometimes (though he never ran out of freshness), his silliness was sophisticated. And it comforted her that he liked her even though he came from a more sophisticated background (his deceased father had been Sam Field, the screenwriter and famous wit) and even though he had twice her brains. He made her smarter, quicker, much more playful and more confident than she'd ever been. She had the nerve with him, was inspired by his company, to imitate people, as she'd been able to do on rare occasion when with Jill in high school. Her parody of the Pembroke "Brokettes"—their flirty, eye-rolling, mass finger-snapping singing style—killed Timothy. When Timothy laughed his hardest, his laughter was a wheeze, frequently accompanied by a helpless stamping of his feet or a kicking of the nearest table leg. Sometimes he fell off his chair. She loved him most, at the beginning, when she made him laugh.

Also, she loved to look at him. Timothy was very boyish, so boyish he seemed almost girlish, tomboyish, skinny from the face down, without his face being bony in the dramatic way, like Andy's. Timothy seemed about two-thirds the size of the other boys on campus, most of whom were such shmoes. His hair and hers were almost exactly the same color. He wore it longer than average, to her pleasure. He didn't dress at all conspicuously. He had regular, nice clothes—button-downs, tweed jackets. He lived with his mother, Pamela, in New York, on Fifth Avenue and Ninety-fourth, sixteen blocks from her.

She felt partly like a lucky, slightly older sister toward him, without being sure she wasn't in love with him. She didn't know precisely what she felt, or even what to feel. It was a luxury, being best friends with a boy (young man). Along with the luxury went the difficulty he provided of being "on" nonstop. He had to be handled, disciplined. He cost something.

You could have described him as intense but not romantic. He was definitely huggable and kissable. They had necked by the Seekonk (Timothy: "Seekonk and die."), but nothing had ignited, maybe because she expected him to interrupt the mood with a wisecrack, or because they were outdoors, or because although she found him adorable, and had dreams and fantasies about their doing everything, she didn't really think of him as mature enough to make it smart to start anything momentous. She didn't know.

During Thanksgiving vacation, they went to *Tea and Sympathy*, which moved her a lot. On the way out of the theater, Timothy couldn't resist making up rapid-fire variations of Deborah Kerr's great curtain-line, "Years from now, when you talk about this—and you will—be kind." Actually, the play had made her feel particularly close to Timothy. On the street, starting to cry, she told him to just stop it for once. He apologized when he saw she was crying. In the taxi, he seemed angry, paying no attention to her. Then he put his arms around her and said, "Come to my house. My mother went to Connecticut." When he told the cab driver they'd changed their minds and gave him the different address, Emily felt like saying, "That's all right, leave it as it is," but she said nothing. He held her hand firmly, then lightly, then firmly. She looked at him. He looked at her in a strange haughty way, a severe way, a totally new kind of expression for him, meanwhile stroking her hair as if he were a serious father stroking his daughter's hair.

His apartment was much smaller than her family's, but much more glamorous, heavy silk drapes in the living room, deep rose and silver. She remembered red roses, a jade cigarette box; above the fireplace, a portrait of Pamela, the absent mother, in a lavender dress. On the walls of Timothy's room was a Hirschfeld caricature, inscribed, of his father smoking a cigarette in a holder, wearing evening clothes, and with a heavy frown and a tiny grin; and framed photographs of scenes from Marx Brothers movies, all inscribed to "Sam," or to "Sam and Pam," or "Sameleh and Pameleh," or "Samuel and Pamuel." Timothy himself, she realized then, could almost have been another Marx brother.

They ended up lying on his bedspreaded bed, her heart spilling danger in all directions of her body. She remembered the spread being thin, a roughish cotton with a design of wide ice-cream-colored bands. She took her bra off, but they both stayed more or less in their underpants. They did almost everything, and the next night repeated what they had done. It was wonderful to be so close, to experience this unbearable squirming pressure building up, as if she were about to freeze and boil over at the same time, without worrying (too much) about getting pregnant. She had once heard the inimitable Bunny say (lessons learned at a stepmother's knee), "The wages of sin are diapers." She couldn't forget the expression, it was so revolting. But she certainly didn't want to get pregnant.

She began to imagine, though, what it might be like to be married to Timothy; she wondered if he would be famous, like his father, if he had it in him to succeed after college, or if he was going to try to coast on his father's reputation and not get anywhere. With all Timothy's brains, she hadn't been sure he would try hard enough, concentrate, risk something. She thought about this so much that she finally came to realize she had been putting on him a possible future problem of her own. But realizing hadn't stopped her from worrying about his future. (He was in fact now a scriptwriter for "The Monte Madison Show"; she had seen it a few times—there was no particular Timothy quality in it. She didn't know if he should be called a success or not, but at least he must be making a lot of money, and it certainly beat being anybody's secretary.)

When they were lying together, he became ideal all of a sudden, completely tender, quiet, serious, his face so loving it brought tears to her eyes, with no danger he would interrupt the mood. He said things to her—surprisingly sexy things, but not at all put on, or embarrassing—that excited her almost as much as their touching did. He had known more than she expected him to know, certainly more than she knew. He was more comfortable about sex than she had expected him to be, more natural.

He referred to orgasms as "orgs." There were two-hundred-volt "orgs," and so on. He also told her he thought masturbation vile, so he hired a masturbator whenever he needed one. That was as Timothyesque as he got on the subject of sex. They did it a third time (somewhat less excitingly, for some reason), then his mother came back. They were both content, she thought, with enough to keep them warm and enough to be scared of. She began to think she must be in love.

Everything was great until they got up to school again. Then all his former brain energy, silly as it had sometimes been, seemed devoted to more sex. He could get hold of an apartment on Bowen Street for the afternoon. She resisted. He bought Trojans. He put one on each of his fingers, telling her he'd bitten off all his nails and had to conceal the unsightly embarrassment. She said she got the message. At the same time, he brought her serious letters, love letters, saying they belonged together. Emily-Emmy-me. They would get married after college as soon as he got a job. He said she understood him. She made him the best person he could ever be, the most likable to himself. She would make him the most productive, the least disruptive possible Timothy, be his muse, his fuse, his lollapalooze.

She said she loved him, but she wasn't ready yet for the biggest decisions, and (she didn't actually know if this was true) wouldn't be no matter who the man was. So please don't rush her, be careful of them, don't wreck it, one thing they had for sure was time. She wanted to sleep with him as much as he wanted to sleep with her, but she needed to wait.

He wrote her: "So listen, don't worry. I've put it all in perspective and I see now that it's only love, sex, life and death. God! How blind I've been!" That day, she went with him to the apartment on Bowen Street. On a stranger's bed, she felt as if she were pretending. She stopped him. "Christmas is coming," she said. It still embarrassed her that she'd said that. She had simply meant that in New York, things would be better again, not to sound like a cute little sexpot full of phony promises. The whole thing had been unfair to each of them. One of them had been too young, that was all she could think now.

At Christmas—between Christmas and New Year's—her father and Bunny went to Miami. And there was the apartment, all alone, except for Margaret, who slept way in the back. They had by far the most exciting of their times, almost out of control. She could so easily have let him slide right into her. In order to prevent herself from letting him, or in order to take her own risk, she put her mouth on him. Her tenderness and excitement amazed her. She loved him or loved both of them so much that she cried. While she was crying, she actually swallowed his semen. He was thrilled and grateful and so concerned for her that they both ended up laughing. It was a combination funeral-wedding-birthday.

Then he wanted to sleep over, with her. How could she let him, with Margaret there? Once he had finally left the apartment, he returned, ringing the doorbell because she didn't hear him knocking, and waking Margaret. She told Margaret everything was all right, and her friend had forgotten a book. Timothy pleaded to stay with her. He swore he would be found in Ellen's old room in the morning. He couldn't help it, he said. Everything that had happened made it impossible for him to leave. Impossible. He didn't care what they did or didn't do, as long as he could just stay with her. I know, she said, but why not tomorrow? Because we were just together, he said, and I can't separate myself from you. I can't be without you. I can't. He made sharp gestures with his forearms, pleading sharply, and twisting sharply on his feet. He kept his voice down, in deference to having awakened Margaret, but even though it sounded as if he had laryngitis, she felt as if he were yelling. Please! he kept saying, please! Tomorrow, she said. He said he wanted to do for her what she had done for him before. She said she'd have to work up to that. He told her he wanted to be stuck to her, he didn't want to do anything or be anywhere without her.

She couldn't say anything to him. She would have liked such talk had they still been in her bed, but now she couldn't stand it. His behavior froze her. All her former emotions were congealed, so that she felt frozenly sick to her stomach. She hated him for whining and for acting as if he had no place to go but her, as if it were her duty to provide him permanent bodily warmth or he would die. She finally made him leave by being as obstinate as he was and repeating until he understood that she would be too nervous if he stayed because Margaret would know and be upset. After he left, she couldn't sleep, thinking he might come back again.

She didn't see him anymore that vacation. She said she needed time to think. To her surprise, she wanted to stay cold; she wanted to hold out on him. She was surely at least as miserable as he said he would be if he couldn't stay with her for one night, but she didn't want to be in his presence.

Back at school, he wrote her notes, plain serious notes without any jokes, begging her to talk, just to talk. By now she hated herself for being tight, almost as much as she hated him for being so needy, and she worried that her reaction to him might seem to be too much her fault if she didn't try to put some words to it for him. So they met, but she had lost heart. Her warmth had gone for good. She couldn't forgive him. She didn't accuse him of being reckless and immature and overtly needy. Instead, she explained that she wasn't ready for what he needed, sexually or otherwise; she wasn't up to him. She didn't say it, but she knew their future was hopeless. He was too desperate and self-indulgent or she was too selfish.

Then he stopped trying. They became strangers until they were seniors, when they kidded around at a distance, like people who talked without knowing each other's names, without quite wanting to introduce themselves. It seemed to her that he had done the going-away. His extremeness, his neediness, intensity, had taken him away, left her behind, not given her a chance. He came to seem to her elusive and undamageable, while she was wounded. She would remind herself that Timothy, silly or serious, was too much Timothy. But she couldn't get rid of him. In the long run, he got what he had wanted that night, without even being there: he had stayed with her. Timothy had been the only serious possibility so far, if not ever. Andy at his most impressive (in high school, unfortunately) hadn't come close to Timothy in uniqueness, at least not worthwhile uniqueness. Maybe her problem was that she just hadn't been interesting since Timothy. But there hadn't been anyone to be interesting to. Was she right to be worried about herself, or just too impatient?

At the moment, she felt dangerously close to calling Timothy tomorrow (he was still in the book). Or right now, and inviting him to the party. He would arrive very late. Mr. Show-biz. Had he grown bigger? Maybe he was no longer unusual. Maybe she had overrated him when she knew him. She might never meet anyone again it would even be possible to overrate. She remembered everything about him so clearly.

CHAPTER FIVE

The Housewarming

When, at the party, Emily asked Byron if he had been in touch with Timothy lately ("Just curious"), Byron answered that Timothy, although friendly enough on the phone when he could be reached, was always busy and never called back. She regretted having thought about him earlier. It peeved her now and made her feel foolish that after he had graduated from college he had then graduated into a separate world, gone through a private curtain into the world of TV, where those plebeians who merely watched TV were not admitted. It wasn't exactly the same, but sometimes she thought her mother was not so much dead as on the other side of a curtain that went from earth to sky. No one could see over it. All the people on the other side had the same secret: they weren't really dead, but were hiding forever. Having the secret made them superior.

Standing beside Byron in the dining area, Emily watched her grandparents being the center of attention. When they had arrived—the first to arrive by about twenty minutes—Emily thought how glad she was they were there, how proud; then she worried who was going to talk to them. But partly just because they were the oldest, she supposed, and also so charming, they were a big hit. Daphne Rice and Wilma were sitting with them on the sofa, Gifford Cotton and Iris standing by. They were all enjoying someone's remark, probably Grandpa Gus's. Grandpa had the sense of humor, despite his severe demeanor and his dark, dark suits. Granny was so lovely and sharp, people couldn't see her sadness and bitterness. In the other cluster, Dunc—the actual Mr. Sinclair!—seemed to be entertaining her father, Bunny, and Ellen. (Her father had come in with four bottles of champagne and looking unusually pleased with himself about something, as if he had a trick up his sleeve.)

It made her teary, it was such a compliment that everyone had come and seemed so glad to be there, enjoying themselves on their own momentum, like old friends having a reunion. What had she done to deserve it? Only Stan stood by himself, staining her ceiling permanently with cigar smoke. And he and Ellen hadn't brought baby Janet, whom she had wanted to show off.

"Your grandparents look like such great folks. Your grandmother, really, she's so distinguished." Byron always enthused in a rather whining tone of voice, sounding as if he were sarcastic instead of sincere, even though Emily knew he was sincere. His voice was part of his not being serious or intense enough in general. For some reason, it seemed to go with his snub nose and ringlety hair.

"She's great, but she's got this perfect instinct for memories that really depress you. When she got here tonight, the first thing she said when she took off her coat—she gave me such a beautiful burnt-orange vase—was how well she remembered my parents' first party in their own first apartment twenty-nine years ago. My Granny is my mother's walking monument. My mother was their only child. I couldn't stand to be that way. But she has the shared history with my mother much more than I do. I may be a slightly bit drunk on the champagne. And I had vermouth earlier. Forgive me if I'm babbling."

"Eat, drink, and be merry, dahling."

It was as if there hadn't been time for her somber mother to get out into the sun, where Emily could get a good look at her. She had imagined her mother doing things in the light, had made up walks, motions, smiles that occurred in the light, had added her mother's presence to occasions that had occurred without her. Sometimes, though, like tonight, her mother moved of her own accord, like a creature waking up at the bottom of the sea. "My mother was always holding meetings at our house because our living room was big. She was like the star. People came to her. She held the meetings and they came to them." Byron was listening with a fixedly serious face, probably slightly embarrassed and not knowing what to say to her. She kissed him on the cheek. "Now don't be rash," Byron said.

"I'm just glad we're friends." In college, Byron had been adorably funny on stage, mostly because he was always being miscast, although he could be very funny when he intended to be. But Byron wasn't going to make it as an actor. She knew it. She suspected he knew it, too. He didn't have the ambition or the uniqueness.

"I'd be glad to be my grandmother at her age, but not grief-stricken. Sometimes she looks at me as if I'm Li'l Orphan Annie. But she's amazing, really. She has all this spirit and generosity despite her sadness. She's a lot nicer to my stepmother than I am. I think she's so disappointed she figures she has to be pleasant. She keeps up with everything. She keeps herself up. She knitted that gorgeous suit she's wearing. She's extremely well-read. Everything in her apartment is beautiful. In the country they have the most beautiful garden you can imagine. They'll be married fifty-seven years in June."

"Listen, Emilia, I'll take her anytime. My grandmother looks like a dago Aunt Jemima." He laughed—a short, victorious laugh.

Emily laughed with him, at his remark and his laugh. "That's so funny, Byro."

He laughed again, in almost exactly the same way. "Poor dear. She can barely speak English and she's a terrible cook." He wiped his eyes. "What fun."

"By the way, do you want to go standing with me tomorrow for *Anne Frank?*"

"I'm all atwitter."

"My friend Jill is seeing it right now, and coming here later. With Steve. Steve Farkas."

"Farkas! Good Lord, I hope they don't marry."

"What's in a name, I ask? I haven't met him."

Her chest and stomach stiffened, as if she were holding her breath, as she saw Bunny approaching her in basic black and bracelets, and with her silly smile, half-smug and half-shy, and her usual wobbly steps, which made her seem as though she were thinking of turning a corner, even though she was coming right at you. Because of her curly hair, she looked to Emily like a blonde sheep on its hind legs. In one of her paws she carried a sheet of her pink stationery.

"Are you ready for my opus?" Bunny asked.

"You have an opus? Sure."

"Your father also has a few well-chosen words."

"God, I'll leave."

"You can't leave your own party, honey."

"Then I'll move."

"Oh, Lee," she called to Emily's father. "You have to hurry. She's threatening to walk out on us." Bunny tapped the neck of a chianti bottle with a knife.

Everybody was silent and smiling at Emily, suddenly her own guest of honor. Her face was hot. With a geeky grimace she couldn't seem to undo, she looked at her father, at least giving herself an excuse for not having to look at the others, especially the Partridge people. Why would they care about this family stuff?

Her father said to her, from a ceremonial distance, "Emily, when you were sixteen you wanted to be on the stage, but thank goodness I see you've gotten too bashful. I may say that both my daughters, as well as my baby granddaughter, who is unable to attend tonight due to extreme fatigue, are as modest as they are beautiful, and I couldn't be more proud of them. Anyway, Cookie, the welcome mat is always out for you at your former address, so you should always feel free to come borrow a cup of sugar."

"Cubed or granulated," Bunny said.

Emily always had to remind herself that for her father Bunny was an "understanding, fun-loving companion." He was entitled, God knows. "And much more sensitive and intelligent than you or Ellen seem to imagine. Everyone's not a genius," he'd said, after she'd stupidly made a teenagey face when he'd told her, visiting her up at the Greenway, late in the summer, six whole years ago, that he and Bunny were getting married. "So don't be so snooty." She couldn't stand it that she'd provoked him to say that to her, although poor Bunny had never failed yet to do at least one moronic thing every time she saw her.

"And sweetheart," he said, "I know you're not lacking for escorts, but if you ever need a young man to go to the theater with, give me a call. We had great times." They walked toward each other, the guests lightly applauding. Emily could have sworn she and her father had rehearsed this moment, but she knew they hadn't. They embraced; he kissed her forehead. They stood together at the side of the room, leaving Byron incongruously closest to Bunny by the square dining table.

Bunny said, "I promise I have a very short poem for Emily." She read from her pink paper with, Emily thought, whatever the opposite of a straight face was—some strange kind of smile that made her look as if she were announcing surprising good news.

> She says her apartment is small,
> But we don't think so at all,
> 'Cause the tenant who lives here's a big-hearted
>   gal,
> And that makes the love wall-to-wall.

Bunny bounced her head to the loose, sparse claps. At Pembroke, Emily realized, Bunny would have been a Brokette! Bunny then veered over to Emily, saying, "May I?" and kissed her cheek. "And you'll definitely be moving to a two-bedroom before long," she said into Emily's ear.

"I guess you never can tell," Emily said, looking at Ellen (standing with the bored Stan) for a sisterly sign of disbelief over the poem. Ellen, however, called "Speech, speech," throwing her arm twice into the air, as if she were at a rally.

"Thanks a heap, sis," Emily said. The worst was over, though. It wouldn't hurt for her to open her mouth and say something nice. "Okay. Speech. I want to thank my father and stepmother" (lest there be any doubt in anyone's mind) "for their many cups of sugar, without which this party wouldn't have been possible. Thank you for the speech, Daddy, and the poem was delightful, Bunny. Ogden Nash is quivering in his boots. And by the way, Daddy, I'm not loaded up with escorts, as you refer to them, so anytime you say. I'm especially glad my truly wonderful grandparents are here. I'm very flattered that my boss, Mr. Sinclair—Dunc—came, and Wilma, my other boss, and her husband. And all of you. I've sort of forgotten what this party is for, but I'm glad I gave it. I mean, glad I'm giving it, since the evening is still young. And thank you for your extremely thoughtful, generous gifts."

"You're welcome!" Dunc said, to the laughter of the relaxing group. Dunc had brought cognac; Wilma and Gifford, a gorgeous bright blue-and-yellow floral Spode cup and saucer; ever-creative Iris, one of her watercolors of irises, inscribed but unframed; Byron, copper masks of comedy and tragedy to hang on the wall; Daphne, a large, floppy pink throw pillow; Ellen and Stan, a bottle of red wine and a bottle of white wine. And the champagne from her father and the vase from her grandparents. "This evening is young no longer, my dear; not for us," said Wilma. "We had a marvelous time. I am mad about your grandparents." Gifford patted Emily's hand. Then Dunc was saying, "Great, great, see you Monday." And Emily was showing them into the corridor, wanting to say, "But it's so early." They helped themselves to their coats from the coatrack. Out of the elevator, far down the hall, came a man, or grown boy, carrying across his arms a tall cone of paper. He was marching fast, right at them. "I'm looking for Mademoiselle Emily Weil. Is that Emily there?" His voice was warm, deep, and ultrarefined. "I'm Emily." For some reason, she thought of Thom Blake on the dressing-room stairs at the Greenway; then she was

thinking, My God, I don't believe this, this person is George Koenigsberg. Why is this person George Koenigsberg?

He was wearing a dove-gray, double-breasted overcoat, open. His
hair hung on his forehead, a sleepy pompadour over sleepy eyes, the
way it usually was in his photographs. "I have found you," he said,
stopping before her with glowing brown eyes and presenting the
flowers while smiling as if he were proud of her, seizing her shoulders,
kissing her left cheek, her right cheek. The smell of his cologne seemed
to her like a secret she wasn't quite supposed to know, personal instead
of from a bottle. She felt as though surrounded by hubbub, cameras.
She held the flowers to her chest while he introduced himself to her
departing guests. Wilma said, "We think you're the most talented young man in the world." "Yes, indeed," Gifford murmured.
Dunc added a few hurried, hearty words. Emily now took in George's
maroon silk bowtie, tattersall shirt, gray double-breasted suit.
"We must be off. So happy to meet you, Mr. Koenigsberg," Wilma
said. As they walked away, Gifford turned to wave to her with a
charming bob, making Emily feel better about her relief at seeing
them go. What would they think of *this* at Partridge? Would she be
promoted?

"So how *are* you? You look fantastic," George said. "You were a
perfect princess of a girl and you've improved."

"How are *you*?" She was about to re-enter her apartment with George
Koenigsberg. Byron, Iris, and Daphne would pass out. "And to what
do I owe the honor? My father must have told you I was having a
party, obviously."

"But I'm overjoyed! You look so great." He grinned and held his
grin.

She saw, under the cone's inner paper, a large bunch of roses.
"Thank you. These are beautiful. I'll put them right in water. Do you
want to hang your coat out here? I don't know if you're staying, of
course."

"Of course I'm staying." He removed his coat.

Was he lonely since his divorce from Constance Shipp, about three
years ago? "There's room in my closet, but not for everyone's. That's
why the rack."

"Might as well make use." He hung it up.

"How do you want to be introduced?"

"By my name will be fine. Don't worry, bubbeleh. I put my pants
on nine legs at a time, like anyone else."

But he seemed to straighten, as if her apartment were the stage of

Carnegie Hall and he about to appear. So here goes, she thought. What have I got to lose? With a warm face, she led him in.

"Say, Dad, look who I found outside. Aren't you clever?" Iris, in her black sweater, made a face of amazement and congratulations mixed together, with her mouth closed, her jaw down, and her eyes up.

"Hi, Lee," George said. Her father greeted George by grasping his shoulder, patting his back.

"This is George Koenigsberg," Emily said, doubting that she sounded as matter-of-fact as she wanted to. She called off her guests' names. George went among them, each handshake deepening the silence in the room. He sat down on the convertible sofa, Grandpa Gus fussing deferentially and unnecessarily to make room for him. George was wearing dark gray socks and gray suede shoes. Gray underwear? "Would you like champagne?" she asked him. "You have a choice of champagne, sherry, chianti, cognac, scotch, coffee, tea or milk and cookies." The onlookers were nervously amused.

"How about a little of each? I'm not greedy." More amusement. He took out cigarettes—Pall Malls; Timothy had also smoked Pall Malls. "I'd love champagne. How can I turn down champagne?" He asked Granny and Grandpa if his smoking would bother them. Granny, with a typical smoky chuckle, said, "Oh, goodness, no," and put one of her Lucky Strikes to her lips. Having lighted his and Granny's cigarettes with a lighter that did not look like any Zippo, George said to the small assemblage, indicating Emily, "This angelic creature, with her beloved father and my folks, came back to see me in the green room at Carnegie Hall after a concert when she was a child. I've never forgotten her. How could I forget her?"

The feeling was mutual. She handed him his glass of champagne. She said, "I had just had my fourteenth birthday. You were only twenty-two and you'd just been in *Time* magazine as the 'Dreamboat of classical music.' It was the premiere of your piano concerto with the Philharmonic, and you said to me, 'Isn't this marvelous? I must find some way of making it last forever.' "

"As a matter of fact, I am finding ways. I am going to find ways."

"Let us in on the secret, Mr. Koenigsberg," Granny said.

"It's George, please. It's what my new piece is about."

Emily had left the roses leaning against the dining table. If she didn't put them in water it would be clear she was willing to let them wait because she was so eager to hear George's every word. She forced herself to excuse herself. She poured half a glass more champagne

and took a sip. She felt sharp, not fuzzy. She asked Byron to open a
new bottle, there were two left, and to ask people if they wanted more
of anything. Using the sink in the kitchenette, rhe went about the
business of transferring the evening's mums from her large glass vase
to her grandparents' new ceramic vase, putting George's roses in the
glass vase.

George was saying that he had become obsessed with reincarnation
and was reading everything about it he could get his hands on. George
Koenigsberg was revealing his obsession in her little apartment. One
of the gods of the world—it was the equivalent for her of Adlai walking
by surprise into Ellen's apartment. George was also the son of her
father's (and mother's) friends, Bernie and Flo. But everyone started
somewhere.

She had thought, eight years ago, when he had said he must find
a way of making it last forever, how natural it seemed to her that
someone so talented, handsome, famous, and young should talk that
way. She had always felt exactly the same way, and she didn't even
have any talent or fame, or any kind of looks that would make her
famous. All she was was young, then and now. All she wanted was
never to die. She had wanted to live forever from way before she had
met George Koenigsberg and, she was quite sure, from before her
mother had left home. But she had thought at times, very privately,
that she had inherited the desire to live forever from her mother,
that her mother wouldn't have gone to Shanghai, done something so
extreme, unless she was the kind of person who believed that by making the sacrifice of leaving home to help the refugees get settled, she
would return home to live forever. Only it hadn't worked for her
mother. That's why it would work for her mother's daughter instead.
Emily had never told a soul these thoughts, including Timothy. It
would endanger her chances of being right if she said anything.

Emily placed her grandparents' gift vase, with the mums in it, on
the coffee table in front of the sofa, and the roses across the room
on her lamp table. George was differentiating between the Buddhist,
Hindu, and Celtic beliefs in the transmigration of souls, or metem-
psychosis, referring to himself as "an absolute metempsychotic." He
went on to Jewish and Greek beliefs. Daphne and Iris were at his feet.
Emily was pleased with herself for having thought, without thinking
about it, to give her grandparents' vase a more prominent position
than George's roses; at the same time, the roses, though not center-
stage, were on a higher table, like a featured actor "also starring."

She retrieved her champagne glass from the dining table, ready to participate. The buzz of the doorbell—Jill and Farkas—rerouted her. Maybe it wasn't Jill and Farkas. Maybe it was Marilyn Monroe and the Actors Studio. Maybe it was Bill Haley and the Comets. She had a star here, so she was herself a star. Anything could happen. She wished people would keep coming all night. But it was Jill and, beside her (unless it was someone else; she felt slightly disappointed), the tall Steve Farkas.

Jill, in her new bright green coat, with her hair looking golden, was a bit more glamorous than usual, less just-plain-wholesome. "It was incredible," Jill said. "You have got to see it. Emily, Steve, Steve, Emily."

"Please to meet you, Emily. I've heard a lot about you."

"Welcome to my abode," she replied. After all, what difference did it make to her if his remark sounded too personal instead of flattering? Anyway, he reminded her of the regular boys she had usually disliked at college.

"How's the party, Emileeee?" Jill asked.

"Much better than I thought. So much better."

As Steve took care of the coats (his was a middle-aged-man's gray tweed), Emily wanted to tell them who owned the dove-gray coat, but how could she? When they came in, though, they'd meet George, and then Jill would think her affected for not having told them he was there. Emily always worried that Jill would think her affected or pretentious for this or that, yet Jill always seemed not to care or not to have noticed. Steve was wearing a blue herringbone jacket, white button-down shirt, and a navy-and-yellow striped tie. Somewhere between square and mature. His cheeks were pink, as if he'd slept on them.

Emily fingered the velveteen collar of Jill's plaid dress. "Very becoming. Looks familiar. This way, folks." They had bought the dress the previous Saturday at Franklin Simon. Emily had bought for herself what she thought of as a less girlish outfit, jet black with horizontal sapphire stripes. She was waiting to wear it.

The room appeared tense, with everyone, including George, standing, because her grandparents were standing, evidently about to leave, as were her father and Bunny, and Ellen and scintillating Stan. Emily realized, as she hurried the introduction of Jill and Steve, that she was scared George might leave too. She wanted the family to leave fast, so George wouldn't have time to think about leaving with them— with the "grownups." She wanted everyone to leave. She had to talk to George. Here he was. She would never have another chance. She had to ask his advice about her life, her future, what to do, what kind of job. He would know. He would know about her. But how could she find a way in front of the others of making sure he would stay awhile, without being stupid or forward or indiscreet? And how could she talk to him while the others remained?

But George seemed to be staying, as did the younger crowd. Did he have an eye for bohemian Iris and her sexy black sweater, or career-girl Daphne in her sophisticated gray sheath?

When she returned again to the room, after seeing her family out, the remaining group, in sluggish conversation about *The Diary of Anne Frank,* seemed poised to disintegrate. George had conveniently wandered away from the others to examine the food on the dining table. Emily barely had to lower her voice: "I'm so glad you stayed. I was wondering if you could stay for a minute after the others left so I can pick your brain about something."

"Soitanly. What's on your mind?"

"Just my life. Life in general." She shrugged, and laughed slightly.

"I adore brie. *La brie. C'est la brie.*" He cut a messy wedge and laid it on a Carr's cracker and popped it in. "Perfecto." He helped himself again.

"Isn't it good? I'd talk now, but there's no place to talk. Maybe they won't stay long. It's no one thing. I just want to know what to do with myself, but I think you'd understand what I mean."

"I'd love to hear your problem. Not that I'm such a venerable sage, you know. When you come right down to it, I'm not that much older than you are. And I'm sure you're far wiser than I am."

"How can you say that? Actually the problem may be that I have no problem. Everything seems sort of flat. It's exactly what I promised myself would never happen. I believe in having someone to look forward to. Sorry. I mean something. Did I say someone?" She smiled at him, frowning at herself.

She was off balance. She couldn't stop being conscious of his fame; it didn't make any difference that she knew he was a mere mortal (who put on his pants nine legs at a time). He had rather hairy fingers. Did hairy fingers help you to be a great pianist? Otherwise, his fingers didn't seem out of the ordinary. His hands were bigger than his fingers were big. Daphne came over. She said she had to get her beauty rest; thank you for the lovely party, she could find her own way out. Emily warmly let her go. She visualized George standing in the kitchenette doorway while she washed dishes and talked. He would dry, if drying was all right for his hands.

"I'll try to hurry the others along tactfully." She couldn't wait for them to leave.

"Don't worry about it. I do have to practice tomorrow. Practice-practice. But I'm fine. Did you know I am going to Australia and New Zealand next week? For the second time? And other parts."

"Everything sounds as if it's still marvelous for you." Emily, with self-conscious footsteps, accompanied George Koenigsberg toward the middle of the room. Steve Farkas sprang at them.

"I must admit I'm quite an admirer of yours," Steve said. (Emily was almost positive he didn't mean her.) "I'm really impressed to meet you. By coincidence, two days ago I bought your recording of the Sonata for piano, flute, and drums and the Stokowski recording of the *Urbs* Symphony. I've got everything you've written now and everything with you playing. What do you think of that?"

"What do I think of that? What I think is, thank you very much."

Emily was surprised at Steve's interest in classical music; it didn't seem to go with his looks or his outfit.

"May I ask you one question?" Steve asked.

George shrugged. "Absolutely."

"How does one person get to be a top pianist as well as an unusually successful serious composer? It amazes me."

"And I also do needlepoint. I'll tell you a little secret. Composition is the great gift, the God-given gift. There are pianists as good as I am and one or two who can play even better. Don't let anyone tell you different. But no one can play my own music for piano like me, after all; so I'm very lucky that way. You see, as it happens, I approve of audiences. I'm one of those strange birds who like it when people like my music and my playing."

"That's very fascinating. Not that there's any comparison, but I understand something about reaching an audience. I'm in the toy business, and if we don't reach an audience I'm not in the toy business."

"What toy business? You seem to be young to be in the toy business."

Emily laughed.

"Farr. It's the family business."

"I spent half my childhood in your store. It's all play. We all play. *Homo ludens.* That's the joy of it."

"I guess it depends on your viewpoint," Steve said. "Come down to the store anytime. We're still there, old Fifth and Thirty-sixth."

"You bet," George said.

"May I ask how you two know each other?" Steve asked Emily.

"We go way back," she said, noticing that Byron, Iris, and Jill stood watching her, George, and Steve from the sidelines. Maybe Byron and Iris, at least, were on the verge of departure. "Just kidding," she

said. "We've only met once before, but it was way back. Mr. Koenigsberg is the first man I ever had a crush on."

"Uhh! Why did you never tell me?" George complained.

"How? And what good would it have done me?"

"It might have done me some good, dear Emily. Now, will you see
me to my coat?"

Her heart slipped. Looking at George, she was about to risk murmuring, "I thought you were staying," when he said, as if explaining,
"Just see me to the door."

Then Byron did say that he and Iris were going to take off. Emily
saw that she wouldn't even be able to see George to the door privately,
whatever he wanted to say to her. With a frantic bluntness that sounded
strange to her, she said, "I have to do the dishes anyway, so it might
be just as well to wind it up, if you'll all promise to come back soon."

"Why don't we all help with the dishes," Steve suggested, "and then
we'll vamoose."

"That's very kind. It's just always faster with one." She smiled blindly
at Jill, praying that Jill would interpret everything at once, without
being hurt, and take away herself, Steve, Byron, and Iris in a flash,
shazam, leaving George.

Then George was saying, "I get up very early to practice. Emily
and I were going to take a little time to discuss a song I'm writing for
a surprise party for my dear friend, her father. Such is the sitch."

Genius! Emily thought.

"Love to be at that party," Steve said. "Emily, I hope to meet you
soon again. It was too brief."

"Brief! I'll say," Jill said. "I think my coat's still on. But it's okay,
Emmy, we'll go to Hamburger Heaven instead."

"I know, I'm sorry, but there's a little crisis." Emily thanked and
apologized and made arrangements with Byron about *Anne Frank* (Iris
was considering coming along). In a minute, the four of them were
actually gone. "See you soon, see you soon," Emily had reminded them.

George Koenigsberg stood by the dining table, Emily on the other
side, her hand under the cheese platter, to clear it. "I don't understand
why you asked me to see you out."

"Oh, well, I didn't want to know too much about the toy business.
I thought I'd leave and return. I thought some of them might leave
when I did. I was hurrying things along. I wasn't going to desert you."

She looked past him into the emptied room. There were his roses;
he was still here too. "That was clever, about the song." Because for

some reason she suddenly felt so sad she feared she might cry, she went around George to collect ashtrays and glasses. He was like something very expensive she could never have afforded on her own. Why had she asked him for advice? What advice? What did she want to know? What could he tell her? Why was he being so attentive to someone so young and unimportant? Family loyalty only? Could he possibly be interested in her fair white body? She imagined he must still think of her as a girl, but maybe not. Actually, Constance Shipp had been only twenty-three when she and George had gotten married. But Constance Shipp was a famous beauty. Cold as ice. Within the last year sometime, she had married some British politician, Sir Colin someone.

Emily carried two ashtrays in a bigger ashtray, in the other hand two glasses. "I forgot a tray," she said, passing George again.

He was lighting a cigarette. "What can I do?" he asked.

"Sometimes I wished I smoked." She felt she would have to entertain him. From the kitchenette, she said, "You can observe while I clean up a little, or you can wrap the cheese, la brie and so forth, but it's going to stink up the fridge. I'd better just get rid of it. Scusi." He stepped aside in the kitchenette doorway so she could pass him again. She scurried to the table and piled dishes onto her teak tray.

"It would be easier to talk if we stayed in one place," he said.

"I can see that." She turned around with the tray. His eyes were now his most prominent feature, they seemed so self-confident. They looked as if they'd been shined. She felt he was in her way to some extent. She carried the tray to the kitchenette. She wiped pâté, cheese, and pastry remains into the garbage and put the dishes in the sink. In the doorway, he said, "I cannot begin to tell you what a delight it is to see you again."

She glanced at him. "Did you really remember me?" She ran water.

"Are you mad? You were indelible. Ineffable."

She frowned, trying to think, against the distraction of his compliment, what to say. She turned the water off; with her back against the corner between the sink and the counter, she faced him. She felt like a wilting stalk in a garbage can, but she didn't quite want to move from the kitchenette, either. "There's probably nothing that can be solved. I think I'm taking unfair advantage of your time." His long ash dropped to her parquet floor. She rinsed out the small glass ashtray with the scalloped lip and extended it to him. "I think I'm having trouble knowing if my problem is real, or if it's only that I'm young. I don't know what's supposed to be true. I guess it's what's called not

having perspective. I lack perspective. I need someone to tell me if
things are supposed to be how they are. My father is a wonderful
man, the best, but. . ."

"Not Socrates."

"Well, your standards are very high. But let's say he's not particularly
analytical about people. And my sister is interested in political problems, not personal problems. She thinks problems are meant to be
eliminated. Hunger, poverty, prejudice, you know, those little things.
It may be silly, but sometimes I actually think there are supposed to
be problems, that problems have to exist so people have them to solve.
Do you know what I mean, or is it just trivial?"

"But of course. An artist requires problems."

"But I'm not an artist, I'm afraid, even if I wished I were. I don't
have the talent or I don't have the guts. It doesn't make much difference what I don't have. I'm not an artist. So I don't require problems. Meanwhile, I don't know how to change my life, or if it's
supposed to change, or whether I'm too picky about friends. But having a boyfriend, which I don't happen to have at this point, shouldn't
make all the difference anyway. I'm so petrified of being a nothing,
a waste. I don't know what of, but a waste of something." Amazing,
that she was saying all this to him. She couldn't decide if he was concentrating on what she was saying or squinting from his cigarette
smoke; maybe it was both. But he certainly seemed to be paying very
close attention. "I don't know what else to say. I don't know what
anyone's supposed to say. I don't know where to go next." She looked
at her hideous speckled linoleum floor. "I probably need a new job,
even though I have a very pleasant job, but it doesn't really amount
to that much. Do you need a secretary?"

"Got one, sorry." He smiled, putting out his cigarette. "What did
you study at college?" He gave her her ashtray.

"Oh, English. I hung around the theater as much as I could, though.
I acted quite a lot. And I'm not bad, either, but I know I'm not good
enough. The only really bearable people up there for me were the
theater group. There were lots of rah-rahs to avoid. When I was
younger, I really thought I might want to be an actress. I suspect it
was probably my own way of trying to make something last forever,
but otherwise I don't think I really knew what it meant. I went one
summer to summer stock and I didn't think I fit in very well."

"I'd say congratulations."

"But in the meantime, I may be a completely ordinary person in
the making. When I say it aloud, it makes me chilly inside, it makes

me think I may be predicting the actual truth about myself. I think
the worst thing in the world is being typical, just like the people I
hated at college, who played bridge all the time and didn't know how
to stop laughing. I'm not like them, but what am I instead? I don't
want to sit around all my life like everyman with all the other little
everymen, watching the stars glitter. I want to be recognized for
something. But all I am so far is someone whose mother died overseas
in a noble cause when I was young. That's my sole claim to fame."

George Koenigsberg said, "Listen to me." So intense was his shape,
so sharp to her eyes, he looked as if a line of light had been painted
around him. "People who are ordinary cannot begin to express themselves the way you do. So you're already far, far ahead of the game
in that respect. Most people your age don't begin to understand themselves. I assure you, I didn't. I guarantee you your life cannot con-
ceivably be ordinary. You're far too bright, sensitive, aware. You're
too vital, too passionate. But here's the point. You cannot accomplish
anything without ambition, without appetite. You have got to attach
yourself to something huge, something magnificent, complex, enthralling, magical, art or religion or love or philosophy." He made
each word sound like a soft shout. He reminded her a little of Andy
Propper. "You have got to be involved in something that deserves you
and that you deserve, something that will give you identity. You can't
be anything unless you belong to something. You can't have identity
all by your lonesome. But angel, you have to make things happen for
yourself. You have to take certain risks. You have to try things to see
if they work for you or not. You've got to attack something with zeal.
With zeal! Have you traveled?"

She was thinking that she might be the kind of person who only
took the right kind of risks, risks that weren't risks. But what did he
mean by risks? "I've been to Europe once, France, Italy, and England,
two summers ago. But I don't want to be a travel agent. Or a traveler.
I can't just keep traveling."

"But go to Scandinavia, Czechoslovakia, India, Germany. Go to
Russia. Go to Japan, go to Africa, Israel. See the world."

"Join the army?"

"Fill yourself up. Get fat on the world, on foreign places. I'm sorry
I can't take you to Australia with me."

She smiled. "I can't take off from work."

"I know it, I know it. Have you ever gone to a headshrinker?"

"No. I've never thought I needed to. It's like having an excellent attendance record. I'm a better person without going. Do you think I need one? I hope not."

"You don't need one at all. You're an incredible young woman, as intelligent and beautiful as can be. If you weren't Lee's daughter, I don't know what I'd do with you." He looked at his watch. "Now I have got to scram. Will you be all right?" His shining eyes flickered. "I recommend going straight to bed, and tomorrow start deciding what you want to love, what you want to learn about, what's in store for you. Maybe when I get back I can sit you down beside me at the piano and give you a little demonstration of how themes get trans-formed. How would you like that? Transformation being, you see, as a very wise old German gentleman said, the life of life. 'Verwandlung ist des lebens leben,' or Krautness to that effect. It's a matter of watching changes and connections while they are happening, right before your very eyes." He spoke almost in a whisper, and stretching words dra-matically. "Learning to see messages concealed and revealed. Right there is the secret of everything, you see—concealment and revelation, simultaneous concealment and revelation, something always about to be born and being born." It was as if he were trying to hypnotize her. "It's life-saving, understanding such things. It's life-making. It's where the fantastic mystery is, the miracle. It's having your finger on the pulse of the universe, the secret throbbing, the transformation energy, the little bundle that explains everything."

She nodded prematurely and cautiously. "It would be great if you could do that for me, if you ever have the time."

"Get some sleep." He stepped to her, kissed her cheek. His hand was beneath her hair, stroking her neck, which was damp, but that was his problem. Her cheekbone rested against his breastbone. She left her arms by her sides, so she wouldn't make a mistake she couldn't take back. She heard her breathing: it sounded frightened, though she didn't feel frightened. She felt calmly suspenseful, and suspended.

Pressing her shoulders, he leaned away from her with a down-turned smile, the same kind he'd given her when he'd arrived—proud of her, it seemed, congratulatory. She didn't understand it. She looked at him straight, trying to smile back at him, while rapidly changing the position of her lips (a squishing motion she had used to make when studying, with a pencil in her mouth). Above all, she felt it necessary to be neutral.

At the door, when he had his coat on, she said, "I thank you for your advice. I don't know what I can do with it exactly, I'll have to think about it. It sounds right, about attaching yourself to something. Anyway, you cheered me up. It was wonderful just to talk to you and listen to your words. I still can't actually believe you were here."

"Kilroy Koenigsberg. I was here. Get some sleep."

Why was he so worried about her sleep? Did he think the rest of her life was going to exhaust her? "Thanks again for coming." Something, impulsive poise, allowed her to kiss him quickly on the lips. But the kiss made her heart rush.

He stroked her hair, once. "Goodnight, you angel. I'll call you when I have a chance after my return. And I shall return."

She herself returned to the kitchenette, where she rubbed dishes with a sponge and soap powder very slowly under very slowly running water, imagining his hand leaving the back of her neck for the bow of her blouse, everything swelling, impossible to resist; they moved into the room, where the sofa was somehow already pulled out into the bed. She leaned against the sink. In her trance appeared rapid dots of noise, like perforations of reality. Without otherwise moving, she turned off the water. She waited, holding the plate, to see if she had been having a hallucination. It came again, it was a tapping at the door.

She gasped. She dried her hands on a dishtowel. She went to the door pretending no one was there, that there had been no knocking, that she was on her way out to work. Though she knew who it was, she asked, so she wouldn't be disappointed, "Who is it?"

"I forgot something." His whisper sounded like notepaper being stuffed through the door's crack.

"Okay." Maybe his lighter. She almost started back in, to look, before she opened up; but then she unlocked. And there he was again, George Koenigsberg.

He looked very serious. "May I come in?"

She smiled in the quickest, tiniest way. She let him by, closing the door without locking it. She followed him, past the kitchenette, into the room. He sat on the sofa in his open overcoat and lighted up a cigarette.

"I'll get you an ashtray." Was he in some kind of trouble? She brought him an ashtray from the sink. She was about to deposit herself in the chair nearest the sofa (a chair she was learning to dislike, modernish, with a slanted seat covered in a pale purple woolen weave—more cheap than chic), when he said, "No. Here, beside me."

"No piano," she said. She sat on the sofa, perhaps a foot from him.

She smiled, with her hands flat together, pointing out, on her knees. He was sunk into his coat and into the sofa, shrunken, timid, dark. He wasn't very big anyway. He looked like an aged little boy, Master Koenigsberg. She remembered something she hadn't thought of earlier. After his concert, when she'd met him eight years ago, in the green room, he'd looked as if he'd drowned in his music and then been rescued. He hardly looked rescued at the moment, but because he seemed as if he'd been through something, she remembered anyway. "Is anything wrong? Is there anything I can get you?" Was she trying to make up for her coldness to Timothy the night he'd come back for more?

He waggled his head at her, against the back of the sofa. With his left hand, he took her right hand, off her knee. He held her hand on the sofa between them. She looked at his hairy fingers that had to practice tomorrow. She imagined herself as taking his pulse, a nurse at a bedside. The thought was so unfamiliar to her it was like a joke on seriousness. If she were a nurse, she would do everything wrong, break everything. From his nostrils and mouth flowed light-beams of smoke. "May I have one of your Pall Malls?" Not letting go of her hand, as if depending on her hand, he reached for his pack, lighted a cigarette, and delivered it to her mouth. She bent slightly to receive it. She puffed out smoke immediately, without inhaling.

"You can't believe how many times I've thought of you over the years. Do you know that I ask for you every time I speak to your dad?"

She thought, whatever is supposed to happen here, please don't let me stop admiring you. "It makes sense I would remember you. But I don't understand what I was to you except your broker's little girl. You must have hundreds of backstage visitors. I couldn't have been that special."

"Thousands of backstage visitors. You underestimate yourself. How you underestimate yourself. You need self-esteem. You must have self-esteem. Sue me, angel, I remember you. You weren't a little girl, you were a young woman. And unforgettable."

"What did you forget? Just now, I mean, tonight." She smiled again, so she wouldn't appear tough or suspicious.

"Our talk—let me try to tell you. I wanted to be the vitality of what I was describing to you. I had the feeling that I'd given myself to you but left myself behind. It left me feeling fantastically close to you, without the closeness being closed."

She tapped crumbs of ash, concentrating on the ashtray. It gave you something to do with your hands, they said about smoking. Her throat made a noise that sounded like the noise people make in their sleep in the next bunk in the middle of the night. She was thirsty.

"It is the way I am," he said. "I get violently caught up in what I'm doing."

"But you're so lucky. You're so full of life."

"Listen to me. I am enchanted by you."

Her head fell.

"You are the most articulate, intelligent, natural, delectable young woman I have ever seen." He pulled himself off the back of the sofa, blowing smoke, and killed his cigarette. Her chest was tingling; she felt that her blouse was tingling. He was kissing the pit of her neck. His hair touched her throat beneath her chin. It was ridiculous—she had to get rid of her silly cigarette. She found the ashtray. Feeling as if she were turning off the light, she placed the ashtray, without moving her head, on the coffee table, by her grandparents' vase with the mums in it. He lifted his face. His lips arrived in warm air. His hand on her cheek seemed to press open her mouth. It was too much. Her heart had melted into spreading blood, a mess. She broke the kiss, holding onto him and herself at the same time, her head in his shoulder and her eyes shut. Her blouse was being drawn from her skirt, from the front and from the back. She couldn't stop him. She thought, if this is it, at least my period ended three days ago; then she thought, even if no one in the world ever knows about this, I will be famous to myself.

Having been hugged as if she'd won a swimming meet, while George said, "I can't get over you, you're so marvelous," she'd watched him fall asleep, on his stomach, beside her on the pulled out sofa-bed, his arms under his chin. Once she had realized he was actually sleeping, she had tried to review his features, the way women did in mediocre novels. He displayed his very hairy back. His face faced her, squashed. Had her father known this would happen? Had he arranged it? Told George to go ahead, then to marry her? Emily has only a year to live and she doesn't know it. You are her shining idol. You'll make her happy for a little while.

Falling asleep, George hadn't explained or apologized. Maybe he was really exhausted. He'd made a lot of noises during the sex. She didn't know the etiquette. Maybe he was doing the normal thing and there was something wrong with her for not falling asleep. Maybe when he woke up he would tell her he was so comfortable with her that he felt as if he were in his own bed, and that's the only reason

he'd drifted off. A compliment. She didn't have the nerve to wake
him anyway, but it also occurred to her that he might be faking sleep,
because he had been disappointed in her sexually or embarrassed to
realize she had been a virgin. If she woke him and he were faking,
she would be able to tell he was faking and that would bother her
more than his sleeping did. She knew he wasn't faking, though. His
sleeping meant to her that it was finished, she'd had her chance. She
hadn't been able to concentrate the first time. She would only know
what she had felt, or what to feel, a second time. She had worried so
much about whether it would hurt, about being aware of the pain
(not much), about getting the movement right, the coordination, that
she might as well have been practicing.

After he'd been asleep for ten or so minutes, she went to wash herself
off, returning with her ivory nightgown on, lying down with her back
to him (carefully, so she wouldn't wake him), facing his roses, which
didn't talk either. She closed her eyes on them. She saw her body
wafting, exploding way up in the air, specks of flesh rushing upwards,
backwards, into the universe, like something being flushed in reverse,
disappearing, except for spots of blood drying across the sky. Try that
one out, Andy Propper. Or T. S. Eliot. If she had been dreaming,
undoubtedly the blood would have been about her "lost" virginity. Or
it was anyway. But she didn't think of her lost virginity as the problem.
She didn't feel ashamed of having done it, or proud. The trouble was,
she felt so unemotional. She didn't feel different, either. In fact, she
wished it had been more noticeable that she had lost it, that it had
hurt more or that there had been more blood, so she would be entitled
to feel different.

Her shoulder jumped when he kissed it. He patted it. "Angel, I
must leave," he was whispering. "It's unbearable, but I must leave."

She wished she could bury herself under her own weight. She felt
him getting up (how could he not have noticed when she'd gone to
wash and put her nightgown on?). She listened to him getting dressed.
She kept her eyes closed. It would have made no difference if she'd
opened them. She couldn't look at him. She had spent the evening
giving him the benefit of a doubt, many doubts, without admitting it.
All his praise had turned into an insult. She opened her eyes, hoping
he would take her overwhelming glumness for sleepiness. He looked
at her immediately, while continuing to tie his bowtie. "You are glo-
rious," he said. "Wondrous. Don't you dare forget it, either."

She closed her eyes. A minute later, she opened them again; she
didn't want to miss seeing him depart. He was dressed, just getting

into his overcoat. She had the strange feeling he was stealing it. "Do you have everything?" she asked.

"Yes. I can find my way out. Please go back to sleep."

How thoughtful of him to whisper. "Have a good trip," she said.

"I'll call you. Take care."

At least he knew better than to sit down and kiss her goodbye. His footsteps didn't sound at all regretful or indecisive. They just went, as if he'd discovered he'd entered the wrong apartment. He wasn't going to forget something this time. She hadn't even been able to ask him why, if leaving was so "unbearable," he had to leave. He might not want to be seen leaving in the morning? Maybe he'd been invited to another party. Her door shut.

Strangling her pillow, she started to sob, the sobs beginning as wails. Uncontrollable and profuse, her sobbing nevertheless allowed her to picture George hearing and ignoring her all the way to the elevator. Observers appeared in the room behind her—Daddy, Granny and Grandpa, Ellen (holding baby Janet on her shoulder), Wilma, Dunc, Mom. They watched her sob as if her unhappiness were a rare illness, or a rare talent, or as if she were sobbing in her grave. No one moved, no one touched her.

CHAPTER SIX

Her Mother in the Dark

Emily's reaction to *Anne Frank* was so perverse, perverted, she could never have expressed any of it aloud, though privately she got a kick out of being so disgusting. Her bad taste entertained her. Emily said to Anne: What do you know about suffering, spoiled bitch? You died in a concentration camp when you were fifteen. Big deal. Did your mother die when you were ten, trying to help people just like you? Did your mother go away for good when you were still seven, leaving you alone with your silent father and unsympathetic older sister? Did your first lover *(lover!),* your former idol, the very famous George Koenigsberg, ditch you in the middle of the night, humiliating you and making an ass of himself in the process? You never had to work for coolies' wages as a secretary. You never had an incredibly pathetic stepmother with the I.Q. of a donut, whom I tolerate for my father's sake because he had such a raw deal when his wife left while I had this blissful, one-big-happy-family childhood. And you never had to see the simpleminded shit-hit play they made about you. The whole world feels sorry for you and admires you. Once the Nazis found you, Anneke, your problems were over.

To say such things to herself was a little like picking her nose, or something along those lines. It was like trying not to be Jewish, or practicing to be anti-Semitic. It was even worse (or better): it was the thought equivalent of being a Nazi, when you had complete freedom to do anything you wanted to, and what you did was the worst a human being could do. In her teens, she had imagined herself as a comic-book Nazi sometimes, sauntering nude among cowering Jews, sneering, with a whip and a snarling dog, taunting them with herself and the dog, then letting the dog jump on them, tear off their clothes, tear their bodies. The victims wanted to embrace her, but instead got the dog "embracing" them.

Anne Frank moved everyone, but not her. It was like breaking the law not to be moved by it. It was officially moving. She wished she could review it somewhere and call it "officially moving." To think that she had thought of the phrase herself was like taking a breath of unfamiliar strength. She wanted to wake people up, make them see how fake and tearjerky the play was. All it had done for her was allow her her amazingly nasty reactions, which she chewed on like too many sticks of gum. Anne was a real saint, a Jewish saint. Anne had hope for everybody. "In spite of everything, I still believe that people are really good at heart." Not too moving, Anneke! And as a matter of fact, I think I believe it too. Maybe I'll start saying it too. But why should you say it? I know why, Anneke! To give your surviving Daddy his officially moving curtain-line: "She puts me to shame." Emily Weil arrested for exiting *Anne Frank* dry-eyed. Rest of audience all mush, stunned, murmuring, My God, what a girl Anne Frank must have been, what a love of life (sense o' wundah!), and here we have life, but do we appreciate it? She hadn't read the actual *Diary of Anne Frank*, but she certainly wasn't going to now.

Emily hadn't criticized the play to Byro and Iro, because she suspected they'd think her criticism was sour grapes over Susan Strasberg's performance (even though, of the three of them, she was the only one who no longer wanted to act). So in the Mayflower coffee shop, she said she thought Susan's (Iris called her Susan) performance was excellent. In fact she thought it was fine, but not that hard to do. Byro and Iro were knocked out by the play, their chance to suffer and be Jewish. She let them assume she was too subdued to say much, that the play was too personal for her, not only because of her being Jewish (at least born Jewish, which was more than Byron or Iris could claim), but also, as they might have been thinking, because the play reminded her of her mother, the war, refugees, et cetera. She preferred them to think she was suffering silently than to tell them she thought the play was a piece of *merde* (despite Susan's excellent performance). She didn't have the nerve; she might have spoiled their pain.

Of course she had been suffering silently anyway. She had almost not come to the play because of the night before, but she hadn't wanted to get more depressed, so she thought she'd let Anne Frank take her mind off George. George had been like running into someone's arms in order to be tossed through the window. She was undeniably embarrassed by her eagerness to overlook George's ever-so-obvious faults. She was also embarrassed by her dislike of him now, by how asinine he had become in one evening, after eight years of being God. She had to force herself not to think about what uncomfortable strangers they'd been afterwards. The sexual experience itself was wasted, virtually. The actual intercourse was less important than what had happened, not happened, when the intercourse was over. But even all by itself, the intercourse seemed, by Sunday, like a quick movement, as if he had somehow gotten his penis into her while they'd collided coming around a corner—a collision with a private wetness in the center of it. She wasn't certain she'd had a complete orgasm (certainly not what Timothy's finger had accomplished).

She would never tell a soul about George. She thought she might tell George himself, when he got back from Australia, "down under," that he was going to be a father, just to see what his reaction would be, because he hadn't asked or said anything about taking any precautions. At his level they probably didn't worry about such things. He wasn't listed in the phone book, of course, but she could have gotten his number from her father. She thought dozens of times of calling him right then, on Sunday, and asking him if he'd caught up on his sleep. She wanted to ask him why he'd stayed after the party. Had he known he was going to sleep with her? She wanted to ask him how many women he slept with during a week. Seven? Fourteen? Twenty-one?

She also avoided calling Timothy ("This is Emily Weil. From college? I've been thinking about you lately for some reason and I'm wondering if we could get together for a drink sometime, so we could catch up with each other") by starting to dial his number twice, and hanging up before she got a heart attack, and finally going out for a sunny autumn walk with Jill.

Jill, who admitted she had been peeved enough by Emily's behavior Friday night not to call her on Saturday, now told Emily that Steve Farkas had liked her. She might hear from him sometime; also, she might not, because Steve feared Emily would be too sophisticated for him. It seemed Steve and Jill weren't going to be anything—"no sparks." Jill said they were too much alike. Emily said she didn't know why Steve Farkas should like her particularly, no less think her too sophisticated for him (unless it was because of George's being there), but she was flattered. While she spoke, she was thinking that if Jill and Steve were too alike, wouldn't she and Steve be too different? Jill then asked, "Did you and George" (she emphasized "George," slowing it, as if she were making fun of him, while at the same moment she was being presumptuous in using only his first name) "make much progress with that song?"

It took Emily a few seconds of silence to remember what Jill was referring to. She said, then, panicky that the few seconds had been fatally revealing, "Sure. He only stayed an hour. We got most of it done." (Could an offhanded answer afford to sound as sad as she thought hers had sounded?) "By the way," she said, rushing to insert her *Anne Frank* opinion, "my frank *Anne Frank* opinion." Emily had known Jill for so long that she could afford to astound her with her opinions. Jill was the ideally astoundable friend—she got astounded, but she stood her ground.

Jill said, when Emily had finished, "I think you're crazy. It's one of the most moving plays I've ever seen. I just think you can't afford to react to it."

Emily went to bed Sunday night planning to start out again—after the not exactly typical weekend of housewarming party, George Koenigsberg, and *Anne Frank*—as someone good at making the best of things, and as someone to whom things happened. Friday night, before the party, she had thought of her life as flat, stalled. Bumpy was preferable to flat. She felt, at least, more grownup. In bed, she read twenty-five fast pages of *Marjorie Morningstar,* another piece of *merde*. Now Marjorie was a girl who knew about suffering. Too bad Anneke couldn't read about Marjorie. At midnight, Emily turned off the standing lamp by the sofa-bed.

In the dark, her mother's naked body lay across her entire mind. It happened now about twice a year, her mother melting with her dysentery, turning into sick liquid, sick sweat, diarrhea-gravy; turning yellow, Japanese, like a traitor; her skin like chicken fricassee, pimply yellow skin loosening, beneath it what looked like packed wet dirt in the shape of a body and was really packed diarrhea. Her actual Eightieth-Street-and-Park-Avenue mother, her only one. The school outside of Shanghai, where her mother had been held by the Japanese, melted. Her mother had died in a hospital over there, but in Emily's mind the school collapsed from heat, as if the school were sick, with a high fever, crushing her mother and the other women in the room under school desks. (There had been no desks, in reality; the desks had been replaced by beds.) When the school collapsed, arms went up to protect heads. Emily's arms went to the top of her head in bed. Then, after her mother was crushed, and nearly invisible, her mother's arms were reaching out. In every death that Emily imagined, her mother's arms were reaching out after she was dead. Her mother had lived in the school when the Japanese interned her, with about forty women in one room. Emily knew this from Henrietta Fish, who had been another social worker over there and who had come to visit after the war. Emily recalled little Mrs. Fish at the dinner table, with her anxious yet reserved manner, reporting to Granny and Grandpa, her father, Emily, and Ellen.

The mother who had knelt on the pale-green living-room rug to say goodbye, in the navy-blue suit, white blouse, and little hat, was no realer than the mother Emily imagined wanting to get home, with her arms out, saying, Take hold of my hands, bring me back, let me start again, give me another chance, help me. Her mother's narrow, somber face with the short, sleek hair, the face from the silvery photograph, said, You can't know how much I loved you, how precious you were to me. Help me. Bring me home.

According to Daddy, when Mom had gone to Havana in 1939 for the JRSA to get the Jewish refugees from Germany off the ship and the Cubans hadn't allowed them off (America also refused them), Mom had stood on the dock, with some of the refugees' relatives, as the ship sailed back to Europe. It was the most terrible story in the world, even worse than Mom could have known at the time, because Mom didn't know that most of the refugees would be murdered in concentration camps. (Emily had written a short story in school about the scene in Havana, trying to describe the feelings of the refugees, of the character of her mother, of the hard-hearted bureaucratic Cuban officials. She had thought the story might seem overemotional—she had, daringly, referred to the Cubans as "bastards"—or farfetched, but Miss Moody had called it "exceptionally moving and sensitive"; and again Emily had felt that she was misusing her mother.) The true story was so hard for Emily to believe, it seemed to have happened in another world, in the world's imagination. She didn't understand how the Cubans could have been so cruel to the refugees, or why America hadn't let them in either, and her father's answers had been vague or else she just didn't remember them well enough. In any case, she didn't want to bring up the subject again now. All she knew was that even though the story seemed so impossible that you almost couldn't believe it, it was true. Her mother had ended up just like the refugees on the boat.

To try to help her mother, Emily remembered moments from her small selection of their life together before her mother had left for

Shanghai. Her mother was made up of moments (seconds, really), probably a total of less than three minutes of memories. Tonight she remembered her mother and Granny and her mother's two female cousins and their mother (Granny's sister, Marie Hirsch), all of them in blue-and-white or white-and-blue summer dresses, strolling arm-in-arm in American safety (the cousins, unlike her mother, hadn't been born in America but in Vienna) around the lawn in Newbury—one of the real outdoor memories. She remembered her mother demonstrating the rumba for her and Ellen in their living room, where she had held the serious meetings, where she had said goodbye, kidding the rumba, calling out the rhythm in a very strict way, with a straight face (her usual face), as if it were a military dance-step. When their mother had done the rumba for them, she and Ellen had laughed so hard they capsized and rolled around on the living-room floor. She and Ellen had never laughed as hard together at the same things since.

Her mother had been like someone making a short visit, Emily thought tonight. She and Ellen had not been born to her, were not her daughters, but were simply present when their mother had visited. The memories were memories of a visit. There were some snapshots and one very short sepia home movie. (There must have been memories she had lost, too, like dreams you knew you'd had without being able to remember them. She must have also forgotten dreams of her mother. She remembered only one dream, a repeated one, from long ago, of her mother sinking on a ship.) She felt she couldn't get close to her mother, but not because she was dead and far away, and had been for a long time. She couldn't get close because the few memories of her that existed had been drained of impact, if they weren't simply too trivial in the first place. Either there wasn't enough to remember, or it didn't want to be remembered.

She remembered her mother reprimanding her and Ellen for playing with their mashed potatoes. She remembered a winter Saturday afternoon walk to the Metropolitan Museum; she thought that was the day she had learned that winter smelled like cold wool. She remembered her mother playing Schubert on the piano. She remembered the perfume on the brown fur collar of her mother's bottle-green coat. She remembered her mother saying, "Goodnight, sleep tight, see you in the morning light." She remembered her mother staying home from work to take care of her when she was sick on another winter day, her mother knowing how to take care of her, as if she'd learned how at a mother school. She particularly remembered realizing that her mother didn't seem to mind at all taking her temperature rectally, didn't seem to notice.

After her mother had left for Shanghai, Emily went through a stomach-ache phase. Doctors could find nothing wrong. It astonished Emily when Ellen had to go to the hospital to have her appendix out, and once again with a possible concussion from field hockey. It broke the rules that she didn't get to go to the hospital, while her sensible, sickness-pooh-pooing sister did. When Emily caught colds, Ellen would say things like "Cough, cough, Camille," and "So-o-o psychosomatic." Emily had been convinced she'd had a brain tumor when she was fifteen. Nobody did anything about it. (At times, the brain tumor had returned, expanded, because it had been ignored when she was fifteen.) Ellen said, "It's all in your head. Get it?" When Emily announced a sickness, her father would give his little frown. "Let's see how it is in the morning," he'd say, or, if she didn't have a fever and could go to school, "Let's see what the nurse says." If Emily did have to stay home, her grandmother usually came to be with her, calling her "dear heart." When she or Ellen had mumps, measles, chicken pox, her grandmother, along with Margaret, would take care of them. Her grandmother's being around had been the best of being sick. In Newbury, the summer she was four or five, she'd been stung by a bee. She remembered that the sting had been like an award, a prize of pain; she'd been surrounded, briefly, by the family, including her mother, and once she'd stopped crying, it was impossible not to smile, like a creep, at the corner of her mouth, from being the center of attention.

She remembered her mother applauding her for something, something early, athletic—a run, or somersault, or cartwheel, in Newbury, on the lawn behind the house, her mother applauding and calling "Yay!" She remembered performing *Little Red Riding Hood* for her mother with Juliet Bibby in the living room in the city, throwing herself into it, trying to make it as real and frightening as possible, making a production out of it, as her father would say. Emily had played the mother and the wolf, Juliet had played Little Red Riding Hood and the grandmother. Emily remembered preparing the performance, the costumes, rehearsing, making Juliet be serious, figuring out which furniture would be what in the play, and she remembered drawing the drapes for the forest scene during the performance. But she didn't remember her mother's reaction. A somersault and a kiddy performance of *Little Red Riding Hood* that had seemed monumental, as if directed by Stanislavsky himself, and had probably lasted four minutes. That was it. She had not had time to do anything important in front of her mother.

It was the worst thing she could think of. She had never done anything important in front of her mother. No one could say, Emily, that just isn't true. It was true. It was like being told everything was over. She turned on the standing lamp and sat up in her silly red-and-white-striped cotton nightgown, a knee-length T-shirt left over from college. She wondered if something was in the process of happening to her, in her veins, if she would pass out in a minute, or die, or vomit, or change into someone else. She thought, for the first time, that she had as many memories of her mother dead as she had of her alive. In addition to her mother's never coming back, her mother would never leave. Her mother would always be there, forever, with her arms reaching for her, wanting to come back, but it was no help.

PART
THREE

CHAPTER SEVEN

Steve

Steve brought up the embarrassing subject himself when telling Emily about his family origins. "My pop likes to say that the family name was Farr in Hungary and his father changed it to Farkas when he got over here." He laughed through his nose, smiling with his mouth open.

"What's in a name?" she said, while remembering that she had asked Byron the identical question as a joke about "Farkas" two-and-a-half months ago, before Farkas had arrived at her party. This time, she knew the answer. The *name* was what was in the name. A rose by any other name might smell as sweet, but a rose couldn't do a thing for "Farkas." "Just lucky it's not your first name, I guess." He smiled again. She smiled too.

They were in a plushy Italian restaurant whose name she wished she weren't uncertain how to pronounce. Just because Steve, sounding very in-the-know, had said on the way over that the place was "Probably Mafia, but great cannelloni," didn't mean he'd pronounced the name correctly. Some of the male customers did look like Frank Costello—Italian Joe McCarthys—and the women were on the showy side. The restaurant reminded her of a musical-comedy set of a restaurant. While Steve talked about his family ("impossible") and the family business, she watched his face more carefully than she listened to his words, as if she were testing the texture of a food rather than its flavor. She couldn't figure him out. He was smooth, he acted sophisticated. He had handsome, even features, brown eyes. He made her think of a naval officer, an Annapolis graduate. Still there was something a bit awkward about him, something unsmooth, exposed, naive-seeming. She couldn't forget the way he had sprung at George at her party (not that she was embarrassed for Georgie-Porgie any longer). Steve had intensity in his face, brightness in his eyes, along with the permanent innocent ruddiness in his cheeks (a natural rouge she found rather attractive). He was quite direct, but occasionally during the conversation he'd look self-consciously away at nothing. He moved his hands a lot, slowly, indicating and illustrating. He'd graduated from the Wharton School only three years ago, and then been in the army, and was already an executive (though nepotism might have had a little to do with that), and he seemed to know restaurants, and he'd ordered a delicious wine, Soave, which she could have drunk a whole bottle of by herself. He was wearing a gray flannel suit and a navy-blue tie. She was wearing her jet black dress with the sapphire stripes; she worried she looked garish against the scarlet banquette, as if she belonged here, a Mafia daughter or daughter-in-law.

She told him about her still-newish promotion at Partridge to assistant in Publicity, how hard everyone worked, herself included, and at the same time how hard it was to take the job too seriously, at least at her level. She worked hard because she wanted to do well—she wanted to keep the job—but what she worked hard at didn't seem that worth doing well for any other reason than to keep the job. "My claim to fame so far is a caption I wrote that appeared under the photo of one of our books, *Good-lookin' Cookin'*—I'm sure you've read it several times—on the women's page of the *Cleveland Plain–Dealer*. And the caption i-i-izzz . . . 'Taking a gander at sauce for the goose.' All mine. The collected works of Emily Weil Dickinson. Actually, everyone liked it, but how excited can you get about it? How do you get better at writing captions? And should I start a scrapbook?"

"Shouldn't you be pleased? You're just beginning."

"Of course I'm also worried I won't be able to do it twice. I shouldn't complain. I'm not complaining. Everyone's very nice around there. It's a comfortable place to work."

"How did you come to this job?"

"In Publicity or at Partridge?"

"Whichever. I'm interested."

His smile looked to her as if he thought he was interesting for being interested, but she could be wrong. "Partridge because I was a typical English major"—she gave "typical English major" a singsong weariness—"and because I had no particular idea what to do. I'm not a writer and I didn't want to become a professor. So why was I an English major? Anyway, Mrs. Partridge, Lady Blanche, as she is known, although I don't know her, but she's the wife of the president, who's the son of the founder—still interested?—went to Pembroke, where I went, so they favor Pembroke graduates. They must imagine it gives class to the dinkier jobs. And Publicity because my original boss at Partridge, Mr. Sinclair, you probably met him at the party—actually, you didn't meet him because he left before you arrived." Mr. Sinclair had left as Georgie-Porgie arrived. "He suggested Publicity when there was an opening. Captions and press releases are a big step up from secretary. And in Publicity you get to go to such glamorous parties." She wrinkled her nose.

"Let me ask you something. What do they pay you over there?"

Was it bluntness that made him seem on the naive side? But the question also sounded confident, or experienced. "It's sixty-five a week now."

He did one of his self-conscious look-aways; it was abrupt, as if a waiter had bumped his far arm. He returned his attention, saying, "That's a crime, if you ask me. If you came to work for us, writing our catalogues and stuff, we could do a lot better for you."

Her thoughts turned into dancing dots. It seemed so strange for him to offer her a job on their first date. If he were a doctor, he wouldn't offer to examine her. "Publishing salaries are famous for being low, I keep hearing. I really appreciate it, your suggestion, but I think I should try to last it out for a while, don't you?" (She hadn't wanted to say, "Stick it out for a while.") "I've been there barely six months. But thank you. Really." He didn't even know if she was any good. Was a job available at Farr Toys, or was he going to bounce someone for her, show off his muscles?

"Don't mention it. They're not doing you a favor by employing you, you know. You should probably go into advertising. But"—he smiled sort of mischievously, wittily—"I'm not sure you're the type."

"I'm not sure, either. But who knows?" She thought of Page Gibbon, an advertising drip she'd been out with the previous week. As long as Page Gibbon was in advertising, she couldn't go into it.

"What's your ambition? Do you have an ambition for yourself?"

God, did she! But what was it? Georgie-Porgie had the answer. Her face steamed. "I don't know. What do most people say to that question?"

"I don't ask most people. I asked you because you're doing what a lot of girls do out of college, but your attitude is obviously more skeptical, I would say. So that makes you challenging. Okay?"

"I guess so. I'll have to think about it. I think I'm the most ambitious person in the world, but it's not for any specific thing." She felt as if she might be about to flunk the conversation. "I can think of some things I don't want to be, or won't ever be. I like to think about things other people are, real people, that I won't ever come remotely close to being, even though I'm a member of the same human race as they are. Do you ever have that?"

"Such as?"

"The duchess of Windsor?"

He made a sour face. "But she's so trivial."

"That's not the point. Or maybe it is. She's so far away, she lives in a different world, but we're both women and we're both on the same earth. Or I'll never climb Mount Everest. I'll never be First Lady, or a president's daughter, or president. I'll never be on 'What's My Line,' either as a guest or on the panel. I'll never be famous for anything. What about you? I might be famous for captions. Captain Caption."

"I'd like to be president."

"Of anything? Everything?"

"Of the U.S."

"Do you think you could do a good job?"

"Of course." His expression was relaxed; unless he was being dead-pan, he wasn't kidding. "Sometimes I have a yen to go to medical school, too. I like to help people. What did you mean, you're the most ambitious person in the world, but not for any specific thing? That's an intriguing concept, I must say."

Did he always pay such close attention? She wasn't used to being quoted. "I'm thinking." Immortal longings. But didn't everybody have those? "I don't know, maybe you're more ambitious than I am." By ambitious, she meant—she had to remind herself, because it was so much a part of her—that life should be of electric importance at the moment you were living it. Something you knew at each moment you wanted to hold onto forever. You wanted to hold it in your lungs, as if your lungs could remember experiences. If things stayed electrically important to you, you had the freedom to live forever, not just the desire. She wanted it to be the way it had been when she went to the theater with her father on Saturday afternoons, when everything in the day was unusually distinct, mysteriously intense, as if she were living to the fullest in a world realer than the real world. She said, "I have strong desires, let's put it that way. Strong wishes. They're not necessarily realistic. They're just strong." She swallowed. They might not see each other again. She didn't want to spill her guts to him.

"Would you mind giving me a for-instance?"

"I'll try." Maybe he was so interested because he thought her saying she had strong desires meant she was oversexed. "I'm sorry, but it's so general. Do you remember George Koenigsberg?"

"Yes, I happen to recall the man. Have you seen him recently?"

"Not since the party, no." Her lips seemed to be Novocained.

"I don't imagine he has too much spare time on his hands."

Uh-uh. Wrong things to say, Farkas. But she had dropped the name of someone she despised. It was too late. "He says people have to attach themselves to something bigger than they are. It's easier said than done, but it sounds true. I just have to find out what I'm supposed to attach myself to. I think I'm waiting for it to come to me, which is undoubtedly a big mistake. Like waiting for a golden carriage to come down from the sky and pick me up and carry me to whatever it is I'm supposed to attach myself to."

"Are you religious?"

"I'm Jewish." It came out as if she were saying, Isn't that enough? They both laughed. She heard the laughter as the surprised sound of people caught in the act of getting to know each other. It wasn't that she had anything she knew of to feel guilty about; rather that the laughter was friendlier than she had thought she felt ready to be. "Are you religious?" she asked. Farkish? A Farkee?

"The High Holidays, more or less. And Passover and Hanukkah. It's really more family than religious, in a way, more a matter of tradition."

"By the time my sister and I came along, most of the religion had been weeded out of our family."

"Isn't that rather ironic? Jill Strauss told me your mother passed away helping the refugees in Shanghai."

Passed away was an expression she couldn't stand, like *little girls' room.* Bunny-type expressions. In Steve's favor, accidentally, she had never considered how accurate it sounded in her mother's case. "She died on the job, you could say." She felt the familiar mild ray of reflected glory, a lukewarm featherweight flush on her forehead. "But my mother wasn't religious either, as far as I know. And even her parents aren't, my grandparents. They're first-generation atheists." She was sounding smarter to herself at the moment than she usually did. "My mother just happens to have been a devout person, I guess, as a person. And a Jewish person, obviously. She is someone who certainly found something larger to attach herself to. My father fasts on Yom Kippur, but he doesn't go to temple. We don't really do anything else. My sister vows she's going to bring her daughter up Jewish, though. Actually, I am religious, in a way. I don't think about God, but I think about religious spaces. Not churches, but where people are hiding when they're thought to be dead, but are actually alive. In my religion, there is no afterlife. Nobody dies." She laughed again, by herself.

"You're too much," he said.

Thousands of people on the slopey meadow in Newbury, a secret elite, the vanished living, including her mother, eating cold roast chicken through eternity. "I talk too much," she said. And she walking among them every few hours, picking up their picnic garbage.

"You don't have any idea how interesting you are."

"Thank you. I'm trying to become interesting, I hope. That's the best that can be said at this time."

"Well, if that's the best that can be said, how about some zabaglione?"

"I'm stuffed, thanks." She'd had a taste of his cannelloni appetizer; a half-portion of fettucine Alfredo; veal marsala; and salad. Also, a vermouth, and a goodly amount of wine. He'd had squid as his main course, which impressed her no end. She had tasted that, too, without courage or pleasure.

"Would you like coffee? Espresso? Cappuccino? Maybe some fruit? They have a great fruit bowl here."

"Just coffee, please. You know what? I just thought of an ambition. I wake up with it sometimes, but it gets away all the time. In June is my grandparents' fifty-seventh anniversary. I've thought a few times of trying to put on a performance of *A Midsummer Night's Dream* for them at their place in Connecticut. It's a perfect setting. Everything's there. I mean everything but the cast, lights, costumes, and trivialities like that. It may be insane, but you have to admit it's ambitious. I even used to think about building a summer theater on their property and running it. I still do, sometimes. Anyway, *Midsummer Night's Dream* is my grandparents' favorite play. They always talk about a production they saw years ago as the most magical thing ever on the stage. So that's my ambition."

"Sounds fabulous." Steve scratched the back of his neck and squinted, appearing to be in intense thought, or bemused. (Was that what bemused looked like?) "I wonder if there's anything I can do to help," he said.

"Can you act? I don't even want to act in it myself, except as a fairy or something. My heart is set on Moth, actually. I think it's the smallest part in the play. What I really want is to put it on, to see it *be*. I want to surprise my grandparents. I want to enchant my grandparents. I want to wave the magic wand. I want to see them on the front porch, side by side, sitting in armchairs from the living room, not the porch chairs."

"You really have it down to specifics, don't you?" His question rubbed her the wrong way, but his look seemed to be taking her seriously enough. "I'm just thinking," he said. "You know, the way I met Jill in the first place, at her settlement house, was when I went there to talk about giving out toys to the kids at Thanksgiving and Christmas. We have a policy of doing that. On pediatric wards, also. It's heartbreaking sometimes, but I can't resist the kids. Some of our employees like to help out and sort of entertain. I was just picturing Doris Gregorio and a few of our other people in your cast. Doris is our office manager. She's the sweetest gal in the world, but she weighs in at about two hundred pounds."

"That's perfect. She can play Puck. Do you mean it? It would take at least twenty people to do this. I don't know where I'd get twenty people willing to rehearse and go up to Connecticut and so on. It's crazy. Unless they all want to get their own grandparents up there to sit on the porch too."

"I'm sure you know plenty of people who'd do it for you." As their waiter passed by, Steve got his attention with a sharp gesture, not a hail, not a finger-snap, something in between that Emily didn't quite catch, except for the definite commandingness of it, something like the hand saying, come here, you. It embarrassed her for the same reason she was always so polite to waiters—because of the age difference. Steve's gesture was what you would use to beckon a child of your own when you were irritated. The waiter was at least fifty. The waiter had acknowledged the command on his way to another table and now returned. Steve asked for the fruit bowl, zabaglione, an American coffee, and an espresso. Her father was not rude to waiters, but rather indifferent.

"I think I might get a few friends from college who were in the theater up there." Timothy as Puck; better as Bottom, going against type. Byron and Iris and two or three others. "And maybe a few people from Partridge. And members of my family. When I start thinking about it seriously, it seems so hard to bring off, and yet the idea of it seems so perfect."

"Maybe you could just do some scenes, or one big scene. Can you do that?"

"That's possible. I hadn't thought that way. Maybe just Pyramus and Thisby."

"I have to confess, I've never seen it."

"I was in it at college, my senior year. I played Helena. My swansong. A big success, as a matter of fact."

"I'm sorry I missed it. I mean it."

"Would you be in it?"

"For the right money, like that! Just kidding. I'd be flattered, only I wouldn't do you any good. I can't act to save myself."

"Anyway, it's fun to think about." She felt so sad. "Will you excuse me?" She had to use the little girls' room, the bathroom. Toilet. Terlet. Toilette. She paraded past the Mafia court, feeling as if they had all stopped eating to watch her go strolling in her Maidenform bra. The ladies' room was much brighter and airier than the restaurant, with wallpaper, like a bedroom. She thought then of the restaurant's plushness as restaurant marinara, and then she thought, The theater is a body, the aisles are bloodstreams. The first time in years she had thought it, her own line of personal poetry from her teenagehood, which she had never told anybody and which had finally disappeared one day, had finally stopped plaguing her. If she ever had a tombstone, that's what they would put on it. "Emily Weil, 1933–10,033. The theater is a body, the aisles are bloodstreams."

She thought of her grandparents sitting on the porch in chairs from the living room, watching her production of *A Midsummer Night's Dream,* the performance beginning during a sunset, then she saw her mother standing between the two chairs, watching too, only Grandpa Gus was watching her, his returned daughter, instead of the performance. And Emily thought then that her mother was not only a dramatic sort of person—whether or not she had meant to be theatrical in her life—but an actual theater. Her mother was a whole plush house inside, just by being a female, a mother, even a departed mother, so that's probably where the line had come from in the first place. Emily couldn't decide if she was having the revelation of a lifetime, or if the thought was obvious, or if it was a revelation and obvious simultaneously. Everything and nothing.

Steve knew the way to her heart, but she wasn't positive how much of her heart was present. He took her to *The Matchmaker, Uncle Vanya, Middle of the Night, My Fair Lady,* as well as to dinner, to movies, to a Philharmonic concert of Beethoven's Ninth. By accepting his continual invitations, she felt she was making up her mind about him while he paid, in effect, for her time. It was as if he had already made up his mind about her to a greater extent, or he wouldn't keep asking her out. On the other hand, if she didn't feel the equivalent definiteness of interest, she was definitely interested. He was definitely interesting. He was not nearly so obviously right for her as Timothy had been, or seemed to have been, but in some ways, such as overall maturity, he was much righter. Not that Steve didn't have his immature moments. He could get extremely upset if a restaurant gave him a "bad" table, or if their theater tickets were not the best.

At *My Fair Lady*, the hit of the century, as they were going in, they heard a woman saying to her husband, "Eddie, do you realize we may be seeing the greatest thing in the world tonight?" Emily was amused by the woman's excitement, but she was unusually excited herself. When they were directed to their seats, way in the rear of the orchestra, and way on the side, Steve stopped short, as if he were going to argue about the tickets with the usher, as if a terrible mistake had been made. Hadn't he ever bothered to look at the tickets? When they sat down, he fidgeted, boiling, insulted, looking toward the front center of the orchestra as if he wanted to identify those who had outdone him through cheating or favoritism. Emily said, "We're going to see and hear just fine, like everyone else. What's wrong with these?" Steve didn't answer her. She wondered if he might be putting on some kind of act. "We're here. At the greatest thing in the world, Eddie. Let's be happy, okay?"

"It's like sitting in right field. Why did Evelyn tell me they were the best? I'll have to speak to Evelyn."

Evelyn, his secretary, had stood in line to get the tickets. "She obviously meant the best available. Please promise me you will not say anything to Evelyn other than thank you."

"Let's drop it."

"Promise me."

"Okay. Let's drop it."

It interested her that she didn't like everything about him that interested her. She certainly wasn't stringing him along because he invited her to the theater; she was trying to figure him out, put him together. She liked being with Steve. She looked forward to being with him. Sometimes, so he wasn't always taking her out, she cooked them chicken breasts or her shrimp-and-rice dinner or her beef bourguignon dinner, at her apartment or at his, on Fifteenth and Fifth, walking distance from the Farr store and offices. She was a so-so cook at best.

It also interested her that for someone who seemed to be used to getting what he wanted, including girls, as she gathered from his reports of his past, he put surprisingly little extra pressure on her sexually. He persisted, but he was fairly friendly about her refusal to take the final step, maybe because her refusals were friendly and the final step was all she refused.

She was attracted to him, but not ready to lose complete control. Among other reasons, she didn't want to start gaining distinction in her own mind by sleeping with men like a twenties' woman. Two men would lead to four, four to eight, eight to sixteen. She wouldn't have been ready all that quickly for Steve, she suspected, even if it hadn't been for George. But George didn't help. Each time she thought of him, she still got angry. Sometimes she got angrier than she'd been right after it had happened. Occasionally she still imagined playing a horrible joke on George—getting his telephone number from her father, luring him to her apartment, seducing him, them telling him she had VD, or having her father appear from the kitchen and arrest him. At college, she had heard about a girl who had actually made a bowel movement on the chest of a boy who had fallen asleep drunk right after intercourse.

The second time that there had been quite a bit of petting, she said, "I just want you to know I feel a little silly. I'm not a tease. I'm too serious to be a tease." They were nearly naked.

"I'm not going to think less of you if you give in, you know."

"But would you think more of me?" she asked. That had made him laugh. She blushed. "Truly, it's not a moral issue. And it's not that I don't like sex. And it's not you. I don't know. I don't have a diaphragm yet. We have time, don't we?"

"Five minutes. Can I ask? Are you a virgin?"

She rubbed her forehead, no, against his cheek. Her heart beat as if it were coming loose. "But it was a bad mistake."

"Traumatic?"

"I wasn't raped."

"Do you want a diaphragm for your birthday?"

"Ask Evelyn to get it for me."

"Who was the guy? If it wasn't madman Timothy. Was it Timothy?"

"No."

"A secret."

"Not necessarily. It's embarrassing. As I said, it was a mistake."

"Was it before or after Timothy? BT or AT?"

"After."

"Was it only once?"

"Sort of three-quarters of once. Four-fifths."

"Be mysterious. Do you think I care?"

"I want you to care. I just don't want to talk about it yet."

"I understand. Really."

She had secrets. Her mind was a messy bedroom with the door closed. That she had secrets behind her forehead amazed her. The forehead, smooth or wrinked, didn't show the secrets behind it. The forehead was like a curtain that never rose. Andy Profound. *The fore-head is a curtain that never rises.*

Andy Profound, naturally, would have called someone like Steve a clod, without bothering to know him. She thought of Steve as a healthy blend of conformity and eccentricity. She wanted men to be complete individualists without being nutty. While she might be average herself in most ways, she wouldn't settle for averageness around her. She didn't seek out distinction in order to make up for her own average-ness, she felt, but because she knew, or she hoped, that distinctive experiences were waiting in her life for her to find, unforgettable surprises slipping from their disguises, terrible or wonderful. As long as you got out alive and intact, terrible could be wonderful, she was sure. She had already had two bad experiences with men. Thom Blake, even though she'd been very young then, and George, a whopper, even though she could see why she'd done it. But at least both ex-periences were unusual, memorable, unexpected. Perhaps she was in love with experience.

She could not see herself as any unforgettable surprise. If she were distinguished, would George have crept out in the middle of the night? At her lowest, she saw herself as the daughter of Queen Janet the First, but without the qualifications to assume the throne. (Ellen had the qualifications but would be lackluster.) But at least she cared about her life as if her life were life itself. That might be her only distinction. Because she didn't know what to do with how much she cared. That was her failure. But at least she thought about things.

She lacked distinction, but her standards were high. She had used to wonder if she was so picky about boys because Thom Blake had ruined her for life. Jill scoffed at that, saying Emily was picky about everything. But the fact remained that unless you counted Andy, and she didn't, she had never had a boyfriend in high school—just "dates" and some heavy necking. Timothy had been her first truly serious boyfriend, even in college. Nevertheless, having managed to refrain from going to a psychiatrist, when a lot of girls in her family situation would be camping out on the couch, she'd have been damned if she'd ever go to one to learn if Thom Blake had made her cold. She thought she was very curious about sex, more curious in a way since George, with normal desires. She'd shown herself she could be sexy, to a point, with Timothy and Steve. Still, she worried. She might turn out to be different from most women, in a bad way.

Glenn Monash, an older man—thirty-two—and an intellectual, was the only man she'd gone out with whom she'd met through work— at a party Partridge gave at the Pierre for Duvall Rodgers's novel about FDR. Glenn Monash, a historian, an assistant professor at Columbia, hadn't been in Steve's league as a person. And Page Gibbon, Steve's other recent predecessor, was much less so, except for his name, which was by far his best feature. She had met him at a semi-bohemian party at Iris's eighth-floor walkup on Prince Street. Page Gibbon, a copy-writer at Kruskin and Murphy, was a mannequin. Page Gibbon had one-hundred-percent zero sense of humor.

The difference between Page and Steve was that where Steve would affectionately say, "You're too much" if she expressed herself slightly off the beaten path, Page Gibbon had said, two or three times, "I don't get you." He didn't get her at all. Or want her. She hadn't had to turn down any more dates with him. If she had told Page Gibbon her *Midsummer Night's Dream* idea, he undoubtedly would have said, "I don't get you." Her *Midsummer Night's Dream* idea wasn't exactly the kind of thing that Steve Farkas thought about every day of the week, but Steve's first reaction had been to ask if he could help.

The front porch in Newbury looked onto an oval flower bed of perennials, containing, in late June, when the festivities would take place, pansies and impatiens at the border, lupines, lilies, astilbe, Siberian iris, bachelor buttons, and daisies. Purples, pinks, blues, yellows, orange, white. Summers ago, at Emily's request, Granny Luise had taught her the names of all the flowers to be seen around the house from June through early September, when Emily was there. Emily had quizzed herself on the names. She loved flowers. Not that she knew too many people who went around complaining about them, but she felt she loved them more than most people could because of how much it amazed her that natural things could be so beautiful you'd think they had to be handmade. Flowers were so colorful, graceful, and subtle, and so thrilling to smell, it was nearly impossible to imagine that they just grew, the way grass and trees just grew. They were rare, no matter how plentiful. It seemed to her she had been meant to understand flowers.

Behind the flower bed, an apple orchard extended back to the stone wall running alongside the Senns' meadow and down to the dirt road on the right. It was on the bars of lawn before and after the flower bed, and on the deep stage of the orchard behind, that Emily imagined *A Midsummer Night's Dream* magically taking place.

Lanterns illuminated the orchard all the way through. In every tree, microphones were hidden. Stagelights were fixed in the branches of the front trees, directed at the bars of lawn-stage. Granny and Grandpa were no longer sitting on the porch, but on the walk in front of the lawn, on their living-room thrones. A complete cast, letter-perfect and with perfect enunciation, performed the complete play. The costumes were the same colors as the flowers. Aside from directing, Emily took the three-word part of Moth. Otherwise, she watched her grandparents and her returned mother—the miracle she had wrought. The production (not the miracle, which was private), got written up in the *Newbury Weekly*. The production had to be repeated for neighbors and townspeople. The *New York Times* reported the story. By popular demand, the production had to be repeated again and again for larger and larger audiences from farther and farther away. A company of the highest quality was formed, under Emily's directorship. Newbury became a world-famous repertory theater, the equal of Stratford-on-Avon.

Emily could not get the production out of her head now. The problem, as a matter of fact, was precisely how to get it out of her head. How could she unroll the fantasy onto the lawn and into the orchard so the colors and the words would begin to move in the lanterns and stagelights, Mendelssohn's music appearing as naturally as a breeze, the orchard actually populated by fairies?

So easy to imagine and so hard to imagine making it happen. Steve kept asking, "How can you know unless you try?" (It sounded to her as if he were wondering underneath, Are you a phony? Are you just entertaining yourself or will you put yourself on the line?) She drew up a list of technical problems. She drew up a list of the play's characters along with some names of possible performers. No amount of practical thinking made it seem easier to do. The problems were a fantasy all their own. If it was easy for her to talk, it was also easy for Steve to give her pep-talks. She began calling the project *A Midsummer Night's Nightmare*. Steve again suggested she do selected scenes, but the idea embarrassed her for some reason. It would be too amateurish. She could imagine people forgetting their lines or having to read from scripts. Granny and Grandpa smiling through. It would be a grown up version of her old *Little Red Riding Hood*—childish, no illusion.

She went so far as to mention the full-scale plan to a few people. Bunny was gung-ho. Even Ellen said she liked the idea. Steve spoke to some Farr people. It sounded like fun to them, he said. But what did that mean? Steve also thought he knew how he could get the costumes made cheaply. But each time Emily pinned herself down, thought through to reality, she saw herself organizing something as huge and cumbersome as a circus or World's Fair or political convention, an exhausting shambles. There weren't three months left. It would take a year.

She tried again to think about scenes, a scene, Pyramus and Thisby, needing only Pyramus, Thisby, Wall, Moonshine, Lion, and Prologue. Even a scene would be very hard to do well. Unless she gave up and had people do it informally, no lights, costumes, music, orchard, or fairies. She began to settle in her mind, after all, for amateur hour. The realistic approach to life. Fun, but no enchanted Granny and Grandpa, and no miracle. Herself doing Prologue, maybe, or divide it with Ellen. Her father as Thisby, definitely. Bunny as Pyramus. And she would decide between Ellen, Stan, Steve, and Byron for Wall, Lion, and Moonshine. Stan would make an ideal Wall, if he would deign to do it. Byron would make an ideal Lion. Using Steve might make him seem like a family member. But he might be hurt not to be included, even if he couldn't act to save himself, as he said; he had been so patient and good. She suggested June thirtieth, in Newbury, as the date for the performance. Ellen said she and Stan were in and Bunny said it sounded fabulous and they'd all have a ball.

After more than three months with Steve, she hadn't yet brought him home to her father and Bunny, nor had she been to the Farkases' on Madison and Eighty-eighth, in Sue Freund's old building. She and Steve talked half-jokingly about meeting each other's family. Without quite saying so, neither of them wanted to incite rumor, it seemed to Emily. Neither was quite "ready." Emily liked denying Bunny the pleasure of knowing or supposing anything; also, the George episode made it more possible than ever for her to keep her private life from her father.

Steve kept referring to his folks (Jack and Mona) as "real characters," Mona in particular. Mona stayed out of the toy business; she was a broker for a fancy real-estate firm. Emily was curious, naturally, about Steve's family, but for some reason not all that curious; she wished she could be interested in Steve without having to be interested in his background. When he called his family "real characters," or "impossible," it was obvious he wasn't being as affectionate as she imagined people usually were when they used terms like that. But the terms were ambiguous, and his tone in using them was not revealing. She didn't seem to want to know what he didn't want to tell her; whatever it was made her uncomfortable. She sensed that Steve needed to keep somewhat of a distance between himself and his parents. Emily wondered if his parents embarrassed him, the way Bunny embarrassed her. Or did he embarrass them?

Steve was a peculiar, unpredictable mixture, thank goodness. Maybe his parents couldn't take it. He could be more or less an outsider in the family, not exactly a black sheep, but not the adored son, either. (His sister, Debbie, had died as a baby during an operation for mastoiditis years ago.) Maybe what she had once thought of as his awkwardness bothered them. Maybe his parents were ultrasophisticated. But unless they actually disliked him, why would they notice it at all, if she had gotten so accustomed to it in the few months she'd known him that it had almost dissolved into his being, into his skin? Maybe he was too interested in music. (Steve's record collection was the biggest Emily had ever seen, though Steve said it wasn't much at all.) Maybe his parents knew that every once in a while he mocked the toy business for being trivial and fad-crazy and imitation-crazy and in certain cases so money-grubbing as to be irresponsible about safety. Maybe he talked to his parents' faces about these feelings, and they resented him for having them or for having the gall to express them. When he talked about wanting to go to med school so he would be doing good in the world (his hero was Albert Schweitzer), did his parents think of him as naive and idealistic?

In the meantime, she and Steve ("Stevie" on occasion) coasted along, with hardly a cloud in the sky. Emily was liking her life: career girl with apartment and boyfriend. She liked her life without liking her job or her apartment particularly. It was the Job and the Apartment she liked, rather than the job and the apartment. But it was the boyfriend rather than the Boyfriend. The boyfriend not too strange but strange enough; loving but not too mushy; needy but not too needy; strong but not too strong; money to spend on the right things; thoughtful; could be funny; could be temperamental. He could also be so sweet. Tender. When she had told him the details of her mother's departure and subsequent death, he couldn't say anything at all. He had simply looked at her, biting his lip, and slowly shaken his head while tears appeared in his eyes. That had given her a tremendous pang.

At moments when she was not so pleased with him—when he was, without even realizing it, bossy, or suddenly moody, distracted, obtuse, or insensitive—she sometimes resorted to reminding herself of the pang, or of other kinds of reassuring moments. Boyfriend's girlfriend was considered by boyfriend to be much smarter than she knew, prettier than she knew ("even prettier," he teased), far sexier than she seemed to have any idea of; and the most outspoken, imaginative, and interesting girl he had ever known. All the others had been ordinary by comparison; many of them, however, he had to say in their defense, did compensate for their relative dullness by having slept with him.

"I'll just have to try to keep you happy by using my feminine wiles until I give in." If her self-confidence wasn't coming from him she didn't know where it could be coming from. She felt, without thinking hard about it, that for some reason he was going to wait for her; that he needed or respected her enough in general to wait for intercourse. She didn't say so to him, but she knew intercourse wasn't that far off. More and more often in her mind, he was inside her. She was getting used to the idea. At the same time, tiny quick thoughts, like squeezes of light, hinted at what helped to hold her back. It wasn't just fear of getting pregnant. It was her fear that once they did the real thing, she would be a woman-in-training or a wife-in-training (which was at the same time exactly what she wanted to be). Although she knew it was silly in a way, because having sexual intercourse wasn't necessarily a conclusion of anything, still it connoted a bit too much maturity to suit her. She had always thought being mature was the most desirable of all characteristics. It would definitely be premarital, sleeping with Steve, whether or not they ever ended up marrying each other. She didn't want having intercourse with him even to seem final. She wasn't worrying (maybe she should be) that he would drop her once he got what he wanted; instead she was worrying that, once she slept with him, she would need to stick with him forever. And that might be just fine, but it was forever, and forever wasn't necessarily fine. Forever in this context meant marriage, children, getting older slowly—or rapidly. It meant changing in the same way everyone changed, then dying. Forever, in other words, meant not forever in this context, and she didn't have any idea how to solve the problem, so she tried not to think about it too much. Her mother had solved the problem.

CHAPTER EIGHT

An Encounter at the Theater

Emily's life right now seemed to her to be a story. In the story, she was enviable for what she did all day and all evening, despite her not being distinguished. No two ways about it, she was one of the crowd. No one who didn't know her knew of her. But since Steve, she felt more shaped.

Though she wasn't ready to bring Steve home, she'd been thinking she might be ready to show him off to Ellen, anyway. She asked Steve if he had any interest in going to *Waiting for Godot* for her earth-shattering twenty-third birthday. It opened Friday, April twentieth, two days before the big day.

"It's supposed to be very obscure, right? In case we don't understand it, we'll console ourselves at Sardi's after."

"Thank you. You know I would adore that." She slid onto his lap (he was sitting in his butterscotch-colored leather armchair) and kissed him three times. "I thought I'd ask Ellen and Stan if they'd like to double with us. Stan will probably fall asleep as soon as the curtain goes up."

Steve gave a that's-his-problem shrug. "Wouldn't your parents be hurt—your father, if it's your birthday celebration?"

"Not if he doesn't know. I'll try to get tickets for the second night, the Saturday, if Ellen and Stan can make that. If not, then the next week."

"Since it's your birthday, why not let me handle the tickets? I'll send someone from the office or we'll use a broker. No big deal."

"Not Evelyn. I'd prefer to go myself and make sure the tickets are satisfactory to your royal highness. Your royal heinie."

"That's not very funny." He smiled anyway, little-boyishly, with his mouth open.

"I was just teasing, Stevie. I can't wait to go, and to Sardi's. I just thought I'd get the tickets myself so you wouldn't be laying out the money for Ellen and Stan. Would you let me take you for my birthday present to myself? I'd really like to."

"That's very considerate of you, but it's hardly necessary."

"I didn't suggest it because it was necessary."

"If you're going to bother to stand on line with your incredibly beautiful legs, just see to it that you get decent seats, okay?" He took hold of her hips between his thumbs and fingers and wiggled her back and forth a few times.

"If I don't, I won't return to civilization."

Ellen insisted that Daddy and Bunny had to be invited. Emily gave in. There wouldn't be that much time for Steve to be reviewed during an evening out. Everyone would be at the same level, more or less— no hosts and no guests—and in fact, she and Steve, being the youngest and hippest, would probably understand the play best. Anyway, what did she have to hide? Ellen sent her a check, her father likewise, and Steve gave her money for their two tickets. She bought excellent seats for the last Saturday in April, when everyone was free.

She usually arrived early at a theater, but since she didn't want to be waiting nervously with new Steve for the others (the quick meeting at her housewarming didn't count) she managed to arrange that she and Steve got to the Golden at ten of eight. She had the tickets, after all. In the bubbly lobby (Timothy called theater lobbies cocktail parties without drinks), after cheerful, breathy introductions, which she had of course rehearsed in her head, she dispensed paperback copies of *A Midsummer Night's Dream* to her father, to floppy Bunny, to Ellen, and to prim-mouthed Stan, reminding them they had agreed that on June thirtieth, in Newbury, they would be doing the Pyramus and Thisby scene from scripts. Stan made everyone chuckle by saying the scene sounded familiar because he had clients in Paramus, New Jersey. Bunny punished him with a slap on his overcoat. Emily said she thought they should all meet at least twice for run-throughs. In the meantime, they were to please look over Act Five, scene one, and see what they were in for. When they met, they would decide on the casting. Everyone nodded obediently, as if it were all taken care of. Everyone listened to her. It seemed so easy. She couldn't remember ever having been in command of anything involving grownups. Maybe being twenty-three meant having automatic control of your life. Even the introductions had been smooth. She was wearing a brand-new teal taffeta dress she was crazy about, black pumps, and a black coat (all courtesy of her father), and she would never look better in her life.

In they went, occupying most of row I in the side section on the right, off the center aisle. Stan the farthest in, Ellen, Bunny, Daddy, birthday girl, and Steve, on the aisle. "Close," Steve whispered.

"Close," Emily said. "You like the seats? You don't like the seats?"

"Stan may not like the Exit sign looking over his shoulder." Steve helped her spread her coat behind her.

"There were no seats for six people closer and in the center. I'll switch with Stan at intermission, if you like, or you can."

"I think you did fine. And you look so sexy, it's unfair."

"I like being unfair." To her father, on her right, she said, "Old times, Daddy."

"I love being with you, cookie. We don't see enough of you." He quickly kissed her forehead.

Bunny leaned forward toward Emily and Steve, saying, "I'm hoping I love it, Steve, don't you?"

"I'm loving it already," Steve said.

Steve should have been in the diplomatic service. Emily was feeling freely warm toward Bunny; Bunny's Bunnyness seemed to make no difference all of a sudden. Wasn't this the very first moment she had ever felt friendly toward her? She said, "Bunny, I promise you any part you want in June as long as you make sure Daddy participates." Emily noticed Ellen looking on, trying to keep herself entertained from the periphery. Stan was reading his program. Did Stan ever feel left out, or did he want to be left out?

"He'll be there," Bunny said. "I have ways." Bunny presented her typical uncertain-looking smile. It was almost as if she were trying to be coy, practicing to be coy, and not quite making it.

"Of course I'll be there," her father said. "I'm directing."

"I'm directing, Daddy. You're in it. You've got to promise. We don't have enough people. Family's got to help out."

"I won't let you down, Cookie."

Emily glanced at Steve's reliably handsome profile. He was also reading his program. He'd behaved with complete charm and composure meeting her family. She'd be lucky if she did a tenth as well. She sat between her father and Steve. Her neck shivered. Her father and Steve had shaken hands in the lobby. She connected her father and Steve. She was their common subject. "You're very good," she said into Steve's ear. He smiled, continuing to read. His nudginess about seats was childish, but there were worse crimes. So he liked the best. He didn't ask that much for himself. The houselights were going down. The moon of the stage would be appearing, with people on it. Steve encouraged her. He was patient with her limitations, but he didn't think she should settle for herself. The curtain rose.

The act ended without Godot having come, naturally, and with Bert Lahr and E. G. Marshall waiting—saying they were going, but not moving. Emily looked at her father first. "And?"

"I never had a better time in my life," he said.

"Do you like it?" She laughed. She was disappointed in it, actually. Most of it seemed too obvious instead of too difficult. The best parts were the least understandable.

"I'm impressed that someone could spend his time thinking up a play like that. It's a free country, of course."

"I think Beckett lives in France, Dad," Ellen said.

"France is also a free country. Good for him. People are amazing." He slapped his kneecap once lightly.

"It's sort of like Alice in Wonderland without Alice," Steve said. Emily looked at Steve. Before she had a chance to decide if his comment was as smart as it sounded, she saw Timothy Field, or someone just like him, in hornrimmed glasses, coming up the aisle with a blonde in black. "Timothy?" She felt as if she were grabbing to restrain her leaping voice, face, and heartbeat.

He looked hard and stopped, smiling welcomingly, as if he were older than she. He was wearing an impressive blue blazer. "The lovely and talented Bala Kinwood, aspiring actress," he said of the blonde. "The lovely and talented Emily Weil."

"Hi, Emily," the blonde said. Talk about Alice in Wonderland; her hair came down to her tushy.

"Timothy Field," Emily said. "Steve. My father, my stepmother, sister, and brother-in-law Stan. God. It's been so long. How do you like it?"

"Steve Farkas," Steve said, rising to shake hands with Timothy, and remaining on his feet in the aisle.

"Steve," Timothy said. "Got it"; then, to Emily, "We're going to have a quick soda or perhaps even scotch-and-soda across the street. Join us?"

"There are too many of us," Emily said. "Thanks, anyway. We're going out for something after."

"I'll call you," he said. "Byron says you're well."

"I didn't know you'd spoken to him recently." Mistake. Stupid mistake.

"Well, he said you were fine once, I swear. How is he?"

"I think he's okay. I haven't seen that much of him lately. Are you famous?"

"Not really. Just a household word. Liss-en! It's so nice seeing you!"

"Bye-bye, Timothy."

He and the blonde vanished.

"Who's that?" her father asked.

"College friend."

"He seems like a friendly young man," Bunny said. "Is he in the theater?"

"TV. He writes for Monte Madison. Ugh." But even the *ugh*, she knew, was a kind of bragging.

"Of course," Bunny said. "I'm sure I've seen his name."

Steve had sat again. Emily looked at him. She sensed that her mouth was slightly open, as if she were expecting to swallow his reaction, whatever it might be.

"Seems a bit arrogant, if you ask me," he muttered, trying to lighten his criticism by darkening it.

"So show-biz!" she exclaimed. All she could think of was how unemotional the encounter had been, and how quick. It didn't connect at all with how she'd known him. But she supposed it did actually connect in one sense—with his speed and his glibness. She was disappointed in a way that she hadn't liked him better seeing him again, that it didn't disturb her more. Something she had not really thought would ever happen had happened so fast it wasn't even worth it.

She wondered if instead of going for a soda or scotch-and-soda (he talked just the way he used to) they'd gone right to the lovely and talented Bella Kinwood's apartment. (It had to be Bella, not Bala, but who was named Bella anymore?) They'd been in a hurry. He didn't seem to be liking the play that much. He hadn't answered her question. They weren't coming back for the second act at all. Instead they were doing what Timothy had wanted to do to her two years ago when she'd been too impatient with him to see him anymore. Steve did it to her. He did it in a delicate way. She loved having it done. It was exciting and it was safe. But while she had nothing to compare it with, his delicacy sometimes seemed to her close to holding back, like caution in disguise. He did not hold back when she did it to him, and neither did she. She put a lot of thought into it. She loved hearing him gasp, making him gasp, this slightly proper young man who was fussy about his theater seats. Steve put her in the category of slightly improper. She was proud to be a swallower. She knew some women who would just as soon die. Timothy's penis had been thinner than Steve's was, wirier, making an umbrella of his jockey shorts. (Steve wore boxer shorts.) Steve's was fatter and stumpier, "older." She couldn't remember George's. She wasn't positive she had seen it. Technically, would she be a three-penis or two-penis girl, and which was it better to be? How often did people have thoughts like these at the theater? She visualized turning to her father and Bunny and passing on her reflections to them. Maybe Bala-Bella was an expert. Lovely and talented.

By the time the houselights went down again, Emily still hadn't seen them return. How could they miss the second act? Had the reunion bothered Timothy? Was that why it had been so quick? Or had he been indifferent? Would he call her? (Don't call us, we'll call you?) Did he ever think of her? Was he thinking of her now? Of their reunion? Had he and the blonde gone to their seats from the other aisle? Had they just disappeared? Maybe the Timothy had been a different Timothy, who had once known an Emily who looked exactly like her.

When *Godot* was over, Emily pleased herself during the applause with the thought that in the second act there had been less not to understand, so she had liked it less. She had been secretly scared before the play that she wasn't going to get it. Now that she had been most intrigued by the parts she didn't get—loving the indefinable, unique flavor of their strangeness, their comical strangeness—she was going to have to decide if she was a mental coward, since what she didn't understand she didn't have to ponder if she didn't want to. She thought the audience had been overly appreciative, as she found it usually was. She would never have the nerve to say so, but she sometimes suspected that audiences were suckers and were treated like suckers by plays, not *Godot* necessarily, but many plays, *Anne Frank* being the best example. Even plays that were on the audience's level talked down in a way, because they put themselves intentionally at the audience's level.

As her party pooled in the aisle (no Timothy or blonde to be seen), Stan said, "I thought it was a pure crock, myself. Emily, how about a scene from this one for your grandparents' anniversary? They won't know what hit them." Everybody laughed. "Stanley expresses himself very forthrightly," Ellen said. "I didn't mind it. I thought it was sweet." Emily saw her sister's mouth twist into sweetness. Ellen shook her head, at herself or at the play. Ellen talked about the play as if it were a child. That's how she got the upper hand. What did "sweet" mean, anyway? Her father said, "I don't know what's wrong with Mr. Beckett. It wasn't very dirty. The man wants to be boring but not dirty. He's supposed to be avant-garde. He's not taking advantage. I must have a talk with him." Emily thought that for someone who usually said the same kind of thing, her father was surprisingly amusing. As a matter of fact, there had been an erection in act one and a fart in act two. Both words had gotten a big laugh from the audience, naturally. Even she had laughed at "Who farted?" because of the way Bert Lahr had said it. She was embarrassed that she had laughed along. Bert Lahr had clowned too much, obviously aiming for laughs.

Outside, under the marquee, they finished putting on their coats. Bunny said, "What about a play with not one single female in it? In my book, you need both sexes."

"Bunny, we read the same book," Steve said, chuckling.

Emily glanced at her boyfriend, the charmer.

"Don't you know it?" Bunny said.

"I liked that aspect, though," Emily said to Bunny. "I don't know. It's unusual, I admit." It hadn't even occurred to her that there were no women in the play. Did that make her dumb or smart?

"What do you think Godot stands for?" Bunny asked. "God?"

"God is dead, Bunny," Ellen said. "Hadn't you heard?"

Actually, Bunny, Emily thought, Godot is a kind of dough. You say "Go" to it and it moves into the shape of pies, bagels, bread, the dough of life, and also money. It's a play about not having any dough. That's why they don't go anywhere. They're too weak and poor.

Emily put her arm in Steve's. They all started down to Sardi's. What would they talk about once they got there? She was just as glad the *Godot* conversation had evidently finished. Everyone coming out of the theater had probably said the same dumb things they had all just said. She, Bunny, and Ellen—"the girls"—each had an arm in her man's arm. But no matter how much it pleased her to be with Steve, without him there would be no problem of what to talk about at Sardi's. Ordinary, boring family talk. Both Stan and her father were wearing hats.

"I have to tell you," Steve said to her, "in my opinion those characters were basically shmendricks. They could use a little ambition."

He enjoyed playing the gruff businessman; it was a joke of his. "You're cute." She kissed his cheek. She would prefer to go home with him now even more than being at Sardi's. She could tell him about having been scared she wouldn't understand the play at first, and then actually preferring the parts she hadn't understood. He would like her for that, because it wasn't the typical reaction he would have gotten from some earlier girlfriend. They would lie on his double bed. He would play a record of something she had never even heard of. At the moment, she was feeling so grownup, and so grateful that he had fit in so well, so relieved, she thought she would like to surprise him by saying, "Let's pretend that I went and got a diaphragm."

"Anyway," she said, "it takes all kinds, Stevie. Some people wait for Godot and some people just don't have the time. Not everyone in the world can be a hotshot young exec."

"I don't know about hotshot."

"Also sensitive, understanding, charming down to your toes, and adorable."

"It's lucky I'm all those things, since I'm hardly a household word."

"When I think of household word, I think of vacuum cleaner, or range. It was rather pompous of him, but you can't blame him for trying to be witty." She wondered if Timothy had hardened completely into a comic routine. Did he ever think about other people? Hadn't he insulted Bella-Bala by referring to her as an aspiring actress when he'd introduced her? Or embarrassed her?

"Frankly, I can't see what you ever saw in the guy."

"I can't myself, anymore. How could I? I can only see what I see in you." She kissed his cheek again. "You're perfect."

They were given one of the tables near the front. What a waste, in a way; her group hardly deserved the prominence. Steve had made the reservation. Emily sat between him and Stan now, looking toward the pale orange walls covered with the famous caricatures of famous theater folk. Round tables like the one she sat at were distributed between her table and the banquettes beneath the caricatures. Thom Blake, she thought, would not be among the caricatures or the diners. She had heard nothing of Thom Blake since her summer-theater summer. Was he in prison? Dead? She hadn't even seen him on TV. What would become of someone like him? What did Thom Blake do after failing as an actor? She belonged in this restaurant even more than he did. She pictured him digging ditches on a chain gang.

Steve ordered champagne. She started to touch his sleeve to stop him, but instead she touched his sleeve and said nothing. The touch would be understood as gratitude. To say "Thank you" would make her sound like a little girl. She smiled quickly at Stan, on her right, as a substitute for speaking. Stan was looking at his menu. She picked up her menu. She loved champagne, but she didn't want to be over-celebrated. She'd been given presents already—from Steve, a pink cashmere sweater set and a sexy note; from Ellen, a copy of the book, *The Diary of Anne Frank,* which Ellen had insisted she read because she had hated the play so much. Ellen had been so right; the book was completely different, amazingly mature. It had caused her cheeks to tingle many times. At the end she had burst into tears. The book made her hate the play more. Bunny had sent her a short poem accompanying the nightgown—alternating yearly with a slip—from Bonwit's: "Whee, whee, twenty-three. Skidoo, skidoo, we love you." Emily had told Steve she was going to get Partridge to publish Bunny's complete works. *Skidoo and Other Poems,* by Bunny the Bard.

Her father said, "I'm having the club sandwich," and closed his menu. Emily couldn't concentrate. The menu was so large and her head already so full. She thought she might have an omelette. Eggs and champagne rang some kind of glamor bell in her head. She looked at her father. Beyond her father, she saw Timothy and the blonde sitting at a banquette. How could she not have noticed them? Had they just slipped in? They were like Banquo's ghost. "Household Word is here," Emily said to Steve.

"Ask them to join us," Steve said, not looking for Timothy, but rather smiling at her in a quick snide way.

"There's not room."

"They can sit on our laps."

"Very funny."

"Mr. Farkas," her father said to Steve. "It's the toy business, isn't it? What's new in the toy business?"

"Steve, please," Steve said. "What's new? Well, Davy Crockett is old. He died on us. I could tell you all about extrusion molding and instrusion molding and blow molding, but I wouldn't want you to be up all night thinking about it."

Stan, of all people, let out a surprised laugh, loud even for a noisy restaurant. She noticed Timothy looking; she thought then that she saw him start to get up and his knees decide to stay put. She wanted to find out what was going on with him; there didn't seem to be anything wrong with that. In a way, it would be much easier for her if he came over. But since Steve had just scored a triumph of wit, he might not mind if she went over to Timothy for a minute. A minute was all she wanted, anyway. How could she miss the opportunity?

So she stood up, patting Steve's arm, feeling a blush arriving, and said, "Excuse me a sec. I'm not going to let him be so hoity-toity." She explained to the others, "My friend I saw at the theater before is over there. I'm going to have a quick reunion. I'll be right back. Order me an omelette, Stevie?"

"Yass'm. Get his autograph."

So she took herself, smiling like a TV personality, across the room, with numb feet and bumping heart, thinking, Ah, show biz is such a small world. "Hi again."

"Didn't want to disturb the family party," Timothy said. "Nice to see you after all these minutes."

"That's such a beautiful dress, Emily," Blondie said.

"Thanks. I bought it for my birthday."

"It's your birthday?" Timothy asked. "Happy birthday—I write all my own material. It's so hard to get help these days."

She wondered if people were wondering who she was, who they were. "How'd you like the second act?"

"Was that the second act? I thought they'd forgotten and done the first act over again."

"I really came to find out what you're doing these days. Are you writing for Monte Madison?"

"I'm also doing the book and lyrics for a musical. Sorry there's not room for you to sit."

"I can't stay. That's wonderful! Is it being done?"

"Next winter."

"On Broadway?" She sounded like a moron to herself.

"The great white whale itself."

"A musical of *Moby Dick?* Oh, I get it. The Great White Way."

"I'm not supposed to say anything about it. This is not the place. But it's definite."

"I'll certainly keep a lookout for it."

"What about yourself?"

She laughed. "I haven't made a name for myself yet. I'm in the publicity department at Partridge House."

"Hey!"

"I make names for other people, I guess. Anyway, I'm thrilled to hear your news."

"Liss-en. I'm really going to call you. I'll fill you in. You're in the book?"

What did he think? "Of course." She frowned lightly. "Why not?" She smiled at Bella-Bala as if to explain that Timothy was just being friendly. Probably Bella-Bala knew he didn't mean any of it anyway.

Soon Timothy would have an unlisted number. "Congratulations on whatever the show is, Timothy. I can't wait."

Timothy hopped up, kissed her cheek.

"Thanks for coming over, Emily," Blondie said.

Emily patted Timothy's elbow and walked back to her table, feeling better. Steve wasn't watching her return, but listening to Stan. The waiter was pouring the champagne. As she passed behind Steve to her chair she ran her fingers along his hairline as if her hand were chiffon. A woman of the world. On the stage of Timothy's mysterious musical, the stage lights shone out of high darkness, jewel-colored gels, topaz, emerald, sapphire, ruby, amethyst. The singers and dancers in the beams of light were the chosen, the singled-out, cavorting with magical finesse on the floor of heaven.

Nobody asked about her talk with Timothy. Here she was, sitting with a Broadway scoop, and they were all on "Steve's side." They all disapproved of her going to see her "ex." If they only knew how little she cared about her ex, despite his news (which might not even be true, or might not turn out to happen). Timothy's news, if true, was exciting. It was more than exciting. But Timothy seemed more ordinary, more glib, than he had been in college. She wanted to go with Steve by taxi instantly to his apartment, and use his bed like grownups, so that this time, when she woke up beside him in the morning, she would feel married.

While the conversation continued around her, without needing her, she slipped her left hand beneath the table and onto the top of Steve's rock-solid right thigh, making a slow scratching motion. Under her dress she felt restless. Stan was describing a law suit against a board-game manufacturer. With her right hand, she brought her champagne glass to her lips. No one was proposing a toast. If Timothy were in Steve's shoes, meeting her family for the first time, he would feel above them and not talk enough, or he might try too hard and be embarrassing. In any case, he wouldn't know how to make contact with them, she was sure. For all his glibness, he'd be out of it. His joking ways wouldn't work for such a situation, and everyone would be stranded. She couldn't get over Steve's ability to fit in. He fit in so well, he hadn't even patted her hand. She let it lie for a moment on his pants, and then she returned it to the table.

Tomorrow morning Bunny would call all agog over this fabulous catch, where did you find him, don't you let him get away, girls will be swarming all over him. Ellen might also call, a little less agog, grudgingly agog, but Emily trusted she would not be home to take their praise, and that the unanswered rings would arouse their curiosity.

She actually had to seduce him a little. Ellen and Stan walked to Eighth Avenue for a taxi. Her father and Bunny got one in front of Sardi's. While she and Steve waited for the doorman to get the next one, she said, leaning against his hip, "I just figured out, your house is much nearer than mine."

Steve smiled, without seeming to pay attention. In the taxi, after he gave the driver his address, she snuggled; he put his arm around her, squeezing her twice quickly, as if he were trying to reassure her or comfort her about something, then murmured, "So tell me, are you sure you're willing to sleep in the same bed with me?"

"Huh? Have I ever objected?"

"I just thought you might have your college reunion on your mind." He looked amused, with a wiseguy smile. Most of the time when something was bothering him, he tried to make it seem like a joke at first.

"Are you kidding? That was a big nothing." Now, she supposed, she wouldn't be able to tell him about Timothy's musical. Maybe Timothy would invite them to the opening and Steve would refuse to go.

"It must have been a big letdown from what you expected. By the way, how come when you introduced Timmy to the rest of us slobs, you didn't use my full name? I had to do the honors myself, you know."

"I'm sorry. I guess because there were six of us. I didn't want to drag it out."

"You notice he got the full treatment, though. 'Mr. Timothy Field.' I got 'Steve.' "

"I never said 'Mr. Timothy Field.' I hope you're just being stupid, not serious."

"It was his full name meet my first name, though, right?"

Still the wiseguy smile and the arm around the shoulder. Was the evening going to go up in smoke? "I just said I didn't want to go through the whole rigamarole with names. I didn't use anyone's last name."

"I think my name embarrasses you. It sounds too Jewish."

"You've discovered my secret. I'm anti-Semitic. Why didn't you bring this up when I did it, if it bothered you?" He was going to ruin her plans.

"I didn't want to spoil the evening."

"So now you want to spoil the night instead." Maybe she should be pleased he could be jealous. "Look, you don't think your name is the most attractive name in the world, either. It's one of the first things you ever mentioned to me. I don't even think about it." Not quite true. But not because it was too Jewish. It was just ugly. "And what could I do about it anyway, even if I wanted to? I happen to like you the way you are, most of the time."

"Maybe I should change my name to Steve Field. Sounds pretty good, as a matter of fact."

With his smile, and his arm around her, he looked as though he owned the conversation and thought he could do anything he wished with it. She raised her eyes to him. She wanted to say, "You're going to lose your chance, dope." She whispered, "In case you hadn't noticed, I was feeling very sexy." She got a sudden lump in her throat and a pain in her eyes, as if her feelings had been hurt. If he said, "You mean toward Timothy?" she would ask the taxi to turn around and take her home.

"How sexy?"

"Figure it out." He was going to have to stop smiling. He did. He looked skeptical and alert. His chin lifted a little, she thought.

"How come?" he asked.

She didn't want to attach it to the way he had behaved with her family. She wasn't rewarding him, she hoped. Or trying to prove that seeing Timothy hadn't meant anything to her. "I don't know. I thought it was time. Maybe it's not." They hadn't even discussed his reactions to her family. Maybe he'd hated them.

He didn't say anything. He looked away, out his window. Then he came back, looked at her, kissed her lightly. He took her hand. They gazed at each other for the rest of the trip. The taxi was hurrying bumpily down Fifth Avenue. They would be at his house right away. The avenue was like a straight clock, an avenue of time. (Andy Profound?) The taxi was carrying her and Steve through the clock in a rush. She was definitely excited. She couldn't wait to get there.

In his bed, with their clothes off, he asked her, "Do you want me to see if there's a condom around?" sounding anxious, as if a condom were something for an elderly lady to sit down on.

"If there were, I'd be insulted."

"I just thought there might be some leftovers from the old days in the draw."

Drawer. "I don't want that. My period is due." The opposite of the

George night. Periods were so convenient! "Believe me, I considered everything." She realized she wasn't giving him much of a say. In a way, this was her event. She was making it possible. "Do you want to talk me out of it?"

"Hardly. I just want to be sure you know how you're going to feel tomorrow."

"How about you?"

He shrugged. He smiled nicely. "I'm very serious about you."

"I'm not making some kind of sacrifice. I must feel safe with you, or I wouldn't want to do it."

"I think you're more than I deserve. I've never said that to anyone."

"Why? I wish you wouldn't feel that way."

"You're too smart and beautiful for me. I'm not kidding."

"That's such nonsense. Are you worried you'll run out on me?"

"I've had months to do that."

"It's not the same."

"Anyway, you might run out on me."

"I doubt it. But isn't this a conversation to have another time?"

"Let's never have it," he said.

His mouth had tightened, sharpened, toughened, in a way she had never seen it do, so that it seemed his mouth was looking at her along with his eyes. He had said the perfect thing. She found that she was staring at him. All she could do was breathe and, with her eyes, ask for his hands.

When he went into her, she heard herself making a huge intake of surprise, sounding as if she had just seen the last person on earth she ever expected to see. Then there was a pause. She thought they must have both opened their eyes at the same time, before they began moving. She gulped, looking up at him. She loved it that he was looking at her, the melted way he looked at her, like an adoring male angel who had descended on her. He was hers.

CHAPTER NINE

The Refugees at Home

It was all connected with fitting, even going to Dr. Lippert to get fitted with a diaphragm. Everything fit. Steve had fitted into her family, and then he had fit into her. He had fit and filled her. She wanted to write a poem about their love and their lovemaking. In addition, she had been able to fit their sex into her life, absorb it. It was a big deal, but it belonged. It had been the right thing to do, even though it wasn't quite supposed to be. She and Steve belonged to each other.

At her desk at Partridge, in a room with three other women who hadn't a clue to what she was thinking, she dwelled endlessly on Steve fatly slipping up her, causing every one of her cells to clench in an upward spread of suspense, and then the grateful, mutual spilling collapse, a shivering or unshivering. (Five-hundred-volt "orgs.") She would call Steve at Farr to say, "I can't wait to see you." She noticed a sensation she'd been familiar with since the beginning of adolescence occurring with great frequency when she thought of Steve—an electric jump high up in her vagina, plus wetness. Known as lust. She thought of herself as pregnant with sex, "radiant," "earthy."

Steve was ecstatic, too, always cheerful and giving. When she finally told him about her and George, he didn't even act impressed, which would have bothered her more than jealousy. He was definitely interested, but concerned, and disgusted for her. It was a grownup reaction. He seemed to be concentrating harder on her since they'd started having intercourse. He looked at her more often, more tenderly, more intensely, for longer. He smiled more often while looking at her. She had done something for him. He looked at her as if he had moved into her soul.

Actually, his apartment was their apartment much more than hers was, because of his bed and more room in general. She kept some of her clothes there now. She felt like a professional human being, she decided. Her profession was that of female person. She fit into the human race and suddenly she was proud to be like everyone else in the world instead of scared of being more or less typical. She looked forward to everything these days, except that she still seemed to be squeamish about going to Steve's parents' house for dinner. "I don't know what bothers me, exactly. I just think sometimes that we should go on this way forever without having to get into family entanglements. Did you ever bring the other girls home?"

"Sure, sometimes I did. In the first place, 'the other girls' are not you. Let me tell you something. You have very little to worry about, as long as you take them as they are. My mother's maybe a little too colorful and my father gives the impression of taking the back seat, which is slightly deceptive. Anyway, what do you have to hide?"

"I guess I worry they won't like me, 'approve' of me."

"Why shouldn't they?"

"I'm sorry. I'm such a little girl about this." Maybe she didn't like mothers; maybe she was incapable of liking anyone's mother. Quick, quick, the shrink!

"Never fear. I have faith in you. You'll be just as wonderful as I was. Just remember how wonderful I was."

He had liked Bunny more than politely ("She seems like a good egg. She has a great sense of humor. You probably expect too much of her. You expect a lot, you know. That's why you like me so much. The more you let her be who she is, the more you'd probably appreciate her."). He'd scored a big hit with Bunny, so why shouldn't he praise her? Yet Emily admired his tolerant attitude and wished she could adopt it. Maybe there was nothing wrong with Bunny after all, and she didn't see her right only because she was her stepmother. Maybe Bunny was a great woman in her way. Or maybe there was something wrong with Steve. "Do you think we're going to get married?" she asked him.

"Who? You and me?"

"You and I, grammatically speaking."

"Well, *excuse* me! Do you think we should get married?"

"I'm asking you."

"You mean you're popping the question?"

"I'm asking your opinion, shmegeggy." She had started to borrow Steve's Yiddish words. Formerly she would have said "silly."

"I have to see if you can learn to cook first."

"Suppose I can't."

"I guess I'd have to send you to wife school. If I sent you to wife school, I suppose it might as well be for overall instruction."

"Well, naturally. What do you think I need to know?"

"You must obey! Luff, honor, unt obey!"

"Yes? And do you have anything to learn? Is there husband school?"

"Anything you want changed, just put in a request and I'll take it under consideration."

"Thanks. Very thoughtful of you."

"I'm going to make a date for us to go to my parents' for dinner. If you're not free, I'll go by myself and talk about how wonderful you'd be if you were there. They'll say, 'Stevie, she sounds incredible, you're making her up. She's a figment of your imagination.' And I'll tell them, 'No, she's for real. She'd be perfect, except that she's embarrassed to be seen with me except at Sardi's and she doesn't like people she hasn't met.' "

"I am allowed to be a little nervous, you know. You don't give the impression that you're always that crazy about them. How often have you mentioned me to them?"

"Never."

"Seriously."

"Once or twice. Why would you care?"

"Just wondered. Anyhoo. I'll try not to let you down."

"Just be yourself."

"To mine own self be true?"

He looked pugnacious. "Yes, exactly, as a matter of fact. They're dying to meet you, Emily. Just don't act too superior, and everything will be fine. All you have to do is smile and talk and be sweet, just like a person. Or in my mother's case, smile and listen." He smiled.

"I'll probably do that one—smile and listen. Meek and mild." She supposed he was being obnoxious, but maybe he had a right to be, maybe she had been making a problem without realizing it, and anyhow, his obnoxiousness wasn't very obnoxious. In a way, it was kind of fun.

In the second week of May, at ten-thirty in the morning of the evening that the first reading of the Pyramus and Thisby scene (family plus a possible Steve) was to take place, Emily received a phone call from her father at work. His "Cookie" sounded like a combined warning and consolation. Obviously he was calling to postpone the reading. "Yes, Daddy, when do you want to change it for?"

"Darling, I'm sorry. I wish it were that. Your granny died."

She laid her pencil on the desk. She put her hand to her cheek and ducked her head so the girls at the desks across the room couldn't see her. What was it like to hear such news? She tried to squeeze it away with closed eyes and a sour face, but it was already throbbing in her forehead. "Daddy?" She felt herself starting to cry. She checked herself as best she could. "I can't believe it. What happened? Where are you?"

"Mount Sinai, in the emergency room. She broke her hip in the bathroom this morning and evidently she fractured her skull at the same time. Gus managed to call their doctor and an ambulance brought her over here, but the truth is, she was dead when she got here."

In such good shape for her age. Just like that. "Is Grandpa with you now?"

"He's in the waiting room, around the corner. Bunny's with him."

"How is he?"

"It's hard to tell. He thinks Luise is in surgery. I'm going to have to tell him she died in surgery."

"Should I tell Ellen?"

"We're bringing Gus to our house when I've finished with the formalities here. Ellen's meeting us there. Why don't you meet us there in an hour, three quarters of an hour, I'd say."

"I want to come to the hospital."

"There's nothing for you to do here."

"I just want to."

"It's up to you. Maybe you should, at that, if you take a cab. Gus will be glad to see you. To the emergency-room entrance." He explained how to arrive at the emergency-room entrance.

"I'll be there, Daddy," she said in a choked voice, hanging up. She realized that she sounded ridiculously as if she were on her way to save him. But she felt so sorry for him. He didn't care nearly as much as she did about her grandmother, yet he had to handle his mother-in-law's death without the help of the wife who had made Granny his mother-in-law. Her father was the man in the family. There was no woman in the family.

Even though she was in a hurry, she called Steve in order to avoid reacting, or to react in his ear—she didn't know which. Spreading the news, even to Steve, she felt yet again that she was making herself important through someone else's death; also, that she was cheating on her grandmother's time by calling him. "I may sleep at my father's or grandfather's tonight. I'll let you know. Anyway, you know where I'd like to be."

"Be sure to let me know if there's anything I can do. I can always come up if you need me there. I might have dinner with Jerry" (Jerry Goetz was a sweet and not too fascinating friend of Steve's from Wharton who had once doubled with Jill and them) "and then come home and wait to hear from you. But why don't you call me again here this afternoon if you can?"

"Okay. Thanks." She was so lucky to have him. They were a separate family of two.

"I'm really sorry I didn't get a chance to know her."

"Me too. She was amazing." The whole *Midsummer Night's Dream* thing would be off, of course. They weren't going to do it just for Grandpa. Grandpa was certainly not the star of the couple. "I'll call as soon as I can. Love you." She made a kiss and hung up.

When she stood, she put her hands on the front of her desk—*to steady myself,* she thought—closing her eyes and lowering her head, and began to breathe hard and shakily, filling with grief, expanding as if she had no skin containing her. She felt that she was breathing her own breath, and her mother's and her grandmother's, that she was all three of them, breathing for them. Inevitably she gave way and began to cry. She wished she could stop. It was too late to hide in the ladies' room. Daphne, who sat at the desk behind her, was standing beside her with her hand on her shoulder, saying, in her cold-cream voice, "Are you all right, baby?" Emily nodded, continuing to cry, and wishing Daphne would remove her hand. Emily wiped her eyes, moving slightly away from Daphne. "It's okay," she said. "My grandmother died. I have to take off." Daphne squeezed Emily's shoulder. Emily looked across the room at Mrs. Poplar's closed door. Laura DiLallo and Mary Beth Davidson were looking at her. She was the one whose relatives died. Emily took her handbag out of her drawer and a monogrammed handkerchief from the bag. "I have to go to the hospital. I'll be back later or tomorrow. I don't know when the funeral is, though." She was staring into Daphne's pretty, vapid, sorority-sister concerned face.

"That's all right, baby," Daphne said. "You're not to worry." Daphne patted Emily.

"I'd better see Mrs. P."

Laura stood sympathetically. "We'll tell her, Emmy."

Elsa Poplar at that moment opened her door and came out of her office, holding a file.

"Emily's grandmother died," Laura said.

"It's all right," Emily said.

Mrs. P. walked toward Emily, large and bosomy, in her chocolate suit, her blonde hair blowsy, loose even in a bun. She was slightly unglamorous-looking for her fancy job and her sophisticated manner, Emily always thought. Mrs. P. kissed Emily on the forehead.

"Thank you," Emily said, crying again, a few spasms, into her handkerchief.

While holding Emily's hand, Mrs. Poplar spoke to Daphne in her underplayed way. "I'm going into a meeting with Bill and Dunc. Will you please call Mort in Chicago and remind him that there's no such thing as laying it on too thick with Charlotte Elgar. She doesn't mind ten tugboats in every port, thank you very much." She squeezed Emily's hand and released it, saying to her, "Let us know if we can help in any way."

"Thanks." Emily then darted to her coat, to the bathroom, the elevator, the street, a taxi uptown to an emergency.

She forgot for a minute that it was her grandmother, not her grandfather, who had died. Which was worse—her dying or his surviving? Her little (smaller that Granny), sweet, nervous, friendly but not especially communicative grandfather. Sort of like Daddy in that way. He was already lonely. What would he do without Granny? Since he'd retired from the art-supply business, he said, he was going to become delegate to the U.N. from his building because he was so well informed from reading the newspapers so thoroughly. Otherwise, he said, all he did was take walks and naps. But that was his kind of joke. Granny had forced him to do volunteer work at JRSA, the organization Mom had worked for. Also, they traveled a lot, as they had always done, mostly cruises. It was Emily's belief that travel, more than anything, brought pleasure to their marriage. They'd gone almost everywhere. They'd been to Japan last year. Granny, naturally, had wished they could go to China so they could visit Mom's grave in the Jewish cemetery in Shanghai. Emily then visualized Granny in her bathroom, just a few hours ago, losing her balance, lurching, cracking her head on the bathtub or the tile, and she flinched and covered her eyes. Granny had the purest white hair, white with depth to it, snow in shadow, as smooth as a plate. She began to think about the blood, and had Granny cried out, was she naked, had she and Grandpa talked, did she know she was dying?

The trio of Grandpa, her father, and Bunny were standing outside the hospital, waiting for her, or looking for a cab, sort of helplessly, as if they had been unable to get into a movie and were trying to decide where to have Chinese food. Though she was sure she looked like a wet leaf, she felt as if she were some goddess flying up in a chariot and reaching out her hand for them. Grandpa crawled in beside her, staring at her as if she were a stranger, red-eyed, dressed in his usual dark suit and tie, Bunny beside him, her father up front. Emily instinctively grabbed her grandfather. In her arms, for a moment, he made high-pitched, coughlike sobbing noises while she clenched her trembling face on his shoulder.

The funeral was held at Campbell's, in a small room, a Rabbi Felix Roth, and a perfect speech, too short if anything, by David Breitenfeld, Granny and Grandpa's closest friend, a dapper Viennese bachelor. He talked about Granny's nobility, how she had taken her daughter's death like a queen (Emily had always thought Daddy thought Granny had felt sorry for herself, and that that was why he didn't care for her so much. Either way, though, there was no question that for thirteen years, her daughter's death had been Granny's main feature), and how her own freakish and, considering her full age and excellent health, ironically abrupt death could not rob her of her nobility. She had been stoical. She had kept gardening in her beloved Newbury year after year, keeping life alive, as she had kept love alive in her husband and her granddaughters. The way she had died was a capitulation only after long resistance; she had been wrestling privately with death for years and winning, and then suddenly let down her guard and been tricked by a deceitful enemy, over which she would triumph in people's admiration and love. Then he read "Death, be not Proud."

Emily cried, remembering Granny, who was so wonderfully elegant without being fashionable, coming to nurse her when she was sick at home, Granny's hand on her forehead or cheek, substituting for Mom's. It was really the end, Emily thought. No mother, no grandmother, no sweet older woman, no wiser woman. Where would she get it from again? It was gone. Not that she had spent that much time with Granny or that Granny had been a mentor; but it had been enough that Granny was around, just there, arriving or greeting in her sad but always loving way.

After the funeral there was a lunch at her father's. She knew the people's names better than she knew many of the people, including some of her relatives. Granny's sister, Marie Hirsch; one of Marie's daughters, Klara (pronounced "Klahra") and "Klahra's" husband Felix, and their short but good-looking son, Cousin Warren, a freshman at Columbia (Emily had met cousin Warren once before in her adult life, at Granny's seventy-fifth birthday party); Grandpa's lumpy niece Sybil and her shmoey husband Martin Neckarsulmer; Gene and Juliet Senn and David and Theresa Streeter from Newbury (Emily had played with Don and Sally, the Streeters' children, during the summer); Benno and Hilda Wiener; Ernestine and Fred Gans; Leo Hampel, Grandpa's former partner in the art-supply business, and his wife, Edith; and a woman named Fannie Benjamin, who had once owned a dress shop off Madison Avenue, where she had sold some of the clothes Granny made. Ellen had brought baby Janet. Stan had left right after lunch. (Steve had come to the funeral service but not to the house, for fear that he would be out of place. She missed him every other minute. He was acting completely, unselfishly thoughtful, almost too ready to be at her service). Granny and Grandpa's housekeeper, Elma, was helping out Margaret.

Emily noticed that she was getting something like an exciting relief out of having all the people there to watch and talk with. There was excitement in the idea of people collecting at all, people who didn't necessarily know each other. The sorrow itself seemed to have a kind of warm, bubbly quality; laughter and tears were mixed together, emotion was all over the place. Baby Janet was the natural focus of the gathering, really. At one point in the postfuneral afternoon, she took a wobbly run at her great-grandfather Gus, who had beckoned her in a tired, good-humored way from the couch, and sat in his lap in her baby-blue dress, showing off her smile. Emily got teary while taking in the scene. She glanced over at her down-to-earth sister, who also seemed to be moved. Emily went and hugged her.

When she let go of Ellen and was standing beside her, saying nothing, she thought, I am standing in a tomb. The thought made her freeze. She might have been standing in icy water. Ellen excused herself to take Janet off Grandpa's lap, and left the room with her, probably for the bathroom. The thought was like a reminder of some truth, a punishment for relief and excitement for having forgotten that death was death and not primarily the excuse for a cozy party.

Emily put her hand on her heart and took a deep breath. She actually felt frightened. She was standing in a tomb completely covered over by Bunny's taste—the furniture so colorful and sunny that the room looked like a patio. (Her mother's photograph had been transferred from the piano to the inset bookshelf; Emily had once thought to complain, but no longer wanted to bother. It was her father's business.) It made no difference how much the living room had been disguised, it was the same room where her mother had knelt to say goodbye. No matter how bright and floral the living room was, in Emily's mind it had stayed dusky, and also wider and longer than it now appeared to be. She remembered the chairs as bushes in the shadows, and the floor as a darkening lawn. The room was permanent that way; it was temporary now.

She didn't want anyone to talk to her. She walked out of the room in a hurry and into her old bedroom, where Bunny's divorced son, Neil, the traveling jewelry salesman, sometimes slept. Except that the cream walls were bare of her old decorations—the high-school poster for *Our Town,* an oil painting (now in her own apartment) by her grandmother of the Newbury house and grounds, a bulletin board crammed with mementos, autographs, silly buttons—it was the same room she had left for college. Some of the funeral coats were on the bed. Emily sat on the covered radiator and looked down at the courtyard, a well of old sun. For Mom there had been a memorial service and reception at the JRSA building. She remembered being concerned that not enough people would come to fill the auditorium; but it had become filled, and then there were even people standing. She remembered the fact of speeches, but not the speeches. And she remembered wondering if by chance her mother might appear at the podium, at the end.

Then she thought of her mother's gravestone in Shanghai, the black-and-white snapshot of it that Henrietta Fish had brought to them after the war. Then she thought of Granny's bathroom. Granny's bathroom had been in her mind for two days. She had been in that bathroom so many times, but not recently. It made her uneasy (as if she could do something about it now) that she hadn't seen Granny since her last birthday, her seventy-ninth, in March, when she had brought her an enormous bouquet of spring flowers. (She spent a ridiculous amount of money on flowers. She bought them for herself or for Steve's apartment at least once a week. Buying flowers, she felt she had captured magic.) Unlike Granny, she had no desire to see the gravestone, even if it were possible to get to China in one day, though maybe she should do it for Granny, if she ever could. She wondered if Granny had chosen to be cremated—cremated!—because she didn't want to be buried, because Mom had been buried, and so far away. Was being cremated a way of going to visit Mom? Was it "natural" to be cremated, or was it bitter, like saying, "I, too, am a victim of the Holocaust"?

The photograph had been a photograph of a marker of disappearance, like the wing of a plane sticking up from underground, the tail of something: this is all there is of me, this is what's left of me. When she'd seen the photograph (where was it now?), she couldn't help but think that it was too bad, but her mother had chosen to be turned into a stone. Now that she was older, and missed Mom much more, she still thought seeing the gravestone would be pretty much the same as seeing its photograph. The gravestone itself would be a photograph of her mother—a stone photo of a name and dates beneath the earth. Her mother and the gravestone and the photograph of the gravestone were the same thing: Janet Mayer Weil, 1900–1943.

It made her feel miserable to have such a thought at such a time, when she had just been reminded at the funeral of the strength of love, and she was alive and her mother and her grandmother weren't. She didn't want to be so hard and so sad at the same time. So close and so far. Steve shouldn't be the only person in the world she really knew.

She returned to the living room, thinking she had been gone so briefly that if anyone had noticed, they would have supposed she'd simply gone off to the bathroom rather than shutting herself in her old bedroom to have deep thoughts. Ellen was back in the living room, too, holding Janet's hand and talking to Cousin Warren. Emily went to her father, who was standing over Grandpa and Fanny Benjamin like a waiter as they sat on the couch. Emily touched her father on the sleeve of his dark blue suit. She didn't know what she wanted to say to him; she wanted to be with him. She kept her hand on his sleeve. A privilege of age. "May I speak with you at some point?"

"I was just asking Gus if he wants to spend tonight here."

She let go of her father and knelt, resting her arms on her grandfather's knees. Her grandfather had been insisting on sleeping at his own apartment. "Do you want me to stay with you, Grandpa? I'll be glad to." The man had no idea that if she didn't stay with him she would be sharing the bed of a man named Steve to whom she wasn't married. Her grandfather patted her hand. "No, darling." He sounded croaky, as if he had laryngitis. "I have to get accustomed." His eyes were shrunken. "Elma is staying. Don't worry."

"It's not worry, Grandpa." What else was it? What else was there to do but worry about him? There was no blood in his face. She imagined him living in Steve's apartment with her, the three of them around the kitchen table, Grandpa and Steve exchanging business stories, Grandpa chattering away, safe and happy, protected by his granddaughter and her fine young man, approving of them. "Anytime you need me, though, Grandpa, will you call me?"

"Of course, darling."

He didn't believe her. "I mean it," she said. "I'm going to call you every day to see how you're doing."

"I always like talking to you." He patted her hand again.

She was making him uncomfortable. She got up. She kissed his cheek.

"What can I do for you?" her father asked her.

"I don't know. I feel out of touch. Can we go in the bedroom and talk a minute? I think I've talked to every single soul but you."

"Lead on, Macduff."

As she left, Emily noticed that Bunny was captivating Martin Neckarsulmer about something or other. Martin Neckarsulmer looked to Emily like a city hick, a hayseed from the city. Ellen, Janet and cousin Warren stood near the living-room entrance. "Care to join Daddy and me?" Emily asked her sister. "Family reunion?"

"Why not? Is princess here allowed?" Ellen asked.

"Sure. Only princesses and daddies are allowed," Emily said.

"Our daddy, not your daddy," Ellen said to Janet. "Your daddy's at his office. We also have a daddy. Your daddy's not the only daddy in the world."

Janet listened to her mother's comment without appearing to register it.

The bedroom was like an ad for an ocean liner or something—white with lots of sky blue. Flamboyant. Bunny had dressed up the apartment, all right, Emily thought, bringing "fun" into Daddy's life, probably. There hadn't been any showiness in the old days. All the drama had been real. A Greek tragedy on Park Avenue.

Emily and Ellen sat on the raw silk bedspread, facing their father, who lay, amusingly, on the blue-and-white-striped silk chaise, beneath the afternoon sunlight in the windows. Baby Janet stood between her mother and her aunt, bouncing her back against the bed. Daddy tipped his tortoiseshells to his forehead, to massage his eyelids with the backs of his fingers. He yawned.

"I must say, you're very good, putting up with all those geeks and geezers," Emily said to him.

"What's the problem? Don't be silly." He fitted his glasses over his eyes so they were snug.

"What are geeks and geezers?" Janet asked, turning to her aunt, ready to be entertained.

"Shh," Ellen said to her daughter. "This is grownup conversation."

"Grownup conversation about geeks and geezers," Daddy said.

Janet giggled boisterously, still bouncing against the bed, looking as if she were revving up to take off on her glee. The glee was a performance, it seemed to Emily, at least as much as it was a response. Emily said to her father, "I just meant that you've given up two days of work and you're behaving like the perfect host to a bunch of people you hardly know." And couldn't care less about.

"I don't see that it bears mentioning. It's my place to do it. I want to do it. They're your mother's family."

That was exactly why she imagined he could resent the situation. "I was paying you a compliment. I'm used to your being wonderful to Ellen and me, but I don't think of you as all that gregarious."

"I'm going to have to study the compliment. You girls don't come for dinner enough."

"We have our men," Ellen said. "We have to cook for our menfolk."

Emily looked at Ellen. "Speak for yourself." Ellen was wearing a navy-blue dress, with tiny, dark red, green-sprigged berries in it. It emphasized her bust and also made her seem a teensy bit dowdy, more a mother than a political aide, which was what she called herself this election year. Emily herself was wearing a black shirtwaist dress and pearls of her mother's. She couldn't be sure if the outfit was too informal or too obviously right for a funeral. "I cook for no man. No mortal man eats my cooking and survives. I must have inherited that from my own mother, I guess. Steve and I mostly eat out."

"La-di-da," Ellen said.

"That's not a very nice thing to say," their father said. "Your mother wasn't all that bad a cook. I survived. She tried. And she always apologized."

"It's nothing to brag about, Emmy," Ellen said. "And furthermore, I happen to be a fabulous cook, from the same mother."

"I'm saying everything wrong," Emily said. "I'm eating my foot in my mouth."

Janet once again turned her Shirley Temple face to Emily, knowing she was supposed to find the remark funny. Emily took her by the shoulders and said, "Do you think that's hysterical, scrumptious? I'm eating my foot in my mouth?"

"I want to see you eat your foot in your mouth. Show me."

"It's not polite," Emily said. "Not now."

"In any event, we always had help," their father said, "even before Margaret. Remember Margaret's predecessor?"

"Oh, God, Gilda," Ellen said. "Somewhat slovenly."

"Matilda Gilda Gildegarde," Emily said to Janet.

Janet laughed, a sophisticated-sounding, comfortable gurgle.

"Gilda the Great Gildersleeve," Emily said.

Janet laughed too loudly this time, banging against the bed as she watched Emily's face, waiting for more.

"Gilda Farrell," Ellen said, holding her daughter still.

"Correct," their father said.

"Okay, Daddy," Emily said. "Here's a serious question. I don't know why I've thought of this, but how much did you and Mom travel together? Did you enjoy traveling the way Granny and Grandpa did?"

She thought he started to answer her, a grunt of beginning that dissolved right away into a short, irritated sigh out of his nose. He frowned a little with his whole face. Then he answered. "We went to Europe on our honeymoon. You know, as I think of it, I wanted to travel more with her. She preferred to be in Newbury with Luise and Gus, and then of course with the two of you. We took the trip with you two to the Rockies once. Why do you ask?"

"I don't know." She didn't know what she was doing. She loved her father just as much as she always had; at the same time, as he lay diagonally facing her from the incongruous chaise, a bit below her, she thought he might have unwittingly moved into the circle of her power, relatively relaxed and unprotected, that now was her chance to ask him questions, even if it bothered him a little. She wanted to get closer somehow. That was the main thing. Yet she felt anxious for him in her chest. "What did you do when she took off for Shanghai?" Emily experienced a bizarre sensation she'd had before—the sound of her words in her head without being sure she had actually spoken them.

"I had you two to look out for. I may not be getting exactly what you mean. What did I do about what?"

"Were you friends when she left?" This time she knew she was speaking. She felt she was robbing him.

At first he looked intensely annoyed; as he held his expression, though she saw that he must be saying: Don't be silly it's not worth discussing.

Janet had turned around. She was bouncing her chest instead of her back off the bed. "Mommy?"

"What?"

"I want to come up with you."

"Okay. We're talking now." Ellen and Emily helped Janet up on the bed. She wriggled into place between them. She continued to wriggle, swimming with her behind. "Mommy?"

"We're talking, Janet."

"Mommy, are we going home soon?"

"No. In a little while. Aunt Emmy and Grandpa and I are having a talk. You'll have to be quiet a little longer."

"I don't want you to talk. I'm very tired."

"Then go to sleep. Here's a whole bed."

"I want to sleep at home."

Emily feared her father would use the interruption as an excuse to leave.

"Listen to me," Ellen said. "When you and I get home, we'll have a bath and I'll read to you and your father will put you to sleep. Stay with us quietly now for a few minutes so we can finish."

"But Mommy," Janet whispered.

"No buts." Ellen kissed the top of her daughter's head. Janet swatted at her own hair, brushing away the kiss. "Lie down on my lap. When you wake up, we'll be going home." Janet placed her thumb in her mouth; she swayed against her mother's shoulder. "In my lap," Ellen said. The child then slid with a thorough slowness an inch every two seconds down her mother's arm, keeping her thumb in her mouth and humming in a bumpy manner. When she finally reached her mother's lap, her head toward her mother's stomach, she was pressing her white-shoed feet against Emily's thigh. Emily picked up the cool legs, laid them across her, and stroked them. Janet yelled "Don't!" She thrashed her feet, but didn't withdraw them.

Emily lifted her hands, stiffly holding them in the air. "My, my," she said. She put her hands behind her on the bed, looking at Ellen for permission to proceed. Ellen seemed to be amused. Emily couldn't be sure if the amusement was over Janet's behavior, or a message of sympathy because their father would be a tough nut to crack.

Emily chose the message of sympathy; it implied approval, in Ellen's older-sister way, of Emily's questions, of her initiative. Emily said to her father, "I've always wondered what it must have been like for you, because Ellen and I hardly ever discussed it, and I didn't want to trouble you. I figured you had enough troubles."

His arms were folded, like cloth, across his chest. She felt he was calmly watching her trying to get to her point. Deadpan.

"There's never been that much to talk about anyway, has there?" she asked. She was getting warm in the neck. She was scared she might be right—nothing to ask, nothing to find out. "I mean, I've always wondered if there was some big mystery to her going we didn't know about. If it was all what we knew or if there was something behind it. Did you love each other?"

"I *think* so." His indecisiveness was so casual and lighthearted that it came across as certainty.

"Were you happy together?"

"I think so." This time the "think" dropped, in a reserved, modest way.

"Okay, thank you, Daddy, that's it. Time's up."

"Your question's not simple, you know. Do you want a serious answer?"

"Sorry. Yes. I'd love one." More than anything, ever.

"I'll tell you what I think," he said. "I don't find happiness all that easy to define. I think we would have been happier, except that your mother was not always so happy herself. She was already overcome by what was happening in Europe, and then seeing the German refugees sailing back to Europe from Havana in 'thirty-nine, as I've told you in the past. She was miserable, I would have to say, from that experience on. She knew, you know, that the ship was not going to Germany, where it came from. The ship went to Antwerp. Your mother herself helped arrange that. But she was terribly bitter the passengers weren't let off in Havana, and then not even here, because we were in the middle of the Depression, and Roosevelt didn't want to admit any more refugees than he could help. We had plenty of anti-Semitism, you know, in the country and notoriously in the State Department itself. On top of all this, although the passengers sailed to Belgium, which was considered a godsend, within months of your mother's return from Havana Germany had started taking over Europe. So she got more and more desperate. Her pessimism had plenty to feed on. I don't deny that. She cried a great deal at times. I had to try to take care of her. She was terribly guilty about the helpless people on the ship and later she was terribly guilty about you girls when she left for Shanghai. She didn't seem to be capable of being consoled. I've always thought your mother wished she were a refugee herself, the way other people want to be rich or good-looking. She couldn't stand being as fortunate as she was in all respects. Most of us can tolerate good luck. Your mother couldn't. She saw what could have happened to any of us if we'd been born unlucky, if Gus and Luise and the rest of the family hadn't emigrated at various times. She just grabbed onto the world's misery and wouldn't let it go. Like her mother. Either she inherited it from Luise or she passed it onto her when she died, I'll never know which. They both had an excuse. The world, unfortunately, is not peaches and cream. But different people handle trouble differently. Most people know it's there and they try to manage it, but they don't necessarily latch on for dear life."

His speech was certainly a record for him. Perhaps he'd had it ready and waiting for years, saving it until she'd asked the necessary question. Maybe he'd always wanted to talk, and her shyness about the subject had prevented him.

"If the war hadn't happened, you might not be married now or you would still be married now?"

He looked at Emily without expression through his immaculate tortoiseshells. "How can I answer that?"

"If it's a stupid question, forget it. Maybe it's none of my business. I don't want to reopen old wounds." Maybe she sounded like a gossip columnist about her own family.

"I don't believe there are any old wounds. I think your mother needed something in her life that was serious and important enough to be worthy, tragic enough to be worthy, if you will, and I didn't fill that bill. Not that anyone could have. Or should have. It never came up as an issue between us, except insofar as she shared her misery with me. I believe I had her respect. We'd had plenty of fun together earlier in the marriage. And she adored you two, of course. But there's no question that Hitler and the rest of it changed her life. If your mother needed something serious and worthy she certainly found it. You have to understand, everyone was concerned all the time over here. Your mother didn't have the worrying all to herself. But she was like a woman with a destiny. She was a sufferer. She took it all onto herself. She took it all personally. I can't say I recommend that approach, but I can only speak for myself. I suppose we all have destinies, even the most ordinary of us, but on most of us it doesn't show. On your mother, it showed. Even though she didn't volunteer to go, you know. There were already a few JRSA people in Shanghai, but they needed more help. Joe Stern asked your mother to go. I told her it would not be feasible for her to go. Then they asked an unmarried man, but he backed off for some reason. Then Joe Stern asked your mother a second time and she came to me in a state. She was feeling more and more helpless and hopeless, and this anguishing had been going on for some time, so I said, 'Go.' "

Silence set in, surrounding them like the black lines in a Rouault. It occurred to Emily that silence, for once, seemed to be putting her father at a possible disadvantage.

Ellen finally said, "So you were really the big sacrificer."

"Not compared to her. I don't know what you mean. I had to let
her go. She was too miserable. She had to go. Half the time she walked
around as if someone had died. I know that she made an effort not
to show it to you."

"She was very serious most of the time," Emily said. "Even for
someone with a small face, she had a long face."

Ellen said, "I'm afraid I don't quite see why you couldn't have insisted
she stay. For you and for us. Or why she didn't just decide it would
be preferable all around for her to stay. It doesn't feel to me that she
adored us all that much."

"Well, she expected to return quite soon, of course. Remember,
when she left for Shanghai it was nearly nine months before Pearl
Harbor. I'll tell you, I did suggest she see a psychiatrist. Her response
was to ask me if I thought the psychiatrist would tell her Hitler was
a delusion. It's possible I should have been more persistent. It's not
easy to judge. Anyway, I can thank God for the three of you there.
I wish she could see that sight."

Emily watched her father's mouth in the process of forgetting it
had been going to smile. Gradually it contracted, until he looked like
someone trying not to sneeze. His Adam's apple lifted and dropped.
He made a dry noise, which sounded like a scraping from his Adam's
apple. "It would be a serious mistake for you to think she didn't love
you—or me. Her letters, you know, before Pearl Harbor, were for
the most part about how terribly she missed us."

Emily remembered only that she had lost interest in the letters a
long time ago. After Pearl Harbor, between Pearl Harbor and the
news of her death, there had been one tiny note from her, that everything was fine.

Her father went on: "It's awful to think she had to die helping others
survive, that she couldn't have come back to us and lived out her full
life." He made the dry noise again.

There was too much going on between the lines for Emily to digest
everything her father had said. The point of her questions must have
been that if her parents hadn't gotten along, then Mom's departure
made a bit more sense. It became less purely idealistic. But she couldn't
decipher yet if they had really not gotten along, or if it was the war
that had come between them. She wanted to go over to him, kneel
beside him and embrace him, but if she did it might set off an emotional reaction in her that he wouldn't appreciate. She was on the
verge of breaking down anyway. Looking at him, she took a deep,
deep breath, letting it out silently so it wouldn't sound like a sigh.

"You know what?" Ellen said. "I just realized."

Emily felt as if Ellen had interrupted her mood. She put her hand on Ellen's wrist, in a compensatory show of interest, because she wanted to maintain the unity she felt with her.

"We were refugees who stayed put," Ellen said to their father. "Who stayed home. We were stationary refugees when Mom left."

"That is brilliant," Emily said. She pressed Ellen's wrist, then took her hand away, keeping her eyes on Ellen. "That's the most brilliant thing I've ever heard." Ellen continued to look at their father. Emily thought how tough and handsome her sister's face in profile looked at the moment.

"I tried to take good care of you girls," their father said. "I would never have imagined I could have done a halfway decent job, except that you both turned out so magnificently, despite everything."

"I don't know how magnificently," Ellen said. "Granted, she expected to come back. But you can't say she adored us if she left us at the ages we were. It's bull. Plain bullshit."

"That's very edifying language."

"Too bad!"

"Look. I resent your speaking that way in front of me and more so in front of your daughter."

"I apologize. She's asleep. My language shouldn't be the big issue here, Daddy. No matter how you slice it—no matter how much Mom was suffering and all that, and no matter how heroic and noble she was, it was selfish of her to take off. And it was a mistake on your part to let her go. She ditched us, plain and simple. She ditched us. And she died."

"I've just been trying to remind you how torn she was."

"If she was so torn, which half did we get?"

Emily felt herself flushing.

Her father raised his right hand, not palm out, but sideways, so the narrow edge of the hand faced them. The gesture was regal and indecisive at the same time. He looked at Ellen quizzically and with distaste. "I really do think . . ." he said, lowering his hand. "What's the purpose of this discussion?"

Emily rushed in. "Daddy, the fact is, you did the best job. You took me to the theater all that time, which was the happiest time of my life, and which I'll never forget, and I think you must have memorized my school schedule. I don't think Ellen's blaming you."

"It's all right. I'm not looking for thanks."

"I didn't say I had any complaints about how you raised us," Ellen said. Emily noticed that Ellen's face was red, too, but she did not suppose it was from blushing. Ellen was simply mad. "I always thought you were on top of everything, and I don't know how you did it. You never even seemed to have to work at it. Sometimes I don't understand how any of us did it. But I have a tremendous amount of resentment, frankly. When I think about Mom, I feel gypped, even though she had the worst of it, obviously. I'm very sorry she died, believe me. She didn't have to die. She didn't have to leave, either."

"If Mom had the worst of it," Emily said quietly, hoping for calm, and hoping her heartbeat would calm down, too, "and we both turned out so well, what does it mean that we were refugees at home? What did it do to us? I might be kidding myself, but most of the time I feel perfectly normal, at least the way I behave. What does it mean to be a refugee at home, I mean?"

"To me it means I'll never ditch anybody," Ellen said. "Anyway, I thought you just said it was so brilliant."

"It is brilliant. I just have to figure it out."

"And I'm not the one who said we turned out so well. Daddy did. I think we were damn lucky—pardon me—to turn out as well as we did. I will never find it acceptable that she left." Ellen made this last remark directly to her father.

"No one said it was acceptable," he said.

"You seem to have accepted it," Ellen said. "I'm sorry. I shouldn't have said that. That's the whole damn trouble with this. It's always been impossible to discuss because it's unfair to you or unfair to Mom because she died in such a good cause. We're all so separated by it!"

"Where do I go to complain?" their father asked. "If I found it unacceptable, what would I do about it?"

"I don't know, Daddy. Let's drop it. I said I'm sorry."

"How come I'm so normal?" Emily asked Ellen, using herself to lighten the mood in the room. All that was unusual about her was hidden.

"You've always been a bit of a nut," Ellen said. "Don't worry. You haven't changed that much, as far as I know. As much as I love my husband and child," she said to her father, "I think that if Mom hadn't taken off and died the way she did, I might be making more of my own life somehow. What did I major in political science for?"

Emily replied instead of their father. He didn't seem about to, and she didn't like Ellen's leaving her out of the problem. "Your life isn't over and neither is mine. What are you going to do? Run for president?"

Ellen looked at her and away without answering.

"I think you should both be very proud of yourselves," their father said. "And if you'll excuse me, I think it's time I went back to the guests." He got up from the chaise.

"Can you stay for a sec?" Emily asked her sister. Ellen nodded with the back of her head, keeping her eyes on their father. Emily wondered what was going to happen. Would he drop a bombshell? Would he burst into tears? Kiss them? They couldn't stand up to kiss him, because Janet was sleeping across them. Bunny was their real mother, he would announce. Bunny had been around, behind the scenes, from day one of their lives.

"I love you girls," he said, coming over and kissing each of them on the top of the head. "It's a shame life has to be so messy sometimes. You didn't deserve it and neither did she." And with that, he left. For some reason, Emily thought of how he usually said "Behave" when they said goodbye. Perhaps "Behave" didn't really mean "Be good," but "Do something! Express yourself!" which he himself never did, since he was so reserved.

Ellen said, "Have you ever noticed how extreme Daddy is? Don't you think 'messy' is too extreme? Life is more like a drop of spilt milk, don't you think? Jesus!"

They were together on this one, all right. "Daddy and I went to *King Lear* when you were in college, and I was so upset afterwards, naturally, and Daddy at least had the good grace not to say anything on the way home, I was so gloomy, but when I asked him how he liked it he said it made him think of an eight-car pileup. I don't think Daddy takes to tragedies too well."

Ellen looked as if she thought the anecdote was unnecessary. Emily saw that their talk might be awkward. They didn't usually have face-to-face conversations. They were hardly ever alone together. So, be bold. "May I ask you something?"

"Why not? Incidentally, I thought it was great you pushed Daddy on those things."

"Thank you. I'm not sure what it accomplished."

"Oh, I'm not saying that it accomplished anything. But it was worth doing, if only to see what it feels like to challenge him about this directly. You know, it's possible that Daddy saved our lives by being so tight-lipped all the time, by making it imperative that we talk about things to other people."

"I don't talk about things that much at all. Do you?"

"A fair amount."

"Who to?"

"Stan. One or two friends."

"Does Stan listen?"

"Sure. Most of the time. You'd be surprised. Stan is wonderful because he doesn't seem to be there, but he is. He puts things in perspective. He's calming. And he adores his daughter even more than he adores me. He thinks you don't like him."

"Why?"

"He thinks you're arty or snobby or something."

"Thanks a lot for telling me. It's not true I don't like him." Lie. "He's hardly ever said a word to me. But he was delightful the night we all went to *Godot*. What do you talk to him about?"

"If I'm sad or upset or peeved. Or happy, appreciative. Anything at all. The way I did with Daddy before."

"But you'd never done that before with Daddy, had you?" Her question sounded alarmed.

"Of course not. I found Stan. And Mom obviously had the same problem with him."

Emily thought for a moment. "I guess that's true." Ellen had pinned it down very fast. That's what Daddy hadn't been saying, and maybe didn't even know—that he had been unavailable to Mom before Mom became unavailable to them. He said she was incapable of being consoled, not that he was incapable of consoling her. Maybe Mom would have been too much for anyone to handle, though. Emily didn't know what to do at the moment but move on. "I tell Steve most things. Not everything. I think I'd like to tell him everything, but I don't have the nerve to tell anyone everything. I think he'd listen to anything, though, most of the time. He's extremely receptive. Steve definitely thinks I'm fascinating. Sometimes he makes me seem more interesting to myself than I usually think I am. I say things he's never heard before."

Ellen nodded, half-interested. "That's a good sign," she said. She didn't ask what Emily told Steve and what she didn't tell him.

She hadn't told him her fantasies about Mom being made of diarrhea, melting, her arms reaching out. Once she'd been embarrassed about possessing weird thoughts. Now she might be protecting her thoughts because they were all she had that made her unusual, and if she told them she'd lose her uniqueness. But also she was scared of being too weird; she wasn't sure yet whether or not there were some things you weren't supposed to tell a soul. "Have you ever been to a shrink?"

"Why do you ask?"

"You don't have to answer. I'm just curious."

"Have you?"

"No. And I don't think I want to, either. But maybe I should. I don't actually have that many friends to talk to. Jill is basically square, and she's all wrapped up in her social work and I'm all wrapped up in Steve. Maybe I need a new girlfriend. Byron and Iris aren't that close to me. Steve knows the most by far." Ellen didn't know anything, not about the fantasies, not about George, not even that she was sleeping with Steve, though she could undoubtedly figure it out if she wanted to.

"What's wrong with you, though? You seem perfectly well adjusted."

How would she know? "How do I know? How do you know? I thought you said I was a nut."

Ellen looked indifferent, as if she'd forgotten she'd said it. "You've got a boyfriend who evidently loves you. You've got this 'in' job. You're seen in all the top night spots with Ernest Hemingway and Gertrude Stein."

"Look, I know you think I think I've got a great job, but I don't. I think I have a dumb job, and I'd like to quit and do something grown-up. Steve is great, but even if I marry him, I don't want to make him my entire life. What did you mean when you said that if Mom hadn't gone off you might be making more of your life?"

"Well, she's a rather hard act to follow. And if you follow it, maybe something terrible happens to you, like you die?"

"Hunh! When did you figure that out?"

"From a psychiatrist." Ellen smiled as if she'd been clever.

"When did you go? This is what I started off wanting to ask you before."

"First in college. On and off after for a while."

"Live and learn. Did it do you any good?"

"A lot."

"Why did you go?"

"At college because I was having some trouble 'forming attachments.' And I was away from home for good for the first time. I was sort of lost."

"I'll be darned. You never seemed lost to me. Did Daddy know you went?"

"Damn right. He paid for it."

"Why shouldn't I go?"

"No one's going to stop you, Emmy. Why do you think you need to?"

"Because I'm scared I'm too well adjusted. Maybe I accept things too easily. I'm scared I'll settle for my job, and maybe that I'll be too dependent on Steve. I worry I don't try hard enough. Steve thinks I under-use myself. And I'm just terrified of being typical. And of ending up liking it."

"Don't you think you should give it a little time? You just turned twenty-three, for God's sake."

"But you're worried about the same thing, apparently."

"Not exactly. I do worry about making something of myself, but I think you can be a regular person and still make something of yourself. I may go to grad school in a year and a half."

"That would be great. In poli sci?"

"Probably. I also happen to be crazy about being a wife and mother."

"Do you think Mom's going away was worse for you because you were the older daughter?"

"Possibly."

"I really think I counted on Granny a lot."

"Granny was a help, no question, but more for you than for me. I really felt deserted by Mom, and sometimes I still do."

"That's sort of what worries me. How come I don't feel that way?"

"Maybe because you did have me around, and Granny."

"No hard feelings, but you weren't really all that interested in me when we were living at home. Between you and Margaret and Granny and Jill and osmosis, I guess I learned what every young woman should know. But you got exasperated with me a lot for exaggerating when I was sick and because I was too excitable, which I don't seem to be anymore, do I?"

"Not that I notice particularly. Do you remember once when there was static on your radio and you thought it was applause that wouldn't stop? You were so excited you were hysterical."

"I remember it all the time. Actually I thought it might have meant the war was already over and Mom could come home." She knew by then, within a year of Mom's leaving, that she had confused feelings about wanting her to come home. "Anyhow, you went off to college and then you got married. You might have had it worse than I did, but sometimes I still have the feeling that everyone's away, except for Steve. That includes me. Sometimes I worry that I'm away too. It's not that I feel deserted. I feel that I'm the one who's removed from people sometimes, separate, different. I worry that no one knows what's going on inside me, including me."

"I wouldn't worry too much. You probably would have had problems by now, if you were going to."

"But I'd like to know what's going to happen to me. I'd like to know if anything *happened* to me. How exactly did Mom's absence affect me? I think I must close it off most of the time so I don't miss her so much. I keep her far away most of the time. Actually, sometimes she misses me."

"Does she phone?"

"No, I mean it. I imagine her wanting to come home." She'd skip the ugly details. "Do you ever do that?"

"No. Of course I miss her sometimes. But I don't imagine her wanting to come home."

"Do you think that's crazy?"

"I don't think you give yourself enough credit for being normal. But if you're really concerned about it, then go to a headshrinker. Don't make such a big deal out of it."

"But the problem is, I think I really want to figure everything out for myself. I want my life to figure itself out. Do you know what I mean? I think I'd prefer to be surprised. But also I want my life to mean something, without its being explained to me. It's sort of like waiting to see what the past is going to do." She loved what she'd just said.

"So don't go. I think it's good you don't want to go."

"How come you called me a nut before?"

"For God's sake! I was only teasing. I think you might want to be, but unfortunately for you you're not. I have to drag this one home or she won't get to sleep tonight. She's going to be a very cranky sack of potatoes anyway. Wake up, Jans."

"I don't want Mom to be the only thing I'm about, either," Emily said. "I want to have a destiny, but not controlled by her."

"Sounds fair. You could do worse than get married and have a bunch of children and bring them up properly." Ellen took her daughter under the knees with her right arm, scooping her legs off Emily's lap, and with her left arm grabbed her under the shoulders, lifting her as she lifted herself off the bed. "Ugh-a-lug," she said. "You weigh a ton, baby."

Janet made a cross, sleepy grunt and shoved her head behind her mother's neck so no one could see her.

"Hold up," Emily said. She joined her sister standing. Instead of kissing her check she laid her head on Ellen's free shoulder and hugged her lightly, then took a chance and gave Janet a quick hug.

Wriggling, Janet said, "No!"

PART
FOUR

CHAPTER TEN

The Evening
at the Farkases'

Early Sunday morning, three days after Granny's funeral, Emily and Steve were lying in his bed, spring sunlight coming through the venetian blinds, Emily thinking how beautiful, how promising the sunlight was and how tremendously much more of it there was outside, an enormous dome of it, a heavenly capitol dome of sunlight. "Let's go to mass," Emily said.

"Have you converted? How can you convert? You don't have anything to convert from."

"It just seems like the right kind of day to go to mass. Then to the Easter parade."

"Unless you have a private calendar, which I admit is possible, knowing you, Easter is eleven months off, kiddo. Anyway, blekfast." Steve made a big deal of cooking breakfast on weekends in his bathrobe, different omelettes, sometimes Frenchtoast or pancakes or waffles, and he also made sausage or bacon, fresh juice, coffee, a big professional job.

"After breakfast, late mass. At least let's go for a walk." Breakfast wasn't a major meal for her, but she didn't think it would be fair not to show how impressed she was with his performance in the kitchen, so she always did her best to eat as much as she could.

"We'll go for a walk." He kissed her and got out of bed nude; they'd just had sex before. He put on his T-shirt, pale-blue boxer shorts and his old plaid flannel robe. "You're allowed to eat breakfast in bed today. Wait here."

"I'm not hungry for anything but you, big boy."

"I'll put maple syrup on certain parts of me."

Before falling asleep again, she mused—wool-gathering, she believed it was called—how Steve frequently went out of his way to please her, satisfy her. Actually, he didn't go out of his way; most often, it was on his terms. He didn't make big sacrifices. Why should he? He hadn't had to. But on his terms, he showed a lot of interest in pleasing her. Being eager to please was one of Steve's boyish qualities in a grownup's body. Someone like Timothy hardly knew anyone else was there except as an audience for him. She dozed off while thinking how at home she felt in Steve's bed, so at home that her side, the side away from the night table, belonged to her. They called it her side. Emily Weil slept here.

"Babes?" he said, rubbing her shoulder. "Chow's on."

Under the covers, she rolled around to face him in the warm-breeze comfort of nakedness. Seeing the crowded tray on the night table, she sat up, as happily bare-breasted as a native, crossing her ankles with her knees angled out to make a place for her plate of scrambled eggs, her favorite kind, and cinnamon toast, also a favorite. He was beside her. "May I have some coffee first?" she asked, wondering if she had literally become one of those who was useless without coffee in the morning or whether she just liked to act that way. He held the saucer for her while she lifted the cup and took a sip. He had already added her cream and sugar. Talk about pleasing someone. "Thanks. Don't hold it. I'll have the rest when it cools off." It wasn't that convenient, eating in bed.

"There's orange juice. That's cold."

"I'll have it for dessert."

"By the way, don't take too-big bites. There's a little surprise in the eggs. I wouldn't want you to swallow it."

"Hmm. The chicken?"

"Not exactly."

"I've got it. A mink coat. Stevie, you shouldn't have." Sophisticated repartee.

He wasn't trying to keep a straight face; he smiled in a cheerful, frowning way, as if he couldn't guess the surprise himself. She had a sudden inkling, but she couldn't believe it. But what else could it be? She wasn't about to betray greedy curiosity by raising the eggs and peeking, or by stabbing them apart, so she took tiny bites, trying to avoid spoiling the fun by hitting anything too soon. Then her fork revealed it—a sapphire in a platinum setting, with two diamond baguettes. She gasped sincerely, even though a ring had been her incredulous suspicion.

"So?"

She put down her fork. She leaned her face against the top of his chest for some time, pressing her tears into his T-shirt, hugging him, and wondering what else her reaction was supposed to be. He kissed her cheek. She leaned her head back against his left shoulder. His eyes were wet too. He said, "You look so beautiful right now." Holding his neck, she kissed him.

"You haven't given me your answer," he said.

"Oh. I don't think you've asked the question."

"The ring's the question. Will you marry me?"

"How can I say no? But I think we have to discuss it. I have to let the reality sink in. Do your parents know?" They were going to his parents', finally, tomorrow night. When had he decided to do this?

"I would hardly tell them before you. Let's see if it fits. I'll wash it off."

"No, I'll wash it off. It's so beautiful, Steve."She finally picked up the ring; she kissed shreds of egg off it. Ellen had their mother's diamond engagement ring.

"Come on. I'm going to clean it."

"It's so dramatic of you. Why do you want to marry me? I don't know what to say. I'm so honored."

"Why not just say yes?"

"I will. When we talk."

"Let me have it so I can wash it." He took it from her.

"I want it back."

"Eat your cinnamon toast," he said, going into the hall, where the bathroom was. He ran water.

She nibbled on the toast. Had he hidden anything in the toast? Steve returned, patting the ring against his robe. "Let's try it on," he said. He sat again, preparing to crown her ring finger. She laughed a little as he lowered the ring, feeling as if they were practicing a magic trick or a scientific experiment. The ring fit a bit loosely. She looked at it, with her fingers splayed, posing, as she imagined everyone did. "If you'll tell me where you got it, I'll have them tighten it."

"I got it ten days ago, the day we had lunch near your office. I was just waiting for the right moment to hand it over. It's from Ernest Fischer, on Madison."

"I'm glad you got a sapphire instead of a diamond. And not from Tiffany." She smiled at the ring, then at the buyer.

"I agree. When do you want to get hitched?"

"After I finish my coffee." Steve handed her the cup. She ate the rest of the slice of toast. She took several swallows of her coffee.

"My eggs aren't the warmest," Steve said.

"I would love to make you some fresh eggs, if you'd permit me. I'm serious."

"It's okay. Really. They're so good it doesn't matter that much."

"Mine were the best I've ever had. Sapphire omelette." What would Daddy say? Good luck, Cookie, behave? Where would they have the wedding? The front garden in Newbury. Their own Midsummer Night's Dream. "Here." She gave him back the coffee cup. He laid it on the saucer on the tray. "How do you know I'll make a good wife? I might be too immature." She handed him her plate, which he also put on the tray, and lay on her side, on her right elbow, while he finished eating.

"I had to be careful not to get the plates mixed up," he said.

"I'm impressed with your romantic touch. I really am." She looked at the ring again, its solid glamor. She had never worn any nail polish other than plain, and for jewelry only earrings and necklaces, her mother's stuff mostly. Her mother had not been a big jewelry person, naturally. Emily, too, didn't like to flaunt, or she was scared to flaunt. Her mother, of course, had ended up flaunting herself anyway. "I love this, Steve. No wonder people get married."

"In that case, you can keep it."

"I think you should wear one, too. We should have matching ones. I'd like to buy one for you and conceal it in my beef bourguignon."

"I'd look gorgeous in it, I'm sure."

"Stevie? Do you think it's mostly sex right now? I don't see how sex could be so great if we didn't love each other, but in thirty years will we love each other? Do you realize how long life can be, in a way? In thirty years, we'll be only fifty-six and fifty-three."

"Life begins at forty."

"As far as I can tell, I really am in love with you. This-is-it in love with you. I love being with you more than anything. I think you're basically very matuah, Mr. Farkas. I love every inch of your body. No inch is excluded. I feel very safe with you, too. I don't know what more a girl could want. A lot of ourselves that are hidden are similar to each other."

"I don't know what you mean."

"Neither do I, exactly. I think we're alike in ways I don't understand. I don't know what they are." Sometimes she worried that the way they were most the same was by not being particularly unusual. Then she'd think everyone was unusual in some way, and by that standard she and Steve were.

They talked for an hour and a half in bed, in complete closeness and reasonableness: how to announce the engagement (enjoy the secret for a few days, then tell Daddy before telling Steve's parents); when to get married and where; a rabbi officiating or who; working and finances (finances weren't a problem; Steve made a good salary, he had some money of his own, and a few investments; and he informed her that he also had a plan up his sleeve to make millions, refusing to tell her anything about it yet, except that yes, it was legal); where to live; how many children (he wanted four, she wanted one-point-five, so they compromised on two-point-seven-five).

She decided it was too late for jokes about the family name. The sapphire meant Emily Farkas. That was true love. Maybe she could persuade him to change it to Farr, like the business. Why hadn't the family done both at the same time while they were at it? It would have been a Farr Farkas better thing to do than they had ever done.

At one point during their discussion, Steve seriously answered her question about whether they would love each other thirty years from now. "Let me tell you something. The sooner we're married, the longer we're married. The longer we're married, the better, as far as I'm concerned. I want to show you off. You're a prize, even though you may not think so. I want to take care of you. I want to get behind you, support you. I want to be authorized to make you happy. I want to stop futzing around with my life. You should also. By the way, can you please leave your hair shoulder-length forever? It's ideal."

"Thank you. How is getting married, even to you, going to find me the kind of job, for example, that will make me sprout blossoms of previously unknown genius?"

"You're kidding, but it might give you the necessary self-confidence. I don't know. I want to be your backer, in a way, invest in you. All I know is, I would never marry anyone else but you."

She didn't understand how he could be that sure. They had known each other four months. It seemed much longer, and Steve was definitely a realistic person, but was four months enough, even if they waited four more months to get married, as they had so responsibly decided to do in their talk? Obviously she thought so, but how could she be sure, either? "I know what you mean," she said. Even though she didn't know anyone else right now, who else in the world would she ever want to marry? If she wanted to get married in the first place.

She didn't want getting married to be a way of getting into enormous problems, or a way of avoiding them, either, such as who was she supposed to be and what was she supposed to do with her life.

On the good side, she'd had the encouraging thought during their talk that getting married, far from meaning everything was over, the way she'd worried about it toward the beginning of their relationship, would instead be a chance—an opportunity—to be grownup. At the moment, being grownup seemed to her like a permanent form of pleasure.

Then, illogically, forgetting that being grownup was a permanent form of pleasure, she thought of herself and Steve as daring—that it would be admirably daring of them to leap into adulthood. "You'd have to be my friend for life," she said. "You'd be the one I'd trust with my personal thoughts. We'd always have to have personal, private talks. Endless talks. You'd have to talk too. As much as I did. You couldn't spend all your time with your ears in your records. I'd want to be your most interesting record. Not a broken record, I hope."

"I'm not planning to get married not to pay attention to you, babes."

"Hmm. That makes sense." His use of "babes" had started in the last two weeks. She wished she could find a way of telling him not to say it even more than she wished he wouldn't say it. Maybe she'd have to find a nickname for him he disliked, so he'd get the hint. He liked "Stevie." So maybe she should try "Fark." She said, "You are literally the only person in the world who knows about George Koenigsberg, except for George Koenigsberg. Even he may not know anymore. I don't seem to confide in people much. And there are things I haven't told you."

"I want to hear everything." He was looking her nakedly in the face. "How come you don't confide in people? How come you confide in me?"

"I don't know the whole answer to the first. I think it has something to do with feeling that in a strange way it's not my place to talk about my mother, and that I'm more admirable if I keep my mouth shut. And my mother seems to be the main thing I have to confide. But since I tend not to talk about her I tend to be not talkative in general. I like keeping things to myself. I like thinking about myself as someone who keeps things to herself. I confide in you because I want you to be the person I trust, I guess. So you'll accept me."

"I accept you, believe me." He hugged her.

"And also, I don't confide in people that much because my mother isn't around that much to talk about. I know that sounds flip or callous, but I don't mean it to be. I mean I don't think about her that much. She's far away geographically, to say nothing of being dead, and she's far away in the years since she died. But I try to get hold of her, and sometimes she just appears on her own, and sometimes it shocks me because it's so vivid, but even then I think she should be closer, that she should appear in front of me, in the flesh instead of in my mind. It's hard to explain. I can't make her real enough. She's not on my mind a lot, but she's under my mind all the time, I suspect. I have really bizarre fantasies about her sometimes."

"Tell me."

"They're sort of disgusting, and I'm not being coy." Even now, with Steve, she felt constrained. She sounded childlike and self-indulgent to her own ears, partly because she was testing him to see how he'd react. But the more difficult it was to tell him, the more interested she was in his reaction. So she told him. It was like part of the dowry. She added to the fantasies a connection she sometimes made with Ellen's description of a newsreel she had seen in 1945 at the Trans-Lux of emaciated dead and living bodies in the liberated concentration camps. She thought telling Steve about the newsreel might make him see her fantasies more clearly, though she herself had never seen the newsreel.

"It's amazing to think of thoughts like that in someone's head. But it doesn't disgust me at all. It's fascinating. It makes me love you more, if that's possible."

"I have to admit, your reaction when I told you about my mother originally is one reason I decided I might really like you."

"It's so terrible for you. It makes me full of sympathy, for you and for her. I wish I could find her. I wish I could bring her back."

"You can't 'find' her. Dig her up?"

"No. I don't know. Discover her. Alive."

"If she were alive I assume she'd have found her way home."

"That's what I mean. I wish she were back here. I wish I could have done something."

"That's okay, but thanks. I might feel the same way if it were reversed. What about you? Tell me something disgusting." She resented how cold and jumpy he'd suddenly made her feel.

"It's not the same. There's no comparison." He seemed in despair that he had nothing equivalent to tell her; then she saw the despair was left over from what she had told him. "Anyway," he said, "I've told you. The worst there is is that after Debbie died, my parents weren't getting along at all, and later I have a hunch they thought

about separating. I don't have any proof, but the atmosphere was very
bad after she died, when I was seven, and it got bad again when I
was nine or ten. It was obvious. I shouldn't say it, but I think my
mother feels neglected sometimes."

"I have to ask you a favor. It probably sounds very touchy and un-
grateful, but I'd appreciate it if you didn't talk about how you wish
my mother could be back and how you wish you could bring her back.
It's no good. It does no good."

"I know. It was just an impulse. I couldn't help it."

"Do you understand?"

"I think so. I'm sorry if I upset you. I didn't mean to."

"You're forgiven. Forgive me. Okay?"

"Don't worry about it. Sometimes I think I get carried away."

"It's okay." She put her hand on his cheek. He was looking dead
earnest. There was none of his intentionally endearing smile, when
she couldn't tell if he was apologizing or not apologizing, a variation
of his wiseguy smile (or was it just his wiseguy smile with a different
meaning to it, a different caption under it?). His earnest quality, which
she hadn't liked much at the beginning, when she associated it with
awkwardness, naiveté, now reassured her. It was like rock-bottom re-
liability, responsibility. It said to her that she didn't have to worry too
much about the complicated, fluctuating parts of him, the fussy Steve,
the bossy Steve, the jealous or sardonic, slightly bullying Steve, the
tough weakness in him that seemed to reveal his "executive" side and
his most vulnerable side at the same time. "May I say yes now?" she
asked.

"You're wearing the ring. It wouldn't be fair of me to take it back
at this late date."

The next night, Steve picked Emily up at her house after work. They
walked hand-in-hand (Emily ringless) the eight blocks to the Farkases'.
Steve's mother's cousin, Helen, and Helen's husband, Laurence
Kornbluth, the well-known avant-garde sculptor, were also going to
be at dinner. Steve was sure Emily would love them. Very bohemian,
he teased. Also rich as sin. Larry Kornbluth did very, very well. Emily
thought she had heard of him. She couldn't decide if knowing that
the Kornbluths would be there made her more or less nervous; probably more. She had changed into her new print sheath, blue and green
flecks on white, bolero jacket. The kind of dress an older woman could
wear, she now feared; in the store, this suggestion of maturity had
seemed a plus, something Emily had earned. The Farkases—Mrs.

Farkas—would approve, but the Kornbluths might assume from it that she was too conventional to be interesting. Steve was wearing one of his two gray suits, with the pink button-down Emily had forced on him, saying it went with his cheeks, and a sort of plum-colored tie she had bought at the same time. His outfit made him look beautiful as well as handsome, she told him.

In the little entrance hall, when they got out of the elevator before Steve rang his parents' doorbell, he squeezed Emily's hand, causing her heart to exhale electricity. A uniformed white maid, mousier than Margaret, opened the door. "Good evening, Mr. Steve." Even Steven, Emily thought. "Gretta, this is Emily. Emily, my friend Gretta." Emily shook Gretta's hand. Off to a good start. Treated the help like people. She would not only be liked, she'd be well liked. The living room was invisible from the foyer. Emily heard conversation coming through the square entrance down the hall. She recognized now that the conversation had weakened when she and Steve were admitted, and that it had picked up again since. The sound of talk was enticing; it altered her nervousness, spangled the edges of it.

Then it was no looking back. Down the hall (huge urn of a vase containing peach gladioli), turn right, and right, and voila! At a distance, two women seated, two men rising. Cream-colored raw silk drapes. Tables covered with doodads, porcelain animals. Emily felt queasy as she crossed the beige carpeting. Her heart thumped, her mouth smiled. Visible in the dining room beyond was a huge dark cabinet showing china like a bemedalled chest. The smiling woman whom Emily took to be Mrs. Farkas knew, Emily was positive, that she had become Steve's fiancée yesterday; Steve had told his mother. The giveaway was that Mrs. Farkas didn't assess Emily, but smiled straight at her face, treating her as an unknown, refusing to be revealed in an appraisal, making use of her knowledge. Drinks had been served. The Farkases and Kornbluths were armed.

"Mother," on the grand, nubby off-white couch, was Mrs. Farkas, as Emily had supposed, cheerful, buxom, chunky, a deep voice, large teeth, like Chiclets, pronounced dimples that gave her an insincere look, dark, smooth hair in a pageboy. She was wearing a short-sleeved white linen dress with cherry piping, some plump jewelry. Helen Kornbluth, beside Mrs. Farkas, had on a magnificent embroidered blouse, like stained glass made of cloth, gold, green, black, red; an amber necklace and earrings, black skirt. Her eyes and eyebrows were gray. Her gray hair was braided and wound around her head. "Dad" was small, formal, shy, a charming cocky smile, beautiful tiny teeth, white hair, though he wasn't elderly-looking; dark blue suit, blue tie with silvery dots, icy black shoes. Mr. Kornbluth's tightly ridged hair was a darker gray than his wife's. His wife's face was rather serious and narrow, but sweet. Gracious. His face was wide but severe. He wore wire-rimmed glasses, a checked shirt, a maroon knit tie, a strange pale sport jacket. He gave the impression of being indifferent.

"Stevie! Make Emily a drink," Mrs. Farkas said. "Emily! What do you want to drink?" Emily had been seated on a small aquamarine chair facing the couch. Mrs. Farkas's question sounded to her like a question she couldn't afford to answer incorrectly. "I'm having a martini," Mrs. Farkas explained to her. "It's good for my arthritis. It's good for something, anyway. Will you join me, or would it knock you on your ear?"

"Dry vermouth?" Emily asked Steve, lifting her face to him; she could feel her neck stretching. She spoke as quietly as possible. Everyone was watching. "With ice and a twist?" It was as if she had just met him, as if he didn't know her drink.

"You've got it," he said, quickly touching her shoulder and not calling her "babes." He looked so rosy and elegant. He went off to the bar, past the couch, in the corner, near the dining room. She was alone with four strangers. The large armchair in which the slight Mr. Farkas sat was covered in a leafy beige-and-cream pattern. His chair seemed to overhang him and surround him. If he were in danger, the chair would close over him, concealing him completely like a thick pod.

Mrs. Farkas, without saying anything, minutely nudged toward Emily, along the glass-and-chrome coffee table, a silver tray that offered a slightly dented mound of chopped liver decorated with parsley sprigs; miniature slices of rye bread; and a dish of celery stalks, radishes, and black and green olives.

"No, thanks very much," Emily said. She did not want to take anything from this woman yet. "I love the room. It's so comfortable." She lied to make up for not taking. Steve returned with her vermouth and his scotch-and-soda. Behind him appeared Gretta, carrying another silver tray and chugging right at Emily. On this tray were three hundred and sixty degrees of shrimp surrounding a fluted silver dish of cocktail sauce. In each shrimp, a toothpick sword. The shrimp made her think of a water ballet. Just a bit nouveau? Emily thought she'd better take one to break the offering-and-receiving ice. Steve was sitting next to her now, in a twin chair. Mr. Kornbluth took three shrimp. Definitely bored.

"I think Stevie told us you were in public relations," Mr. Farkas said.

That didn't sound like Steve's kind of mistake. "It's not public relations. I don't know if that would be better or not. I'm a lowly assistant in the publicity department at Partridge House." Maybe now they wouldn't allow Steve to marry her.

"Still, Emily," Mrs. Farkas said. "Who knows? You've got your whole life ahead of you. The sky's the limit, right?"

"I don't know about that." She smiled and shrugged. "I hope so." Should she ask something about the toy business? There wasn't a toy in sight, not a rubber ball. It would help if the Kornbluths chipped into the conversation.

"Emily is undervalued and underpaid," Steve said.

Then Mr. Kornbluth surprised her. He didn't look interested; he barely looked at her. But he asked her, "What do you do in a job like that?"

"It's not really that interesting. Most of the time I'm writing press releases and other stuff. Otherwise, it depends where the pressure is. There can be quite a lot of pressure. Everything's always important at the moment, trivial as it may be. It's not trivial while you're doing it. Books have to be sent to reviewers, reviews have to be sent to authors. We have to send biographical questionnaires to the authors. We have to get in authors' photographs. Various lists have to be kept updated. There are book parties to arrange. If you're more important than I am, you're running the publicity campaign, authors' radio appearances, interviews, newspaper and magazine coverage. It's endless." Bizeebizeebizee.

"You must meet a lot of famous people," Mrs. Farkas said.

"Not really." She thought of the famous people she had met in her job, and whether they were famous people or famous authors. "No autographs yet." She couldn't tell what Mr. Kornbluth had done with her answer to his question; he was bent over his hors d'oeuvres plate. Mrs. Kornbluth looked serenely polite.

"Have you ever met Katharine Hepburn?" Mrs. Farkas asked.

"Not yet, I'm afraid." But the sky's the limit, right?

"We sat two rows behind her at *Cat on a Hot Tin Roof*," Mr. Farkas said. "A very glamorous lady."

"Emily wanted to be an actress when she was younger," Steve said.

Did he think he was bragging? Joshing? Why had he brought that up? "No talent," she said. "Minor drawback. Oh, speaking of actresses,

I heard at work today that an interesting manuscript has come into the house by the mother of some starlet who's had quite some flings with a few stars, the starlet has, I mean, and the agent wrote to our editor-in-chief, 'This one smells of money.' Naturally, everyone in the house wants to get his hands on it before we turn it down, since of course we're too respectable to publish it."

"Jesus," Mr. Kornbluth said.

What had she done? Could something like that be too dirty, just mentioning it in polite company? Had she said something she didn't understand?

"Helen is the head of drama at Annette Beardsley," Mrs. Farkas disclosed.

"There's not really a head, Mona dear," Mrs. Kornbluth said. "I just direct the plays."

"How great," Emily said. Steve hadn't told her, nor had she asked him, a thing about the wife of the well-known Laurence Kornbluth. "Now that must be a wonderful job." Emily was pleased to be saying something to Mrs. Kornbluth.

"It's what I love doing. It agrees with me. I must say, it's not always as smooth as silk, but the children are full of surprises, and that's the best of all, isn't it?"

Not that it was a controversial idea, but Emily agreed without thinking about it simply because Mrs. Kornbluth expressed herself in such a smooth but sincere way.

"What are you working on these days, Larry?" Steve asked.

Emily was concerned that "Larry" might be showoffy and disrespectful to an older man Steve didn't know that well.

"Me? I'm doing an animal series."

"They really are so wonderful, you must come to the studio and see them," his wife said. "I laugh aloud. And so profuse and varied."

"I didn't know you did humorous work," Steve said. "May I ask what they are?"

"They're antlers. Variations of antlers.

"Why antlers?" Steve asked.

"I probably saw a deer in the country last fall. Who knows? It'd be much easier for you to see them than it is for me to tell you about them."

"I'd love to," Emily said. "Wouldn't you, Steve?"

"We will. I'd really love to."

"I think I'd like to be an artist," Mrs. Farkas said. "It beats working."

Everyone laughed, even the Kornbluths.

"I always thought you were an artist, Mona," Mr. Farkas said.

"With Jack's compliments, you can't always tell if they're compliments," Mrs. Farkas said.

Emily thought she might be starting to have a good time. The "grownups" were talking about the revival of *The Iceman Cometh,* who had seen the original, who hadn't. Steve and she were going Saturday. She thought about the color of dry vermouth, a dress or scarf the color of vermouth. She couldn't make out what the Kornbluths were drinking; maybe sherry. If there were going to be more drinks, she decided, don't have one; she might talk too much or get too chummy. Then Gretta came in again. Dinner was served. She made her announcement in such a quiet voice, as if she had stage fright. Everyone stood up.

Emily looked at Helen Kornbluth. If she could have refrained from looking, she would have. Her eyes acted on their own. She wondered if blushes invariably showed. Helen Kornbluth reciprocated the look with definite pleasure, in complete command of herself. Emily wanted Helen to turn away, but she wanted to speak to her before she turned. "I've been admiring your blouse. You made it, undoubtedly."

"Oh, no, my goodness. I found it in a little shop near school when I was poking around one day. Just good luck. You'd look wonderful in it yourself. Would you like me to try to find one for you?"

It might be too exotic on her. "Thanks. I live about two blocks from Beardsley myself. What's the store?"

"Anya's? Something like that. Anna's? Let me check."

"Thanks. Maybe I'll bump into it myself." Halfway to the dining room, Steve intercepted her, held her back. "Okay?" he asked.

"I think so. You have a better perspective. I don't know how nervous I am." She couldn't tell him how interesting the Kornbluths were.

"You're great. Just looking at you makes me proud." He gave her the quickest possible kiss on the cheek.

"Same here." And how much more wonderful than his parents he was. In the dining room, she thought, she'd meet everyone all over again.

The dishes in the cabinet were a very expensive-looking deep blue, deep orange, and gold. Behind the chair Mrs. Farkas took, at the right-hand end of the table, was a sideboard, above it a portrait of Queen Mona herself, it had to be, maybe twenty years ago, with her mouth closed. Emily was seated between Mr. Farkas, to her left, and Larry Kornbluth. Opposite her, the fabulous blouse and intimidatingly gracious face of Helen Kornbluth; and between Helen and his mother, Steve. The table itself, under a crystal chandelier, was sumptuous. A pale green soup waited for them in gilt-edged cups. The linen tablecloth was a dark beige, embroidered with flowers of the same beige. The centerpiece was of pink and white peonies. On the windows behind Mr. Farkas hung regal drapes (The House of Farkas?), a dark blue background, a pattern of golden shapes, something between fleurs-de-lis and macaroni.

They had begun the soup (asparagus) when Larry Kornbluth, tipping his forehead at the display cabinet, said, "Any of your stuff for sale, Mona? Helen and I are running low on dishes."

No one laughed fully until Mona replied. "It doesn't bother me one bit for you to make fun of my acquisitions, sir. It didn't bother me last time, either. You carve antlers, I'll collect Crown Derby." Steve laughed the hardest, slapping the table with his fingertips and looking at his mother with surprise or admiration or congratulations. Larry laughed aloud too. Mona was half-keeping a fraction of a straight face. Helen's expression was noncommitally amused, as if the exchange had passed beneath her nose for a sniffing judgment she couldn't quite make. Mr. Farkas was spooning his soup. Emily decided that as a guest she wasn't responsible for a reaction. But she thought it was remarkable that Mona would—could—answer back so quickly and cleverly.

Conversation ensued. Eisenhower versus Stevenson that fall. Mr. Farkas still liked Ike. The Kornbluths, not too surprisingly, were passionate Adlai supporters. Emily thought of mentioning that her sister worked in Stevenson's New York office, but what would be the point? She wanted the attention off her. The attention was probably on her, anyway. Silent attention.

Then Helen Kornbluth was speaking to her, focusing on her in public. "Is it true you wanted to be an actress? It's a subject I'm interested in."

"In high school I really loved it. I thought it was the best thing in the world to be. I went to summer stock one summer as a kid and that kind of soured me, but I acted some in college. I still love the theater more than anything. I love to go. I'm very good at going."

"Don't forget, you're also great at getting tickets," Steve said.

"Mrs. Farkas," Emily said. "Do you have any idea how fussy your son is about his theater seats?" She sounded to herself as if she were trying to act like a fawning, gushy new daughter-in-law.

"Emily," Mrs. Farkas said, "I have to admit, I think he gets it from us. Jack and I always prefer seats up front. Front and center. It's just one of those things. Tell me, is it bad?" She was showing her Chiclet teeth, so that she didn't look at all as if she had asked a question.

"I guess no one likes bad seats. It's just not always possible."

"Oh, you know," Mona said, "the impossible just takes a little longer. Isn't that what they say? Or a little pull somewhere on the right strings. Life is short. You might as well enjoy yourself."

"First class, why not?" Mr. Farkas said. "I agree one hundred percent."

Emily had never heard anyone talk this way about seats. The Farkases seemed unusually outspoken.

"Maybe it's just a simple question of seeing and hearing better," Steve said.

"That's right, Stevie," his mother said.

"Let me ask just one little question here," Larry Kornbluth said. "Whatever happened to 'The play's the thing'?"

Thank you, Emily thought. Perfect.

"That's how we show our respect to the play, Larry," Mona said. "By sitting up front."

"Does that mean the people in less good seats are less respectful?" Larry asked. "What the hell are good seats, anyway? Doesn't it spoil the illusion for you if you're too close?"

"Not me, Larry," Mona said. "The closer I am, the more illusion. What can I say? Other people can do whatever they want, whatever they can afford."

"Emily," Helen Kornbluth said, "to change the subject for a moment. Tell me what parts you played."

Helen was like a teacher at the table, diplomatic and motherly. "Helena in college, *Midsummer Night's Dream*, and Emily Webb in high school, in *Our Town*." God, namesakes! "Were you an actress?" Emily asked her. "Are you?"

"No, no. I've always loved the theater and I've always loved children. I used to teach first grade regularly at Beardsley. Then Larry and I had our own children, and I became attached to the school in this way. It works out very nicely, but it's not very interesting to hear about, I'm afraid."

"Helen, tch-tch," Mona said. "Such a braggart."

"Well, we just finished our spring production, *Brigadoon*. Perhaps next year you'll all come. I'm planning on something a bit meatier."

No one responded, so Emily, even though she didn't want to appear too eager, said, "I'll be there."

"I talked to the Beardsley PTA last week on toys and safety," Steve told Helen.

"Excellent. I know they must have profited from it," Helen said.

"I think it went well," Steve said.

"Generating good will doesn't hurt," Mr. Farkas said. "Until Stevie came along, we had no spokesman. Stevie's our ambassador."

"The ambassador from Farr," Steve said. He seemed a little embarrassed. Emily couldn't tell if his father's compliment was gratifying to Steve or an undesirable pat on the head.

While Gretta cleared and Larry Kornbluth was asking Jack Farkas some questions about the toy business, Emily dropped by brain elevator to one of her distant memories, a dark corridor in second grade, a corridor behind the school stage, she and her classmates lined up to go onto the stage in costumes and faces that glowed, human candy. Everyone looking mysterious to each other and important, she and her classmates nearly turned into strangers. Coming onto the stage, it seemed to her in memory, had been like entering a back door in order to appear anywhere on earth for the first time ever. The opening of the curtain was the beginning of life. Her mother had been in the audience, for the last time (also the first time?), in the rows of parents, the parents also disguised, ghosts, dead melons, dead moons (Andy Profound!), distant but watching. Her mother these days was precisely the way she'd been in the audience then, present and not present.

Leg of lamb, roast potatoes, string beans with almonds, salad, a colossal fruit cup, brownies and lemon squares, coffee. Mona was describing a gorgeous penthouse on Fifth and Sixty-eighth she had just sold to a very big bigshot whose name she could not mention, and the conversation continued in the real estate vein, mostly the relative costs of living on various avenues and streets in New York, and in various other cities, including London and Paris; the rent of Larry's studio on Second and Second; the rent the Kornbluth's daughter, Susan, the flutist, paid for her apartment in the Village, and their son Rafael, the graduate student in philosophy, paid for his apartment near Columbia.

Emily was slightly embarrassed by the subject at first, worried that the Kornbluths might think it agreeable to her and beneath them, also worried that Mrs. Farkas would ask her what rent she paid, not that there was any particular secret about it, but she didn't want to be forced. The Kornbluths, however, seemed perfectly relaxed in their participation, and her rent didn't come up. In fact, she began to feel mistakenly passive, then ignored, and she watched for an opening in which she might volunteer her rent as the price of admission to the table talk. If Steve mentioned his, she would, she thought—she'd have to, since she'd be the only one left—but he didn't, so she came out of the conversation uncompromised.

After dinner, back in the living room, what Emily had pictured in a fraction-of-a-second's fantasy at the dinner table happened: Helen Kornbluth asked her to sit with her on the couch.

"Gladly," she said. Two veteran nonactresses exchanging the highs and lows of their noncareers. The others were talking about something, thank goodness.

"It's one of those things, acting," Helen said, "that are free when you're young, and so competitive and costly when it comes time to be an adult. Just like any art, I suppose. It's all so natural to many young people, it seems such a shame that even the talented ones usually give it up when they leave the school."

Emily was instantly absorbed in Helen's subject, but she couldn't help wondering, why the concern? And why expressed to her? Was Helen sympathizing with her? With herself? All she could think of to say was, "Your daughter's a musician, though."

"And a good one. Not a great one, unfortunately. She could use more jobs. But she'll never stop playing. She couldn't. She's an exception. Don't misunderstand me. I think the world is wonderful, as terrible as it can be, and you look as though you're having a fine time in it. I don't believe for a minute that everyone should be an actress or a musician or sculptor. God forbid. But I do think that people as intelligent as you seem to be, as passionate as you seem to be, should not be wasted."

"That's on my mind all the time." Helen really got to the point, didn't she? "But sometimes I must think there's not that much of me to waste, since I'm afraid I'm not that remarkable. Then sometimes I think there's something there, but I don't know what to do with it. As a matter of fact, my sister reminded me last week, only she didn't have to, because I've never forgotten it, when I was little, between eight and nine, I got all in an uproar one afternoon because I heard applause on my radio that was simply not stopping, and I really thought the second coming had happened"—Helen smiled at that—"or what I really thought was that I had just missed the announcement that the war was over, which had just begun for us, and my dinky little radio was carrying the applause of the whole world." She hoped to God Steve hadn't told his mother about her mother and that Steve's mother hadn't told the Kornbluths earlier ("Stevie's friend lost her mother. If you look closely you'll see she's missing a mother.") She would have to ask Steve if he'd said anything.

"It was static, I assume."

"Yes. But what excited me was that the static could pass itself off as applause and trick me. I loved that. Maybe it's silly of me, but I still love it. I don't think of myself as an idiot for having been fooled that way. In a way I think of it as the best of me. It's hard to explain. Maybe it sounds ridiculous. I don't think about how it turned out to be nothing but static. I think about how the static had that talent of sounding like applause, like a mimic."

"Do you know what you sound like?"

"Not an electrician."

"You talk like an artist."

"I'm not, though." An artist with no art. It sounded so nifty, but so sad.

"But perhaps you are."

"If I am, it doesn't make any difference. I have nothing to play on. I have no piano. I don't know how to play. I must be an artist without an art."

Helen made a tiny, thoughtful chuckle, two subdued notes; to Emily they could have signified agreement or recognition or simply appreciation of her phrase. Helen then asked, "What stopped you, in summer stock? You said it soured you. Or is that too personal? I know it could be."

"It's a long unpleasant story. I didn't like the people all that well. I lost my courage, anyway. But if I'd really had the talent, I figure I wouldn't have lost the courage. My reasons weren't good enough for wanting to act. Or they were good reasons, but maybe they didn't have enough to do with acting. I wanted to make sure that everything lasted. I connected acting with eternal exciting life. But then wanting to be an actress didn't last. I don't know. I got modest. I still wish it could be that way, though." Did she sound as if she were sucking up to Helen, to what Helen had been advocating?

"You still wish the excitement were there or you still wish you wanted to keep the excitement there?"

"God." Emily felt a soft knock against her heart raising a deep-seated dust of unacceptable possibility she had always ignored, at least consciously. Or else the knock was Helen herself, Helen asking the question more than the question Helen was asking.

Helen went on. "Is the excitement there or do we have to make it up? Sometimes of course it's there. You can't mistake it. But sometimes

I've wondered if we don't have to make it be there, get excited in order to be excited."

"It's a wonderful question. I'll have to think about it more. I'm pretty sure I want the excitement. And that I don't make it up."

"I should hope so. And I thought so. But it's a question that comes along."

"I think I even recognized it. How about you? Did something stop you?"

"To tell you the truth, I think I've developed some ambition late in life." Helen raised her chin. "I think I'd probably like it to have turned out that I was directing professionals, professionally. I can only think of one-and-a-half female directors. Not that I'm good enough. Only that I wish it. And not less and less, I'm afraid."

"Emily!" Mona called, in her cheerful bray. "Stevie says you picked out his shirt."

"I hope you like it." She so resented the interruption that she had to remind herself Mona was Steve's mother.

"I love it. I could never get him to do anything bold with clothes."

Steve put his hands in front of him, protecting himself. "I make up for it with my imagination," he said.

"I know it. You always played your clothes close to the vest. What do you think of that?"

"Very witty, Mother."

"That's right. Oh, you're being sarcastic."

Emily couldn't help notice that Larry, sitting in the chair she had occupied before dinner, was doing an even worse job of enjoying himself than he'd been doing earlier. Then she watched his face lifting anxiously and gloomily toward Helen, asking, Emily was certain, "Can't we go?" His ridged hair had become an extension of his frown.

"Anyone want a cordial?" Mona asked from the chair to Larry's right, having missed his look.

"We get up with the birds, Mona," Helen said. And she stood, as did Larry. Emily wondered how she was going to say goodbye to Helen, both physically and with what words. Emily stood too, in case Steve wanted to leave, and so she wouldn't be seated when Helen departed.

"You babies, too?" Mona said.

"We have to work tomorrow, Mother." Steve stood, from the end of the couch near his father's chair.

"I don't? Your father doesn't? Jack, let's go to El Morocco."

Jack smiled his petite, beautiful teeth. "This is El Morocco, only a little bit less expensive."

"We'll stay five minutes, Mother," Steve said.

Emily felt bad for Mona; Mona didn't like evenings to end. Steve said to Emily quietly, "Five minutes okay?"

Emily said, "Fine." It would be less rude to Mona, and she wouldn't have to go down in the elevator with the Kornbluths. She couldn't look at Helen, so she shook hands with Larry. Larry looked as if he didn't know he had spent the evening with her, but he did say, "Hope you'll come to the studio sometime."

"Thanks. I definitely will. It sounds so intriguing, what you're doing."

"It intrigues me, too, thank God." He laughed restlessly.

Helen said to Steve and Emily as a twosome, "Please come see us. It was so good to see you again, Steve."

"It was great. See you soon." They kissed.

Then, to Emily, Helen said, "May I?" They embraced quickly, both smiling as they separated. Emily swallowed. "We'll meet again," Helen said.

"It was wonderful talking with you." Emily thought of embracing Helen a second time; the first time had been like bumping into someone.

"Goodbye." Helen gave a farewell nod. "So long," Larry said, on his way to the hall with his wife, escorted by the Farkases.

In the middle of the parents' living room, Steve kissed Emily on the mouth.

"How'd I do?"

"You must have been perfect, because all evening I wanted to get you home to bed."

"Does your mother know?"

"That we sleep together? Probably, if she thought about it. Why?"

"I mean about yesterday. The engagement."

"Of course not. Why?"

"I just wondered. She looked as if she did. Acted as if she did."

"That's the way she looks. Knowy."

"Knowy but not nosy?" Emily asked offhandedly. Was Mona smart? Shrewd? She couldn't be as stupid as she acted.

"I wouldn't do that to you before your parents know—your father. How can you even ask?"

"I wasn't accusing you."

"How did you like her?"

"You can't not. She's so funny."

"You and Helen really seemed to hit it off."

"We had one of the best conversations I've ever had in my life. She dazzled me."

The front door shut. "We'll leave in a sec."

Jack, on his and Mona's return, said to everybody, "There's no one like Larry and Helen, is there?"

"There's no *room* for anyone else like Larry and Helen," Mona said. "Stevie, does Emily want anything to drink?"

"Just some water?" Emily said.

"You, Mother? Dad?"

"Not for me," Jack said. "Keeps me up." He patted Steve's back, thanking him for the offer.

"Mother?"

"I don't drink alone."

"It looks like you're the only one who wants to burn the midnight oil, Mother."

On the way home, Emily vowed, she was going to explain to him the difference between "like" and "as" clauses. She thought of the living room group, herself included, as the weary family after a big party; then she realized the Farkases were staying up just for her. "Steve, maybe we should let your parents go to bed."

"That's all right," Jack said. "It was a pleasure to meet you." He and Emily shook hands.

"Thank you. You too," she said.

"Stevie." He squeezed his son's arm. "See you tomorrow." He left the room without hesitation.

"Jack, your wife says goodnight," Mona said, without turning around.

"Hope to see you inside," Jack called back.

"Emily, talking about my son's imagination, do you know what he did one time when he was in college?"

"She knows, Mother."

"About the records?" Mona asked.

"I'd like to hear it from you," Emily said. Perfect? Excessive?

"This boy," said Mona, placing her arm across Steve's shoulder, "went out in Philadelphia with most of his semester's allowance and bought classical records. Hundreds of dollars. But he knows what he wants. That's the good thing. Jack and I weren't jumping up and down for joy at the time, but I ask myself, how many people in the world would want something that much to do such a crazy thing?"

"At least I didn't ask you for more money, did I?" Steve said. "And I still have the records. So it didn't turn out so bad."

"I love the story," Emily said for Mona's sake, and for Steve's. She did love it. She admired it. She kept it near the top of her mind. The passionate Steve.

Mona drew her arm off her son's shoulder. "Where do you live, Emily?"

Rent? "Eighty-sixth and York."

"That's nice for a working girl. Roommates, probably."

"My apartment's too small." Better than saying she wasn't the room-mate type.

"Studio?"

Emily nodded.

"That's convenient for you. Easy to clean. Lots of young women are living over there."

"I think so. I guess so."

"I hope you'll come to dinner again soon. If Stevie doesn't invite you, come anyway, by yourself."

"Thank you. But we will."

Mona smiled—the Chiclets, the dimples. Emily kissed Mona on the cheek. "That's nice," Mona said. "Steve will tell you I'm not the greatest in the world at keeping my big mouth shut, but something tells me you're special."

"Mother, look, this is really out of order, but it happens Emily and I got engaged yesterday."

Mona's chest and head jumped. She looked at Emily's bare ring-finger. "You're not joking?"

"We haven't told Emily's family yet, but you seem to have super-natural powers."

"Jack! He won't hear me. Let me get him." She took off like a movie reporter dashing for a phone.

Emily was smiling at Steve in a frozen are-you-crazy? way.

He was smiling too. "What was I supposed to do? You were really going to think I'd already told her unless I told her right in front of you now. Your father's not going to turn us down, is he?"

"That's not the point, is it?" She could hear how angry she sounded. Her cheeks were hot. This was an impossible place to have a fight.

"I'm sorry, but what would you have done in my shoes? You helped a little too, you know?" His smile, unfortunately, was cajoling.

"I was just trying to be friendly." Her watch said almost ten-thirty. "Maybe we can still go to my father's tonight." She wanted to have left before his parents came back to the living room. It occurred to her to leave by herself. She walked away from Steve, toward the en-trance to the hall. When she heard what she supposed was his parents' bedroom door clicking open, she stopped. She walked back toward him. He actually looked worried.

"I'm really sorry. I agree, we should go to your father's right away."

She examined his sober face to see if he was making any effort to make it sober. It looked honest to her. But she felt as if a tragedy had taken place. The top of her chest hurt; she had swallowed stone grapes. She stood beside him, taking his hand just as his parents re-entered the room, Mona with her arms reaching out, assuming the embrace position.

CHAPTER ELEVEN

The Flag of Farr

Emily made the mistake of accepting Timothy's unexpected phone invitation one morning to have a drink with him after work that day. A mistake because, lo and behold, he wanted to go to bed with her—he said he still loved her. It seemed clear that he also still resented her denying him two years before. He arrogantly accused her of being a person unwilling to take chances in general and of doing the easy thing with her life by marrying Steve, whom he had met exactly once for less than a minute. He nevertheless said he wanted to stay in touch, as did she. It thrilled her and made her wild with envy that *Big Time,* his musical, was actually coming to Broadway in late November. Little Timothy! It was a mistake also because having the drink caused her to be a little late meeting Steve for dinner at Granada, and because she told Steve where she'd been and what had happened.

"You know something?" Steve said. "I think you're getting back at me for my slip-up telling my mother our news prematurely." Here came his wiseguy, I'm-only-kidding smile, one of his few definite bad points.

"That's ridiculous. I forgave you already."

"Who knows?"

"The whole point is I felt no sexual attraction for him."

"Sounds like quite an accomplishment."

"It's not a big deal for me. You're making the big deal out of it." Why was Steve even a little bit insecure about sex when he was so good at it and it still seemed to be getting better all the time, including his tongue down there. She looked forward to sex so much, sometimes it seemed as though she couldn't bother to think about anything else. But not tonight.

"How come you felt no attraction?"

"I felt no attraction because I'm all taken up by you. Completely. It was no fun for me to listen to him telling me he was still attracted. He told me he still loved me. Can you believe that?"

"Apparently he felt entitled."

"He says anything he feels like saying. He always has. The main thing is that as soon as I left him, all I wanted to do was tell you all about the conversation. I almost felt as though I'd met with him so I could tell you about it."

"You should have phoned and told me you were going to meet him. The only thing that bothered me is that you were late here and I didn't know where you were. Next time I'd appreciate it if you'd let me know your plans. I don't like to wait around worrying."

"I was twenty minutes late. You don't always get home at exactly the same time every day."

"You were more like a half an hour late, if you really want to know. I think it's silly to argue about."

"Steve?" She put the hand Timothy had kissed on the hand Steve wasn't using to eat his shrimp Ajillo.

"What?" He continued to eat.

Timothy had everything she loved going for him, yet he had been no temptation. He didn't even begin to be an alternative. She kept her hand on Steve's. "He's so far beyond me and above me in achievement, but at the same time he seems so far behind. He's really a boy wonder, I guess. But he's a boy. He's a little boy."

"Really?"

She took away her hand. "What do you want to talk about, Steve?" She visualized leaving the restaurant right now, alone.

He looked at her. "I'm listening. Seriously. Are you getting your period by any chance?"

"Yes, by any chance I am. So what?"

"You're irritable tonight, and usually you're not at all. I also have to say I have other things on my mind than your college boyfriend's psyche. Besides, unless he's bullshitting you about his show, he seems to be doing pretty well for a little boy."

"Well, will you please tell me what's on your mind then, and I'll stop trying to entertain you with my stupid anecdotes and listen." She paid attention to her own shrimp, waiting for him to talk. She wasn't sure what he meant by things on his mind, other than their decision to get married, but he had met three times in the last two weeks with Jerry Goetz, his friend from Wharton days, on one of these occasions along with some "other guys." When she'd asked him, the first two times, what these meetings were about, he'd said, almost in a teasing way, "In due time." Once, he'd met with Jerry at home when she was staying over; she'd kept to the bedroom in her nightgown, re-reading *The Great Gatsby* and feeling slightly like a kept woman. "Are you going to talk to me or are we just going to sit here in utter silence?" she said finally.

"You know something? I'm thinking about our future while you're dwelling on your past."

"Hardly. If we can't stop talking about my meeting with poor little Timothy, we're in serious trouble, Steve. You're dwelling on it, I'm not. I'm not marrying you because I'm still in love with Timothy." She decided not to mention the possibility of opening night and whether Steve would want to go. "You really are making something out of nothing, and I want you to stop." She felt as though she were shouting softly. She'd never had a fight in a restaurant before.

"Yassuh, boss." His accompanying look was sarcastic.

She wouldn't say another word until he did, and only if he didn't say anything nasty.

"My mother asked me in today's phone call what our plans for the wedding are."

"So why didn't you say so? What does she want to know?" Maybe he was partly right. Plans had to be made, and she'd been flittering around without a care. She wanted to be in her wedding without having to arrange it.

"Frankly"—Steve raised his eyebrows, but she couldn't tell if it was at his mother or at her—"she wants to know how Jewish it's going to be."

"So do I. Let's decide. How Jewish does she want it to be? I mean— I don't mean I'd necessarily agree to everything she wanted, but I'm not being snotty. How Jewish is necessary for your family?"

"They expect the breaking of the glass, I guess."

"What is that—virginity?"

Steve laughed. "You really know your faith, don't you? It's the destruction of the Temple."

"At my wedding?"

He laughed again, then shook his head. "You really are too much."

In the past, she'd taken this comment as a compliment. Tonight she had her doubts. "Does your mother think this is like intermarriage? Is she going to boycott the wedding if it isn't Jewish enough?"

"My mother likes to noodge, if you know what that means. I told her you and I still have things to decide."

"I appreciate that. But we do still have almost four months."

"That's not as much time as you think."

Her main wish was to be married in Newbury, but it was obviously impractical. *Midsummer Night's Dream* all over again. Also, Grandpa Gus and Granny had usually gone up for the summer in late May, but he refused to go now. The waiter removed their shrimp dishes and served her arroz con pollo and Steve his habitual beloved paella.

"My mother also inquired when she and Dad were going to meet your folks and do we want an engagement party?"

"I'll take care of that tomorrow. Promise."

An evening to relax. Mona and Bunny, the two Einsteins, doing all the talking, Jack and Daddy in silence. Bunny naturally was champing at the bit to organize everything. It would be such a relief to let her take over, but of course it wouldn't be a relief, because the wedding wasn't Bunny's business. Bunny was like an aunt by marriage.

She should speak to Ellen, probably. Ellen hadn't had any trouble handling her wedding, of course. She didn't know where to begin. If Mona wanted to take over the whole thing, then Bunny would be kept out. She didn't want Mona handling the wedding anymore than she wanted Bunny to, however, and she didn't want to be responsible for hurting Bunny's feelings. Bunny was actually quite harmless most of the time. If she hurt Bunny's feelings, she'd be hurting Daddy's too.

When she had told her father about the engagement (the same night Steve had blurted out the news to Mona), Daddy in his monogrammed robe and Bunny in a peach peignoir that looked as if she'd borrowed it from Queen Elizabeth, Bunny had started to exclaim and then had the sense to sit still until Daddy reacted, which made Emily feel bad, because she saw Bunny recognizing that her position was outside. When Bunny did stupid or silly things, it still irritated Emily, but now, when Bunny showed tact or charm, Emily felt guilty. The big thing, though, was that her father reacted in a surprising way. Instead of giving a quiet, light response, "Wonderful, Cookie," and shaking Steve's hand, he sat in his armchair not saying a word. She watched his mouth straining, and then his eyes plainly watering. He took off his glasses to rub his eyes. She had to hug him, come what may. "I'm sorry," he said. "I suspected why you were coming down here at this hour, but still." Then he stood up and did shake Steve's hand, a bit flustered; for that moment he seemed younger than Steve, partly because he was shorter than Steve.

Then Bunny got into the act, saying to Emily, "I told you you wouldn't be in that measly apartment for long and you didn't believe me." To which Emily couldn't resist replying, "We're moving *into* my apartment, Bunny. We're going to live on love." By then Bunny was giving Steve a hug and saying, "This one is the cream of the crop as far as I'm concerned." Emily told Margaret. Margaret joined in drinking some champagne, which happened to be in the fridge. With her champagne in hand, Emily phoned Ellen from Daddy and Bunny's bedroom, waking her up but getting the most enthusiastic response out of her she'd ever gotten from her for anything, as if Emily had finally done something worthwhile.

Before she and Steve left, her father said to him, "I guess we'll be seeing more of each other soon, Steve," at which she felt she had given her father a grown son.

The next day, her father took her to lunch at "21," to find out what was what. She told him she loved Steve more and more and was eager to marry him. His combination of compassion, sensitivity and imagination along with responsibility and maturity amazed her. He was a businessman, but he loved music. "The way you love the theater, Daddy," she explained. She guessed he had some flaws, like everyone else, but she loved them along with the rest of him.

Her father seemed to be amused by her comment about Steve's flaws; she noticed that he didn't ask what they were. He asked if she had anything else to tell him or ask him. She wondered if he meant was she pregnant. She said, "I just want you to know I think I'm in very good hands. Just the way I've always been, Daddy. You don't have anything to worry about. Steve's not a romantic idiot, like me. He's the one with the head on his shoulders." She kissed him on the cheek.

Then she wondered if this father-daughter talk would be her last chance to tell him about George Koenigsberg. When she imagined telling him, and pictured how it would appall him, she realized she absolutely couldn't ever tell him, even though inviting George to her party seemed to be the thing she blamed her father for, not allowing Mom to go away.

As they parted after lunch for their respective offices, her father said, "I can hardly believe it, darling, except that you've always been such a prize person I suppose I knew it would have to happen sometime soon. I hope you'll be as happy as you deserve to be. Steve seems like a very fine young man. Bunny's just nuts about him." He hugged her then. He never hugged her, but he hugged her and said, "Behave."

Daddy's perfectly right to trust my judgment about Steve, she had thought, but how does he know? For such a conformist, he was quite easygoing about her getting married. Maybe just an outgrowth of the attractive fatherly lightness she had been grateful for as a teenager. On consideration, she was still grateful. What a nuisance it would have been if he'd presented an official father's questionnaire for Steve to fill out, like the profit and loss statements at work. Her father knew Steve had a good job in the family business and that Farr was a famous, solid old company. Maybe that was all he felt he needed to know. Maybe that was all he did need to know. She knew the rest.

After dinner, she and Steve took their customary walk from Granada up Washington Square. She wore a red sweater over her blue dress. Steve was wearing his tan gabardine suit and a maroon-and-gold-striped tie. The huge entrance arch to the Square always made her think of the Arc de Triomphe. The early-June evening—the old brownstones, the trees, the square's park—tingled with exciting peacefulness. She felt like a significant person, distinct, at least the equal of Isabel Archer "affronting her destiny," in what continued to be the best novel she'd ever read, or at least her favorite. Now was the time of her future. Steve put his arm across the bottom of her back. She did the same to him, adding a half-turn and a quick kiss. Steve said, "I apologize for before, I really do. I love and respect you so much, it's not fair of me to be tense with you."

"Sshh, I forgive you. I have a confession."

"What's that?"

"I wish we could make love in the park."

"Seriously? Sounds good to me."

"I wish we had a place we could meet at lunch between your office and mine to lie down and luxuriate for two or three hours, a little lawn on top of a penthouse with a wall so no one could see us."

"We could, for a lark, you know. People do it. In a hotel, I mean. We could meet at one of our apartments. You want to go to the Victoria or the Plaza. You want a suite, not a bed. You want room service."

"I want you. I only feel good now when I'm with you and we're being loving, preferably in each other's arms. The more I spend time with you, the more I realize how I'm killing time when I'm not with you, and how safe it is with you. I don't ever want to be with anyone else. I want to eat off your flesh."

"Be my guest."

"Since we got serious, I don't like going home to my own place or even to visit my father's that much. I think when I met you, after a while I felt as though I'd crossed a street in the dark, where there was actually no street, just a street-shaped hole, a big avenue of a hole, which I somehow got across to get to you, and then I didn't want to be anywhere else but with you."

He squeezed her waist. He didn't say anything.

He appreciated her; he let her talk any way she wanted. He admired her and probably even liked it that compared to him she was not exactly strange but said things sometimes that most people didn't say. "I want to live a rich, full life with you, complete, without any bad fights. I want us to become a couple who's a permanent fixture at the theater, like Mr. and Mrs. First-Nighter. I want to learn you and make you happy. And make you proud of me. I want to get even more attached. I want us to be inseparable."

"I'm already proud of you, babes. Let me ask you one minor detail. When do you want to have kids?"

"Five years? We can watch children at the zoo."

"Seriously."

They were now strolling up lower Fifth Avenue toward his apartment. "I don't know. A few years? I certainly want children." Did she? Why not? One child. A genius. "But first I want us to have a tremendously long honeymoon, where we go about our business during the day and come home to our marriage and feed it and pat it and play with it. That sounds silly. But you know what I mean."

"Sure: Look, I love what you're saying. I just think you're being a little bit idealistic. People can't spend all their time in bed and going to the theater, even you and me, and sometimes they're going to have occasional disagreements."

"As far as I'm concerned, we should only argue about what plays to see. I honestly don't mean to sound unrealistic. Obviously, we'll have all kinds of experiences. But everything we learn should make our lives better and make us love each other more. I'm very serious."

"It's probably just as well we're not heading out west in a covered wagon. But really, I understand you. I do."

"I might not be a pioneer-woman-type, but I could have been if I'd had to be. I can tell you one thing. I have a desire to take care of you. I don't just want to be taken care of. I think about us together."

"I know. I feel the same. I just can't express it like you. I wish I could."

She had noticed—since meeting his parents—these glimmers of brand-new feeling in her: protectiveness toward him (once she had gotten over her horror at his blunder in telling his mother) and a fresh sense of Steve as a boy-man (while still a man of the world) who needed her indulgence. When she'd first met him, at her party, he'd seemed boyish too, but in a slightly creepy way. Now the boyishness, mixed in with the rest of him, was enthusiastic and charming, also somewhat innocent, such as when he'd given her the ring. Dinner tonight hadn't been a very good example of charm on his part or protectiveness on hers. But it certainly was great to make up.

He said, "Look, it seems like a good time to tell you. I was going to wait. We may not be able to go on our honeymoon in September."

Nothing could be seriously wrong tonight. When she glanced at him, he gave her a tough, straight, zippered smile—either good news or trouble. She said, "If we can't afford it, that doesn't bother me." She wanted to go back to Europe—she'd been once, the summer after her sophomore year, with Jill—but she wasn't dying to go. At the moment, she thought being married would be Europe.

"We can afford it. My mother offered it as a wedding gift, also on the phone today, first class on the *United States*. But I may be tied up here."

"That's very nice of her. May I ask what's going on?"

"It could be great. It could be."

"Then please don't keep me up in the air, okay?"

"Well, it's this business thing, with Jerry. It's complicated, but the general idea is that he happens to know two brothers who are developing a big shopping mall in Westchester. Where I would just love to establish a suburban branch of Farr."

What first occurred to Emily, as Steve's smile relaxed and expanded, was that he sounded like an explorer or a king, planting the flag of Farr on foreign soil. "If it's a business thing, and you're going to be stuck here in September, how come your mother offered us the honeymoon trip?"

"Because they don't have a clue yet. No one knows. This is the biggest thing that's ever happened to me, not counting meeting you."

"Why all the secrecy? Why haven't you said anything?"

"I'll probably be telling my father and Uncle Ira sometime this week. Right now, I'm waiting for word on one thing before I present it. I don't think there's any doubt the developers want us. It would be a big feather in their caps, the first ever branch of Farr. It's just a question of the terms of the lease, which Jerry's lawyer is advising me about. Knowing my family, they'll have objections. Dad is quiet but very tough. Uncle Ira is even tougher, but not so quiet, I think I've mentioned. To put it bluntly, he can be a rude, tactless bastard." Steve chuckled for some reason, as if he enjoyed his uncle's meanness. "Lots of things could happen. They could like the idea so much they'd want to take it over. It's a great idea, isn't it?"

"It's such a great idea, I wish you'd told me about it." She told him her first reaction, about planting the flag of Farr.

He squeezed her again. "Maybe we should have a flag at that! A pennant! See, I want you in on this. I want you involved in it. The only reason I haven't told you is that I don't want to jinx it. I've been thinking of it as a kind of surprise wedding gift. This was my idea for making millions, remember, when I gave you the ring?"

"I do."

"There've been a few snags along the way, working out a partnership with Jerry, other things, waiting, people changing their minds. But suddenly tonight it seemed stupid not to tell you. I know it's going to work. But you have to swear not to say anything to anyone. Anyone. You can't tell your father or your brother-in-law."

"Of course I won't. How did you mean you want me involved in it?"

"Working for us. Advertising, publicity, which could be very, very important."

"Gee. Isn't it sort of inconvenient, though? How would you get out there every day? Would you have to go every day?"

"Commute by train, or drive, or move there."

"A typical suburban couple?"

"It would be near Scarsdale. Scarsdale happens to be very beautiful. You wouldn't be a typical suburban anything. You're too kooky, for one thing. We wouldn't have to live up there, though. It would be convenient, that's all. But Westchester isn't all of it. There's also New Jersey, Long Island, Connecticut. There's so much territory opening up for shopping malls. We talked about going west in a covered wagon, but it's not so funny. There's the whole damn country. Who knows? Jerry's family has lots of real estate connections."

His excitement was so great, she didn't see how she could complain at the moment about being kept in the dark even though she was supposed to be part of the plan. Or tell him she definitely didn't want to live in the suburbs. She loved the basic idea, it thrilled her, little Farrs spreading through the suburbs, the country, like Monopoly. Little bright-green buildings. "It seems so neat and logical."

"Maybe you should be at the meeting."

"As far as I'm concerned, if your father turns down the idea, it would probably be because he's jealous. You'll convince them. Maybe it'll take a little time." What was making her act so confident?

"I'm sure it will take some doing, but it's going to happen. I'm very glad I told you. I think I'm glad I waited, too. It's nearer. And it's more of a big surprise."

She had a feeling at that moment for why he would have wanted to wait. "I'm just glad I know now." She wanted to exclude all doubts, for his sake. "I'm so impressed. I mean, my God, it's so vast."

"Could be. Could be."

They were crossing the street to the corner of his block. When they got to the corner, he suddenly stopped their walking, right under the streetlight, and kissed her, clutching her face with both hands, startling her whole body into an immediate response. He said, "Thanks for your faith. It means everything to me. I love you." He had never embraced her face before. She held onto him. He made her feel that no matter how much she was his, he wanted her to be even more his. "Let us go upstairs," she said. He took her hand for the half block to his canopy.

She went straight to the bathroom, where she undressed and put in her diaphragm like someone in a race. (Now that she was engaged she'd become even stricter about using the diaphragm.) She even peed impatiently. In the bedroom, she "raped" Steve, provoking his laughter as well as intense interest, helping him pull off most of his clothes, pushing him down on the bed, jumping after him. She swayed her breasts (small was not useless) across his eyes and lips, swiveled them around his chest and stomach for a while, then his penis. He said, "I can't stand it." She kissed his penis briefly; when she couldn't stand it either, she climbed onto him. Iwo Jima, she thought.

He held her shoulders. He shook his head. He said, "You know something? I'm so lucky, it's impossible for any human being to be as happy as I am right now. I've got everything." Smiling, she closed her eyes; she started sliding up and down on him, in slow motion, tuned to her suspense, until she simply lost control of herself, like an exploding engine.

Because they thought they might do it again, they lolled with his night-table light on; she lay on her stomach while Steve stroked her back, her backside, the backs of her thighs, and kissed her shoulders and the back of her neck beneath her hair. She was melting into the bed, so satiated she could tease herself by worrying she might never feel like doing it again.

Had her parents lain like this before they were married? After? Had they done everything before they were married, or "everything but," or were they too conservative? Was Daddy more conservative than Mom? Her guess was yes. She pictured her mother nude. She always imagined her body as similar to her mother's, except that her mother's was a bit shorter. Then she saw her mother as a skeleton. She quickly dressed her mother in flesh from the head down, until her mother was clothed in nudity. Her mother woke up, opened her eyes in her grave, horrified at finding herself there, knocking on the grave, on the coffin, yelling, Get me out of here! The coffin rose out of the earth. Her mother stepped out of the coffin, her mother, but with Helen Kornbluth's intense face. Emily frowned Helen Kornbluth's face away; it came back. It was larger than her mother's, closer. Emily replaced it with her mother's and kept her mother's there by not looking at it. Her mother flew home nude across the Pacific, like Superwoman without a costume, for the wedding. At the wedding she wore a wedding dress, so Emily had to wear a regular office dress.

What did her mother think of Steve? What would she say about him? A very fine young man? How would her mother be talking to her at this age? Up to tonight, Emily had thought only in the vaguest way of her mother in relation to Steve—mainly that as usual she wasn't present to react. Would she disapprove? See something in him no one else saw? Would she be smart about personalities? Analytical? Over-analytical? Accepting? Accepting-tolerant or accepting-resigned? Snobbish? Socially snobbish? Intellectually? Would she look down on the toy business? How would she act toward Mona Farkas? Would Steve like her even though he liked Bunny? Would she recommend prolonging her and Steve's engagement past September? Would she say, my darling, you two are meant for each other? Would she be disappointed that her daughter had chosen a businessman, even though she herself had done the same thing in choosing Daddy? Would she be disappointed anyway, in general, in her daughter—that her daughter was an assistant in a publicity department, lowly and superficial, or would she see that she was far from superficial despite her job?

"Are you asleep?" Steve asked.

"Close." She wasn't going to spoil their perfect mood by telling him her weird imaginings. And actually, she could drowse off in two seconds. She shifted to her side, facing him, snuggling into him. The air was made of the smell of their skin. "I'm completely content."

"Me too. Want to go to sleep?"

"We can always wake up again. Or do it in our sleep."

Steve reached behind him to turn off the bed-light. He returned to her in the dark. She changed positions again, pushing her back against his front, and reaching for his hand to draw his arm over her shoulder. "And good luck," she said.

"What, babes?"

"With your plan. Remember? The Flag of Farr."

"Oh. Thanks. You're my good luck."

"Goodnight, sleep tight, see you in the morning light. My mother used to say that."

He squeezed her hand. "I feel privileged."

CHAPTER TWELVE

"And You Deserve the Best"

Emily began to concentrate on her wedding by giving up and hiring (in the emotional sense) Bunny to help her take care of the arrangements. Emily's father had hinted at their lunch that Bunny would be only too happy to assist in whatever way she could, and such was certainly the case. (Bunny worked part-time as personal secretary to Jerome Sacks, an elderly, famous philanthropist and Eisenhower supporter. Mr. Sacks was slowly fading out, so she usually had some hours in the day for her own activities.) Having allowed Bunny to take the lead in handling all the nuisancy details (Emily herself had placed the engagement announcement in the *Times*), she had to confess that she was enjoying their telephone chats. Emily was making Bunny happy at no cost to herself. In fact, very much to her own advantage. She liked Bunny right now because she was making Bunny happy. Still, when she considered that it was this girlish type of planning that interested Bunny so much, and that she was so good at, Emily thanked God that Bunny wasn't her blood mother. There were things Emily had definitely never wanted to be interested in, like cheerleading or even being in a group of bridesmaids. The thought of girls in groups made her gag in her mind. She had the idea that Bunny would be happy kicking in an amateur chorus line.

So Bunny at the moment was maybe one-tenth of a real mother, for all Emily's gratitude that she was helping her out so generously and competently. Helen Kornbluth might be uncontrollably maternal, if given the chance—two hundred percent. Wilma Cotton, with whom Emily had had lunch twice since moving to Publicity, might be regarded as about fifteen percent—no children of her own, and even shallower than Emily had originally conceded, but sweet and thought-ful just the same. As for her own dead and departed Mom, she would surely qualify as a hundred-percent mother, if only she spent more time at home—unless Mom counted her own coffin as home, having fixed it up over the past thirteen years with flowers, perhaps a little chair and cot, a rectangular section out of the old pale-green living-room rug (where was that rug, anyway?), a photo of her two refugee daughters and Daddy on the little coffin piano, a flashlight, Sterno, cans of Spam and stew, a little radio. Who could tell? Maybe she really lived over there, in the Shanghai Jewish cemetery, in the little hut of her coffin, like a night watchman. Why shouldn't it be nice for her?

Emily had a hard time imagining Elsa Poplar as a mother, but per-haps partly for just that reason liked to watch her dealing with people, her casual sophistication, which Emily took to be the result of so-phistication to spare, to throw away. Mrs. P.'s manner of speech made light of things. She liked Mrs. P., and would like her a lot, she thought, if only she admired what she did. (At the same time, as an employee of the company, Emily felt a bit of pride that her own boss was Par-tridge's first ever female vice-president, generally considered the best publicity director in the business.)

So when Mrs. P. asked to speak with Emily one morning, about two weeks after the engagement, Emily thought (along with, Is something wrong? Is my attitude showing?), I have been summoned by an im-portant, respected person whose work is unimportant and which I don't respect. Doing publicity makes things seem better than they are, including many junky books. It is essentially lying, like advertising. It isn't artistic or scientific, and it doesn't do good in the world. For some reason it seemed necessary to Emily, while waiting for her noon ap-pointment, to remind herself of her low opinion of her own job, as if she were preparing herself to be fired. But getting fired didn't seem possible. Mrs. P. often said she was doing good work; and Mrs. P. had recently praised Emily for her alertness in detecting trouble when Laura DiLallo sent literally half the invitations to the Pelham History Prize party to people on the wrong list, and these people began phon-ing in their delighted acceptances. So Emily didn't expect or wish to be fired, though it wouldn't be the worst thing in the world to have her ambition questioned. Emily could make sense out of friendly doubt, and perhaps in a year, when Mrs. P. suggested it wasn't working out, she could say that she had never been meant for publicity to begin with.

In Mrs. P.'s inner sanctum (with the photographs of Mrs. P. and Truman Capote at the Stork Club; Mrs. P. and Edward R. Murrow; Mrs. P. and General MacArthur; and Pearl Buck; and Lily Lombino; and John Steinbeck), Mrs. P., wearing an unusually becoming outfit— a straw-colored suit and chartreuse blouse—said, "Please sit, my dear. Daphne is leaving us in September for a big job in Personnel at BBD&O, which has always sounded like a railroad to me, but I wish her well just the same. I'd prefer to try to break you in rather than bringing in someone new to replace her. She thinks you have the ability. On the other hand, you are planning to get married in September. However, if you're not going to be making a mad dash for motherhood, I think you deserve a chance to see what you can do for us. You're bright and serious, and being a trifle shy is all right as long as you're not rude to those who need you and whom you need. It's my hunch that behind the reserve are the necessary imagination and confidence and that they'll emerge as you're given responsibility. Daphne would help to train you over the summer. We'd bring in someone competent beneath you, and I'd be keeping a sharp lookout while you get your footing."

During Mrs. P.'s speech, Emily had time to bury the gauchest possible responses, such as, "I can't believe it," or "Do you actually think I can do it?" What she said was, "It's such an honor."

"You look shocked to death."

"I don't mean to. I can't say I expected it. But it's certainly a pleasant surprise." She laughed. What was she supposed to say, or not say?

"You'll really have to want the job. It's hard work, and there'll be extra demands on your time. You'd have to discuss it thoroughly with your fiancé."

"I definitely have to. I'm quite sure I'd want it, but it will require discussion." She couldn't say anything to Mrs. P. about Steve's business plans. For that matter, it might not be such a good idea to tell Steve about Mrs. P.'s offer until his plans were resolved.

Wanting to sound like an adult professional, but not artificial, Emily said, "I'll need a little time to think. I had no idea such an opportunity would be coming my way." Then, not to be too humble, she added, "Not at this point, anyway." Then she wished she could subtract what she'd added.

"Neither did we. I'd want an answer in a week at the latest. I've got to hire someone by the end of June so we can begin to concentrate on training whoever it is. And if it's you, we have to work out the timing of Daphne's departure in relation to your honeymoon."

"Actually, as a matter of fact, we might not be going on our honeymoon right away anyway." She could be sounding too eager to please. But it was worse than that. Because if she didn't go on her honeymoon right away, that would mean she'd be working for Steve, not for Mrs. P. She had to talk to someone. Who?

Without asking Emily why she might not be going on her honeymoon right away, Mrs. P. said, "That might or might not be more convenient, depending on when you go. I'm not going to worry about it right now." She stood up, as did Emily, saying, "Assuming it all works out and you make a place for yourself, we'd try to give you maternity leave, if that ever becomes an issue. Issue is an unfortunate choice of word. I only mention the matter so you can include it in your discussions with your fiancé, if it's relevant."

"We haven't made any definite plans in that department at all."

"I'll see you back in here soon then, and I hope you'll be saying yes. I'd like to see you succeed. And I'm able to see you succeeding."

"I hope so. I'm very grateful for your confidence. It means a lot to me, to say the least."

"You understand that this is strictly between us, except for the obvious people. Daphne is set to have lunch with you today."

Emily nodded. "I understand. And I'll be back with a definite answer as soon as I can. Thanks again." Should she have said "Thank you" instead of "Thanks"? Mrs. P. shook Emily's hand. Emily visualized embracing her, as she'd recently embraced Helen Kornbluth and Mona, stepping up in the adult world. Instead, she looked into Mrs. P.'s ripe, pretty face like a pleased person. In a way it could truly be said that no one had ever paid her such an important compliment as Mrs. P. had just paid her by offering her this job, which, if it stayed the same as it was in Daphne's hands, literally meant second-in-command. Mrs. P., eyebrows up, was now reading something on her desk. She said goodbye to Emily. Emily opened the office door, wanting to say goodbye in reply, but sensing it wasn't called for.

She entered the main room, trying not to smile, and in the process looking, she feared, as if she'd just received very bad news. So she forced her face to relax. On purpose, she ignored Laura and Mary Beth as she crossed the room toward Daphne, though she wondered if they were watching her. Her promotion might be announced in the "Literati" section of *Variety.* Unable to help smirking now, she said to Daphne, "Free for lunch, by any chance?"

Daphne gave her a cheerful smile that was as noisy as an out-loud laugh. "Well, I'd say there was a remote possibility of that. I'm waiting for a tinkle from Cindy Winkler at CBS, and then we can take off."

"Thanks. I really need advice." In her reign, she would banish all cute cold-cream-voice talk, and the people Daphne had nauseated would rise up to praise Emily for her dignity, her reserve, and cry, "Tinkle is dead. Long live the queen!"

She was going to tell Steve about the job offer at the end of the second day following her talk with Mrs. P. if he hadn't had his family confab by then. But after the second day, she waited another day, despite the clump in her stomach that felt like held breath accumulating there. She worried that if she told him, his reaction might be that she had betrayed him (even though she hadn't accepted the offer), or that he would think she hadn't said an outright no to Mrs. P. at the time of the offer because she doubted that his Farr expansion plan would go through, or because she would rather move up at Partridge than go to work for him. Then she began to worry that he would be upset because she had delayed telling him for three whole days. He'd ask why she hadn't told him immediately, consulted him, trusted him with something so important.

The third night she was getting ready to prepare dinner for them in his kitchen. She had bought filet of sole, new potatoes, frozen peas, and salad fixings. Steve wasn't even home yet, so instead of a girlfriend she felt like a wife, a regular, full-time, old-fashioned wife. When she heard his key in the front door, for some ridiculous reason she threw off her blouse and her bra and called, "Good evening, dear, I'm in the kitchen. How was your day? Do you want a drink? Little Timmy's out playing catch in the yard with little Tommy and he wants you to see how well he throws the ball." Why the hell had she said Timmy? Wouldn't he think she was thinking of Timothy? She turned around as he entered the kitchen.

He was neither amused nor angry. "Too warm for you in here?" he asked her. He didn't come kiss her.

She felt a bit silly, but she would have felt sillier getting dressed on the spot, as if he'd caught her about to do something lewd with the filet. "I was just being—what's wrong?"

"Guess."

She walked to him while putting her bra back on. "They said no?"

"They said no. They also said never."

She felt a gasp in her blood. She took his hand. "God. Shit. They didn't." What terrible timing. "Do you want a drink?"

"I've had one, but I think I will."

"You had one at the meeting?"

"In a bar."

"With Jerry? With your father?"

"By myself."

"By yourself? Where?"

"You want the name of it? What's the difference?"

"That's terrible." Then she saw that his eyes were spilling over, and she choked up. "Let's go sit down." They were in trouble together. "I'll make your drink. What would you like?"

"I haven't changed my drink."

"All right." She went to the other end of the kitchen, where she put her office blouse back on and made him a Cutty Sark and soda, thinking, how do I make this all right?, meaning the drink, partly, because she rarely made his drinks and sometimes forgot whether it was with soda or water, but really she meant the situation. How do I make this all right? As if she had done the damage. But she wanted so much for him not to feel bad, to help him feel better. She hated— hated—his parents. Both of them. His mother probably had nothing to do with the turndown, although with her you could never tell, but still, she hated them both.

She carried his drink and a vermouth for herself into the living room, where he lay on his Danish modern couch with his jacket off (he'd dropped it on the floor) and his tie and collar button undone, his head resting on one of the throw pillows. The couch was fairly skimpy, so she gave him his drink and sat on the narrow striped rug, facing him, wondering whether to hold his hand or leave him alone. He didn't look at her; he sipped his drink, staring at the wall. She decided to reach for his hand; he gave it to her. He said in a husky voice, "The future looks mighty bleak all of a sudden."

"That won't last, Steve. I won't let it last. You can't let it last."

"I couldn't imagine trying to get through this without you, but I wouldn't feel quite so lousy if you weren't around, since I was doing it for both of us."

"I fell in love with you before I even knew your plan existed, so it's not a problem for me, in that sense."

"I don't know what I'm going to do. I may have to quit." His voice was on the verge of quavering.

You can't quit, she wanted to say. We won't have enough money. "Can you tell me what happened, or would you rather wait?"

"What happened is everything I worried all along might happen but I didn't want to tell you and I didn't want to think about too much because I got so gung-ho. I started to concentrate on how they'd sound if they basically liked the idea instead of how they'd reject it, and that's what I kept in my head—how they'd accept the idea. What they did was what I knew they'd do—they flat-out turned it down in twenty seconds and said they wouldn't even consider it, out of the question."

She wondered if Jerry had been with him, to back him up. She couldn't ask him at the moment; she wasn't sure why the question occurred to her. He'd take it as an insult. "What was their excuse?" she asked.

"Excuse? They don't need an excuse."

"I mean what was their reason?"

"They have a dozen reasons. I could have predicted all of them. They have a great business going, why mess with it, the store's been around for almost seventy years, its name is golden, expansion would be cheapening. Cheapening was a big point. They don't want to borrow money, another big point. They don't want to lease space. They have a lot of pride in owning the building on Fifth, everything belongs to the family, they don't want anyone else fiddling with it. They ask who would manage a store in the suburbs, they wonder about security, who will the customers be, it's difficult for customers to make returns, they have to drive too far. Ira makes Westchester sound like Death Valley. They don't listen. I reminded them that people are moving to the suburbs in droves, and they all have cars. I told them the name of Farr is much too powerful to cheapen, it can only take its strength with it wherever it goes. I told them it's time for movement, it could be cautious, one store at a time. I said at least why don't you think about it. Here's what Ira said to that. He said, there's nothing to think about. When your father and I are dead, you can try and ruin the business. My father smiled at me a lot, like he's selling me the company. He said I showed initiative, imagination. My own father was trying to soft-soap me. He said it's time I became vice-president for public relations anyway. But I have to quit. How can I work there now? I'm sure they'll sell it someday anyway. They're not going to give me a chance to ruin their fucking business. There are a lot more important jobs than mine in the company, even if they make me a vice-president, but they're obviously not interested in putting me in any of them. Believe me, it's not sour grapes, but I'm not that interested in the toy business as a business. I'm interested in kids. Maybe they feel that. And maybe I don't belong there. But here I had a brilliant business idea, really farsighted, that excited me for the first time, that made me interested, and it was very carefully worked out, and they shot it down like I was some kind of jerk off the street."

Time to be calm. "What will you do?" A dumb question, since he'd already said he wanted to quit. But she didn't want him to quit.

"What I'd really like to do is go to medical school and make them pay for every penny of it. I've always wanted to be a doctor in my better self."

"I know."

"What do you think?"

"I don't know, Stevie. I don't think you can make a decision feeling this way."

"How would you feel if I ended up deciding to be a doctor? That I need a bigger challenge?"

"I'd go along with it, naturally." Easy to say. "I'd be married to you but living without you half the time, because you'd be so busy." She knew this from Bobbie Frost at work whose brother was a radiologist, and from Andy Propper. It got much worse after med school, when they were interns and residents. Everyone knew how hard doctors had to work. "I'm marrying you to be with you, not without you."

His head fell sideways toward her. He kissed her hand. "How was your day, incidentally?"

"Oh, it's very silly. They want to promote me."

"Hey! Tell me! At least there's some good news. When did this happen?"

"Today."

"Why didn't you call me?"

"Why didn't you call me about your news?"

"Because our meeting didn't even take place until quarter to five, and when I found out when they would see me, I didn't want to talk about it beforehand. Anyway, my news is bad news."

"My meeting was end of the day, too." Did being in love turn you into a liar?

The phone rang. Emily started getting up to answer it in the bedroom.

"Let it ring," Steve said. "I'll bet you it's my mother."

"Okay." She sat again. Since their engagement, Emily had sometimes answered his phone. Maybe she was being unfair to Mona in not insisting on answering. The phone stopped after seven and a half rings.

"Every day she asks me when will the families get together, she wants to know about a party, do we want a party, and I'm going to tell her we don't feel like it, we don't know when. Let them suffer."

"The families can't meet for the first time at the wedding, Steve."

"Why not? Why does there have to be a wedding? We'll get married secretly."

"Bunny's been so busy on it already."

"We'll invite her and your father. Ellen and Stan."

"In a way I'm glad we're not getting married 'til September."

"You mean so I'll forgive them by then?"

"The atmosphere might be more friendly."

"The atmosphere might be more friendly, but I can't tell you about forgiving. Ira I don't have to worry about. Ira's not forgivable. All my father did was say no nicely, but that doesn't mean I can ever forgive him. Maybe he just lets Ira do his dirty work. My father's sneaky. He's so quiet, you can't accuse him of anything except being too quiet."

Steve was sounding smart. "I love you." She decided to sit next to him on the couch even though there wasn't room. She made him make a little room for her.

"Tell me about your promotion, babes. We have a lot to think about. Maybe we should go out fancy and get drunk, for the hell of it."

"Not tonight. I'm wifing it in the kitchen." She hummed the beginning of "I've Come to Wive it Wealthily in Padua." *Kiss Me, Kate* was like a dictionary of songs for her. The phone rang again. Emily said, "I'm getting it. This is ridiculous." She scampered and slid, in her stockings, toward the bedroom. Why would she be so eager to answer the phone if it were Monanucleosis calling? Because being with Steve and his news made her nervous? Because she wanted to hold his family together? Because she loved hating Mona and loved hearing what came out of her mouth next? Yes to number three. Unfortunately, it might not be Mona on the phone. Or Mone on the phone. Sweet Moan. "Hello."

"That sounds like Emily. Is that Emily?"

"How are you, Mrs. Farkas?"

"That's nice. Lots of people who've known me forever don't recognize my voice like that. Darling, it's nice you're visiting Stevie this evening. Is he in the room?"

"He's in the living room."

"Don't tell him it's me. I'm sure he's told you the news."

Was there other news? "I assume you mean the meeting?"

"I wish my poor son weren't so restless. A lot of young men would give anything to have his job. Look, I'm heartbroken for him. I want you to do me a favor."

"What's that?"

"Be nice to him. Take care of him. There are times when a mother has to be a wife instead of a mother, so now you have to be the mother."

What am I supposed to do, nurse him? "Steve will be all right." Emily was enjoying sounding terse and grim.

"Jack wants him to know how important to the business Stevie is."

"I think he offered him a promotion."

"Stevie didn't indicate his acceptance. I'm sure he will, in his good time. I'm sure it would be the best thing for him."

"That's not exactly my department."

"You're right, darling. You're a very wise young lady not to get mixed up in it. I just wanted to find out how my son is and ask you to be—it's none of my business, but Stevie needs a lot of encouragement and support. He always talks about how he loves children so much. Don't we all? I should know, I lost a baby daughter. I just hope in your good time you two will have lots of children. Having one is wonderful, if he's as brilliant and imaginative as Stevie, but it can make everything so unpleasant sometimes. You count on one so much more."

Emily thought it safest and simultaneously most direct not to say a word. While listening to Mona, she had visualized Mona's huge white teeth turning to blood, so that she was talking with blood dribbling over her lips.

"I'm so grateful he's got you as a friend and wife-to-be through thick and thin. Do you think it's possible to just have one word with him? I won't take long."

"Let me see if he fell asleep. Hold on a sec." Emily flung the receiver onto the quilted bedspread and went out to the living room. "She wants to talk to you."

From the couch, Steve said, "I want you to tell her I'm just leaving to buy the paper. I'm out the door. I'll call her sometime later. Repeat: sometime later. Got it?"

"Got it." She returned to the bedroom. "He's just leaving to take a walk and he'll call you later. We'll probably have dinner soon."

"He should remember I do not make decisions concerning Farr, so he shouldn't take what happened out on me. I'm just the wife. He could spare a quick hello on his way downstairs. But I know he's not feeling so great, and I'll speak to him after dinner. I have to tell you, Emily, strange as it may seem, toys have never brought this family any happiness, none whatever. Some material benefits, but no happiness. We're not a happy family. But I know you and Steve are going to be happy. Thank God for that. You only live once. You might as well try to make the most of it."

"Listen, I have to finish getting dinner ready for when he comes back."

"I understand. Forgive me for interrupting. Jack's not being very talkative for once. I'm sure he'd like to talk to Stevie, because I know

how badly I want to myself. Jack has too much pride, and he thinks
his son won't talk to him, so he doesn't want to call. Inside, he probably
feels for Stevie as much as I do. It's hard to tell. In the meantime, it's
up to me to keep the lines of communication open. Please give Stevie
my love and tell him to call me later. Thank you so much, darling."

"You're welcome. 'Bye."

Everything Mona said sounded insincere. And yet you could pick
up that everyone seemed to disappoint her—Steve and her husband
each disappointed her in different ways. She wanted Steve to be
everything Jack wasn't, and Steve was everything Jack wasn't, but not
in the way Mona wished. Mona didn't think Steve was enough of a
"man," Emily suspected. Emily despised her even more now, but also,
without wanting to, felt a little sorry for her. In the living room again,
she told Steve, still languishing on the couch, what his mother had
said about toys and happiness, to cheer him up.

"Did she know it was funny?"

"I don't think so. It sounds like the beginning of *Anna Karenina,*
like a takeoff. Each unhappy family is unhappy in its own way? By
Leo Toystoy. Toystore."

Steve smiled, but weakly. He might not be sure what she was talking
about. "Do you want to keep me company in the kitchen while I make
dinner or stay out here 'til I call you?"

"To tell you the truth, babes, I'm suddenly so pooped I can't keep
my eyes open. Do you mind?"

She bent over and kissed his liquory mouth. Had he forgotten about
her job, or just couldn't face it, or wanted to wait 'til later to discuss
it? She wished he would hug her, pull her down, need her. Instead,
he took her hand again, like an invalid. "Your mother mentioned how
important your father thinks you are to the business."

"Yeah. It's crap."

She wouldn't pass on the rest of Mona's remarks to him. "Just reporting."

"Thanks for talking to her, though. I really appreciate it."

"If you're falling asleep, give me your glass so you don't spill it." It
was almost empty, but she took it anyway. "I'll call you in about fifteen
minutes."

"Thanks."

"Are you all right? You look pale." She put her hand on his forehead—slightly sticky, but no fever that she could tell—the first time
in her life she had done that to anyone but herself.

"Do I really look that bad?"

"You'll live." The couch was a stretcher. He would be carried out on it, with a bleeding ego, ego failure.

Steve actually had to go throw up during dinner. "Not your cooking," he said, when he came back from the bathroom. He said he hadn't had that much to drink, either. It was the drinks plus the day. He finished his potatoes, leaving the fish and peas, and asked for some tea. "I really want to hear about this promotion. It could be very important. What am I talking about? It *is* very important."

When he felt better, so did she. "I love you," she said, for the second time that evening. She told him what mixed feelings she had about the promotion because she had decidedly mixed feelings about publicity. She wanted to say that those feelings would undoubtedly have been overcome if she'd gone to work on his expansion plan, but she didn't see how it would help anything to say that now. She told him the job would be demanding. Daphne often had to stay after five, and there were the parties. Emily emphasized that Mrs. P. had insisted she discuss it with him.

"What about dough?" He looked amused, as if he knew she hadn't asked about the salary.

"I'm due for a regular raise now anyway. It will certainly go up when I start the new job, if we decide I should take it in the first place."

"Just tell me, did you ask what the money would be?"

"I was much too flustered. But I will, obviously. I don't expect to be doing it for nothing." She was flustered enough now so she feared she might give away that the offer had not been made that afternoon.

"Did you talk about what would happen if we had kids?"

"All taken care of." She got teary then, because she had an answer that would please him, even though she had no desire to have a child in the near future, which she'd already made clear to him, on their walk. "Mrs. Poplar said that once I'm established and everything they would be able to give me maternity leave. Not forever, but a leave. And I'll have a backup. Mrs. P. is a very progressive woman. She just wouldn't want me to have a baby right off the bat."

"Maybe I'll try to have one all by myself."

"I don't think that works very well. She meant us. Our child, Marcus Aurelius Farkas." She nearly said "Oops." Her silly grimace admitted the possibility that she'd goofed by making fun of his disgusting family name, while it also tried to disarm him.

To her amazement and joy, the conversation then turned so comical they ended up laughing hysterically. He started it off, by replying to

her Marcus Aurelius foolishness, "In school, they used to call me Carcass Farkas. But I wouldn't want to be responsible for naming my son
Carcass. It might do psychological damage."

"Freud Farkas? Fred? Frank? Franco. Phil. Ferdinand. Faith. Farley.
Flo. Phoebe."

"Sarcophagus?" he suggested.

"Brilliant! That's the best." Like the Timothy days, she thought.
"Sarco for short. How about Sarcastic Farkas? Remarkable Farkas.
Erich Maria Remarque Farkas. Harvey Farkas." She had lost all fear.
"Friar Farkas. Froggy Farkas. For a girl, Fleur Farkas. Lacrosse Farkas.
Carafe Farkas. Becky Farkas. Margo and Wells Fargo Farkas."

They went through Marco Polo Farkas, Sophocles Farkas, Focus
Farkas, Ficus Farkas, Phallic Farkas, Farrel Farkas, Ophelia Farkas,
Fandango Farkas, Fungus Farkas, Franz Farkas, Kafka Farkas, Kaka
Farkas, Oscar Farkas, Darcy Farkas, Sophie, Sophia, Sofa, Pasha and
Farouk Farkas, Pasta Farkas, Pastafazool Farkas, Farfetched Farkas,
Step'n Fetchit Farkas, Rufus Farkas, Bre'r Farkas, Frère Farkas, Frère
Jacques Farkas. She had never laughed so hard in her life. Sarcophagus
won first prize, Carafe second, and Pastafazool third. First and third
prizes were Steve's.

After they had breathed again for a while, she said, "So much for
the kids. Should I take the job?"

"Of course. You have to. We'll work out the snags."

"Seriously, I can say no. I don't know what to do about the honeymoon. The problem is when Daphne is leaving. But if I say no, the
problem is solved."

"You can't say no. As long as they're going to pay you what you're
worth and as long as they'll honor maternity leave."

"Right." If she said no, it would look terrible. Mrs. P. would definitely
disapprove of her. She loved Steve so much she could have conceived
right then, under their little dining table in the corner of the living
room. "I think you're the most wonderful man in the world. You get
better every day."

"Let me tell you, you picked the right day to say it. I just hope I
can take care of myself as well as we've taken care of you."

She saw a hand appearing in the future, like a puppeteer's hand
in an emergency, removing Steve's Farr plan and replacing it with
her promotion. But he should come first, she thought; she wanted
him to come first. "I assure you, we will. You deserve the best. You're
such a wonderful husband, I wish we were married right now."

Things got surprisingly calm for weeks. Emily had noticed before: matters always seemed to get set aright. She thought it could be true that her life tried to make up for her mother's loss—apologize in a way—by being generally in her favor.

She was spending more nights at his house; he was spending more time listening to his records, using a set of headphones when necessary. She didn't mind his closing himself off with the music, though, because he behaved so lovingly the rest of the time. One way he insisted on being difficult was obviously in order to irritate his mother (since it was impossible to irritate his father), but in the process he also put Emily slightly on the spot. He refused to be pinned down about the families getting together before the wedding. "But now your mother or Bunny asks me about it," Emily explained, "and I have to say I'll ask you again."

"Fine," he said. "You just keep doing that. I just pray my mother doesn't go and arrange it over our heads. I'll kill her."

Emily wasn't unsympathetic to Steve. Even when his stubbornness made her a bit nervous, she understood why he might feel entitled to hold something back from his parents. Her own father could undoubtedly have cared less about the families, and Bunny would have to accept the situation. Besides, she and Steve had spent a full evening at Daddy and Bunny's since the engagement, with Ellen and Stan, so at least there had been one dinner at each side's house.

Steve said about listening to his music that he liked to be carried away—it stopped him from thinking—but in the long run it would help him decide what to do about his future. So there he'd be, lost in Beethoven, and unusually sweet when he emerged. She found it sexy, both his listening and the after-listening, his being away and his coming back to her. The sad fact was that she didn't seem to be particularly musical. She'd hear some melody that moved her a lot, and she'd think, I'm too sensitive for music. The reason I don't love it is that deep down I love it too much. But that implied she didn't have the courage to endure pain, which was obviously completely untrue. So then she had to admit that she enjoyed music but certainly didn't need it the way Steve did. Her early crush on George hadn't happened because he was a musician per se. It was a matter of his being young, gorgeous, and famous in such a dramatic way, and so nice to her back then.

Of course there hadn't been much music at home; it was Mom who had played the piano on which her silvery photograph used to sit. Ellen had taken lessons without much interest for a while, it seemed to Emily, and she had done the same for a year. Steve said that in his

house there had been no music at all. No records, no books, just Crown
Derby. His father read inventory, his mother read plates. When Emily
remembered his telling her this, she remembered to be impressed
with him. She was sure Steve loved it that of the two of them, he was
the music-lover. And it did give him something over her. All she'd
ever collected was show albums. The theater is my music, she thought.
The theatah.

When Steve got engulfed in music, she read galleys or manuscripts
of forthcoming Partridge books, and reviewed files of publicity cam-
paigns. With Mrs. P.'s approval, Daphne had given Emily two projects
to handle by herself—an important Jewish cookbook and a picture
history of the World Series. Emily said to Steve it was a toss-up which
subject she knew less about.

Mrs. P. had hired a girl named Nina Brooks away from Partridge's
advertising agency to take over the duties Emily would be leaving behind. Nina looked like a twenties' flapper, but she was obviously bright,
as well as a little glib; she was also a year older than Emily, which
Emily sneakily liked. Nina and Emily discussed the possibility of Nina's
moving into Emily's apartment when Emily got married. Nina wanted
out of her roommate arrangement.

Steve had his eye on a two-bedroom apartment right in his own
building. He pointed out that it would give them decent closet space
and a den-study until they needed the room for child number one.

The wedding had been rescheduled for mid-August so Emily and
Steve could take a quick honeymoon—probably out west—before
Daphne left Partridge. Bunny had booked the Balmoral Suite at the
Victoria for the ceremony, reception, and lunch—seventy-five to eighty
guests—and her suggestion of the Reform rabbi from Granny's funeral
had been accepted all around. Husband and wife would spend their
first night at the hotel. Emily had settled on an ivory peau de soie
dress from Bonwit's. (She told Steve it was scarlet.) Her mother's wedding dress had disappeared years ago. Ellen hadn't worn it for her
own wedding; it would have been too small on her anyway, but it
hadn't been around even then. Perhaps Mom was buried in it.

The wedding lay somewhere ahead of Emily and off to her right
(as the Victoria was situated in relation to her office)—an opulent
event shining in a gilded heavenly-worldly way, smelling of flowers,
liquor, perfume: something thrilling being prepared in her honor.
Partly out of gratitude that Grandpa Gus, at least, would be present,
Emily had stopped imagining the wedding taking place in idyllic Newbury. But at times she would mention to Steve how much she wanted

him to see Newbury. Newbury was the summer of her entire past.
She'd been lonely up there at times, and it was where she'd learned
Mom had died, but being lonely in Newbury sure did beat her one
summer away at camp and her summer in summer stock.

Granny and Grandpa were there forever, Mom at the beginning,
Ellen for a while (Ellen liked camp), Daddy as a treat on weekends
(usually parts of weekends), local friends, occasional visiting friends
from school, guests and relatives of Granny and Grandpa. Emily gar-
dened with Granny, she picked berries, rode horseback, biked, swam,
made ice cream, read, went to the movies, to the Newbury Fair. The
comfort, beauty, safety of the place was worth whatever loneliness she
had felt, by far. Over the summers, she had been baked in a sunny
green loaf.

In fact, she recalled her loneliness as a kind of excitement. Her
mother had died, but her mother had left her alive and eager to learn
what would happen to herself. In the early mornings in Newbury,
she'd stand in her tiny rectangular bedroom in the rear of her grandparents' house, watching, through the summer screen of her little
window, the back lawn as long as a field and, beyond it, the upward-
sloping meadow. On gray mornings just as much as on the bright
mornings of dandelion-colored haze, the view meant to her, when she
was a girl, that her life was getting ready and, someday not far off,
would begin. Everything waited. The squeaking of the early morning
birds decorated the edges of the silence. The lonely bushes, trees, and
boulders on the distant rising meadow looked to her as if they were
pretending to ignore each other, but were actually discussing and deciding her future. The silence included their conversation; the distance
made their conversation inaudible to her. As she breathed the morning
air, along with a whiff of the metal screen, the air became a thrill in
her chest. She would tighten her body, both to hold onto the excitement, it seemed, and to prevent its spreading. If it spread, it would
be over.

She had become much too busy at Partridge, in any case, to day-
dream about her wedding day, no less about not getting married in
Newbury. Aside from breaking in Nina Brooks and continuing to do
a lot of her own work, she accompanied Daphne to lunches, interviews,
and other events involving Partridge authors. Once, on her own, she
presided over and paid the bill at an interview-lunch at Respighi's for
a reporter from *Life* magazine and Hal Comneck, the World Series
book author. She went to a book-and-author lunch at the Plaza that
neither Mrs. P. nor Daphne could make. She went to an enthralling

ladies' lunch (her least favorite activity, but her most entertaining experience so far in publishing) at a synagogue in Plainfield, New Jersey, with Sondra Fertig, her important-cookbook author, at Sondra's insistence.

In the mornings, she couldn't imagine being able to do such grown-up things as she was being called on to do that day. But then she did them, and almost all the time people were friendly, grateful, or at the worst, manageable—manageable by her.

On Sunday, August the twelfth, at one o'clock in the afternoon, Emily Jane Weil and Steven Elliot Farkas were married by Rabbi Felix Roth in the Balmoral Suite of the Victoria Hotel, with Jill Strauss as maid of honor and Gerald Goetz as best man, before Lee and Bunny, Grandpa Gus, Ellen, baby Janet, and Stan, Mona and Jack; family friends, aunts, uncles, and cousins from each side, including Helen and Larry Kornbluth and even callous Uncle Ira and his third wife, Matty; the Senns and the Streeters from Newbury, except for Don, who was in the Marines; Byron and Iris; three old friends of Steve's— Mark Franklin, Tony Green, and Rich Gottesman—and an old girl-friend, Denise Feibush, with her idiotically friendly Dale Carnegie husband Chuck.

Emily had wished it made sense to invite Timothy (though he hadn't called her again), and even Andy Propper. Not only Andy, but others from the olden days, like Sue Freund, Juliet Bibby from way back, and people from the Greenway—Dwight Hermann and her crush, Carey Ames, Thom Blake, on leave for the ceremony from Sing Sing, surly, handcuffed, accompanied by two guards. (Also George Koenigsberg, if he were handcuffed to Thom.) Ah, fame!

The Partridge representatives were Wilma (with Gifford); Dunc (still so obligingly friendly for someone so important and formidable), again no Mrs.; Bobbie Frost from Contracts; everyone from Publicity, led by Mrs. P. (Her husband, Alexander, a famously obscure person who did unknown important work that took him to Washington all the time, wasn't expected and didn't appear.) Then there were Daddy's two closest associates, Lionel Wiener (with Mrs. Wiener) and Ben Harlow, and his secretary Nancy Troop and her husband Les; his bridge friends, the Wrights; a dozen employees from Farr, with wives or husbands ("The Madding Crowd from Farr," Helen Kornbluth called them, because they drank and danced so boisterously); Margaret, hugging Emily at the reception and weeping; Gretta from the Farkas household, and Elma from Grandpa Gus's, acting almost like Grandpa's nurse instead of his housekeeper.

Emily had little to do with Helen Kornbluth in the course of the wedding afternoon; from the beginning, however, Emily was conscious of Helen's presence, resentfully so, despite her understanding that the resentment had to be unfair in a way. She could not help remembering Helen's ultrarefined face intruding on her mother's in the nutty fantasy last June at the end of the great night with Steve, what she'd come to think of as a milestone night in her love. Now here was the same too-memorable face at the wedding, as if Helen were a party-crasher instead of especially welcome, as she was supposed to be. Emily was certain, based on experience, that she would have been able to ignore her mother's absence, at least for most of the day, if Helen weren't here, or to miss her mother as she chose to and when she chose to instead of being forced to miss her by somebody else who hadn't the slightest idea that she was an unsatisfactory substitute. It seemed to Emily, much as she could see how illogical the idea was, that if Mom were here, Helen wouldn't be.

It didn't help that Helen's unusual pink, gray, and white silk print dress (beautiful with the gray hair and eyes, but why did she always have to wear the hair like an arts-and-crafts instructor, with the braids wound on the head?) was conspicuous, a performance by itself, though in fairness, if compared it had rivals. And the "madding crowd" remark irked her, not because it was snobbish toward the Farr people (Steve hadn't minded or hadn't paid attention), but because it made Helen appear awkward, sophisticated but out of place, too literary. Still, the woman had done nothing seriously wrong; she'd barely done anything.

At some point, Emily and Steve encountered Helen crossing the dance floor (on her way to the ladies' room or to them?). She said, "When you get back from your honeymoon, I'm going to call to invite you to the studio. Mona's told me how busy you've both been. It's one of my major sources of pride, as a mother, not to interfere."

"Oh don't worry about that," Steve said. "It's a date."

Emily wondered if Helen would know from Mona about Steve's business problem and her own promotion at Partridge.

Then Helen said to Emily, "And I hope someday soon we'll have a chance to pick up our conversation where we left off at Mona and Jack's. I haven't forgotten it."

"Definitely," Emily said. "Neither have I."

For the rest of the afternoon, at moments when Emily happened to glance at Helen unintentionally, Helen was already looking at her, it seemed, involved with her, alert to her.

When Helen and Larry departed, Larry, true to character, acted like someone who wanted you to know he went places in order to leave them. Helen said to Emily (Steve was elsewhere at the moment), "Have a wonderful trip. We'll be speaking."

"After we get back." Emily jerked forward to embrace Helen, thereby apologizing for wishing she didn't have to embrace her.

"All the best," Helen said. She kissed Emily with confident affection on each cheek. "And you deserve the best."

Emily didn't analyze what Helen's words might mean or not mean. Once Helen had left, she put her out of her mind.

After the formalities were over, the immediate families, plus Jill S. and Jerry Goetz, drank more champagne in Emily and Steve Farkas's hotel room. At one point, Emily and Jill hugged hard. Emily had already thanked Jill at least twice for introducing her to Steve; she wanted to say something else, something about how Jill had always been so important to her that Steve was now Jill to her. But the thought wasn't really accurate, and also it seemed slightly insulting to both Steve and Jill. What came out, with tears, was, "I can't believe we're actually still here together, today, in this life! I honestly don't know what I would have done without you. You were always there."

Jill patted the back of Emily's head and said, "Don't be silly, I love you." They hugged again.

Emily wiped her eyes. "You've got to come to dinner the instant I get back. We've really been so out of touch this year I can't stand it, and it's ridiculous. It's all my fault."

"Thanks, sweetie. I'd love to. Maybe I'll seduce Jerry Goetz tonight, Emileeee. What do you think?"

"As long as you're not drunk, I think it's—I don't know. Just be careful." Emily laughed at her own motherly-sounding advice. Jill laughed too. Jill, in her fairly unflattering pastel blue chiffon dress and her short blonde hair was sort of young-dowdy, not exactly flowering. She looked old-fashioned. She just didn't do enough with herself. In another way, though, she did an awful lot, Emily had to admit. What were you going to be a social worker for if you didn't deal with real-life, adult difficulties? Jill would just go on being more and more mature and responsible.

The gathering didn't last long. Emily and Steve were getting up early the next morning for a flight to Los Angeles, where they would stay for two days at the Beverly Hills Hotel, then two days at the Malibu beach house of Sylvia and Bert Cooper, old friends of Steve's parents Steve happened to be particularly fond of, before taking what everyone said was the unforgettably spectacular drive up the coast to San Francisco.

There'd been some discussion about going to San Francisco. Emily had explained to Steve that it was from San Francisco in March 1941 that her mother had left the U.S. for Shanghai, on a ship to Honolulu. From Honolulu she traveled by plane, on the first Pan American Clipper to cross the Pacific, stopping at Wake, Guam, Manila, all those war islands, but nine months before the attack on Pearl Harbor. Emily finally decided, with no pressure whatever from Steve, who had substitute suggestions—Las Vegas, the Grand Canyon—that she definitely wanted to go to San Francisco. She said to him, "That town is big enough for my mother and me. I probably won't even think about it once I'm there." The city was supposed to be unique, varied, and romantic, with great food, and they'd be having sex in the lap of luxury at the Mark Hopkins hotel. San Francisco wasn't for her to brood about, but for her and Steve to love and remember together. He would admire her for not being disturbed by being there.

PART
FIVE

CHAPTER THIRTEEN

His Surprise

Steve's interest in going to medical school was like a symptom that turned into something worse while being ignored. Precisely what had never happened to her (in the sense that nothing she'd ever worried about, on or in her body, had become serious) had now happened to her through her husband.

Without telling her beforehand, he'd seen a dean at New York University about taking the undergraduate science courses you needed even to apply to med school. "I can start next summer. The only problem with summer is it's a real bitch. Twelve weeks, nine to five, because of labs, four days a week, plus preparations at home at night. They recommend doing it in two full academic years instead, which means I couldn't even start until a year from now. So I may take one chem course next summer, to start the ball rolling. At least the school's right nearby." He didn't crack a smile. In fact, he looked excessively serious.

"That's thrilling, that it's so convenient."

"Your enthusiasm overwhelms me."

She gave him a look and went into the bathroom. She needed the excuse of the bathroom not to say anything. She didn't know what to say, and she didn't want to talk anyway. She ran water in the bathroom sink like a teenager covering up the sound of her peeing. During their gorgeous honeymoon, Emily thought she'd noticed that their sex life was getting even better, not more exciting, which it couldn't be, but closer, deeper, mellower, more solid, more embedded. Now, just a few days after their return, he was dropping a slow bombshell on her head without seeming to have the slightest idea he was doing it.

They'd just been lying on their bed (they were supposed to move to the bigger place on the fourteenth floor in a month—if she went with him, she thought), half-undressed, with a quiz show on the TV in the corner, when he'd made his little announcement. Everything had been normal and happy, cozy. He'd gone to a hamburger joint on his way home from work, without seeming to mind at all; she'd had to go to Hal Comneck's World Series book party at Toots Shor's. She was amazed how fast feelings changed, how instantly crushed she'd felt, hopeless.

But now she washed and dried her face because she'd thought of something to say to him, and she came out. He wasn't in the bedroom. "Steve?"

"Out here. Kitchen."

She found him making a drink.

"What are you doing that for?"

"No reason. I felt like it. Want one?"

Not yet, she thought. "Are you coming back in?"

"I'm not going to sleep in the kitchen."

She imagined they were getting divorced. Her head felt queer. There were only bones in it, exhausted bones, no brains. The idea of his going to medical school felt to her like their death, the end. She had no spirit all of a sudden. She said to him what she had thought to say before leaving her bathroom sanctuary. "Would you like me to quit my job? I'll quit. We just got married." Her throat filled with sadness. "If you're resenting my job, I assure you, I'd much rather be married than work, if that's the choice." Then something else occurred to her. "By the way, if you go to medical school and pre-medical school, I assume that means you'd quit Farr, right? Who would pay for it? How do we live until you get your degree, and until you start practicing?" Did he even know what kind of doctor he wanted to be? "I'm sorry if I sound materialistic, but I just wondered."

"Obviously that all has to be worked out. It sounds sensible, not materialistic." He stood in his brown socks with his legs crossed at the ankles, sipping his scotch and soda. His shirtsleeves were rolled up to his elbows. Ready to operate.

She thought: I would really like to talk now, but how is talking going to solve the problem? "Do we have to talk standing here?"

He said, "I have to discuss the finances with my parents, obviously. I'd like them to pay for school, frankly. You'll continue working. Soon you may be making enough to support both of us." He tried to grin. "Or I may borrow some of the money from them to help keep us going and pay them back when I can. I have my investments and stuff. It can be done one way or another."

"Do you know what kind of doctor you want to be?" He was someone she had just met at a cocktail party.

"I'd be glad to tell you if you're interested."

"That's ridiculous. Of course I'm interested. That's why I married you. But that doesn't mean I have to love everything you do. How do you expect me to react? You didn't tell me anything in advance, as usual, and I don't know what it's going to mean. Do you? It's not exactly what I visualized, medical school." Nor would she be able to stand it. She knew.

"I don't expect to be an absent husband, you know. I just got married too. I happen to love you. Also, I'm not planning to open a chain of whorehouses. I want to be a doctor. That's supposed to be good, not evil. And it's not going to be as bad as you seem to think, anyway." He poured some drink into his mouth. All very casual and making light of it.

She found it a strain to raise her voice. Her voice sounded sick to her. "I didn't say it was evil, did I? The point is, it's not what I married. I didn't marry medical school. And I resent your taking me by surprise this way, I really do. How do you know how bad or not bad it's going to be? How do you know how bad I think it's going to be? You talk about this as if you're going away for a few weeks. Two years of pre-med because you never took any science courses?" How did he know he could even pass them? "Four years of medical school, then all the shit that comes after that?"

"The shit that comes after is called internship and residency."

"I know what comes after." She was beside herself, she realized. She wanted to get out of the house so her bones wouldn't break through her skin.

"Believe me, I'm sorry I'm making you so upset. It's not what I expected, frankly."

"What did you expect?" She wished she could say something violent.

"How did I act when you got your promotion?"

"How can you possibly compare them? What's the matter with you? It doesn't take fifty years of training to do what I do. I'm already trained. A few times I haven't been home in time to eat with you or cook for you. You think that's the way it's going to be with you? You'll hardly be around at all and when you are you'll be studying or sleeping. And anyway, I just offered to quit my job. I'll stay home twenty-four hours a day if I have to, gladly."

"That's hardly necessary. When we talked about it in the summer, by the way, after my family gave me the shaft, you said you'd go along with it."

She hadn't believed he'd meant it. She'd never believed he'd meant it. She'd suspected it was a vague romantic desire. People wished they could play the violin, too. "I also said, if you recall, that I was marrying you to be with you, not to be without you." They were still standing at opposite ends of the kitchen rectangle, appropriately. She couldn't believe what was happening, and she couldn't see a way out of what was happening.

"If I'm so miserable where I am, and I've set my sights on something that would make my life definitely very worthwhile, what am I supposed to do?"

"No one's asking you to be miserable, obviously. It has to be fixed. I must admit, I thought I could help make your life a little worthwhile. My life certainly wouldn't be worthwhile without you."

"You're being silly now. You know I couldn't live without you, either. I'm doing this partly because I thought you'd respect me for it, I swear. I was doing it partly for you. And you're not unhappy at your job. I am. I'm really miserable."

"Then you should absolutely get another job, I agree. I may not be unhappy, but it's not my life. My life is my life, not my job. I guess I enjoy the challenge, and it was gratifying to be promoted, but I honestly don't think I'd have trouble giving up the job itself. I'd be a bit embarrassed, but I could certainly live without it. I was prepared not to take it in the first place, Steve. I asked your permission. I certainly didn't take it and then tell you about it. On the contrary." Had he tricked her, telling her to take the promotion so he could spring medical school on her later? Was she going to get an annulment? Charles Wright, Daddy's bridge friend, was a big divorce lawyer. She shook her head slowly.

"What?"

"Nothing. I don't know what's going on." She had started to choke up. She didn't want him coming near her, so she turned her back. She couldn't stand there with her back to him, so she walked on into the bedroom. She put her shoes back on. She put on a beige sweater. She didn't know what to do. She had to get out. Now, just as she had been standing in the kitchen entrance, he was standing in the bedroom doorway.

"Are you leaving?" he asked.

She wouldn't look at him, and if she answered him, he would be able to tell she was struggling not to cry. She decided to pass him, hoping he wouldn't try to stop her. He turned sideways to let her through. She walked by him with her eyes scrunched so she wouldn't cry and so she couldn't see him in case he was smiling in some embarrassed way. She went to the closet by the front door, pulled her suit jacket off the hanger, and left the apartment, letting the door slam.

Outside the door, she started to cry; once she got to the elevator, she had to wait before pressing the button, so she wouldn't appear in the lobby hysterical. In the meantime, she had to hope Steve wouldn't be stupid enough to follow her into the corridor, and that no neighbors would happen to come out of their apartments or come up in the elevator. Then she realized that she didn't have her key. If she rang the doorbell, she'd be like a child who had failed to run away from home. She pressed the elevator button, thinking, the hell with the doorman, she'd rush by him. It was all Steve's fault anyway. The doorman would imagine she was running home to mother.

She walked down Fifth Avenue rapidly. She wasn't used to taking pensive strolls. Even in Newbury, where it would have made sense, she'd never taken a walk in order to think. She didn't know how she thought, anyway, or if she thought at all, in the sense of figuring out private things.

She had judged Steve all the time before marrying him. While she'd judged, her feelings had developed into love (or sexual desire, though she couldn't believe she didn't really love him). She hadn't anticipated him, though. She'd looked forward to everything so much, she always did, but she hadn't foreseen. She hadn't thought hard about what their life might be like. She'd expected everything to stay the same indefinitely—day after day, night after night of excitement and comfort. She'd ignored his hints about med school. But it was his mistake (mistake wasn't the word for it) not to discuss his plans with her beforehand. And then to tell her the outcome so lightly. Incredible! She wouldn't have reacted nearly so strongly if he'd included her.

She had to get him to see what bothered her. But then would he change his mind? She seemed to be thinking that if he admitted he'd made a mistake in the way he'd told her, he'd admit the whole idea was a mistake. He had to change his mind, but also be happy. She had to make him happy. She'd help him figure out what to do with his life, sit down with him, help him find a new career. She'd spend all the time he wanted doing that. She started back to the building.

The whole thing was impossible. If he passed his pre-med requirements and then got into some medical school that wasn't in New York City, would he expect to move to Podunk? Was she supposed to come along to Podunk with him? But none of that made any difference. No matter where he might end up going, in effect he was leaving her behind and behaving as if he didn't understand why she should be so upset. She wouldn't mind if he went to grad school, as long as it was in history or something. He liked history. Political science. He and Ellen could take political science together. He wanted to be president. He'd said so on their first date. Or law school. Three finite years. A compromise. That was it. People always said marriage meant compromise.

Steve answered the doorbell in the green-and-gold silk robe from Sulka she had splurged on before the wedding. It made him look like an emperor, and at the moment she was sorry she'd bought it. "We've got to talk more sensibly," she said.

"You're absolutely right. How about in bed?"

Did "You're absolutely right" mean he'd reconsidered? "I don't know about bed."

"You decide where. Just so we can relax."

She didn't know about relaxed, either, but she'd have to try. She went into the bedroom ahead of Steve. "We might as well go to bed," she said.

"Don't worry. I'd be scared to lay a hand on you."

So, each on an elbow, at a distinct distance from one another, in the lamplight from Steve's night table, they waited to resume talking. Steve was wearing fresh light-blue pajamas. Her white nightgown wasn't fresh, but what did it matter? Maybe, without their knowing it, this was to be their final married conversation.

"What did you think when I left?" she asked.

He didn't answer her. He stared at the sheet. His lips were stretched by his hand, which supported his head at the left cheek. Less than three weeks after getting married, they'd called a conference on their marriage. His lips slipped away from his hand, tightening up sharply, the way she loved, when he looked his smartest; but tonight the look was cold, not necessarily colder than she felt, but colder than she wanted him to be. He drew his head away a little. "We're supposed to support each other," he said. His eyes were on the sheet; his expression seemed haughty toward the sheet.

She gulped, hoping that from his angle he wouldn't notice. "How are you supporting me when you don't tell me something that affects my life one hundred percent, or more than one hundred percent, until after you've done it? And why do you think your doing something like that would dispose me to support you?"

"I don't know. I suppose I really knew you'd disapprove." His face swiveled up to her. They stared at each other, she thought, as if they were both realizing that they weren't remotely in love with each other. Then he looked down again. "The only way I can explain it is that it's something I had to do. And if I'd told you I was going to do it and you'd been upset beforehand, I would have been betraying you too. Either way is wrong. I made a mistake. But I'm damned if I don't and damned if I do. And the timing's been against us all around, to say the least. How could I know what to expect with the business thing?"

"I'm your wife, Steve. None of what you say means you can walk over someone like that."

"I admit, I made a mistake. An inevitable mistake."

"Then why did you say before that I said I'd go along with it? If you thought I'd go along with it, why didn't you tell me what you were planning to do?"

"We've been over this already. You said yourself that you were marrying me to be with me, not without me. You reminded me. Before. Remember? 'Going along with it' isn't my idea of an endorsement. I just said a minute ago that I must have known you'd disapprove. You wouldn't make a very good lawyer."

She could swear that before she'd left the house he'd used her having said she'd go along with it as meaning it hadn't been necessary for him to consult her about his plans, and now he was using it to mean he'd been scared to consult her. If he was being sneaky on purpose, she had to admit he was also being very smart. But she hoped he didn't know he was contradicting himself.

"I think you would make an excellent lawyer," she said. "I thought of that on my walk. If you went to law school, it would be a lot of studying, but it would be over. We could look ahead and know it would be over, and also you wouldn't be stuck in a hospital all the time."

"There's only one trouble. I don't have the slightest interest in being a lawyer."

She suddenly got the idea that even though he didn't know it, he was doing all this to kick her in the face, to hurt her, that that was the sole reason he was doing it, not because he yearned to go to medical school, but to hurt her instead of his parents, because he couldn't hurt his parents, didn't know how to, or because they were incapable of being hurt by him. "I was just trying to think of things on my walk you could do that would fulfill you and wouldn't wreck me. It's obviously not fair that you should stay where you're unhappy."

"I really feel I'm wasting my life. I've fallen into this job with the company, the public relations part, in fact I pretty much made it up myself, but they did all right without it all the years before I got there. The advertising side could start being more interesting now that TV's coming on stronger, but my heart isn't in it. They smile at me at the office, but if I wasn't the owner's son, I'd be working somewhere else. Do you really want to live with someone like that? I don't say they're carrying me, but I'm not imperative, either. I gave it a real stab with my proposal. It could have made a real difference, something big that was mine. I was even a little scared they might say yes, but at least I had self-respect when it was in the planning stage. I'm not going to let them take my dignity away. That's that. When I think about being a doctor," he went on, "they have nothing to do with it. But my fantasy is always with you admiring me so much that it's more than worth it to you. You love me for it." He looked friendlier. He was appealing to her. "You're my muse."

"Doctors don't have muses. They have nurses."

"This one has a muse."

"How can you be so sure it's the right thing to do?"

"I guess because I've learned so definitely what the wrong thing is for me."

"Suppose you don't get into medical school after your two years of pre-med? Or suppose you get into someplace in Montana?"

"That's called looking on the bright side. At least I'd be able to say I tried. I don't anticipate failure. I expect to be good enough to get in anywhere. I was very good in science in high school."

"Don't you ever think about how long it's going to take?"

"If a goal is important enough, then it's worth it, the way I see it. There's nothing wrong with someone having a goal, you know."

"I never found out what kind of doctor you want to be." Why bother asking? Politeness. Her question sounded so sullen she didn't see how it could pass as polite. She must be determined, she thought, to let him know how skeptical she was, but in the thin disguise of interest.

"Sometimes I think pediatrician or a specialty associated with children. Or an obstetrician, maybe. But it's not just kids. It's medicine. I have these fantasies of being involved, being called on in emergencies, knowing what to do and doing it on the spot. Is there a doctor in the house. I'm not kidding. I've got this great needed skill, saving lives. Not the goddamn toy business. Do you mind if I make a suggestion?"

She shrugged. "Go ahead."

"That we let this rest a few days? Nothing dramatic is going to happen for months, anyway."

It had already happened. Didn't he see? And what his suggestion meant was that over time she might change her mind, not that he would change his. "Fine." She resented it that he made her feel selfish and foolish, and that he didn't really see her side at all. She resented her resentment. "I'm going to try to go to sleep." How was she going to sleep?

Raising his eyebrows, Steve brought his head close. She gave him a cold, shrimpy kiss. Was medical school worth a cold wife? Steve didn't make a sarcastic remark or face. He said goodnight in a straightforwardly warm tone of voice she couldn't possibly have achieved right now either as herself or as him. Where did he get the confidence to act as if nothing had happened? She said goodnight anyway, sounding businesslike at best; if she had said nothing, he might think she was indulging in self-pity and trying to get his attention. He had moved back to his side and turned off the night-table lamp. He lay with his back to her, the way he usually went to sleep when they hadn't had sex just before.

The only bedlamp was on his side. He controlled the bedlamp. He controlled her. She had given up her name. She had given up her comfortable name for his ugly name. Steve's announcement was her punishment for having allowed herself to become Emily Farkas. The name itself was the real problem, of course. If her maiden name had been Farkas and she had married a Steve Weil, everything would still be fine. What on earth was she doing in this person's bed? She imagined that she must be learning to think the way Mrs. Poplar talked, ever so urbane and above it all. Unfortunately, it didn't stop her from feeling completely pointless.

She slept for a total of maybe four hours. Though she and Steve never talked much when they went about their early-morning routines, this morning the lack of talk had significance in it that made her throat heavy. Steve did kiss her goodbye (she left earlier than he did), but with his face sticking out challengingly, almost seeming to make fun of the terrible situation.

In the pretty September morning, she thought she started to feel better, her mind turning to work and whether she should walk all the way uptown or take the bus. She started to float out of the ropes Steve had thrown around her. The problems were in the apartment. All she had to do was not think about them.

The early part of the morning at work went as usual. In the eleven o'clock meeting, however, in Mrs. P.'s office, with Mrs. P., Pat Crane ("The Jester of the Midwest") and the advertising director, Brewster Day, planning the intensive campaign for Mr. Crane's *Leave the Cashews for Me*, she discovered herself to be in such a foul mood that she wondered how it could help but show. She had to make an effort not to seem grim, also to stay awake. No matter how many folks loved Pat Crane, and even though he was twice her age, all she could think (like Raskolnikov!) was that he took up space, that he had never had a thought of his own in his life except to use little anecdotes people sent to him, especially cute situations kids got into. (Maybe Steve would like him.) And he was a millionaire. A tall, skinny millionaire with a geeky Adam's apple, thin, pale hair, chipmunkish front teeth that, if they were longer, would be the fangs of a moron like Mortimer Snerd. Du-u-uh. He giggled instead of laughing. His jacket made her think of succotash.

The meeting consisted mostly of Mrs. P. giving instructions Emily wrote down, concerning Mr. Crane's appearances at bookstores, lunches, and on radio programs, in many cities, to be coordinated with newspaper ads, Brewster Day's department. Mr. Crane made some suggestions and incessant, unbelievably feeble puns, which stirred Emily's heart to rage, though she noticed that neither Mrs. P. nor Brewster Day laughed aloud at them, either. Mrs. P. employed a clever smile that looked, every time, unprepared for the extraordinary brilliance of the joke and also seemed to put the blame for her restraint on herself. So Emily didn't have to laugh, either. She winced, head down, while writing her notes. She asked a few questions, just to demonstrate her interest.

When the meeting broke up, Brewster Day escorted Mr. Crane to the men's room on the way to the lunch the Partridge brass were throwing for the Jester of the Midwest at the Brussels restaurant. (Mrs. P. had asked Emily to come too. She was glad to be going, curious. Dunc went there about twice a week. Daphne had said it looked like the first-class dining room on a small but supremely elegant ship.) Mrs. P. held Emily back for a moment in her office door to say, in her svelte manner, "I'm getting such glowing reports about you from lots of people here and there that I'm positively proud of myself."

"Thanks. I'm—thanks." She wanted to kiss Mrs. P. She wanted to tell Mrs. P. that Pat Crane enraged her because he was a rich and famous nothing. Mrs. P. would say, "We'd be out of business by teatime if everyone we published were Proust." Emily had heard her say such things. She wanted to talk with Mrs. P., the mother of two sons, about

Steve. She had to find someone to talk to, to talk to her, to help her figure out what to do, how to behave, how right she was and how wrong she was in her reaction to Steve's news. Not someone who would be too easily on her side, as she suspected Helen Kornbluth would be.

At lunch, in his boyish midwestern voice, Pat Crane told anecdotes about celebrities he knew; these did produce laughter among the brass. Emily, the little girl at the table, felt outside at the same time she felt privileged. She mostly kept her mouth shut, not that she was asked to open it much. She had only one vermouth and one glass of wine. Her compromise with the laughter was a full smile. As far as she could determine, the anecdotes were not nearly as significant as Pat Crane or his listeners thought they were, but because they concerned Eisenhower or Doris Day or Bishop Sheen or Bing Crosby, she stuck her ears to the stories as if she were being permitted to hear the world's secrets and must take advantage of the opportunity. Pat Crane completely ignored her; she felt he had done the same in the office, though her note-taking could have prevented her from judging accurately. Now she found his ignoring her in his favor. It didn't seem to occur to this jerk to notice her, to try to include her or please her. His superior air might be misplaced, but at least he was capable of acting superior.

During some of the lunch, she fantasized about each person at the table listening to her on the subject of Steve's announcement. She thought it was sort of pathetic of her but not that strange, since she had married Steve to talk to, never expecting he would be a problem she'd need to talk to others about. If she asked Pat Crane for advice, he'd say, "Your hubby wants to be a doc? My uncle's a doc. He'd be successful, but his waiting room can only hold four dogs and one horse at a time."

Why couldn't she be big enough to let Steve try to do what he said he wanted to do? Had she been mature when she was little, and now turned immature? Tune in tomorrow. Why shouldn't she be able to get used to Steve's going to medical school when she had gotten used to so much worse in her life? Or was the problem that she worried no one would give her credit for being a medical student's wife. She'd always thought of herself as so strong. She'd often heard herself boasting about her strength in her mind. But maybe she only felt strong because she supposed the world was silently giving her credit for being strong. Motherless equaled strong. Maybe all her life she'd actually been weak. Her sudden sense now of her overwhelming weakness didn't mean the weakness was new. She'd felt weak at times, naturally, but never like this. She'd felt too ordinary, too weird, superficial, incompetent, over-inhibited, naive, emotionally stingy, standoffish, but never everything all at once. There were so many strands combined in her weakness at the moment, she wished her weakness were strength.

Then, for the rest of the day, despite having loads to do, she couldn't get out of her head the picture of Steve as dumb, the kind of person you catch with his finger up his nose. The kind of person who insists on lifting something much too heavy, then drops it, breaks it. She thought of the rosiness on his cheeks as marks of naiveté, like decals of blind, destructive innocence and ignorance. It was funny. The reason she imagined him as being dumb was that he wanted to do something that would require him to be extremely smart. Did she really think he couldn't do it? Did she want to protect him against failure? Against success?

Even with grocery shopping, she got home before Steve did, which pleased her until she began to worry where he was. On the other hand, she didn't know what they would talk about or how they would talk about it once he did get home, so when she finally heard his key, its crinkling made her shiver inside. He came into the kitchen while she was washing the lettuce. He said "Hiya"—no "babes"—and put his hands on her shoulders from behind her. She twisted her head so he could kiss her cheek. "Good day?" he asked.

"Yup." Sometimes he pressed himself against her backside sexily when he came home. If he had done that this time, she would have taken a glass from the dishrack and smashed it in the sink. She heard him at the cabinet where he kept the liquor. She wanted a drink now herself, but she didn't want to join him or ask him to make her one. She turned very quickly, without his observing, to see him opening the scotch. If he couldn't become a doctor, he'd be an alcoholic. She washed the two tomatoes. After she washed them, there'd be nothing to wash but the two potatoes. She heard him getting the icetray. She moved away from the sink long enough for him to extract his ice cubes. He didn't ask her if she wanted a drink. She forced herself to tell him about idiot Pat Crane and her fancy lunch with the bigwigs. She felt like her own ventriloquist. "How was your day?" She made her voice dry, to counteract the friendliness of her question.

"About what you'd expect. I worried about you. I thought a lot about you."

Without enough warning even to try to control herself, Emily began crying, making a giveaway wet gasp.

He came to her side. "Are you all right?"

She covered her face, crying harder, wondering why he'd asked that stupid question, and left the kitchen. She went into the bathroom, once again. If she were to lie down on the living-room couch or on the bed, he might try to stroke her or hold her. She stood shuddering at the bathroom sink, with the door shut, in the dark, waiting for the crying, which sounded so much to her like a little girl's, to ease. Letting the problem rest a few days was really a brilliant idea of his, almost as smart as wanting to be a doctor. If he had such dumb ideas, what kind of doctor would he make? His patients would all get sicker. When she came out of the bathroom, although she had technically stopped crying, she could feel herself vibrating with leftover tears.

From the bedroom, Steve said, "Come in here." He was sitting with his drink in his big butterscotch leather armchair. She wanted nothing so much as to get out of the apartment, never return, disappear. She flopped onto the bottom of the bed on her stomach, facing Steve. Her face felt uncomfortably complicated, like more than one face at once. She looked straight at him without really seeing him. The light in the room was a lot like the light in her old bedroom at home, when she would talk to Jill on the phone at night, or Andy, or Sue Freund, or others she was some degree of friends with at the time. She thought again that the person in front of her named Steve Farkas was the person in her life now for talking to, and that instead he had suddenly become the problem, unless she was the problem.

"What are we going to do?" she asked him.

He had slid way down in the chair, so that he was half-lying on his back. By being at ease, he seemed to be in control. In an uncharacteristic fatherly sort of way (not her father, but fatherly in general), he was pondering her, with a grumpy chin, or pondering everything. "Obviously we have to make some sort of adjustment. If I've made you this unhappy, I feel terrible. I really do. Terrible."

She wanted to say, "Oh, Stevie," fall on top of him in his chair, have everything solved. Her lips tightened sourly. Again she had to cover her face. She shook her head. She was like a baby in a highchair preventing someone from feeding her the inedible. He was sitting beside her, with his hand on her back, near her neck. She couldn't stop herself from sobbing. She couldn't stop thinking, either. She was aware of everything, inside and out. She had cried when Mom went away to Shanghai, but not like this, because after all, Mom was supposed to come home within months. When Mom had died she hadn't cried as hard as she'd cried when Mom had left. She was squeaking like something being unscrewed. Steve kept trying to lift her head, as if he were a lifeguard or something, but she kept it concealed. The phone rang. "I'll leave it," Steve said. She said, "No. Get it." She didn't try to make out his end of the short conversation. When he hung up, she asked him to bring her some Kleenex. With her face still down, she blew her nose and wiped her eyes. He stroked the back of her hair like someone not sure how to do it.

"Who called? Your mother?"

"No. Helen Kornbluth, as a matter of fact. She wants to make a date for us to come to the studio."

"Well-timed call. What did you say?"

"Said I'd call her soon. I will, too."

"That's all?"

"What do you mean?"

"Nothing else?"

"Do you mean did I tell her we're having a problem, or Emily's busy crying her eyes out?"

"I'm just checking."

"Do you want me to make dinner?"

"It's okay." Why didn't she say yes?

"Do you want to eat at Granada?"

"Are you hungry?"

"Hungry, not starving. Are you?"

"I still have that big lunch in me. I got you steak." She moved her face sideways, out in the open, and opened her eyes. "I must be very blotchy."

He ran his finger across her cheek; he bent and kissed her where he had drawn his finger. She smiled, closing her eyes. She opened her eyes again, breaking off her smile. She had no reason to smile.

Eventually they went out to Granada, where she listened to him explain, in a much slower, graver voice than his usual one, what he wanted from his life. "I understand why you're upset, mostly. I put myself in your place. I really thought about it. I have to tell you, I'm very, very serious. It's not being a hero so much, like I said yesterday, like being a fireman in an emergency. I don't want a medal. I really want to do good. I want to help people. I want to be good at helping people. I admit, I don't mind if I'm paid good money for it." Brief grin.

Pinpricks in the skin around her eyes from where she had cried before started to tingle. "What happens if I can't accept it, Steve?" The bulge of a new sob formed way down in her throat. Enough!

"It's my job to make it possible for you to accept it by always finding ways to show you that if I didn't have you then medical school wouldn't be worth doing. That's the gods'-honest truth." He looked as if he himself were about to cry.

Emily felt helpless. As far as she could tell, the situation was getting worse, not better—calmer but worse. "Maybe my problem is I don't care about doing good to anyone but you. I never think about wanting to do good, as a purpose. Not doing harm is about as far as I get."

"You're being silly. You're so much better than that. What's more, I think you know it. You could do an awful lot of good by letting me give it a try." His voice was husky. "I'm doing this to be worthy of you. At least that's a very fundamental part of it."

"Worthy of me? Because of my noble profession, you mean? You're competing?"

"You know perfectly well that I mean the person you are." He leaned self-consciously away from her. "Fascinating, unusually intelligent, sensitive, perceptive, strong, courageous, well-adjusted. I might add that you'd probably respect your profession a hell of a lot better, and maybe yourself, too, if you got paid what you're worth."

"Thanks." He refused to understand the pay scale in publishing. Also, it was he who had pointed out to her, when she accepted the promotion and Mrs. P. had told her what she'd be making once she started, that one reason they'd probably promoted her, other than her brains, talent, and hard work, was that it would be more expensive for Partridge to bring in someone at her new level from outside the company. "Did you tell your parents about your plans, by the way?"

"I was too upset about us to bring it up today. I don't see how my father can turn me down, though."

She thought that was quite funny. She wanted to remind him that his father had already turned him down once, which was the whole problem.

"I want to say something else. This is not going to end up being nearly as bad as you think right now. It just isn't. Nothing is. We'll both get used to it and you'll be surprised how easy it'll be. You will."

Maybe she should say to herself, it's only love, sex, life and death— Timothy's immortal observation.

In bed, she and Steve tried. She barely got wet. She was like a cold clamshell. It had never happened before. How did she know it wouldn't be permanent? "Sorry," she said. She was at least able to let him kiss her goodnight, more or less, and half be held by him.

"I'm not worried." He patted her back. "Everything's going to get better. I'm going to see to it. You'll see. Sleep well."

She put her hand on his shoulder; she took her hand away.

He turned over, turned off the night-table lamp. The lumpy rectangular shape an arm away from her in the dark looked dead. It wasn't Steve. Under the covers lay her mother, disguised as Steve. Her mother was in the bed with her, with her back to her. If she drew down the bedding, her mother, with her loose pimply chicken fricassee skin, would be lying there. If she drew down the yellow skin, she would expose the diarrhea mud. Steve's body could have flown out the window while she'd blinked and her mother taken his place, as fast as that, by some arrangement with Steve. Steve had once said he wanted to bring her mother home. Steve had phoned her mother in her grave and arranged to trade places with her.

Emily learned that if Steve rubbed her back, she could soften enough to have sex. While it relieved her to know she could respond, she remained aware of being capable of responding. For the first time, she felt, during sex, as if she were keeping one eye open. Up until now, they'd almost been two people being the same person, loving in the same skin. Now she thought of them as two separate people doing it together at the same time.

It was better than nothing only because she couldn't stand the thought of getting used to being cold. She feared being able to leave him, maybe even becoming an old-maid career woman, not having the heart for someone else. She feared being ungenerous, or being thought of as ungenerous. Not only wouldn't she get credit for sticking it out as a med student's wife if she stayed with Steve; if she left him, she'd be regarded as definitely in the wrong, a spoiled brat. She'd never been a spoiled brat.

The pain had lessened a little because the shock had passed. His wanting to go to medical school nevertheless stuck in her as being the end of the world. Each had figured out that his decision was connected in her head to her mother's leaving to help refugees. Very Freudian. Nothing really helped, despite Steve's optimism and constant reassurances of love.

In one of their numerous conversations, he suggested that she might be jealous of his having an ambition, and that if she wasn't fulfilled enough in her job, she might at least consider taking over his job at Farr. Especially with her promotion, she'd be all the more desirable. He'd bet she would increase her salary by twenty-five percent over what she made at Partridge.

"Are you crazy? First of all, you're saying I should quit Partridge just after they've given me all this responsibility. Second of all, are you saying I should take a job that's not good enough for you?"

"Hey, come on!" He laughed. "It was only a suggestion. You don't think your job's good enough for you, either. At least you'd be making money."

She couldn't pursue his blunder. They couldn't afford it.

As it turned out, Emily was invited to dinner at her father's, with Grandpa Gus and Ellen, for the same night Steve planned to go to his parents' to discuss his future with them. It was a relief to her that Steve didn't ask her to accompany him, and that she had an out in any case. She couldn't stand the thought of being present while Mona vomited insincerity all over her, and Steve asked his parents for money she didn't want him to get. Nor could she have stood it if they said no to him.

On the way up to her father's after work, she pretty much realized that she wasn't heading for an ordinary family get-together either, and she was right. Before dinner, while they all had drinks in the overdone living room, Grandpa told her and Ellen that he and their grandmother had left them the Newbury house. He no longer cared to use it. If they didn't want to share the use of it, then he was going to sell it now and give them the proceeds. They should think it over and let him know.

In sisterly solidarity, without the slightest consultation, they told him they didn't want the proceeds, as if they were saying they loved him far too much to be interested in his generosity. He said they'd be getting the money whether they wanted it or not. The only question was, did they want the house instead. Their father pointed out that as much as he understood their not wanting to talk about it, the fact remained that Grandpa had to make a decision and he needed their help.

Grandpa's usual dark suit made him look to Emily tonight as if he were dressed in a shadow. She dared to think he probably didn't have that long to live; maybe he didn't even want that long. Ellen said, "Grandpa, I can tell you right now, Stan and I aren't country folks." Emily immediately asked herself, If I say I do want the house, won't that complicate matters since Ellen and Stan don't want any of it, according to Ellen, but would have to be reimbursed for their half? She thought how she and Steve hadn't been up there, with all her thoughts of showing it to him. She and Steve might actually be finished anyway, if things kept going the way they were. Realistically, she wouldn't be living up in Newbury or going there on vacations by herself. And if they stayed together, she was sure Steve would have no more interest in that much peace and quiet than Stan did.

She was not going to discuss it with Steve. She said, "Grandpa, I don't want the house, thank you. You know it meant everything to me, but no one can take away my memories." She felt like an adult. She had arrived already feeling like an adult, because not a soul in her family knew what she was going through with her husband.

At dinner, Emily remembered that she and Steve hadn't made arrangements about going home together, which would be logical since they were only blocks from each other. After dinner, Ellen went home with Grandpa. Emily hung around for a few minutes waiting for Steve to call her, while Bunny told her that Mr. Sacks, her philanthropist boss, had written the president of Emily's company, James Partridge, inquiring as to Partridge's possible interest in Mr. Sacks's autobiography. Mr. Sacks had known many notables over the decades. "Including himself, naturally," Bunny said. Bunny seemed to understand that she was not describing a future best-seller. Even Mr. Sacks understood. He had guaranteed to buy enough copies to make it worth Patridge's while. Hey! Emily thought. I should write an autobiography!

When she gave up and called the Farkases', Mona answered. "How's my hardworking daughter-in-law? Stevie says you're running yourself ragged. I'd love to see you so I can remind myself what you look like. I wish you'd give me a call for lunch sometime. Stevie's already left. He'll be home soon. I probably shouldn't tell you, but he's got some wonderful news. Wait up for him, darling, so you two can talk." Obviously Mona didn't know Emily was at her father's.

Aside from making her angry, it bothered her that his going home without her hurt her feelings. In the taxi, she was almost in tears. She told herself, you're sick of crying, switch to something else for a few days.

Steve wasn't home when she got there. He arrived half an hour later; she was in bed, pretending to be asleep. He undressed in the dark. She pretended to wake up when he got into bed. "Are you trying to play hard to get or something?," she asked him.

"I don't know what you're talking about."

"Did it slip your mind that I was at my father's?"

"Of course not. I needed time to think. I walked half the way home. You could have called me."

"I did call you. You'd already left. You had wonderful news for me, according to your mother, so I came home to hear it. To await it. I assume they said yes."

"They did, more or less. Do you mind my asking what you mean by my playing hard to get? You're the one who's distant, if anyone is. I wanted to come home alone so I could think through what they said and what to say to you. You think I'm enjoying knowing you're unhappy?"

"What do you mean? There's an obvious way to make me happy. Which will make you unhappy. Which will keep me unhappy anyway. What's the answer to this, Steve?" She wanted to add, "You've ruined our life. Mine, anyway."

He didn't answer her question. Instead he said, very calmly and evenly, "I proposed to my father that he loan me the tuition for pre-med and med school, and that in place of my salary he give us the basics of what we'll need to live on. All that has to be worked out. He wants to see a budget. But he seemed to be pretty agreeable. He can afford it, we know that. He also said if it didn't work out I could always have my job back, unless they sell the company, which it turns out they may do someday."

Emily thought of asking him to turn the light on. Then she decided it was appropriate to be having this talk in the dark. "Then maybe it's just as well I don't go to work there after all."

"They wouldn't sell for at least ten years."

"What are the basics of what we need to live on? And does what we need to live on include my salary, by the way?"

"I don't think necessarily. Basics are basics. Rent, food. We wouldn't be able to eat out much. We couldn't go to the theater as often."

But with her salary they could. And her father would resume his financial help, if asked. He'd stopped it only at her request, with Steve's strong agreement, when she'd gotten married. "Did you discuss including my salary? Was it mentioned? I could stand not eating out, but I wouldn't enjoy not going to the theater." Of course he would have almost no time to go to the theater.

"I understand. We'd work that out."

"What about including my salary? So we can continue to have a few luxuries. So I don't have to live like a complete puritan for ten years. What was said about my salary?"

"Well, my mother asked if we planned to have a baby—when we planned to."

Her heart failed to jump clear of the surprise. "And?"

"I said we hadn't talked about it lately."

"I see." She might have been willing to have one if it kept Steve from going to medical school, except that she wanted to have one even less than she'd wanted to before. And she wouldn't have one out of spite, even though her husband was turning her into a complete bitch. She refused to tell Steve about Grandpa and the house until she had to, if she ever had to. Grandpa's money would just make Steve's situation easier. "Did your parents think anything about your wanting to be a doctor?"

"Well . . . they certainly indicated they'd back me. My mother said, 'You only live once.' "   Mona liked to say that. And life is short. The woman had wisdom to spare.

"To get my father not to say no is a big accomplishment. He didn't pooh-pooh it. I can't read my father. He might still feel guilty about the other thing."

"Did they ask what I thought of the idea?"

"I said you were behind me."

"It came up?"

"I just said it did. My mother asked what you thought. I said you were behind me if they were."

"How could you do that? That's like taking over my brain." That's what he was doing—taking control of everything.

"Look, I don't want them to think you're not backing me. They wouldn't understand."

"What wouldn't they understand?"

"I don't want them to know we're having trouble, that's all."

"You think they'd disapprove of me? Are you trying to protect me? Or do you think if they knew what I thought of your idea they might not go along with you?"

"It means bringing up the connection between your mother and me and my ambition versus your ambition, all the personal stuff. It's not their business, it's ours."

"You think my mother is the only reason I object to your starting out on all these years of studying and training? You don't think there's any reason at all for my not liking it other than its happening to remind me of my mother?" With Grandpa's money, she could leave Steve. "I'll say one thing. You're certainly determined." To the point of being oblivious to anyone else's feelings. Maybe she should admire him for his stubbornness. Maybe she did.

"It's really ironic. One of the reasons I liked you from the beginning was you were your own girl. You didn't think like everyone else. Most women would be proud of their husbands having the determination to change careers and wanting to reach for something. Especially something like medical school."

All of a sudden he had developed the habit of turning points back and forth, on and off, for his convenience. "You admire me for something and then you're sorry I possess that quality? If anything, what's happened is that I'm acting far too dependent." And maybe without even knowing it, he'd liked her in the first place because he sensed she'd be dependent, because of her mother. Beneath what he said he liked, maybe he'd seen someone to walk all over. She didn't know what she looked like to him. "Do you want me to be dependent on you?"

"I want us to be dependent on each other. I'm depending on you for your support."

"You've said." Perhaps he had opened up independence in her, too, by doing what he'd done. He'd brought out dependence in her, but also resistance. Maybe she had an independent streak, like Mom. Her resistance was like Mom's insistence.

"Do you mind if I ask you something?"

"I think that's a funny question, don't you? What is it?"

"Do you think you'd ever leave me?"

She liked him for asking it. "How come you haven't asked me that before?"

"Do you think it's possible?"

"I suppose anything is possible. I certainly hadn't been planning on it when I married you."

"But you've thought of it since this trouble started."

"It's crossed my mind fleetingly, yes. What would happen if I did?"

"It would be the end of the world."

What a coincidence. Just what his wanting to be a doctor meant to her. "Meaning what?" Would he kill himself?

"I don't know exactly. But nothing would be worth anything."

They should have been violently embracing, but a clinch at the moment was out of the question. She didn't have the nerve to say the truth—Steve, we're in trouble. All she could say was, "I hope it never gets that far."

"It can't. How can it?"

"I don't know."

Then they embraced after all, Steve initiating it. The embrace led to unusually intense sex. Without sex, there would have been no way to end their talk, no way to get to sleep.

CHAPTER FOURTEEN

The Star of the Audience

About a month later, in the early evening, Emily sat in the waiting room of a headshrinker, Dr. Arthur Wachspress, five blocks up Park Avenue from Daddy and Bunny's, the last kind of doctor she'd ever thought she'd be seeing.

Steve, timidly for him, had suggested the psychiatrist. She had agreed to think about it. She couldn't deny she felt low a majority of the time. Their sex life, with the strange exception of the one recent night, at best seemed to be temporarily preventing the total collapse of their relationship. Emily could tell that Steve could tell, and that he was holding back from saying anything about it. She tried to behave politely to him, but she was often irritated with him in her head. Also, she'd had a stupendous dream that wouldn't leave her, some of which was so mysterious she wondered if it might not be interesting enough for a professional.

She had said to Steve, "All my life one of the things I've been proud of is that I've never needed a psychiatrist, when lots of people were going to one—people with complete families. Maybe that's what saved me from going. If my mother had stayed around, maybe I would have had to go to one. I don't even know the name of one. I don't know how to find one." Steve mentioned that he was quite sure his mother had gone to one for a while once. Emily reminded herself that Ellen had used one, but that was in college, in Ohio.

Then she thought Jill might be able to help her find one. Jill still hadn't come to dinner. Emily wasn't sure anymore if Jill wanted to come to dinner. It was dawning on her that under cover of the nine or ten months they had barely been in touch, Jill had been drawing away of her own accord and not through being somewhat ignored by Emily, not even necessarily for any reason at all other than her desire to pursue her own path. Jill had decided that Emily was not a serious enough person for her any longer: once you were out of college, if you had any brains to start with, you did serious work with them, certainly not publicity work. Married or not, you got involved with something useful. Some kind of altruism, sacrifice. Social work, naturally, or medicine. Emily had become, in Jill's eyes, fluff. Jill had approved of her when they were young because something so serious had happened to her; but now Emily's tragedy had evaporated over time, leaving Emily almost worthless. True, Emily had arrived at these conclusions without talking to Jill. But it was hard to get together. Lunch wasn't convenient for either of them, and Jill had turned down the one dinner invitation—"Thanks, sweetie, I have a big paper to finish, give me a raincheck?"—Emily had been able to offer, right after returning from San Francisco, as promised. Since then, she and Steve had not exactly been in a state for entertaining.

She didn't even have a definite reason why Jill would know how to get hold of a psychiatrist—maybe through someone at social-work school—but she called Jill because she couldn't think of anyone else she wanted to ask. And because she wanted an excuse to call her. Of all the people she knew, Jill, her contemporary, seemed to her her most natural advisor.

Jill said she might be able to help, give her a few days to work on it. Emily told her she didn't care particularly if it was a man or a woman (as far as she knew), but she didn't want one of those who sat and listened while you lay down on a couch and droned on. She wanted to talk to someone who answered. Jill called back in a week with Dr. Wachspress.

"How do you spell it?" Maybe with a name like that Jill was pulling her leg.

Jill spelled it. "Very famous. Very good. He's going to fit you in. He's very busy, believe me."

"Is he German?"

"Why? He's American, I think."

With a name like that, Emily thought, I should marry him. Emily Farkas Wachspress. "I really thank you. How'd you find him? I'm impressed."

"I asked an acquaintance who's a psychiatrist. He knows only the best. Let me know how it turns out."

"I will. Thanks again." Why didn't Jill ask her what the problem was? Then Emily thought, I want to see a psychiatrist; he doesn't want to see me. He's doing Jill or someone a favor.

"Mrs. Farkas." A large bald head, a long straight mouth, a lot of blue suit. Dr. Wachspress's bulky top half alone had appeared, at a tilt, through his office door, as if the bottom part weren't dressed.

Emily smiled, forgiving him for having to call her Mrs. Farkas, standing in her newish beige tweed suit and moss-green sweater, her handbag a suitcase for a trip of unknown duration. He opened the door wider for her without opening his mouth at all to smile or to speak further. "Thank you," she said, deciding she'd better not smile anymore. Maybe she didn't know how serious things were.

Under his blue suit, over his white shirt and blue tie, he wore a blue V-neck sweater. Why not a vest? Unlike Daddy, no perky, three-peaked white handkerchief in the breast pocket. Maybe this doctor was really a mortician luring her into a coffin. Maybe the dreaded couch she spied along the left-hand wall on entering his living-room-sized paneled office was situated above a trap door. She crossed a persian rug on her way to the dark leather chair to the right of his mammoth desk. Visible on the desk from her seat were ornate silver implements; weird, ancient-looking little animals and other figures in ivory, bronze, gold; tiny drawings or etchings in antique frames on tiny stands; gorgeous polished stones or minerals—a throng of exotic objects. On inset shelves behind the doctor, among dark old tomes, were more of the same, along with an occasional terracotta pot or urn.

Emily had planned to start off in a direct way with a line about her husband and medical school and her mother and Shanghai—two "disappearances"—wishing to intrigue him with the cleverness of her spadework, but now that she had arrived at the moment, her approach seemed glib to her. Instead of flattering herself, she flattered him, fearing she might be revealing something about herself unofficially. "Everything here looks as if it comes from the Metropolitan Museum or was dug up by archeologists, it's so old and beautiful."

"Thank you."

The collection of objects seemed to her the result of supreme knowledge and experience she would be unable to attain in five lives. On the waiting-room walls there had been prints of ancient maps and cities.

"Will you fill me in about yourself?" He had a rather heavy, solid voice. He was definitely American. Like an idiot, she must have expected a sinister German accent and a creepy, overinterested manner.

"Well, it's a long story," she said, and laughed.

He actually seemed slightly amused himself. "That doesn't surprise me. Why don't you try to summarize it to begin with."

She told him the facts: her mother and the war and refugees, Shanghai, and Havana before that. Steve and medical school and the connection between her mother and Steve, including the fantasy (un-revealed to Steve) about her mother in the bed in Steve's place, and then the previous fantasies about her mother, Emily providing all the details frankly, but with her head down and feeling confronted by tremendous sadness. She told him she thought she had managed suc-cessfully in her life up to now, all in all, that if anything she might have been too normal. What a wonderful job her father had done with her and her older sister, especially considering that you wouldn't think he was cut out to bring up two daughters by himself. (She re-ferred quickly to Bunny.) And suddenly, now that she'd gotten mar-ried, she wasn't managing. Then she described her confused attitude toward her job, toward her promotion itself, the combination of her disdain for the work and pride in being asked to do it and in being praised for doing it well. She told him about her once wanting to be an actress and her belief that being an actress would allow her to live forever. She told him about her possible jealousy of Steve for having a serious ambition, and her possible fear of ambition, and her sister's similar fear, along with her distrust of Steve's ambition and of him. She went back, mentioning Steve's business trouble with his father and uncle during the summer, before the wedding, leading to his medical school maneuver after the honeymoon, and her resentment of it and of being taken by surprise, and Steve's justifications for doing it and how he'd done it.

Dr. Wachspress made notes every once in a while with a silver pen. She was sure she was talking too fast, saying too much. She didn't see how he could make much sense out of her rushed history, but he didn't interrupt.

She had expected to tell him her great dream near the beginning. Then she'd passed by it, as if forgetting her lines. Now she was glad she'd skipped it earlier, because she thought of the dream (which she'd eventually told Steve as part of trying to be friendly, and in place of telling him about Grandpa's money, without his being able to provide any insights she hadn't had herself) as her *pièce de résistance*, the most important thing she had to report, the most "intelligent" (despite her own failure to understand most of it, or perhaps because of her failure; the dream was bigger than her mind).

"I have the fantasies about my mother I told you before, but I don't literally dream that much, at least not major dreams." She laughed. "Sounds like publisher talk. 'A major novel.' " The doctor made a note instead of smiling. "Shortly before I made the appointment with you, I had this huge dream. In a way, almost the best thing about it was being reminded of the amazingness of dreaming. I felt as though I were watching a play taking place inside myself, but the play was a movie, a three-dimensional movie. Everything was life-size and lifelike, but even realer than reality, clearer. You couldn't show what was happening in the dream on the stage as clearly as a movie would show it if the movie were literally three-dimensional. The dream was a movie that was not on film. It was so amazingly clear, it's impossible to forget, even though nothing in it ever actually happened." She must be sounding, she thought, as if she were the first person ever to have a dream. He was listening in a neutral, friendly way, not impressed, but not bored, either, as far as she could tell. Of course, he was getting paid.

Emily explained again that her mother had gone to Havana two years before Shanghai, and she told Dr. Wachspress that her father regarded her mother's watching the boatful of refugees sailing back to Europe (even though supposedly at the time to "safety") as the beginning of the turning point of everything for her, because not only wouldn't Havana let the refugees in, even the U.S. wouldn't. She then told Dr. Wachspress the dream she'd had a few times when she was young of her mother on the refugee ship instead of the refugees, her mother all alone on the deck, way high up, sailing out of Havana, facing away from Emily, but waving with one arm to Emily below on the dock (definitely not waving ahead of her), and steering the ship with her other arm; Emily crying, waving as hard as she could at her mother's back, her strenuous waving an attempt to stop the ship from leaving; the ship sailing away, her mother continuing to wave, Emily continuing to wave at her mother's back, crying, while the ship sank, and her mother and her mother's waving arm disappeared.

"What happened when you'd wake up from that dream?" the doctor asked her, looking at his pad, not at her.

"I don't remember too well." His question suggested to her that she might have entered the privileged ranks of those whose problems were more significant than their self-effacement allowed them to know. "I don't mean amnesia. It's just vague. I know I must have been upset, because I remember at least once going into my father's bed, and also my sister being sympathetic. Maybe I went into her room once instead of my father's. My sister usually acted impatient, like an older sister, but I distinctly remember that when I was upset from this dream she didn't treat me as if I were making a big fuss over nothing, which is the way she treated me most of the time when I was upset, but as if she understood. My father was never impatient. He didn't go around lavishing hugs and kisses, but I assure you, he was always there in his steady way."

The psychiatrist made quick notes. She was turning into a case.

"Your mother wasn't around when you had these dreams, then? Did they occur after she left for Havana or after she left for Shanghai? Both?"

"They were all after she left for Shanghai. Left for good, though we didn't know it at the time. We thought she was coming back from Shanghai the way she came back from Havana."

"Did the dreams occur after you knew she had died or before?"

"Before, I'm almost positive. Between the time she left for Shanghai and the time she died. But I could be wrong. They might have been spread out past her death."

"In any case, you had the bulk of them before she died."

"I'm sure of that." She was moved by his questioning her.

"Do you want to go ahead?"

"With the new dream?"

"Whatever you wish."

In the new dream, she told him, the ship from the old dream had changed into a large fat rowboat she thought of as an ark. On the side of the ark was its name, *SS St Francis.* The ship in the old dream had no name Emily could remember. The ark was open at one end, with a plank for passengers. One thought she'd had, she told the doctor, was that the ark was sort of womb-shaped. She assumed psychiatrists liked to hear that sort of thing, but he made no comment or expression. Her observation wasn't even worth a note.

Animals and people were climbing up the plank onto the boat in twos, the men and women as naked as the animals, except that some people wore bandages in different places, soaked with blood and pus and God knows what. The people were filthy, even those without the bandages—soiled, miserable, sorrowful, many of them shuffling and limping on twisted walking sticks, many of them with ropes around their necks or waists, but no one holding the ropes. None of the passengers had any belongings. The animals were also wretched, slow, somber. Giraffes, elephants, camels. Every figure was silent. The boat was jammed but completely quiet. No one she recognized was in the dream. Noah wasn't in the dream. No one waved goodbye to anyone. She assumed the animals and people were refugees, she said.

The ark started to sink. No one made any noise or any effort to avoid sinking. Overhead, as the ark sank, a tremendous storm took place, but silently and with no rain, just silently booming spasms of black clouds and vast but silent lightning flashes. "That's all I can think of," she said.

He wrote in his pad.

She looked at her knees, then at the near corner of his desk. She feared he would have hardly anything to say to her because the dream was so obvious and ordinary, despite its length and her excitement about it. She had decided that Dr. Wachspress was careful and kind. She worried anyway. Even though he was a human being, his surroundings awed her. She felt she might be in a sacred room, a temple, and that she was the only unsacred thing there.

"What are your thoughts?" he asked her.

"Oh. I hoped you were going to tell me."

"I might have something to say a little later. But I'd like to hear your own reactions. Your interpretation is important. It's your dream."

"I see. Well." He actually knew all the answers to her dream and was testing her intelligence by asking her her thoughts. "I mentioned the refugees. And it's obvious, the connection between the boat from the old dream and the ark. I know Saint Francis of Assisi loved animals, so that could be the reason for the name. But I don't understand why the ark, why the biblical connotation. How did I ever get from me to Noah's ark, even though Noah's not in the dream? I'm ashamed to say, but the Bible isn't something I've paid much attention to. I'm dreaming about something I'm ignorant of. Is that permitted?"

He showed reserved amusement. "It's expected." He looked at her from a reticent angle. "I think you understand that I'm not free to take you as a patient right now. Not that I'm saying you need a psychiatrist, either. We'll come back to all that in a moment. Your dream is a wonderful dream; but I don't know enough about you to understand it all myself, no less feel competent to explain it to you."

Emily was simultaneously flattered and disappointed.

"All I can responsibly do," he went on, "is make a few suggestions about it. It interests me that you were so pleased to have the dream, the pleasure you take in describing what it was like to have it. I suppose dreaming your own variant of a Bible story indicates the importance you attach to your mother's departure. Your mother and the refugees are history to you, as important as the Bible, not in the sense of ancient history, I think, but more in the sense of world-famous history."

"God." She laughed.

"An appropriate word."

"That's not what I meant. I was just exclaiming."

"But Noah's ark is in Genesis, after all. Your mother's departure and her involvement with refugees was certainly a beginning for you, a point of origin."

Then here she was again, at the old problem. "I don't want to be a person whose only distinction is what happened to her mother or who's shaped by her mother that much."

He nodded as if to say, why should you want to be? "We'll come back to that when we finish. You're probably somewhere on the right track with St. Francis of Assisi. Does the name Francis ring any bells with you?"

"I don't know any Francises. I was in France once. I came back from San Francisco not long ago, where I went on part of my honeymoon. That might be something, because my mother left the U.S. when she went to Shanghai on a ship from San Francisco. The connection didn't occur to me. That's amazing."

"The ark itself I thought might also be associated with a name in your life. Does it sound like anything to you?"

She saw that he was offering her her own answer, and at the same time she saw the answer. "You mean Arkas? That's very funny. How could I be so stupid? It was right in front of me all the time. Especially if I'm connecting my husband and my mother."

"You understand, that's often the case. A lot of my job is letting people see what's in front of them."

On the other hand, she thought, shouldn't there be more? There would be more if he knew her better, but he didn't have time.

"I'll have to begin summing up now," he told her.

She assented with her head, as if it were up to her. Childishly, she gulped. She was excited at the prospect of his verdict. Her fortune was about to be told in the most high-class way.

He looked at her, with his right hand resting on his note pad. "First off, I would recommend against your undergoing analysis or any kind of extensive treatment. On the whole, I get the impression that you're doing too well, have done too well, to justify stirring things up more than they get naturally stirred up from time to time. You show anger toward your mother, which is appropriate enough, but also the appropriate respect. Naturally you're angry at your husband too. I give a lot of credit to your father. People behaving the way he evidently did under extraordinary circumstances like yours make most of the difference. The rest is what you were lucky enough to be born with, which of course includes what your mother herself gave you, along with other good luck that helps people win out over the bad luck. I certainly have the sense that all in all you've won out over the bad luck."

Her two immediate thoughts were regret that she hadn't told him about her grandparents, especially Granny, and the security of the country summers, as part of her good luck. And then—despite her still shimmering streak of pride in what he'd said about her having done so well—that he might be too confident about her. "Thank you," she said. "But" (was this too nervy a question?) "what do I do about me and my husband? It seems to me I've been optimistic all my life, maybe too much, and now I'm here because I don't know what to do, and I'm worried about the future, that it might collapse, or that my past has caught up with me."

"I understand. I'm not saying you don't have a problem. I'm saying that your reactions on the whole are healthy ones. You have the choice, if it's necessary, of coming back to see me once or twice when I can find the time, or of going to someone else I'd find for you. But I think you're remarkably sturdy, and so my inclination is to leave well enough alone. You'd make some psychiatrist a fascinating patient, but that's not a good enough reason by itself to embark on treatment. In the meantime, it seems to me, from what you've told me, you should try to bear with your husband, even though he didn't present his decision to you in the wisest way. Nothing is final. You don't have to—one doesn't have to—approve of his method to remember that he has a life to live too, after all, and that he wants to get the most out of it that he can get. I think you do have to be careful that you're not trying to limit him for just the kinds of reasons you've suggested, equating ambition and medical school with Shanghai and death. Shanghai and death are farther away than medical school is. You have an unusually dramatic history, but there's a way in which everyone has a dramatic history, including your husband. I don't happen to know what his is, but if he's alive he's got one."

"Oh, he does. His sister died when she was little. He's very tied up with his parents, and I don't think they love him right, or well, or enough, or at all, though I really can't say that. But there sure is something wrong there. They don't support him, even when they seem to.

I know all this, but it's possible I haven't acted on it enough, paid close enough attention to it. I don't know."

"Of course none of that means he shouldn't be more careful with you, too, and discuss his plans with you before they become decisions. It would make sense that you're not the kind of person who enjoys surprises. You've had enough surprises."

"But I love surprises." She felt definitely defensive. "That's what I love. I hope I still do."

"Well, I mean the kind that upset you enough to bring you here. No one enjoys those. And your early ones—I'd say they were on the singular and significant side."

Nevertheless, she thought, she hadn't put herself in Steve's place enough—what he had done to her had seemed to her so much more important than what he wanted for himself. It wouldn't surprise her if she had failed him, even taking the irresponsibility of his behavior into account, by not recognizing that his life was just as important as hers, though she was the one with the "famous" story. Famous to her, anyway.

Dr. Wachspress, in his tall, bulky blueness and baldness, stood up, and Emily immediately with him, to make it clear that she didn't need more of him than he had time to give. He walked past her chair; she followed him through the room. "You're the last of the day," he said, "so you may leave the way you came in." He opened the door to the waiting room.

"I see." She hadn't noticed another door, but she assumed there must be one, for the use of those who didn't want to be seen by the person with the next appointment. She decided to be flattered that he was showing her an office trick. He wanted to treat her as a human being, not as a patient. But if she was just a human being, she'd have less excuse for coming back. She was eager to report to Steve; at the same time, she didn't want to leave. She stood once again within the waiting room, he more or less within his office, when they shook hands.

"Let me know if things don't ease up, and we'll take it from there. But I think you'll be okay."

"Thank you very much."

"I don't often get the chance to say this, but I enjoyed meeting you. I believe you're someone with a lot of reason to be proud of herself."

She was much closer than he knew to falling into his arms in tears. "Thanks. Oh, the bill?" Or was she too unusual to be charged? Or too healthy?

"It'll be mailed to you. My secretary's gone for the day. She took your address when you called?"

"She did."

"Goodbye, Mrs. Farkas."

"Thank you for seeing me."

Looking friendly, saying no more, he closed his office door.

She hadn't had time to tell Dr. Wachspress about George, about Timothy, about Thom Blake in summer stock, about some of her father's drawbacks, about the conversation she and Ellen had had with Daddy after Granny's funeral, or that she and Steve had moved only the week before to the larger apartment in their building just when things were going so badly between them.

But now, tonight, describing to Steve in detail her session with Dr. Wachspress, Emily was feeling like her former self, returning to her pre-medical school-announcement husband. They were in the new apartment's den, Steve with his usual Cutty Sark and soda, she with her vermouth. They sat on the ultramasculine plaid couch (green-yellow-black-blue) Steve had bought, with inexplicable delight, off the floor at Sloane's on a shopping trip with her. She was trying to dislike the couch less; she'd had to give in to his choice so she wouldn't add to her reputation for resistance. (The living room, though, would be hers. She had ordered an off-white fabric with a pale blue thread in it for reupholstering Steve's rust couch and his two modernish blue-green tweedy chairs; also a robin's-egg blue rug and off-white linen drapes.) In the den, along with the plaid couch (meant for a sports-trophy room, Emily thought), were Steve's butterscotch leather arm-chair, his records and phonograph, their combined books, and an old wooden desk and swivel desk chair from the Farr offices. Feeling like a guest in the den didn't cut a bit into her relief at telling Steve every word of Dr. Wachspress's and hers.

"I'd like to go over there and kiss him," Steve said when she had finished the whole narrative. He kissed Emily.

Emily visualized Steve kissing Wachspress on the cheek, on the bald head, Wachspress acting as if nothing had happened, showing Steve out of the office. "Send him a Rembrandt. He has beautiful rare objects. Intimidating." If Dr. Wachspress visited their den, he might admire her much less. Even though she had seen very few dens in her short life, she knew this one was typical. Probably all dens were typical.

She and Steve went strolling to Pete's Tavern for dinner. They walked with their arms around each other, as they'd done the night in June when he'd told her his business plan and she was ecstatic about him; he'd kissed her standing on the corner, holding her face in his hands, and she'd carried her ecstasy in all of her body right upstairs to bed. She hardly wanted to remind him of that night, though, since his plan had gone bust. She wasn't as ecstatic tonight, but their future could actually be better than it had appeared to be on the ecstatic night, once they settled down and got used to real life, and started making the best of it. They were really very lucky, after all, when you compared them to most of the other people in the world. "I have a surprise for you," she said.

"You're pregnant."

"Quintuplets."

"What's the surprise?"

"I'll tell you during dinner."

"You mean it's so astounding I have to sit down?"

"I just want to have it a little longer. I've had it for weeks."

"You're a real tease."

Once they had been served drinks, she told him about Grandpa Gus wanting to sell the Newbury house and insisting on dividing the proceeds between her and Ellen.

"Gee. That is nice. What a sweet guy. Why didn't you tell me?"

"It was the same night you were at your parents and went home alone."

"Never again." He put his glass on the table, took her hand, looked into her eyes, and made a sexy kiss while gazing at her. "Babes, I have to tell you something. Whatever mistake I made toward you—mistakes—I want you to know I never loved anyone until I met you. Not this way. That's literally true."

The sight of his eyes welling up made hers do the same. "Maybe I've been a selfish bitch the last month."

"All I know is, I expect to love you more and more the longer I know you."

"Then what happens?"

"I don't get you."

"How long does it go on, getting to know me longer and loving me more?"

"Until death do us part, I guess, or until I burst, whichever comes first."

"If you burst, you couldn't love me forever, or I you."

"I won't burst, babes. It was just a figure of speech."

"I also don't believe in death do us part, personally."

"Death is part of life, so they tell me."

"What's the point of dying if you have to part?"

"I don't quite follow your logic. But maybe we could arrange to have our skeletons locked together, like kids kissing with braces."

"Ick." She wondered: when she used to think it was imperative to live forever—when living meant living forever to her—and she thought that excitement could keep you alive forever, and that nobody died anyway, most prominently her said-to-be-dead mother, had she actually been less happy than when she eventually forgot about living forever and instead just lived, as she'd been doing pretty much since falling in love with Steve? Until his bombshell after their honeymoon, the present had been plenty, all that counted. It was as if the present were itself the future and would just go on happily and indefinitely, so that living forever didn't even get considered. Did having the conversation they were having at the moment mean that she was less happy again, or that she was too happy? Were they the same thing? "Don't you ever think about living forever?"

"Obviously, I'd like to live a long, full life. Living forever is probably asking a lot."

"What's the point of being born if you can't live as long as you want to? Why die?" She realized she had just rhymed and might sound tipsy to Steve. She wasn't tipsy; however, it was probably preferable if she sounded slightly under the influence, in case she was being too silly while she was being too serious.

"What's the point of continuing when you're ninety-seven and you've lost your marbles and have no control over your functions?"

"Well, we haven't solved that problem yet." She smiled, but she refused to let the subject go. "I'm talking about being alive forever as you are at your best, living forever at whatever age you choose, or being reincarnated, on earth or in heaven or whatever. Being in heaven would be no different from moving to a different state of the Union, moving out west, where there's plenty of room, except upwards."

"There's a joke about that. Look, the point is, you have to clear out at some point for your fellow creatures. If everyone lived forever, there'd be no room for you and me. We wouldn't exist. We wouldn't know each other."

"I understand that principle. But it could start now. The rule could start now. I'd settle for heaven, as long as I could be the same as I am right now. Heaven is supposed to absorb the excess population. Extra space for the still-living. There's no end to it. The space just expands as needed. Fields and fields and fields."

"People probably don't feel that way so much when they have kids, because they know their children will carry on the name and the genes."

"It's not the same."

"True. Anyway, this isn't going to get us very far. I'm more pragmatic than you. I'm going to live to the hilt while I'm on this earth. You only live once."

He'd said it. Mona's other very own phrase. Life is short. You only live once. "Either way," she said, "I'd like us to live to the hilt together, the short hilt or the long hilt. The eternal hilt. But do me a favor please. Your mother says two things I can't stand."

"Just two? You're lucky."

"When she says 'Life is short, darling' and 'You only live once,' I keep thinking, why is she telling me that and how does she know? It drives me crazy. It's as if she's God instead of your mother. So since I'm married to you and not to her, I would really appreciate it if you could avoid using those expressions."

"If you're going to ask a favor, at least ask something hard."

"That's it for now."

Steve's calamari and her veal came, with salads, and a bottle of Verdicchio. Steve toasted her. She would have been embarrassed, but she could see how sincere he was, because he could barely look at her. "I want to thank you for putting up with me the way you have and having the guts to go to the psychiatrist like you did. As I've said many times, I don't think I deserve you, but I'm trying. You're as precious to me as my own skin."

"That was very nice. Thank you. Why do you think it took guts for me to go to the psychiatrist?"

"I guess I would have been nervous. You don't know how someone like that is going to see you, what they'll think."

"Did you think he was going to think something?"

"No, come on, I'm congratulating you. I just thought it might help get us out of our rut. And it did."

"I've always really wanted to know how normal I was, I guess. I liked going." She'd been the one with the problem, yet she'd received Dr. Wachspress's commendation. She'd impressed an eminent authority. "This wine is delicious." Maybe Steve would end up as a great doctor. She visualized him sitting in the den, studying. (As long as he had to use the den to study in, they couldn't have a child.) "What happens when I interrupt you before an exam with a pain in the strangest place? Can you please help me right away, doctor dear?"

Steve laughed. "I hope I'll still be desirable, slaving over the books. I hope you'll still want to seduce me. Anyway, I'm going to have to make it worth your while, because the one thing I'm sure of is if you stopped loving me it wouldn't be worth it."

He had said more or less the same thing to her so many times since the trouble had started, it must be true. "It was very good I went to see him." She could now feel the vermouth, plus the Verdicchio, catching up with her. "It was very good he told me there was nothing wrong with your wanting to be a doc. It knocked some sense into me. If the sense can last for the next decade, we'll be in great shape. Once your school starts, everything will probably take care of itself."

"Who knows? Maybe you'll even be a little proud of me."

She put her hand on the back of her husband's hand. "Don't worry." They smiled at each other in a glowing way. The peacefulness of their gaze, and its intensity, said to her that they had to be meant for each other, no matter what.

Now that their crisis seemed to be over, Emily had moments of imagining their future more specifically than she'd been clear-headed enough to do during the crisis. What she imagined would have been depressing if she were still depressed—Steve sitting at the desk with his books 'til two in the morning, or in the library, while she had nothing to do but watch TV or go to the movies or eat dinner at Daddy's (or her "in-laws," God forbid). Unless—and this prospect she saw as the most desolate, for some reason—she started allowing herself to stay at the office later and later, and to attend more business-social events than she was required to, forced herself to become more and more the complete professional publicity gal, a workhorse, a Mrs. P. without Mrs. P.'s reputation or Mrs. P.'s pleasure in the job. Or she might drift, start to drink too much, or sleep with authors, so that (if she wasn't fired first) instead of replacing Mrs. P. someday, which would be frightening as well as a little embarrassing, she'd be passed over, which would be decidedly humiliating. Steve himself had been busy reassuring her; he hadn't volunteered to spell out what it would be like. Had he imagined her sleeping alone in their bed because he was sleeping at the hospital or working forty-eight hours straight?

But she was reluctant to mention her more frequently specific thoughts to Steve. She told herself what she'd told him at Pete's Tavern, the night she'd come home from Dr. Wachspress: once the medical stuff began, she'd be all right. Once she'd had a chance to adjust to the reality. That's what she'd done with her life to begin with. And, according to Dr. Wachspress, with remarkable success.

Still, after she'd finished reassuring herself, sometimes she couldn't help but feel that ten or fifteen percent of her had been removed from her body. But it would grow back. She was positive that she was supposed to believe it would grow back. She wondered where her eternal optimism came from. Suppose the missing part never grew back? The rest of the time she believed that the missing part had grown back already and it was up to her to find it. Steve was at his sweetest again. The sex was usually about as full as it had been at its fullest. She began to remind herself of something she knew everyone knew—that life didn't consist of one continuous state of bliss.

She would think (the original cause permanently forgotten) of the famous family moment when Ellen had screamed at her that everything always meant too much to her, why did everything have to mean so much to her, and she had screamed back that she wanted everything to mean too much to her. Now that she was more or less grownup, it concerned her that if things didn't mean too much to her, then they could mean nothing. Without consciously relaxing her expectations she seemed to have started to risk accepting life as it existed for her, instead of resisting so much what she couldn't change.

Her increased tolerance didn't apply only to the Steve situation; it applied also at the office. It wasn't hard to get lost in her work and to forget what it didn't amount to (in her opinion), because she usually had too much to do every day and because she had to use her wits every other minute—to keep her mouth shut at certain times and open at others, for instance, whether she wanted to or not. She needed to persuade, to sell—to get her authors airtime, magazine or newspaper space, or a public appearance. Sometimes she had to turn down requests for authors to appear.

At her proudest, she thought of herself as a young diplomat, learning discretion and manipulation on the job. But she couldn't shake—didn't want to shake—the idea that to be halfway respectable in publishing you had to be an editor, next best thing to an author. One of her authors crossed her up when they were having a drink. Graham Duckworth, a definitely mediocre novelist (from Hemingway High—Nina Brooks's witticism) said to her in his breezy, blunt (gauche) way, "This is probably the only kind of job you're qualified for, kid, and you're too good for it, but it sure beats writing novels." How phony could you get? His comment made an anecdote for her, which she told wherever she tactfully could.

She hardly had time to remember any longer that Timothy had never called her again, after all his intensity (including criticism) in the bar. Then *Big Time* had opened in Boston, getting a rave in *Variety* that predicted the show would be a solid smash on Broadway after relatively minor out-of-town tinkering. Timothy had his full share of the rave. She started to think about him a lot. She knew him so well (and his penis had been in her mouth!), this immature but obviously exceptional ex-boyfriend of hers in a huge shiny Broadway-bound musical limousine. (She couldn't resist noting that she had known about his show before any critics or audiences had seen it.) Timothy's dream was coming true. It had once been her own dream. In her autobiography, Emily would write about her college love affair with Timothy. (And her "night with George.") The book would smell of money.

She told Steve—no more secrets—about the *Variety* review. "Great," he said. "Let's get tickets as soon as possible."

"Maybe I'll be able to use pull through the office."

She had a fantasy she couldn't get rid of for days of being in the audience for Timothy's show opening night, almost never with Steve at her side, leading the applause as she stood in the fifth row center, the star of the audience. Part of the fantasy was Timothy coming out for a bow, slight Timothy, looking modest and, despite his tuxedo, still boyish, pointing at Emily and blowing her a kiss, so that everybody wondered who she was. Murmurs of curiosity around her. She leaves the audience (she's in her teal taffeta, but it's new), audience heads turning row by row like lights switching on, the audience ignoring the curtain calls to watch her exit. Or she is onstage somehow, holding Timothy's hand, but her hamminess and greed in this version is too much for her, so she reverts to her mystery-lady exit. She is going out to a limousine or to the stage door to visit Timothy backstage.

Then she and Steve went to *Long Day's Journey into Night,* soon after it opened. She had hardly ever in her life read such reviews as the play received. She was tickled they'd gotten their seats—seats fit for Steve—early. The play knocked them both out. At the end, Mary Tyrone's speech, concluding with, "Yes, I remember. I fell in love with James Tyrone and was so happy for a time," Emily was awed by the scene and by her presence at the scene. As one of the cast of privileged worshipers in the theater, she contributed to the standing ovation, shouting "Bravo" (maybe for the third time in her life) to the cast on the stage, where the light was.

She didn't feel like going anywhere after to eat, but ending such an unforgettable evening made her uneasy. On the way up the aisle, Steve held her hand, without saying a word. She said, "It's so strange. It was so exciting to see, but it's so depressing. It's exciting to get depressed, as long as you're at the theater." An interesting idea?

"I agree. It was absolutely tremendous."

"The characters aren't even that significant or important as people, really, but they're made important. The actors make them important. The playwright helps a little bit too. Do you know what I mean?"

"I think so, babes."

Once outside, Emily knew she wanted to go home and curl up in bed, with or without sex. She felt cold and sad. She and Steve walked east, looking for a taxi. Tomorrow night, at long last, Jill was coming to dinner, with a newly announced boyfriend, of all things, a psychiatrist (a real full-fledged practicing psychiatrist, thirty-four years old, named Peter Price. His wife had died in some horrible way.) It might have been through Peter Price that Jill had found Dr. Wachspress, Emily thought. She feared in her heart that tomorrow night would be the last time she'd see Jill, that she was forcing Jill to come. What would happen if she ever needed serious new friends? She hardly h; 1 any old ones. In the taxi, she asked Steve what he was thinking.

He put his arm around her, looking away from her, out his window. "Nothing much. I think I'm under the influence of the play. It really cast quite a spell."

She said, "I'm just interested in what goes on in your head. That's part of the point of being married, isn't it? Getting to know your mate?"

"It should be. I've always thought so. What are *you* thinking?"

She laid her cheek on the shoulder of Steve's blue overcoat. She couldn't tell him the thought that came to mind. She made a singsong hum that sounded coy to her; she hoped he'd take it as meaning "nothing worth mentioning." It was, unfortunately, the same thought she'd confided, like such an idiot, to George when cleaning up after her party, falling into his trap, making her own trap, because she was so thrilled he'd come to her house and because she'd figured that if he was friendly enough to come, why not take advantage of his presence? The thought being that she was worried she was nothing, would turn out to be nothing, always, and that even expressing her worry increased the risk of making her worry come true. It wouldn't be fair to Steve or to herself to tell him. What answer could he make? "Don't worry, babes"?

Emily said, "When I see a play like tonight's, I still wish like anything I'd had the courage to be an actress. But I know I would never have been good enough to be in something like this, not even the maid, so it doesn't make any difference anyway. I would never be what I wanted to be, because I could never be good enough. At least I've always had very high standards."

"Maybe too high."

"But your standards aren't too high for you." President!

' Well, I finally decided to latch onto the right thing. That doesn't mean you couldn't. Anyway, I've got the best idea in the world."

"For me? What?"

"I'll tell you when we get home. I don't think this is quite the place."

"Oh?" A baby. God. A baby? She couldn't say it aloud.

He rubbed his nose against the middle of her forehead.

She liked the new bedroom better. It was larger and it faced Fifth Avenue and it held the possibility of a hopeful future. The old bedroom had been spoiled by the talks they'd had in it after Steve's announcement. For the move, Steve had bought a new two-way lighting fixture that attached to the wall over the headboard. Once they were in bed tonight, with both bedlights off, Emily slid her nightgowned body over to Steve and, in an unladylike way she knew he loved, dropped her upper leg over his. "So, now. Will you tell me your thoughts?"

"I can't concentrate. Help."

She withdrew her leg.

"Don't. Stay there. It kills me."

"I shall return."

He placed his hand on her hip. She heard him make his little breath-laugh. He said, "I'm just afraid my suggestion's going to aggravate you for some reason."

"You have to tell me. So I'll try to control myself."

"Okay. I want us to have a child very badly."

"That was your idea in the taxi?"

"It's not that unnatural. Women occasionally have children."

Maybe I'm not a woman, she thought. "Do you want a boy or a girl?"

"Oh, a boy, I guess, but I don't care. I'd love a girl. The point is, I'd love a kid. And I think it would be great for you. You'd be a fantastic mother."

What he'd just said sounded so stupid—ignorant—it felt insulting. She didn't want to be mad. She'd just gotten over weeks of being mad. "You want to do everything all at once all of a sudden. Why are you in such a hurry?" When would he stop coming up with these surprises? Since their marriage, he'd been pushing in all directions.

"Maybe I am in a hurry, in a way. Unlike you, I don't happen to believe people live forever."

"That doesn't make any sense. We have years to have a baby."

He didn't answer her. He pressed her hip with his palm, whether in annoyance or friendliness she couldn't tell. She didn't ask him why he thought having a baby would be great for her; she was scared she knew why: a child would occupy her while he was otherwise occupied at school. She didn't want to ask him who he thought would take care of the child while she was at work, either. She had no intention of breaking her promise to Mrs. Poplar.

The only safe substitutes for talk at the moment were sex or sleep. The one thing in the world that made her magically powerful was putting her hand on his penis. Of course the power lasted only minutes and the result didn't vary much. Nevertheless, she was capable of enjoying the power for its own sake among the other nicer reasons. At the moment though, she resented her sole form of power. She said, "I'd like you to hold me and go to sleep holding me." She refused to let things get bad again.

"Fine."

"Without being peeved."

"I'm not peeved. I don't understand you sometimes."

She didn't want to talk, but she couldn't stand the idea of his being cold to her or of their being cold to each other. At the moment, the sound of words would be warmer than his arms around her, even if the words might be unpleasant, because his arms would be at her request. "What don't you understand?"

"I'm not a moron. I understand some reasons why you might not want to have a baby yet, but I'm interested in knowing what they are. It's a subject we've just sort of let lay there. But it lurks around. For one thing, it's a damn big job having a child. For another, you've got a job, but you're not what I'd call all that wild about your job."

She was convinced he was testing to see if he'd married someone crazy. She wished she could correct his "lay there," but she still didn't know how to approach his weak grammar. "But just a minute. If you're going to med school and your father's going to help you out, where do we get the money for a child? I mean, aren't there expenses? Farina?"

"Can you imagine our child's grandparents not going crazy with joy?"

"Financially?" She always expected Steve to be realistic, because he was a businessman, and a man, yet sometimes he seemed to act so impulsively instead. Maybe it was self-confidence, boldness of vision. Or maybe he was always being calculating.

"At first there wouldn't be that much expense. Eventually you could go back to work if you wanted to, and later, when the heavy expenses start, I'd be making plenty myself, remember."

"Uh-huh." She remembered Grandpa Gus's money. That was what had given Steve the idea to have a baby now. She tried to visualize an infant in different infant positions and activities—on her breast, against her cheek, being burped, being changed, by her, on a layette. The baby fell off the layette, out of sight. Each picture dissolved before it had a chance to stay. She couldn't hold onto the pictures. "Do you think I'm abnormal?"

"Don't be ridiculous. To tell you the truth, if you had a kid, I suspect you'd love it so much you'd want more."

How did he know? Why did he say that? "When we got married, I thought of marrying you so I could be your wife and you be my husband. I didn't think of being someone's mother." She didn't dream of having a child. She never had. It wasn't her hunger. Not yet. Ellen had wanted a baby almost right away. "I'm not saying I don't want to have one. Or more. Please don't get me wrong. But I want to be married to you for a while." She put her hand on his pajama shoulder. He hadn't taken his off her hip. She hoped now he'd hug her, but he didn't.

"Let's talk about it tomorrow," he said. "I'm getting sort of sleepy."

"Sorry." She took her hand away. How could he be getting sleepy?

"Don't worry about it." He kissed her near the mouth, then on the mouth.

She was really angry all of a sudden. What did she need to be forgiven for? She felt violently jumpy. She felt like turning away, or turning on the light, getting dressed and going to work at one in the morning. She thought of lowering her hand to stroke him with her fingertips outside his pajamas, driving him crazy, then stopping. She didn't know what to do or not to do. If she touched him and got excited herself, she'd have to get up to put her diaphragm in, which she didn't want to bother doing. She touched him after all.

"You're a witch, do you know that?"

She did it by mouth instead, giving him the slow, full, tricky treatment, with bites, a few of the bites sneakily too sharp, and thinking, "Why does he want me to love anyone else?"

The next morning Emily called Jill, anxious over the possibility that Jill was going to cancel, and said, "Steve and I are expecting you and Peter in the vicinity of approximately sevenish."

"Sweetie, is there anything we can bring?"

What kind of a way was "sweetie" for a social worker to talk? "Just yourselves. I can't wait to see you and meet Peter." She refrained from mentioning the new living-room rug, at last arrived, and the newly reupholstered living room furniture. Too housewifey.

"Peter, I just want you to know, is so wonderful he should be bottled, except I wouldn't want anyone else to have any of him."

Was that a hint? No hints were necessary. "Sounds serious."

"I feel so lucky that when I'm not deliriously happy, I'm petrified."

"Oh, Jill." She was moved, stirred, envious, a bride of less than three months feeling a touch of envy. "I am so happy to hear you talk that way. I'm very, very happy for you. Steve and I are really looking forward."

"Same here. See you later, Emileeee. Gotta go."

Emily had not spoken to Jill since thanking her the day after Wachspress and inviting her again to dinner during that same call. Jill still hadn't asked what the trouble was (respect for privacy?), and Emily still hadn't told her. Partly she didn't have the heart, partly she wasn't sure enough of her own position, and partly Jill always sounded too busy.

In her slippers and her honey-colored Viyella robe, an anniversary-of-their-very-first-meeting-at-her-housewarming-party present from Steve, Emily went into the kitchen, where Steve was busy making Saturday morning pancakes and sausages. She had never been that much more popular with the boys in high school than Jill (because of her pickiness or her seriousness? Or was she just kidding herself?), which was possibly one reason Jill had once liked her so much. Now Jill might be getting ahead of her in every department.

Emily poured herself coffee from the Chemex and over her cup watched Steve at the frying pan, waiting for a clue to his mood. Had he awakened appreciating her expert ministrations last night, or was he still bothered because she wasn't gung-ho to have a baby? She had seen on her way from the bedroom that he'd already set the drop-leaf table for breakfast in the so-called dining area between the end of the living room and the front door. "Anything I can do?" she asked.

"Just relax. There's fresh orange juice in the fridge. What's the dinner menu?"

"I thought steak, baked potatoes with sour cream and chives, string beans with almonds, salad, and I might try my hand at an icebox cake."

"Sounds okay to me."

"Any suggestions?"

"Well, we had steak for my parents."

"It's just something I know I can do well. They liked it, I thought."
It was kind of cheating to say so. Mona had raved meaninglessly (as usual) about the steak, as if Emily had invented steak.

"They did. But you're turning into an excellent cook. I think you should be diversifying, that's all."

"I'll see." She wanted to ask him if he was sorry he'd married her. She wished she knew what a marriage was supposed to be like. They ate their breakfast sharing the newspaper.

Later, Steve, who was already dressed in his sweatshirt and old blue jeans, went uptown to play touch football with Jerry Goetz, some younger Farr people, and other buddies and acquaintances. "Perfect football weather. See you in a few hours, babes."

Emily took a shower, phoned her father and sister to say hi, dressed in a gray skirt and green sweater-set, and went out for a stroll that would include errands and wind up in marketing for dinner.

The November day was so sunny, so comforting, and Emily felt so fortunate wandering around her charmingly formal, grownup, lower Fifth Avenue neighborhood that she couldn't believe she and Steve wouldn't straighten themselves out somehow. Part of the purpose of such weather and surroundings was to give people the hope that helped make what you hoped for come true. At Gristede's she bought a small sirloin roast instead of steak. Just because she'd overcooked one roast didn't mean she'd fail again. She wouldn't fail in front of Jill.

Back home, she peacefully put groceries away. In the bedroom, she removed her shoes and her outer sweater. Returning to the kitchen, she tied on an apron and washed her creative husband's breakfast pans and the dishes. Then she stood at the counter, reviewing roast beef in *Good–Lookin' Cookin'* as if she were studying for roast beef finals. She turned to Desserts after a while and the recipe for icebox cake.

With Steve's trusty eggbeater she was whipping cream in the brown-banded tan bowl when she thought she heard a noise at the front door. She remembered how much she disliked being alone in the apartment; she so rarely was. She stepped out of the kitchen and peered into the foyer. Possibly someone had dropped something off outside. Dry cleaning. An infant orphan! George Koenigsberg leaving a box of candy.

Holding the bowl with the eggbeater in it, she walked the five steps to the door and listened. She looked through the peephole. Nothing. She must have heard a neighbor coming home. She checked that the front door was locked. She checked the hall closet for a rapist, burglar, or lion, and then the whole apartment, thoroughly, carrying the whipping bowl for protection. If she stood doing her whipping outside the front door and neighbors saw her, they'd think she was insane, or she'd look like a baker-prostitute soliciting customers.

She went back to the kitchen. She would have liked to turn on the little kitchen radio, but then she might not be able to overhear noises. She started her whipping again. She saw Granny. She dropped the eggbeater. It was as if Granny had entered beneath the front door minutes earlier and only just now appeared. She jiggled in front of Emily's eyes, off the ground, in a dress made of ashes, the ashes from her own cremation, a long ashy dress. The dress was Granny's body. The dress moved like a kite, yanked by the breeze across the ocean to the Jewish cemetery, floating above Mom's grave and descending like a parachute, the ashes wrinkling as their hem touched the grave, and disappearing below-ground.

Emily felt sad to the point of weakness. She held onto the counter, in case she started to crumple. It didn't make sense, but it seemed to her that she was sadder about Granny dying than about Mom, because Granny was older. The older you were, the less you deserved to die. She also felt sorrier for Granny's sadness about Mom than she did for her own, because Granny had been so much older, and because being the mother of the one who had died was worse than being the daughter. She stood still for a moment more, taking in the creepiness and unexpectedness of what had happened.

Then, seeing herself as too stoic to brood, she made herself begin the actual assembling of the icebox cake, pasting the chocolate wafers together with the whipped cream, very high-school home economics.

She heard Steve at the front door. She called hello. He called back. She was glad he'd come home, and on the early side. But she noticed she was a bit anxious about not knowing what he'd do or say. He had her somewhat nervous. She kept at her work while he arrived behind her, saying, "Hi, babes." He smelled pleasantly of leaves, dirt, and autumn air. She turned her face enough for him to kiss her cheek. He rubbed her shoulders. He said, "You don't know how great it is to have such a terrific, gorgeous girl in my very own house who belongs to me."

"That's nice." She smiled and gulped, without his seeing, and tried to continue pasting the wafers while he held her. Was his good mood sarcastic, forgetful, or based on confidence that he'd get his way, because wanting to have a child—"a kid"—meant you deserved to get your way?

"That looks scrumptious," he observed.

"I hope it will be. It requires exquisite skill and profound concentration."

"I can take a hint."

"I got roast beef instead of steak. You're right. I have to branch out."

"Great. I think I can use a quick shower. Maybe I'll put me on a little music. I'll be around somewhere if you want to find me."

"I'll bear that in mind. How was the game?"

"Fun."

"Who won?"

"We did. As a matter of fact, it was such a slaughter, everyone got silly and we quit, but to tell you the truth I don't care that much who won. I just enjoyed myself." He kissed the top of her head and left the kitchen, whistling "Buckle Down, Winsocki."

Instead of examining his last statement for believability, she wondered if she should tell him about Granny, if it was childish to tell him or cheating not to tell him. She completed the cake by coating its exterior meticulously with the whipped cream, painting it, texturing the whipped cream, amusing herself.

She washed her hands. By now, the distant noise of the shower had been replaced by the blast of music from the den—raw, icy, windy music, very vigorous and bleak at the same time, definitely outdoors, a rocky coastline, and freezing cold.

Steve was lying on his prized plaid couch, barefooted, in a clean white T-shirt and fresh chinos, with his eyes closed and his arms folded on his chest. He looked dead, as well as clean and handsome. Maybe the music had killed him through the ears. If he were dead, what a waste their short marriage would have been, most of it spent trying to regain their premarital happiness. Steve opened his eyes. "Who's the cheery composer?" she asked.

"Mr. Sibelius."

"May I turn it down? I have to talk to you."

"Sure. Turn it off. Something wrong?"

She lifted the needle arm from the record and turned off the phonograph. "Do you want a sandwich?"

"I'll have something later. Don't bother, thanks."

"Can you move over a little?"

He made full room for her. She sat down, frowning, unable to figure out how to tell him about her fantasy or why she should tell him.

Steve's left arm lay in front of her. She stared at the curls of hair-bark covering it, Steve's arm, also a stranger's arm. She put her hand on his wrist.

He rubbed at her hand, then took it. "You look upset."

She thought: I miss Mom. Since getting married. Since getting involved with Steve, I've thought of her more and more. And since Granny died. She didn't look at him. She knew he'd be sympathetic if she told him the fantasy from before. She wanted him to be that way, for them to be on the same side. But not because of her fantasy, and not just sexually, either. She wanted him to be more sympathetic and tender without having to appeal to him. Also, the fantasy was too private. She didn't feel about to let him know what had happened. When they'd gotten engaged and she'd insisted they had to tell each other everything, that was before she'd learned how much he acted on his own. At the moment, she wanted to keep herself separate by not telling him the fantasy. Maybe it was resentment, maybe it was maturity.

"Babes, I wish I were a mind-reader, but I'm not. If there's something you want to talk about, I want to hear it, but you have to tell me what it is."

"I know. I'm sorry. Can we just lie peacefully for a little while?"

"Be my guest."

She stretched out beside him, embracing him lightly, as he did her. She rested her forehead on his shoulder. Within seconds of closing her eyes, she saw into her mother's grave, where Mom and Granny were having tea, in tiny coffin-chairs, like the chairs from Granny's dollhouse in the attic in Newbury. They were waiting for Emily to join them, just for tea, for the afternoon, not as a member of the dead, but as one distinguished from them by being alive, honoring them with her brief living visit.

Perhaps to get the picture out of her mind, or simply to say something, so she wouldn't annoy him with her continuing silence, or possibly to bring up the subject of having a baby so there was a chance she and Steve could understand each other completely and be close and safe, a couple in love, by the time Jill and Peter arrived (though what came out of her could not have been what he'd want to hear), Emily said, "I think I'm too lonely to have a baby." She opened her eyes. What did it mean, what she'd just said?

He opened his eyes a crack.

"Were you sleeping?" she asked.

"Not really. How the hell can someone be too lonely to have a baby, if you don't mind my asking? And what do you mean, 'lonely'? Shouldn't I be offended?"

"I don't know. No." She was half-embarrassed and half-impressed with herself. "It just emerged from my subconscious. All it means is I want you, not a baby." She couldn't say anymore; it would sound as if she were literally, actually lonely for him, or nagging about medical school again, when she really thought she meant something different right now, even though she didn't understand it—that she missed her mother too much to want to have a child. She felt as if she had been told the truth about herself, by herself, but in a foreign language that no one in the world knew.

"I think part of you doesn't want to do what everyone else does, frankly. Having a baby's too common. It's too ordinary."

"I got married, didn't I? I wanted to do that very badly, and that's common."

"I appreciate it. Really, I'm grateful, since I asked you to marry me." He gave her a mildly challenging wiseguy smile. "I have my theory about you, though, which is that you have unrealistic ambitions but you don't have realistic ones."

"Oh. That's interesting." It really was. She knew there might be something to what he said. "Can you give me an example?"

"It's hard to put my finger on it. You think you can live forever, but you don't want to have a baby. I don't know. It's a hunch."

She was silent. She wondered about his own examples of a possible lack of realism, such as medical school, getting married so soon, wanting to have a baby so soon. For all she knew, the business plan he'd proposed to his father and uncle might fall into the same category.

Steve patted her shoulder. "I don't know, babes. I don't know."

"What do you mean?"

"Things shouldn't be so complicated, that's all."

"I know," she said. But who had started it? Was he suggesting that she was complicated and he wasn't? "Things will work out." What happened if their disagreements kept interfering with their lives? She didn't know what else to say. She wished she felt sleepy. She said, "I'm a bit snoozy, do you mind?" He'd gotten sleepy on her last night, until she'd exercised her powers.

"Go ahead. You're the boss."

His remark irritated her irresistibly. "I don't see myself as a boss, somehow."

His expression was surprised and a little unfriendly. "I'm only trying to lighten the atmosphere. It doesn't mean anything. It's just a silly phrase. Forget it."

"I'm sorry. If you want to do something while I take a short nap, I'll understand. I'm not trying to get rid of you. You might not feel like lying around, that's all. I have to get to work on dinner in a little while myself."

"I might make myself a liverwurst sandwich. I should check and see if we need some vino. If we do, I'll go get some. Want a sandwich?"

"No, thanks." He let himself off the couch. She rolled over to say goodbye. Squatting, and smiling slightly, he kissed her mouth, withdrawing his face before she had time to decide how much she wanted to respond. She wasn't interested in sex, but she wished he would stay. "Don't go too far," she said.

"Sleep well." He waved as he left, very devil-may-care.

Lying on the plaid couch, Emily stared at the doorway of the den. She was a person, she thought, who knew something was going to happen to her.

CHAPTER FIFTEEN

Her Mother Kneeling

Jill and Peter arrived at seven-thirty, about a half hour late, Jill affectionate, exuberant, and trim-looking: navy-blue silk dress, pearls, pretty pearl earrings, a little makeup, altogether the best Emily had ever seen her in her grownup version. Dr. Price, skinny and quite tall, stood back; he stood back even when introduced. His clothes were all brown but for his white shirt—dark brown pants, heavy, hairy tweed jacket, brown wool tie, not the knit kind, the nubby kind. His shoes were wing-tip, okay, not especially well shined. He had curly dark hair, hornrimmed glasses. He couldn't compare in appearance to Steve, who had on his navy blazer, gray slacks, and a navy tie with scarlet and cream stripes she had bought for him at Saks the day after Wachspress.

Presenting a wrapped bottle of something, Jill exclaimed how elegant and prosperous the newlyweds looked. "We live on love and clothes," Emily replied. She realized she was being superficial, and reminded herself to watch it. "Breathtaking," Steve had said in the bedroom, referring to her in her new black velvet skirt and ivory faille blouse. "You, too. Divoon," she said. One thing she had learned she could count on since their marriage. Dressed up, Steve was always as spiffy as an ad.

In the living room, where pâté, cheeses, crackers (and white mums, to go with the new upholstery) had been set out, Steve took drink orders—sherry for Jill, ice water for Peter. Emily decided she wasn't allowed to announce to her guests that because of their lateness she'd removed the roast beef from the oven at a quarter past seven; that she would now put it back in the oven for its final fifteen minutes, prior to removing it again and letting it rest before carving; that she'd originally planned to serve dinner at eight, with an hour for drinks beforehand, but that now they'd eat at approximately eight-fifteen, with a forty-five minute drink period. In other words, it didn't thrill her that they were late. If anything went wrong with the roast, she wasn't going to be able to blame it on them.

Once they were settled for a while, Jill, holding Peter's hand on the couch, pretty much carried the conversational ball (social work?)—chattering away about grad school and her choices of where she would go to work after getting her MSW and how she and Peter had met (at a party given by one of her psych professors). She reminisced about Emily in high school and at summer stock—Emily's wild excitement over her teeny part and her crushes on Carey Ames and Thom Blake. Emily felt Jill's manner had a slightly snide undertone, implying that Emily used to be an overdramatic if unusual girl who had grown up and settled down like everyone else.

Of course Jill wasn't going to mention Mom; Emily assumed Jill had filled Peter in on that part of things already. She felt warm toward the world, knowing that an aspect of her life couldn't help but produce a sympathetic, respectful response in strangers. Maybe she wasn't worried tonight about respect she hadn't earned because she had new problems now and needed consolation. Or maybe because as a psychiatrist, Peter (who, she noticed, though very quiet, seemed to listen with his eyes, with deep, still attention that went way beyond politeness) would be especially impressed, now that he'd met her face-to-face, at how healthy she was—the way Wachspress had been impressed. And it might be that she deserved respect for her healthiness that she didn't deserve for the early loss of her mother, which she had always assumed to be the source of unspoken, widespread deference. Would she be able to find out tonight if Peter had been responsible for Wachspress? Had Wachspress himself spoken to Peter about her?

Jill, really acting like the hostess, asked Steve what he was up to these days. (She still hadn't asked Emily about her own job.) Steve's answer was reticent or modest—he might not be crazy about discussing the subject in front of his wife. His wife couldn't blame him. (Of course if he'd been even more reticent, he would have avoided mentioning his medical plans at all.) In any case, he announced his news casually. Jill's response was the opposite of casual. She jumped off the couch and went over to his chair to kiss him and then to Emily's chair to kiss her, saying to her, "Why didn't you tell me? I'm so pleased for both of you," just as if they were having a baby. Emily felt that her blush must be showing in some ornate design, like fireworks.

She stood, smiling, about to excuse herself. It would shortly be time to boil the string beans and reheat the sauteed almonds she'd serve with the beans. "We were waiting 'til tonight," Emily said.

"When did all this happen?" Jill asked her, still excited, resuming her seat beside Peter on the couch.

"September." She managed not to say, Just after our honeymoon.

"It's so great, isn't it, Peter?"

Peter raised his water glass to Steve. "You're a brave man. Congratulations."

The remark sounded forced to Emily, like bad acting; he was trying to be friendly, though.

"I hope not too brave," Steve said, "but thanks."

When Emily was dumping the string beans into boiling water, Jill appeared in the kitchen. "Anything I can do?"

"Everything's under control. And you had better be knocked out by my cooking ability." She kissed Jill again, grateful for the comfort of her extraordinarily familiar face. "It's so good to see you. Peter seems so intelligent."

"It's simple. He's the greatest man in the world. But aren't you proud of Steve? Who would have thunk?"

"I *am*. Steve's very unpredictable. It's never a boring moment." Emily started to fuss at the almonds with the spatula, but stopped herself immediately so she wouldn't appear evasive.

"Sounds like fun. Are you okay?"

Wouldn't it even occur to Jill that the med-school business might have coincided with her calling her about a psychiatrist? "Don't I look it?" She smiled, making sure her smile lasted longer than a fake smile would last.

"You always look it. And you happen to look stunning, by the way."

"You too. Do you think the two of us could catch up sometime?"

"We really have to. I spend most nights with Peter, but not all."

There was an answer to an unaskable question.

"How was the psychiatrist you went to? I didn't want to be nosy."

"Did Peter find him?"

"Yes, as a matter of fact, he did."

"He was very helpful. I mean the psychiatrist. Peter was, too." She laughed. "I think I'd like to tell you about it sometime, if you wouldn't mind."

"No. I'd like to hear."

"Jill?" She wished she could say, I have to talk to you. "Are the boys talking in there? 'The boys'?"

"They were when I left. I said, 'Talk doctor, fellows.' "

"Okay. Will you please return to them? I have become a chef supreme, but I'm not experienced in giving dinners yet, so I'm better off keeping myself organized in here. I'm almost ready. But I'd really like to talk sometime. Just with you."

"Sounds intriguing. Anytime."

"I don't think you'll find it boring."

"How's the job?"

"Hectic."

"Tell us more at the table? Peter wants to know all about you. I told him a lot, but he's always curious about everything. The table looks exquisite, by the way."

"Your candlesticks, my mother-in-law's tablecloth."

"Do you get along with your mother-in-law?" By drawing out "along," Jill tried to make a little joke out of the difficult-mother-in-law cliché.

Emily, however, wasn't going to lose the chance to answer Jill's per-functory-sounding question. She answered with a cliché of her own, laying it on so thick that she hoped it would be impossible for Jill to see she wasn't kidding. "My best friend. We talk first thing every morning and last thing at night and we have lunch and go shopping and laugh and laugh like two little schoolgirls."

It was plain Jill hadn't been prepared for so much bitterness. "I'm sorry. It sounds terrible!"

"She doesn't bother me that much, actually. I mean, she bothers me a lot, but she leaves me alone, mostly. She's very insincere and very needy. I think it's very tough for Steve."

"What a shame. Anyway, I don't want to hold up the chef supreme."

Alone, Emily wondered if Jill had given any thought to the possibility that Peter, like Steve before him, would move from Jill's life into Emily's life, though not as a "gift," obviously, in Peter's case; or did Jill stop short of such a worry by reassuring herself that Emily wasn't in Peter's league.

Soon, Jill and Peter were sitting at the table. Amidst applause, Emily brought the roast beef to the sideboard (where the wine had been "breathing") for Steve to carve. "Having fun?" she murmured. He responded with a nod of pleasure and curtness in which the curtness cancelled out half the pleasure, it seemed to her. Maybe he was just nervous about carving. Ha-ha, cadaver practice.

"It looks great, babes, if I may say so."

"Thanks." He seemed to be behaving intentionally in a confusing way at a time when explanations were unavailable. Had he wanted her to crow over medical school in front of the others? Was he mad that Jill hadn't known about it?

When the serving had been completed, and Steve had poured the burgundy (for Peter, too), Emily raised her glass in the candlelight and, looking at Jill, said, "To old times and new."

"I second the motion," Jill said. "And to your wonderful-looking dinner and your life and"—she stopped, censoring something—"good luck to everyone." Everyone clinked glasses. Peter's participation in the clinking struck Emily as slightly *noblesse oblige;* he seemed to look on the ritual as if it were a children's game.

"Jill," Steve said, holding his glass up a little way. "I don't want to be maudlin, but let me tell you, you're a wonderful young woman in your own right, with a great future ahead of you in your chosen profession, but I hope you can understand that as far as I'm concerned, the best thing you've ever done is introduce me to my wife, just a little over a year ago, as a matter of fact. She never ceases to amaze me. And I must say"—here the wiseguy grin—"it looks like she's learning to cook so magnificently, there'll be no stopping her."

"Bravo," Jill said.

"Let's eat and see if he's right," Emily said. She blew Steve a kiss from her chair; then she got up and kissed him directly, a warm peck on the mouth, "setting a good example," she thought, and wondering exactly what kind of a compliment Steve had meant his toast to be.

The roast beef received raves. Emily had to admit she'd never tasted better. She explained to Jill that she'd used a secret recipe of garlic, salt, and pepper. Steve said how concerned he was about the Russian squashing of the Hungarian uprising and how it bothered him all the more because his family had originally come from Hungary. They commented on how terrible the Russians could be. Then Emily, trying to draw Peter out a little, asked him if he minded listening to patients all day long.

"It's not the kind of thing you should mind too much if you're in my profession."

"I mean," she said, after everyone had laughed, "don't you ever want to burst out, talk a lot, to make up for it?"

"He talks to me," Jill said. "He also asks me the most wonderful unexpected questions, but he talks about himself, he really does."

"How can they tell?" Peter asked Jill. He stopped cutting his beef to smile at her through his hornrims.

Jill said, "Sorry, dear. I'll shut up. It's just that you're so modest."

The old conventional Jill, Emily thought, would never have said, "He asks the most wonderful unexpected questions." It sounded so sexy, for one thing, but also, Jill had never been the kind of person who liked unexpected questions. Emily loved the sardonic but friendly way Peter had just dealt with Jill.

"Peter, what would you say if you were going to talk about yourself?" Steve asked, with hostly courtesy.

"Oh, I'd probably ask questions anyway. Much more interesting."

"We'd rather hear about you, but feel free," Emily said.

"I had nothing specific in mind, really," Peter said.

"Steve just mentioned Hungary," Emily said, feeling she'd better push matters along herself. "My company just signed a book about the revolt by Andras Hegyi." Serious enough, folks?

"Very impressive," Peter said.

"You never told me you signed that," Steve said. "That's great."

"We sign so many. But I'm bringing it home for you as soon as it comes out in two years."

"I know you work at some glamorous publishing job," Peter said.

"Partridge. I'm assistant director of publicity, believe it or not. A parasite on the body of creativity."

"Appetizing," Jill said.

"You certainly are some publicity for your company, darling," Steve said.

"I know, you're right, but it's a weekend, and I'm in my own home."

"But you publish Andras Hegyi," Peter said. "There's nothing else you're not ashamed to be associated with?"

"Oh, sure. As a matter of fact, we recently published a book by a French woman anthropologist who got lost in the Sahara desert. You might say it was careless of her to get lost in the first place, but it was worth it, because she got out and wrote a most wonderful and unusual book, and very suspenseful." When she'd shown Steve the galleys, he'd wondered if Margot Neveu's adventure had been faked for the sake of a book, making Emily furious, then causing her to doubt Margot Neveu and finally to decide not to take Steve's cynicism seriously. It was some need he must have to be smart and worldly, ahead of the game.

"There are others," she continued. "And plenty of stuff we publish isn't junk, like cookbooks, photography. Lots of it is really embarrassing, though—childish, cheap humor books, and, you know, typical commercial novels. Junk. Fluff. Trash."

"Emily would like everything to be great art," Steve said, looking as if he were joking.

"Well, it would be better, wouldn't it? You don't like junky music."

"You have an excellent point. It just happens that the majority of great music is in the public domain. And I guess it's much easier to make money on a trashy modern novel than it is on Stravinsky. Anyway, if you're a consumer you have rights you don't have in business. If I'm listening to music, I expect to be satisfied. If you're on the business end, you have to do what you have to do to make a profit, especially if it's your own money in the business. Unless you happen to be so rich you can afford to publish anything you want. That's it."

"We don't completely agree," Emily said. "I'm more idealistic and that doesn't make me completely wrong." She knew Steve must be thinking idealistic and unrealistic were the same thing. "Anyway," she said, returning to Peter, "I enjoy my job. Sometimes I'm afraid I may like it too much. I just wish it were important." Did she sound like an arty high-school girl or a person with integrity? She looked from Peter to Jill. The answer wasn't on Jill's face. Jill seemed to be listening to her food.

"I have a question," Peter said.

"Fire away."

"Why can't you think of your job as one in which you're getting paid to bring books to the public attention, which is what I assume you do, and therefore being helpful to your company and your authors, otherwise known as being important?"

Emily replied, "That's easy for you to say, isn't it? Being helpful is what you do, only you do it on an exalted level."

"Isn't getting paid to be helpful the best possible combination? I don't say it just because that's what I do, or try to do. In fact, I'm often unable to do it, or much of it. There goes your exalted level."

"A manicurist gets paid to be helpful."

"A manicurist probably feels better about her job than you do, from the sound of it."

Did psychiatrist-guests have special conversational privileges allowing them to be as frank as they cared to be? Or was she just so fascinating that he couldn't help but get too personal? "I have to think about that," she said. Was he saying it was better to be a manicurist and unfrustrated? Was he opposed to striving? She was opposed to striving. She had been pushed ahead in her job. "Let's just say my job in tangential."

"Tangential to what? So is everybody tangential."

"Who wants to be everybody?" That got a laugh from the table. "Enough about me," she said. "Definitely time to change the subject." She felt like a hog of modesty.

"Everyone is also central," Peter said. "Almost everyone."

"I appreciate your interest very much," Emily said. "It gives me some things to ponder. Truly. I know a lot of people would love to have my job. Also, I could be unemployed." Steve would probably not like it that she'd said she could be unemployed, since he wanted her to be unemployed so she could take care of their tyke while he was off studying to be Albert Schweitzer.

Steve had been listening neutrally while eating; reserving comments for later, no doubt. But then, thank goodness, he brought up *Long Day's Journey into Night* from last night. The talk turned into a four-person relay of opinion on recent shows, movies, political events, and Elvis. When Steve insisted he had to have seconds on the beef, Peter followed suit.

Jill helped Emily clear. "Peter must be a very good doctor," Emily said. "You really feel he's giving you his attention."

"I couldn't put it better myself."

"He's very serious, isn't he?"

"If he's interested. But he can be hysterically funny, too."

Emily squeezed Jill's hand and looked happy for her. Peter could do no wrong, apparently. She started for the refrigerator.

Jill followed her halfway. "I want you to be happy, too, sweetie."

Emily pulled out the cake on its platter and turned around. She didn't say, "I am happy." She said, "Don't worry."

Jill's face revealed no concern. "Yummy. Look at that."

"What I'd really like is to call you Monday from the office and make a date."

"I'll call you tomorrow. How's that?"

"Either way." But Jill would have to call anyway, to say thank you for the wonderful evening. "Do you and Peter drink coffee?"

"Peter doesn't. Do you have any milk?"

"Sure." Was Peter square or an eccentric? And what difference did it make?

The cake went over as well as the roast beef had. After dinner,

Steve offered liqueurs. Only Steve accepted—brandy and soda. Emily continued with her dinner wine, Peter drank another glass of ice water, and Jill had club soda.

Emily thought the evening might end too early; it seemed to her that the conversation had become dangerously superficial. But everyone got a second wind. Steve asked Jill some questions about what was going on at the Morningside Settlement House, where he had originally met her; he talked a little, disparagingly (and not for the first time), about the toy business he would soon be leaving for good. Peter then told an astonishing anecdote about the childishness of a celebrated child psychiatrist who had died recently. Emily, with such a handy opening, couldn't resist describing Pat Crane, of *Leave the Cashews for Me* fame, as a specific example of why she occasionally had contempt for her own job.

The after-dinner talk all connected to children or childishness in some way, since her point about Pat Crane was his childishness. Not Timothy's kind. Timothy was childish, all right, but she knew from the past without understanding why that Timothy wouldn't be talented if he weren't childish, although she supposed not everyone talented had to behave childishly. She could forgive Timothy his childishness (and his talent). The energy behind one attribute seemed to be the energy behind the other. Pat Crane was unforgivable. Pat Crane was in the business of being childish. Childish, silly, cute, corny. And telling his readers to be the same. To be morons. If Pat Crane ever got his national TV show underway (a definite possibility, as yet unknown to the world at large), he would surely wear Dr. Dentons on it. Timothy's show opened on Broadway at the end of the month. She couldn't wait. To think about it almost gave her butterflies.

Second wind or not, by a quarter past eleven Jill and Peter, after the thanks and kisses (including one for Peter from Emily), hugs, handshakes, and Jill's "Call you tomorrow," were gone.

A friendly, businesslike atmosphere immediately occupied the apartment. Steve took the dessert plates to the kitchen and said to Emily, "I want to tell you, you put together some fabulous dinner," before kissing her, briefly but sexily, and excusing himself to go to the bathroom. "I'll be right back." She changed her blouse for an old shirt of his, put on her apron and a pair of long yellow gloves, and got to work at the sink. Steve returned after a while, having shed his blazer and tie, to help her dry.

"What did you think of Peter?" she asked. What advice, if any, had been solicited and given about medical school?

"He takes himself a bit too seriously, but I think he's a good guy. I loved what he said to you about your job."

"It was interesting. Do you think Jill and he are good for each other?"

"Looks that way. Can't really tell. He seems much smarter than her."

Than she. Please! "I think Jill's plenty smart. I loved seeing her. I think Peter might be too intense."

"Too intense for her? It doesn't look that way. What do you mean?"

Did she mean too intense for herself? He thought about things twice as hard as she did. Would she like Peter in private? As a patient? As a friend? How would he be different if she knew him? "I don't know. Too intense for his own good, maybe. She's really crazy about him. That makes me happy. I liked how he handled her at the table when she was talking for him. He was fine. Unusual. Do you mind my asking if he gave you any advice?"

"About you?"

"About medicine. Medical school."

"He told me to take two aspirins and call him in the morning. Not really. He told me what I already know."

"Did he ask what I thought about it?"

"Nope. Yes! As a matter of fact, he did. Sorry. I told him you weren't crazy about it at first, but you were accepting it better now."

"What did he say to that?"

"Nothing. That was it."

"I just wonder what he thought."

"Beats me. What's the difference?"

"How come you didn't answer my question?"

"Which one? I answered everything."

"I asked you if he asked you what I thought about your becoming a doctor."

"I did answer it."

"But first you said he hadn't asked you what I thought. Then all of a sudden you changed your mind and remembered."

"To tell you the truth, I didn't think it was any of his damn business what goes on between you and I."

"You and me. It's between you and me, not between you and I." She felt some apprehension enter her heart.

"So solly. You and me."

"Maybe it isn't his business, but I'm asking you why you weren't going to tell me his reaction at first. Why is the answer to that that you don't think it's his business? In that case, you wouldn't answer him, not not answer me. I'm talking about your not answering me, pretending at first he hadn't asked."

"Are we in a courtroom? What's going on with you here? I didn't want to start up, frankly, because other than the fact that it rubs me the wrong way to hear you be so hoity-toity about your job, it was a very pleasant evening, I thought, and a great dinner, and I have to admit I'm in a somewhat sexy mood, or at least I was a minute ago, and I didn't want to spoil my chances by adding to a delicate subject. So I started to avoid it, but then honesty triumphed."

"You could have just said that without telling me it was none of his business, which has nothing to do with it."

"You're right. You're a hundred percent right. You get me flustered, I swear. Let's drop it, can we?"

"Okay. I'm sorry." She felt too embarrassed to kiss him. She wasn't used to pushing him so far.

"I'm glad there's some roast beef left over. I could eat that for days."

"I'll make it again sometime, now that it's so easy." She snapped her fingers. Actually, she also wanted to point out to him that he talked about the toy business with less respect than she talked about publicity. But he could always answer that at least he was leaving the toy business, with the implication (becoming predictable) that if she didn't like what she was doing, why didn't she quit (for Farr, or for motherhood).

The sex was better than she'd expected it could be tonight; only she'd have to say it was more about sex than about them. Which didn't stop her from being sorry, as always, when they were done and he pulled out. They lay in their bedlight's dim illumination (one bulb on and its cone turned sideways), sort of squinting at each other, not embracing, but touching.

"Man!" Steve said.

"Same to you."

"God had to make it so good for some reason."

She couldn't believe he was starting in again about a baby. "God made it so good so people could enjoy themselves at night without having to go to the movies all the time."

"Then why did he invent TV, babes? Got you there."

"Obviously TV came along so late in history that it has nothing to do with your silly point. People aren't going to stop liking sex for its own sake because God finally broke down and gave them TV."

Steve was being amused. He said, "God is my co-pilot."

"Congratulations. Would you mind telling me what you're talking about?"

"I put a hole in your diaphragm before."

"Brag-brag-brag."

"With a safety pin, while you were doing the dishes." He hadn't stopped being amused.

"I know you're kidding."

"It's the only means available. What can I say?"

She thought, he's kidding, but I have to know for certain and I can't take the thing out for six hours, seven o'clock this morning. She had a sleeping bee inside her. "Do you know something? If it were true, what you said, if you did it, I'm actually in the middle of my cycle, so you might get what you want."

"Too bad I didn't do it."

"Do you mean it?"

"I was kidding, obviously."

"This isn't funny, Steve. Did you do it or not? I have to know."

"How could you think such a thing? For God's sake!"

"How could you even say it, though?"

"Do you really imagine I'd do something like that?"

"Look, you said it. Saying it is like doing it. I don't understand how you could do that, especially right after we just had such a close time."

"I didn't do it. I just said something silly, as a joke. Believe me, I regret it. I'm doing everything wrong these days."

"But why would you want to scare me about something like that?"

"Because it should be obvious it was a joke. I was pulling your leg."

"But why? Because you're mad I don't want to have a baby, right?"

"I hate to tell you, but you're getting so damn serious about everything. You're acting like you're the only important person in the world and your job's not good enough for you and now I'm not good enough for you and a kid's not good enough for you. You're really being rather pompous and pretentious, I have to say, Emily."

She looked at him as he spoke, then she looked down. She hadn't budged from her position in the bed since they'd started talking after the sex (except that she wasn't touching him any longer, nor was he touching her), because she was too upset to do anything decisive. Now she wanted to leave the bed, without knowing what she'd do once she did, and not knowing what to do while she stayed there. But she couldn't just stay there or merely turn away like a bawled-out child.

She took her white nightgown with the violets on the bodice from between the pillows and got out of bed, facing away from Steve, to slip it on. She sat on the edge of the bed, with her back to him, still not knowing what to do, now that she'd put her nightgown on. She couldn't sort out what had happened. She didn't know how any accusation of his could be right after he'd played such a disgusting joke. She then thought that he might be trying to force her to leave him, trying to get rid of her. And what was the point of staying married? "Do you want your freedom?" she asked.

"Isn't that a bit melodramatic?"

Having started to talk, she now feared she might start to cry, so she got up and put on her Viyella robe and walked out to the living room, where they had been entertaining Jill and Peter two hours before. She sat on the couch, in the dark, with both feet on the floor, gazing to her right at the window, which was still waiting for its drapes. The late-night city light, at the level of the fourteenth floor, made the outside a murky adjacent living room.

She heard the hall light go on, and Steve in the hall, and she turned her head. She couldn't see the hall, only the hall light, announcing him, then his shape crossing the foyer. The foyer light went on. She watched him standing at the far edge of the living room, barefoot, in his blue pajamas. "You don't want light in there?" he asked her.

She shrugged. "I'm not reading."

"Do you mind if I turn it on?"

"I don't care. Why do you ask? Go ahead."

The overhead living-room light went on. She thought how much she would have preferred sitting alone in the dark, collecting herself.

He didn't come into the room. "I made a dumb mistake," he said. "I apologize. Maybe I had a little too much to drink tonight, I don't know. It was insensitive, to say the least."

She had the impression that he apologized a lot more than he changed his ways. "It's like what a fraternity boy would do," she said, "if a fraternity boy knew what a diaphragm was. I don't know how you can behave this way. What's wrong?" She meant, What's wrong with you?

"Except I didn't do it, Emily. You've got to get it into your head that I didn't do it, as stupid as what I did was, I admit. Your diaphragm is safe. If it's not, it's a pure fluke. May I just ask what's happening? Are you going to sit out here all night?"

"I might. You've got to get it into *your* head that I don't think it's wonderful that you didn't do it. It's bad enough that you said it. I'd like to know something. I'd like to know why you keep talking about having a child when you know I'm not ready. Maybe there is something

wrong with me, and I should want to have one more than I do"—she
left out *right now,* to keep herself as honest as she could—"but I would
also like to remind you that we've been married a total of less than
three months, so at this point I don't see how you can blame it on
some neurosis or something. It's completely normal not to want to
have a baby yet. Maybe you want one so badly because you think you
can control it. Maybe you're guilty about going to medical school and
you think a baby will keep me company. Are you acting like such an
infant so that if I have a child you think I won't notice the difference?
Or are you just trying to break up the marriage so you can do whatever
you want without having to worry about me at all?"

"You're talking a bunch of fancy nonsense, you know? It fits right
in with the attitude I was talking about before."

"Which attitude is that?"

"Just the way you ask that question is a very good example. You
are so superior! I'm sorry, but you are. You're very superior and con-
descending, but you never follow through on a damn thing. It's the
one thing about you I don't like. Seriously."

"Why do you say 'seriously'?"

"What are you talking about?"

"I didn't think you were kidding. Follow through on what? What
do you mean, follow through? I have a job. Don't I have a job? I go
to work every day. You want me to quit my job to have a baby. Is that
what you mean by following through? What's with you? If I don't
earn my salary while you're studying, we're down to basics, as you put
it. I'm working so when you go to school we don't have to live off
nuts and berries."

"I said we might have to cut back some—a little."

"And if I'm not earning any money because I'm staying home with
your baby, then what?"

"It would fall into place. There's other money if we had a baby. As
I said, I can't believe the families wouldn't love to help out. But what's
the point of discussing it? You've made it clear we're not going to have
a baby. My baby, as you sweetly put it."

"I'm asking you what you mean by my not following through. Which
is it? That I have a job? That I don't want a baby three months into
our marriage?"

"It's just a whole picture, Emily. You resist my wanting to do something worthwhile with my life. It's like you're trying to prevent me
from following through on something because you don't do it yourself,
but this is certainly a major thing in someone's life, their work. You

happen to think you're too good for your job, but I don't see you doing anything about it."

"But I've stopped resisting you. I've accepted it."

"It's obvious your heart's not in it. Don't think it's not obvious. I'm not that insensitive."

"It's true I don't love it. But I'm convinced you should do it. I'm still concerned about its possible effect on our marriage. Anything wrong with that? And in fact, basically I'm all in favor of your being ambitious. I'd still like to know where I'm guilty of not following through. I'm really curious to know what you mean." She would have liked to bring up the little matter of Steve's not following through on visiting Larry Kornbluth's studio, but she couldn't bring it up, because secretly and embarrassingly she remained squeamish about seeing Helen.

"I notice you seem quite defensive," he said. He was in a peculiarly casual position, with his palm against the corner of the wall that separated the hall from the living room.

"If I want you to give me some of your examples, I don't see how that makes me defensive."

"Okay. Some of them are little things, but they're signs of what I mean. In my opinion your problems are all connected with wanting to do things you never do, saying you want to do things, like the big, fancy plan you had when I first met you about giving a play outdoors for your grandparents. Lots of talk and enthusiasm. You think things can get accomplished by talking about them."

"My grandmother died. That cut the audience in half."

"But by then the whole idea had gotten down to a little shrimpy thing. You start off with these big plans, then nothing happens. It's a pattern."

"But the plan was completely unrealistic. You're absolutely right. I wanted to give a huge outdoor production of the whole play. It was ridiculous. My eyes were much bigger than my stomach." But the fantasy had excited her, it had seemed real for a while.

"So if you don't think on such a grandiose scale, you can get more accomplished. That's my point. And you don't seem so arty or phony in the process. You wanted to be an actress. You weren't an actress. Your whole life has been like that."

Steve was Thom Blake in disguise. "I think I'm perfectly realistic when it counts. I wasn't an actress precisely because I had the sense to realize I wouldn't have been good enough. I don't see why you're picking on me. I'm really scared I'm losing my understanding of you. You don't realize something. You might be more unrealistic than I am, by far. You wanted to get married right away, even though I admit so did I. You want to have a baby now. However brilliant it may have been, your business plan was felt by some to be unrealistic. Your medical school idea might be unrealistic. You may be more ambitious than I am, but I think I'm much more realistic. You know what you are?" She thought not to say it before she said it, but she said it. "You're like some kind of empire-builder, but the only trouble is, you don't even have a map. You don't know what countries you want. Sometimes I think you don't know what you're doing." Maybe he'd have to go to Wachspress.

"Really? That's nice to hear. The only thing you've done that I know of where you've put your money where your mouth is was sleep with George Koenigsberg so you could feel like a big deal."

His lips were open. He seemed to be waiting for her response. "You may be right," she said. "Except for marrying you." She stood up and walked quickly in his direction, to get to the bedroom, not looking at him. She would pack and leave. She would go to Daddy and Bunny's, or her sister's, or to her old apartment with Nina. When she walked by him, she shivered. He followed. "Where are you going?" he asked.

She didn't feel obliged to answer him. She first went into the bathroom, where, while she peed, she thought she'd remove the diaphragm and flush it. Let her be pregnant. She'd have the baby, on her own, and bring it up at Daddy's, or give it to Ellen and Stan for a cousin-sister to baby Janet. But she restrained herself. When she came out, Steve was waiting for her.

"I shouldn't have said that," he said. "I was just getting back at you for hitting below the belt. I honestly didn't mean it. You know I've never held Koenigsberg against you and what a bastard I think he was."

Emily went out to the foyer. She dragged one of the dining-table chairs into the foyer closet and stood up on the sides of the chair so as not to break the caning of the seat.

"What's going on?"

She was having trouble reaching her large lightweight navy suitcase on the top shelf. Steve's suitcase lay on hers. She could hardly walk out carrying his initials. Finally she was able to reach the handle of his suitcase. She pulled it off hers and let it fall. Then, with another grab, she got hold of hers and let it fall too.

"You don't think we should talk, Emily?"

She had gotten down. She carried the suitcase to the bedroom. "I don't have anything to say."

"Where are you planning on going, anyway? There's nothing that's been said that can't be straightened out if we talk reasonably and stop being hurtful. I lost my head there. We both did. You can't just walk out on someone because they've said something in the heat of an argument."

She zipped open her suitcase on the bed and went to the bureau. She heard the suitcase being zipped closed. She turned around to see Steve sitting beside the suitcase with his hand on it. "Where are you going to go at this hour?" he asked, frowning in an embarrassed way.

"I have places to go." She knew she felt self-righteous; that didn't mean she wasn't right. She took a handful of underwear and one of stockings from the top drawer, and two good sweaters from the bottom. She walked to the bed. "Please let me pack."

"You're taking a big step without thinking. It's very childish. We should be talking."

"We talked. You talked." She would not listen to him. She couldn't stop. "I'm following through," she said.

"Fine." He put up his hands in a truce gesture and got off the bed.

Unzipping the suitcase again, she placed the underwear and sweaters in it and went to the closet for two skirts, feeling that she was under guard, that she must make no mistakes or she would be penalized, punished by the very person she was leaving.

"It's what's known as using judgment, Emily. In this case it would be wisdom not to follow through."

She brought the skirts to the suitcase. She removed the sweaters and underwear, laid the skirts on the bottom of the suitcase, and put the sweaters and underwear on top of the skirts.

"It would be out of wisdom not to follow through," he repeated. "Not out of lack of stick-to-itiveness."

"You don't think I have any wisdom. You truly treat me like shit. I keep thinking it's going to stop, but it starts again in some different way." While talking, she packed a sheath dress and a blouse. Her pace to and from the bed was getting faster.

"Look. Can I make a suggestion? Sleep on the couch tonight. I mean I'll sleep on the couch. I deserve it. And in the morning we can talk everything out when we're clear-headed and then you can decide what you want to do. My mother once called my father a cocksucker and they're still married."

"No they're not." She took another set of underwear from the bureau, and a black sweater, and a gray skirt from the closet and went into the bathroom to dress. She'd have to call Daddy or Ellen or Nina from the street. She expected to see her clothes dumped from the suitcase when she re-entered the bedroom, but instead there was no suitcase and no Steve.

She walked to the foyer with her handbag. Her bulky-looking suitcase was parked by the front door. Steve had taken her place on the living-room couch. She opened the closet door and got her camel's-hair coat. She put it on.

Steve stood up and came slowly across the room to her, looking at the floor.

Standing by the front door, not knowing what he might do, with tears beginning to rise in her throat, and above all determined to leave, Emily was convinced that she and Steve were not alone in the apartment, because the moment was too important to go unwitnessed. In the middle of the living room, right in front of her, she saw her mother, in her blue farewell suit and hat, interrupt the old grouping, leave off hugging her and Ellen goodbye on her knees and look up to watch her daughter at the door, watch to see what she would do, if she had the nerve to leave, the strength. All of a sudden, leaving was something she had to do to show her mother that she could do what her mother had once done. Having such a thought made her suspect her own motives for leaving. She picked up the suitcase before she could think again. Heavy, but not too heavy.

"I want to know two things," Steve said.

"Okay." She put down her suitcase and leaned her back against the door.

"Where are you going?"

"I don't know exactly."

"Why don't you phone someone from here, if you don't know."

"Because I haven't thought, and I was in a hurry."

"You admit you haven't thought, but you're walking out just like that? For all I know, you have a place to go that's all planned."

"For all you know. But I don't. How could I have anything planned, Steve? How did I know what was going to happen tonight? You're not making sense." She reached for the suitcase. He knocked it out of her hand. She jumped away from him.

"I'm not letting you go until we talk."

They looked at each other like beasts who didn't know each other. "All right, but that's not a very good way to talk, if you're forcing me."

"I'm certainly not forcing you. If you want to leave, leave. I swear I'll never let you back, though. I'll change the lock."

Her suitcase was just out of her reach, nearer to his leg than to hers. "One thing I don't understand about you. Why do you care so much? You're married to someone who's not thrilled you're going to medical school and who isn't dying to have a baby. Let's just say we're not getting along so well lately. So I don't understand why it's so important that I stay. Pride? I don't understand what's in it for you. The fact is, I don't know where I'm going right now, but I'd rather go anywhere than stay in this house." She noticed that she didn't care if she was scared of him. If he tried to stop her from going, she would fight him. If he tried to kill her, she would certainly fight him. If he succeeded, there'd be nothing she could do about it. He was shaking his head. His bottom lip had disappeared under his top lip. She thought he might be shaking his head not at her but at the situation. "May I have my suitcase, please?"

He kneed it to her.

She picked it up, watching his face. She turned toward the door, expecting his hands to grab her shoulders, expecting a fist on the back of her head, a crash to the floor. The end. She turned the latch, put her hand on the doorknob and turned it, and opened the door to the corridor.

There was a rush beside her, at her right, and a violent slamming of the door out of her hands. "Don't," he said.

They were standing side by side without looking at each other. He had prevented her from going without seeming to realize the marriage was over. There would be nothing to keep her here if she stayed. Her head hung. "What's the point, Steve?" She put the suitcase down yet again.

"If you'll spare me a few minutes, then you can do whatever you please. I think you at least owe it to me to hear me out."

If she tried leaving again at the moment, it would make them both look silly. And their neighbors might be making something of the noise. "Go ahead," she said.

"In the living room, sitting down, if that's not too much to ask."

Following him, she unbuttoned her coat, assuring herself that she wouldn't be taking it off. He sat on the couch again, and she at right angles in one of the chairs. She crossed her legs. "What do you want to say that you haven't already said?"

"Okay. I have news for you."

She was too weary, and too weary of him, to say "What?" But she said "What?" anyway, simply fulfilling her conversational duty.

"I'm going to quit."

The marriage, to beat her to it? "Quit what?"

"Medicine. Medical school. I'm giving it up."

At least he had the sense not to act as if his news were simply a great relief to her, a hoped-for surprise (though she was of course surprised) that would make everything all right. His face, in fact, was disturbingly upset.

"You can't, Steve." Despite his expression, he was saying that giving it up meant to him that she'd have no choice but to stay.

"I can't? I can if I want to."

"But you should pursue it. You're right to. That's been understood for a while, I thought." Nor did she want any responsibility for his quitting.

"It's not going to be worth it to me. I don't know what I'm going to do with myself. I can't stay at Farr. But I don't feel like throwing my life away on medicine. That's for sure."

"When did you decide all this, may I ask? Tonight, or in the last fifteen minutes? Did Peter say something you're not telling me?"

"No. For God's sake. I really am capable of making my own decisions. Obviously, you have a little something to do with it. But it's too much. It's too long, it's too hard, too unwieldy. The end is too far away. Everything you've been saying, I guess. All I'm doing with it is ruining my marriage. I can't let you go."

Of course he didn't understand that it was no longer medical school that had spoiled things. By now, he was better off sticking to his ambition—better off and better. Because what had happened after he'd made his I'm-going-to-be-a-doctor announcement had become much worse for her than the original announcement itself. After his announcement he'd turned into a boss. It was plain to her now that getting married must have seemed to him the chance to be a boss. Really, his original announcement was the beginning of the bosshood. She hadn't seen any of it coming. "I don't think your going or not going to medical school should depend on my staying or leaving. Anyway, why can't you try the pre-med, at least, and if you don't like it, then quit."

"Maybe. What does your leaving or not depend on, by the way?"

"What did you mean, you can't let me go?"

"I mean I can't afford to live without you." He tried to smile and he failed.

"But why?"

"Because I love you."

How did he know? What did he mean by love her? She didn't know what to say to him. So much of her important conversation with him since shortly after their marriage began had taken place in her head. "What would happen if I left?"

"My life would fall apart more than it has already."

Would he kill himself? "You would survive, don't you think?"

"I know you would. You're much tougher than I am. You have much more strength than I do. Without a mother you have more of a mother than I do. My mother's fifty going on two and my father's a cold prick. I'm not saying it's an excuse for the way I've been behaving. Things started falling apart for me after the business deal got shot down. When I came up with a replacement, I began losing you. I need some time. I need some of your strength. Sometimes when I think about you, I think how you came through so strongly without a mother, but that not having a mother might be what made you tough enough to come through. But most people couldn't do it at all, what you've done with yourself. I think you can take care of yourself much better than I can."

"Maybe that's true."

"Look. I don't deserve you, but I want you to know that no matter how dumb or careless I've been, thoughtless, self-centered, insensitive, whatever you want to call it, there's no one in the world like you—I admire so much." He was shaking his head.

She was going to say, "It doesn't help when you say you don't deserve me," but Steve had started to sob on the couch, covering his suddenly lowered face. The noise—*uh-huh-uh-huh-uh-huh-uh-huh*—was so unexpected and strange, it made a sickening chill across her heart. This time, she thought, she wasn't doing the crying. She worried that if she went to him she'd give away all her strength at once. If she remained in her chair she'd be callous. She watched him sobbing like a little boy in his blue pajamas. She heard him squeal into his hands, "Forgive me! Please! You've got to give me a chance!" These words pulled her to the couch immediately, as if she'd been waiting to hear them forever. She clutched him, in tears, with her head against his head. She had to save him. The cloth of his pajamas became for a minute the smooth hard finish of her mother's suit. Then it was Steve again she was holding. He had no way of knowing the message she was squeezing into his bones: I will leave if I have to. But if I give you a chance, you're giving me a chance. I have to try to stay.

PART
SIX

CHAPTER SIXTEEN

Two Women

Her mother's grave was empty. Inside the earth were bones. The cemeteries all over the world had dumped their bones into the earth, filling it from top to bottom and side to side, making an indoor garbage dump of bones. Outside the earth, dissolved in the sky, were Granny and now Grandpa Gus mixed with her and everyone else who had ever been cremated.

Steve lived in their former apartment. She thought of him back there as walking very slowly around the place, all alone and dangerous. The danger of the flammable scotch-smell on his breath stayed in her mind.

Daddy and Ellen fully trusted her decision. (It would have been hard not to. Even Bunny the Steve-lover had understood right away that there was no choice.) Daddy had arranged for a young lawyer in Charles Wright's office, Bruce Kling, to handle the separation and divorce. Bruce Kling was stocky but handsome, slick, and, Emily suspected, very conceited.

Emily had done the only thing she could do, everyone had been upset, and that was about it. Ellen expected her second child in two months. Daddy never changed. Life went on, blah, blah, blah. But she didn't like it going so fast, as grateful as she was to be away from Steve, finally, and back in her old apartment, thanks to Nina Brooks's impending marriage. Daddy and Ellen thought she could take care of herself, and they were right. But their confidence in her judgment and maturity, along with their life-goes-on attitude, meant they weren't treating the break-up of her brief, disastrous marriage as a momentous event that continued past itself. Despite their and Jill's perfectly adequate sympathy and support (Daddy as usual guaranteeing whatever money she needed), Emily visualized herself as alone on the earth. The surface of the earth was empty but for her—a bare earth and a deep, permanent winter twilight.

Early one evening in winter, Emily sat at her desk at the office, working up the nerve to call Helen Kornbluth, hoping to make a date. (It was a whole year and a half since she'd seen her, at the wedding.) Emily doubted very much that Timothy would have been able to understand how much calling Helen was taking a chance—what he had cheaply accused her of never doing with her life—and for that matter that marrying Steve had been taking a chance bigger of its kind than any chance little Timothy would probably ever take, no matter how miraculously successful he had become on Broadway.

Helen had herself once phoned Emily, at Partridge, for lunch, nine or ten months ago, shortly before life with Steve had gone out of control for good. This call had come half a year after Helen's last invitation (on the sobbing night) to the studio (Steve had subsequently urged Emily to come with him, and she had stalled), and many weeks after the fancy invitation in the mail to the opening of Larry's exhibit at some prestigious gallery or other. Steve had attended it with Mona, Emily having the excuse of a publishing-party obligation.

So Helen's phone call to the office last spring had startled Emily, not only because it was from Helen, but because it was so unexpected. Emily, hurriedly begging off, had exclaimed her regret, like a bird shouting it; she gave too many excuses and swore she would call Helen back soon. She feared that before hanging up Helen would ask her bluntly if she had in some way offended Emily without realizing it. But instead Helen said a cool, polite goodbye; following the goodbye, Emily heard a single tiny note of bewilderment, a clipped sigh, as if Helen were turning away from the phone she was hanging up to say to someone, I wonder what the trouble is. More than feeling guilty after the call, Emily wanted to be left alone; she wanted to be left as she was, familiar to herself. She had lived for so long now with her own strength and weakness, and without her own mother.

Then Emily had developed a fantasy, like an infection in her mind, of Helen as a human balloon, snaky braids, breasts, open arms, and the rest, all naked, balloon belly, legs, rear end, expanding and expanding until it exploded into wet rubber shreds, the wetness a watery milk, enabling the shreds of burst balloon to stick to the sky. Whenever it wanted to, the Helen-balloon occupied Emily's head, about to envelop her but without moving toward her, while she watched it expanding as if her eyes were blowing it up, until it exploded again before it could overcome her.

When the irrevocable trouble with Steve swamped everything, Helen had pretty much faded. Now that Emily was out of the marriage and on her own again, Helen's presence had resurfaced, not in the fantasy form (Emily remembered the balloon without experiencing its danger or its destruction), but still sending out pulsations, though milder than before, of the possibility that she was a smotherer, or not as smart as she had seemed, along with the suggestion that Emily had invented or greatly exaggerated her fear, and that to avoid Helen might be wasting the chance of a lifetime.

She had, finally and simply, needed to tell herself to decide: Helen's interest in her had not been too interested, nor had it been the interest of someone too interested in everyone or anyone. She needed to believe that regardless of her elaborate anxieties about Helen, and behind Helen's interest—if it still existed—she would find the apparently extraordinary woman she'd first met at the Farkases', that it was this woman she would be trying to save for herself from all the Farkas rubble. Helen and Mona were opposites. Mona's mouth was a hole for any garbage to fall out of, smelly chunks of rotten cauliflower. Mona's brain needed diapers. The other woman Emily had met that night asked amazingly serious, imaginative questions and had thoughtful thoughts, deep, original thoughts, so that she stood way above the crowd and made Emily stand out in her own mind. Emily now conceived of Helen as a living statue of a wise woman. She might have faults, but they wouldn't count.

So she grabbed the receiver and dialed the Kornbluths' number, recalling that Andy had once told her in high school how terrified he'd been to call the sexy and haughty Barbara Socolow for a date— how in his terror (Andy bragging about his terror), when he finally plunged, his heart felt as though he were dialing it, his heart, instead of the phone. Helen's "Hello?" seemed to take the time to be gracious.

"Hi. Surprise. It's Emily Farkas. I'm just calling out of the blue because I wonder if you'd be free to have lunch some day soon, as my guest."

"How nice. My goodness. Well of course. Can you meet this evening, by any chance? I can do that, if it's convenient. And let's do Dutch treat, in any case."

If she was offering this evening then she was being way overeager, especially considering Emily's past rudeness, or she must know about

Steve and the separation. Emily's forehead had moistened. "It doesn't have to be this evening. I'd just like to get together. Steve and I are no longer together, if you hadn't heard. If that puts you on the spot because you're Mona's cousin I'd fully understand."

"I don't even see why she'd have to know."

"I don't want you to inconvenience yourself tonight, though."

"But it happens to be particularly convenient, you see. Larry is having dinner with his dealer, whom I cannot bear. Larry can't either, but that's another matter. Then they're going to a club to hear some jazz. I was planning to stay home by myself. Is tonight possible for you?"

"I could see where I can get us a reservation. I'd like to do it nicely. Do you mind coming to midtown?" The Kornbluths lived on Riverside Drive.

"Not at all."

"Let me call you right back. Thanks." Oh my God, tonight! Inspired by Helen's availability and soothing tact, Emily pulled a bit of rank and got a reservation at Sirènes, where she had some of her fancier business lunches these days. To feel the improbability of her power was how she felt her power. The not-quite-yet-twenty-five-year-old Emily had reserved a table, late, at a particularly posh restaurant. She called Helen. The reservation was for seven. Never having met alone, Emily thought, they had never met at all. They would recognize one another by hearsay.

Then at Sirènes, Emily was across the table from Helen, Helen against the pale peach wall in a black suit, coral blouse, onyx brooch, coral earrings, overwhelming Emily's perfectly respectable office outfit— her black-and-white houndstooth dress and matching jacket with the black velvet collar. They had clinked glasses, Helen's dry sherry to Emily's dry vermouth.

Helen's spring production at Beardsley would be *The Madwoman of Chaillot,* of all things. They talked about that. Emily was sipping her vermouth too fast. She wanted to stay at the beginning of the evening for a long time and in the middle indefinitely. Helen told her that Susan, her daughter, would be giving flute recitals at some high schools around the city. Rafael, the son, the philosopher, had astonished everybody in the family by getting engaged.

"I thought of you for him when I first set eyes on you at Mona and Jack's, nearly two years ago, but I quickly reminded myself that quite aside from the probable significance of your being with Steve at his parents', you might have done wonders for Rafael but as wonderful as Rafael is he might not necessarily be wonderful for anyone to marry. And now he's found himself a painter, Charlotte. We all love her and she loves him and seems to understand Wittgenstein into the bargain. I mention this not as much in passing as you might think, but rather clumsily to get to the subject of you and Steve, because I'm concerned about you and want to know how concerned I should be. There." Helen took a swallow of her sherry.

Emily was unable to prevent herself from smiling. "There's no need to worry. I'm flattered, though," she added, not wanting Helen to think the smile meant that Helen's concern was completely point-'ess. She couldn't help wondering what Helen knew. "Why are you worried?"

"Because I was told that you and Steve were having serious difficulty and that you left him a month or so ago, but one can't necessarily trust Mona's reports fully, and I didn't want to ask for details. I suppose I don't want to be on anyone's grapevine, really. So I had reason to be concerned because I had liked you so. But I had no butt-in rights whatever and I was reluctant to call you."

"I'm very sorry." Emily gulped. Maybe someday she'd be able to tell Helen, as much as she understood it herself, why she hadn't been friendlier, even the balloon part, and how much courage it had taken for her to call her this afternoon. She looked right at Helen's gray eyes.

"Nor need I know anything now. I was happy you called. We can talk about anything interesting at all."

"Probably I'd like to talk about it, or some of it, anyway. I don't want to spoil the evening, though. I'd like to ask you something on a different subject for a minute, I don't know why, I'm just curious. Did anyone ever tell you about my mother?"

"That she died? Yes."

"And where she was, what she was doing? Did Mona say something that evening, before Steve and I got there?"

"I think so. Is it secret?"

Was that a joke? "No. I just wonder how it gets talked about. I don't like it to interfere."

"With?"

"People's perceptions of me. It makes too much of me and not enough of me at the same time, or something."

"I have to admit it interested me to know it. I'm a mother myself, after all. It's not *what* made you interesting, but it might have to be part of the combination, you know, because my awareness of it made me wonder how it affected the rest of you, whether your thoughts about eternal life and excitement, for instance, didn't have something to do with your mother's early death."

"Your memory is amazing. I'm sure those thoughts are connected to my mother. Sometimes I don't know how, or I forget, but the connection's always in my blood. Do you remember what Mona said when she told you? Obviously, you must!" Emily laughed and reddened.

"Something along the lines that Stevie was bringing home an unusual girl, not a 'typical, superficial Park Avenue girl,' whose mother had died during the war overseas. It was very respectful, I assure you. Your mother was presented as a heroic woman. I think Mona said she died of malaria."

Emily laughed again. "It wasn't malaria. And the Park Avenue part is exactly what I mean. Not a spoiled, superficial Park Avenue girl, but a poor little rich girl."

"No, that wasn't the implication. And I'm quite certain she would have been quoting Steve about the Park Avenue girl, in any case. I may have remembered the malaria wrong."

"I'm sure she said malaria. It's just what she'd say. I never have the feeling she gets anything right. I'm also willing to bet you she thinks our marriage broke up because I refused to have a baby. Or the main reason. The worst of it is, though, that whatever Mona thinks about me doesn't really make any difference anymore anyway, if it ever did. What's truly terrible is what she thinks of her own son."

Helen appeared to be concentrating on what Emily was saying in a calm, neutral way. Her chin and her gray eyebrows were raised. She looked aristocratically detached.

Emily said, "This might sound bitchy, but Mona wants Steve to save her from Jack's coldness, but you get the feeling she thinks Steve isn't man enough to save her or do much of anything. And Jack and Mona seem to have that in common, at least. They both seem to think Steve doesn't add up to that much. They pretend to encourage him, but they don't. They discourage him. Tell me if I shouldn't be talking this way, please. I don't know how to talk about this, what the etiquette is."

Helen said, "Why not just talk the way you feel like talking, and I'll do the same. I don't think this is a time in your life for you to be worrying much about etiquette." Then the captain arrived with the menus and wine list and some recommendations.

Emily hid behind her menu's wide wings. The Helen she had spurned did not exist. It was the real Helen sitting across from her, the first, distinguished Helen. Maybe she wasn't even entitled to her.

Helen ordered moules ravigotte and scallops Sirènes, Emily moules ravigotte (for the first time ever) and sole amandine. They would have a salad after the entrée. They agreed on a bottle of chablis.

When the captain had gone, Emily said, "I feel worse tonight than ever for Steve. Steve is miserable. He is really miserable." A small, sympathetic laugh came out of her. She feared it sounded vengeful. "Now I'm away from it. Steve can't get away from himself. At least I have a chance for a decent future. I have a job I've come to like, or love, mostly I think because it puts me in demand. People twice my age depend on me, or sometimes three times my age, and I can do something for them. I got an offer last month from the publicity department at another publishing house, a job with a better chance to move to the top sooner than the one I've got now, or that's what they told me, and I turned it down, because I hate their books and I really like my boss and owe her a lot. But I got a raise out of it. And there's actually an offer that may come up soon from an ideal place that I probably couldn't turn down. I have the feeling now that I was born to do publicity, for other people, God forbid, and that I can't help it if I happen to be good at it." She was yacketing like a runaway train; she couldn't stop yet. "When Steve left Farr last spring, we were very hopeful. He went to an ad agency. Crockett and Major."

"Yes, I knew about that."

"As an executive on a retail-furniture-chain account, where he's even unhappier than he was working for his father and his uncle. The marriage really started failing after he finally changed jobs. He expected Crockett to switch him to a more glamorous account, but they wouldn't or they couldn't, and then he began thinking it wouldn't make any difference anyway, he'd still be unhappy. At least my ego's being satisfied. Steve has no idea what he wants to do with his life right now except make it worse."

"Oh, dear."

Become an alcoholic. Try to kill himself. He'd nearly killed her. "He's still working there, more or less, but I don't know what's going to happen. Except I know we're going to have to get onto a different subject. You and I, I mean."

"You were talking so urgently, you reminded me of my daughter when she's excited or upset about something on the phone with me, only at such times a daughter isn't likely to suggest changing the subject. Not only am I used to listening, but I'm sure I wouldn't know what to do without it. Naturally, I'm always sorry when Susan has reason to be upset, as I am that you are. But I think I should explain to you. I'm someone whose life seems to have settled nicely. I have a husband I love and admire, who returns the compliment in his peculiar way. And the same with my children. My regrets haven't disappeared. I know how fortunate I am, though, on balance. I think I've learned to understand my luck. What all this means is that if someone like you, who interests me, wants to talk to me, then I want to hear it. I have some room to spare for someone like you. And I know when I get bored. But I'm not bored. As far as I'm concerned, it's not necessary to change the subject unless you're finished."

"I know. Thanks. But enough's enough. I feel so much better than I did when I called you. You don't know."

"I feel better, too. I was disappointed when you couldn't have lunch last year. I supposed it was the difficulty with Steve. But I didn't think I'd hear from you."

"It was my own fault. I think your invitation was more flattering than I could manage. More complimentary, I mean." Would that do for a quick version? Why did she interest Helen? Why did Helen need her at all, with two children and a husband she loved and admired? "Is it fair to ask why I do interest you? I'm not fishing, but I'd really like to know what's there, what you see." She giggled slightly.

"I'm sorry you can't know it for yourself. I think you seem to be ... ordinary is not the word, but usual, conventional, perhaps, and you're not. You're unusual. It's partly that you're a surprise. But the surprise is only part of it. What the surprise is is the rest of it."

Emily couldn't look. The words had been so direct and so deep and in her favor. She lifted her head, without quite meeting Helen's eyes. "Isn't everyone somewhat unusual, at least inside?"

"That may very well be. In fact, I suppose I count on it. But it doesn't make any difference if it doesn't show. You express it."

"To you, maybe, to people like you." What people? Who else was there like Helen? "People like you bring it out in me, of me, from me. You did the night at Mona and Jack's. But what do I bring out in you? I'm not your daughter, so I have an obligation to bring out."

Helen was amused. "I suppose you bring out my interest."

"Interest or interestingness?"

"Both. Both. And I think we care about some of the same things."

Emily wondered if Helen feared being disappointed in the evening. "We're back to the same old problem, then. Would I have a chance of being interesting if I weren't my mother's daughter? I know you don't like this question. I'm withdrawing it."

Helen's head made a little hop as she smiled. "That's all right, since we've already established that you're not fishing for compliments. Don't you accept that you have to be somebody's daughter? I think of you as rare. You are rare. Our conversation that night was rare. You told a remarkable anecdote about the static on the radio, the static and applause. I've told that story to people. I'll never forget it."

"Thanks. I don't know what to say. I'd like to say something else about Steve. And me. I don't know why, exactly, since you're not related to me, but it's very important to me that you know I tried hard with Steve before I left. A lot of the problem was how hard he tried not to be helped." Every night too much drinking, and ridiculing and criticizing of her, along with a whole lot of self-pity. Once he'd said he would commit suicide. The cocky Steve unraveling right in front of her, still to her disbelief. "Maybe I worry that Mona doesn't know I tried hard. Mona and I have pretty much stayed away from each other." Emily checked the proximity of the tables on either side and the surrounding table-noise. "I really wanted to be married to Steve. Neither of us knew what we were doing. We were both very impetuous. Also, neither of us could predict what would happen. Some of our problem had to do with his family rejecting a big idea of his for the business. According to him, they turned him down badly, and I really have to believe him. They didn't give him any credit. They didn't consider it."

The moules ravigotte were served. Emily watched Helen take the first bite. "As far as I can tell," she went on, "his business idea was wonderful—practical and adventurous. Other people were interested, too. That was Steve at his best, and he got squelched. Then he suddenly decided he wanted to go to med school, and I couldn't stand it, right after our honeymoon. I handled it badly. I didn't think it made sense, and it scared me, the prospect of all that absence. Then later I encouraged him to do it. In the long run, he didn't want to go anyway. He thought it was a pipedream himself. But I was too upset to stand back and be generous about it in the beginning. So in a way, I might have helped to squelch him, even though I told him I would have been perfectly happy for him to go to grad school in something that didn't take ten years. But that wasn't for him. We both made terrible mistakes. I think my instincts were right, but I can't escape that I behaved selfishly at times. I brought selfishness into the marriage I didn't know existed in me. But nothing I did could have prepared me for how Steve started to destroy himself." And tried to destroy her. "I just can't believe I'm responsible for that." He had destroyed their hope, just like a vandal. Some of the things he'd done and said were too embarrassing for her to think about anymore.

"Mona did say last month she thought you and Steve should have had a child. I think that's probably nonsense. But I must tell you, she doesn't talk as if she blames you for Steve's unhappiness. If anything, she blames herself and Jack."

"What's she doing about it?"

"She takes it very seriously that Steve's lost you. Mona respects you more than you'd like her to. What she's doing about it is trying to keep herself in control, trying to get Jack as involved as possible, and making sure Steve keeps his psychiatric appointments. Look, Mona has to fight a lot of problems, including herself, to manage at all. I know she often has an obnoxious way of dealing with reality. But Mona's quite courageous. Even Larry likes her. It's easy to see how childish, selfish, and silly she can be. I let her entertain me in her brassy manner and wish I could love her as much as I feel sad for her wretchedness. I'm sure it's not easy being her daughter-in-law. I just wanted to say my piece."

Maybe now she'd like Mona, Emily thought. She patted a squeeze of tears with her napkin. She did it so rapidly she imagined that people who noticed at all wouldn't have time to see she was crying. And she sensed that no one noticed. "Does she know any of what went on between Steve and me? What the trouble was?"

"She knows about the drinking. Whatever else there is either she doesn't know or she hasn't told me. Aren't you going to eat this? It's superb!"

"I will." Emily took a tiny sampling taste. Strange and delicious. She showed her pleasure to Helen with her eyes. She wasn't all that hungry. She took a few more nibbles. She'd wondered often: did Steve's family know about the night she'd told him she didn't feel like having sex with him anymore and he'd run her backwards by the shoulders across the bedroom, shoving her into the wall so hard she'd had to have stitches in her scalp? That was the last thing he'd done to her. "Has Steve ever called you to talk, by any chance?"

"Goodness, no. You have too much imagination. Are you in touch with him?"

"As little as possible right now. But I get worried he's going to do something to himself. He talked about it. I call him much more than he calls me, which is now not at all. He's stopped asking me to come back. He's stopped apologizing. He's agreed to the divorce. He's silent.

I do feel guilty sometimes, even though I really believe I loved him until he forced me to stop. If I ever find another man to love, I'll be sure we won't make the same mistakes."

"Of course you'll find another man. He'll find you."

"I mean the right kind. I'd like to make it last." As it never could with Nicky Becker, three novels, two marriages, currently single, forty. She had resisted, so far. And he was very appealing. Even his inappropriateness was appealing. It always frightened her, the thought of starting to screw around. "I'm concerned that it won't ever be possible for Steve to be satisfied, that he won't find out how to do it. I want it to turn out right for him, and I can't see how it will. And I can't save him." Tears gushed from her like blood. She pressed her napkin to her eyes again, pressing hard. She didn't belong in a restaurant tonight. If she got up and went to the ladies' room, she'd be even more conspicuous. If she were alone, she'd probably be sobbing.

"The wine," she heard Helen say. Emily stuffed her tears back. She brought her napkin down and glanced at the waiter. The waiter worked at opening the wine, paying her no attention. A man at the table to Helen's right was sneaking peeks to see if the fuss had stopped. The waiter poured. Emily tasted and nodded almost simultaneously. The waiter poured for both. He deposited the bottle in the ice bucket and left.

Demonstrating recovery, Emily said, "I'm sorry about the public display. It's ridiculous. I'm filled with sympathy for Steve and I'm scared for him. But I'm relieved, too. I'm sad and happy at the same time."

"Maybe the alternative is unbearable. I think people often use whatever they can to remind themselves how important it is to be alive. How important it is to want to be."

That was a perfect example of the Helen who thought and spoke the way most people didn't. Was she talking about everyone or herself? Was it literally difficult for her at times to want to be alive? Did she have a burdensome secret? An illness? What were her regrets (other than not being a Broadway director)? In any case, it was obvious that Helen had a thousand times more intelligence than she was probably able to use.

"I wonder if my mother ever felt happy and sad at the same time," Emily said, "because frankly I doubt it. I think she was too sad for that, too sorrowful. I'm not."

The entrées were served. Looking at Helen in a normal way, Emily examined her face to see if she could see significant hints of her mother in it. She couldn't. There was undoubtedly a rule against reincarnating into people while they were already living. "When I had my world-famous experience with the static and applause and thought it was the end of the war, what I didn't tell you was that by then I think I already didn't want my mother coming home that much. If it was the end of the war, the applause was for her as well as for peace. I'm sure the idea of her returning made me uneasy. It's terrible to say it. But what I got from her instead of her returning, aside from what I inherited through genes, was that she spread into the world after she died. She became everything. My mother is what makes me feel everything matters. Maybe she's the applause in the static." Yet if it weren't for Helen, she wouldn't be talking this way to begin with. "I hope I don't sound nuts."

Helen hadn't picked up her fork. "Please don't spoil what you said. I hope you'll tell me the details about your mother sometime. Your father is alive, isn't he?"

"Alive and well. I'd like to know about you, too." Everything. "May I ask questions?"

"I'm asked fewer and fewer questions about myself the older I get. I love questions."

After dinner, they decided to walk up Fifth Avenue for ten blocks or so, before separating to go home. Helen had put her arm through Emily's. Emily, at first, looked at the sidewalk or stiffly ahead. She feared that she would squeeze Helen's arm by mistake. She had never walked arm in arm with a woman before. In answer to a question of Emily's, Helen was indicating some of the challenges and rewards of her marriage. She declared her confidence that one day Emily too would learn how dramatically satisfying it could be to live in a marriage, having gained deep, though never quite complete, knowledge of a loving husband, while knowing that the husband, in his own way, had done the same with her. Relaxed now, Emily sometimes looked at Helen, or at the apartment houses, thinking how spiffy the canopies always were on Fifth, out of a Fred Astaire movie. Before her, the streetlights and the building lobbies glowed on the repeated stages of the sidewalk. Arm in arm, Emily and Helen walked uptown, conversing, a young woman and an older one.